STRONGER THAN SKIN

STEPHEN MAY

SANDSTONEPRESS
HIGHLAND | SCOTLAND

www.sandstonepress.com

The publisher acknowledges subsidy from
Creative Scotland towards publication of this volume.

ISBN: 978-1-910985-40-3
ISBNe: 978-1-910985-41-0

Cover design by Brill Design
Typeset by Iolaire Typography Ltd, Newtonmore
Printed and bound by Totem, Poland

For Caron, with love

1

This is the hardest part of the journey home: a long, slow climb up Pentonville Road. Sharp pain along the backs of my calves and thighs. Sweat on my back beneath my rucksack. My breath coming in ugly rasps, but I can't hear it. I have Rachmaninov loud in my headphones. Sonata for cello and piano, Ashkenazy and Farrell.

I always listen to classical music when cycling these days. It makes the most mundane trip filmic somehow. A little melodrama injected even when, like now, I am just making the trip from work to home.

This bike is a new one, only the second time I've been out on it. An anniversary present to make up for the fact that Katy will have first claim on the car for the next however long. Also because she knows I want to lose a few pounds, drop a jeans size, get the BMI sorted. Be fit for the baby.

It's a serious machine. A Bianchi XR1 road-racer in a severely adult matt black: it is the sleekest thing I've

ever owned. £2,200 worth of hand-tooled precision engineering. Beautiful.

When I was a kid I would have flown up this hill, hardly noticed it was there. It's harder now but, despite the pain in my legs, despite the effort to get proper breaths, despite the uncomfortable stickiness under my arms, I am still glad to be out in the sun and the breeze, looking forward to seeing my family. It's been quite a day. The lessons have been all right - but there's been coursework marks to enter into the system, plus a moany faculty meeting, plus an appointment with parents disappointed with the progress their kid is making. I didn't know what to say. Charlotte Phillips is a grade B student making grade B progress. She's doing all right. But all right is just another word for failing as far as Mr and Mrs Phillips are concerned. They want an A star child and it's just never going to happen. Difficult.

But that's over for now. Let's worry about poor Charlotte Phillips and her ferocious tiger parents on Monday. It's the weekend. It's all about Katy, the kids, the Bump. Katy's given up work today, started her maternity leave, left the solicitor's practice behind for a while, so she'll be in a good mood. She might have made a cake.

I am just minutes away from getting sticky, giddy hugs from Ella and Jack. My favourite part of the day. Our kids are at the stage when they're always thrilled to see me. Daddy! Daddy! Daddy! Daddy's back! Yay! Look! Daddy! Look! I get a version of this every day and it never gets old.

I wonder about the random facts I'll get from Jack. Because there will be some. He'll tell me there are only two sets of escalators in Wyoming or that a slug's bum is

on its head, while Ella tells me who her new best friend is and all the hundreds of things that are absolutely mega awesome about her.

As I get closer to home I'm thinking about what I'll cook tomorrow. Saturdays I like to do something adventurous, something a bit complicated. This weekend I think it might be lamb shawarma with saffron rice. Something Middle Eastern anyway. That's the cuisine I like playing with at the moment. It's good that Ella and Jack are prepared to experiment with food too. In this – as in so many things – we are lucky with our children.

Maybe we'll have some people over – maybe Katy's best mate from the solicitor's, Amanda and Nick Campbell and their twins. We haven't seen them since the summer. About time we all got together again. Short notice though, should have sorted it out before this.

Finally, I am past the Tube station, heading into City Road, easier going now, getting ready for the to turn into Haverstock Street. Only a couple of hundred metres to go. A handful of happy, more or less freewheeling seconds before I am back in the bosom of and all that. Now that I have conquered the hill I feel strong. The good old endorphins of exercise chasing away the bad old cortisol of stress.

Here's where I see something that should alarm me, but it doesn't. Not at first. I have maybe lost the habit of wariness. Lost the ability to hear the universe speaking, to recognise its way with signs. The universe will always punish that.

Two people, a man in police uniform and a woman in smart casual but with an obvious law enforcement walk, are emerging from either side of their Vauxhall Astra,

and all I feel at first is a kind of curiosity. Oh my goodness, police in our road. One of them plainly a detective. Not something you see every day.

I am just seconds from home, the wild sparring of Ashkenazy's piano and Farrell's cello at its most passionate, the police already making their ponderous, almost reluctant way down the driveway, when an instinct for self-preservation kicks in. When I realise what it means. What it might mean.

I am almost level with my own front door. A reclaimed door painted the brightest holiday yellow. The male officer has his hand on the doorbell. He straightens his shoulders. He has the look of a man with a difficult job to do. I take that in.

Instead of turning in to my drive, I put my head down and, with my face covered by helmet, goggles and scarf, coast past without glancing to my left, though in my peripheral vision I see the door open. It will be Ella doing that. Opening the door to callers is a job she insists is hers. I can't see her worried frown beneath her dark fringe, but I know it must be there. No one opens the door to the police without anxiety, do they? Not even a child.

Less than two minutes later I stop and dismount. I am in a cul-de-sac I've never been in before, a brownfield development, built where workshops or a factory or stables once stood. Tall skinny houses in some kind of fake cotswoldy stone. Walls the colour of low-fat spread, five-year-old hatchbacks on the driveways. Basketball hoops on the side of the garages. Trampolines filling the back gardens.

I take off my headphones and discover my mobile is going. Katy. This phone is still quite new and still on

factory settings which means the tune is absurdly jaunty, like the fanfare for a news programme that only reports the happy stories. The dogs rescued from a fire, the EuroMillions winner with his beaming fat face and his over-sized cheque, the baby prince being shown off in some distant part of the commonwealth.

'Mark, can you get here now?'

Katy's voice is on courtroom mode. Even, well-modulated. Every word bitten out clear and distinct. Which pretty much tells me all I need to know. Tells me that it is what it looks like. It's not just routine and neither is it a cock-up. I turn the phone to vibrate.

I guess that the police must have been there while she made the call. I can picture them – the male cop's bulk, settling himself comfortably into our old sofa. The female, plain clothes cop less at home, perched on the edge of her seat, not wanting to stray into the personal space of her colleague. Nor does she want to look too relaxed. She'd be working hard on showing empathy. The modern copper's best weapon. I see her smiling shyly at my wife. The woman she hasn't expected to be quite so good-looking, quite so obviously clever, or quite so pregnant.

But maybe it wasn't like that at all. Maybe they were both simply watchful, careful, professional, refusing tea, neither of them smiling. Not even at the kids.

The kids. Ella will want to ask questions and Jack will be hanging back fearful, timid – afraid to go, afraid to stay – wondering if something terrible has happened. Being sure it has. Being right.

No sense in postponing the call any longer. But I do anyway. There's a small patch of green between the houses and the road and a wooden sign in the middle of

the grass that reads 'No Ball Games on the Greensward'. I wonder at the curiously archaic language. Greensward. Like something from Thomas Hardy. A big word for a glorified verge.

I wish I still smoked, that I could spend a few minutes rolling a fag, that I could lose myself in a simple task that nevertheless still requires concentration and dexterity, something that leaves no room for other thoughts. I was an expert at rollies once. My tattoo itches, which it does at moments of stress. I take my gloves off, roll up my sleeve, scratch at it, those letters that have faded to a dull grey inside the love heart which itself is the brownish colour of long-dried blood rather than the vivid scarlet it was when I first had it done. The cheap inks of that Colchester tattoo parlour a lifetime ago.

I put the headphones back on and listen to another few minutes of the music, let it roil around my head. Let it surge and crash and storm around me.

I prod at the numbers. She answers before the end of the second ring.

'Mark?'

'Katy. I'm sorry.'

There is a long pause. Then, 'Is that it? You're sorry?'

I wait. Nothing I can say just now will help. Katy sighs noisily, but when she speaks again her voice is soft, almost a whisper.

'Did you do it?'

I hardly pause at all. 'No.'

I haven't judged it quite right. There's a brittle quality in my voice, a thinness, a lack of authority. A fragility, which, astute lawyer that she is, Katy is bound to have picked up on. I close my eyes, take a long, slow breath. I need to be calm.

'Katy,' I say. 'Really, I didn't.' Now I think I sound too deliberate, too self-consciously firm. I think it sounds like acting. 'What did they say? The police I mean.'

'They said... They said that they just want you to help them with their enquiries into a very serious historical offence. Then I waited. When they told me what it was. I think I was meant to go to pieces.'

Seeing her go to pieces is a pleasure Katy will never give anyone, least of all a couple of low ranking plods.

'But they've gone now?'

'Yes, they've gone now.'

'I'll come back then. I'll explain everything. Don't worry. It'll be fine.'

'Will it?' There's a pause. 'I made a sodding cake too. My last day at work. We were going to celebrate.'

2

In Ella's bedroom the children are dividing up the last of the bags of sweets their granny brought them when she was over. Liquorice Allsorts and they left them till last because sorting out who gets what is hard. Jack only really likes the white and black ones. He'll tolerate yellow and black and pink and black but he really hates the ones with brown on them and the ones with the crunchy coating. Ella prefers the same ones her brother does and doesn't see why she should miss out just because Jack acts like he has a disorder all the time. But they manage it in the end.

'Do you think Mummy and Daddy will get divorced?' Jack says, his mouth full of Allsorts. He likes to shove them in a handful at a time.

Ella makes a face. The way Jack eats revolts her sometimes. It also annoys her that he still calls their parents mummy and daddy even though he's eight years old. It also irritates her that he sounds kind of hopeful and she

knows why. He thinks that if they get divorced he'll get more presents, that'll he'll get two of everything. He'll have two birthdays, two Christmases, that his guilty parents will buy bigger presents apart than they do together. He doesn't understand anything.

She makes him wait.

'No,' she says finally. 'But I think Daddy – Dad – will go to prison.'

Jack looks gutted. Which is what she wants. But as soon as she sees his face crumple, she feels bad. She pushes her remaining sweets towards him, all except the brown ones. He is surprised out of his gathering grief. 'Go on, you have them,' she says. 'I'm trying to cut down on sugar anyway.'

Jack grabs the sweets and puts three in his mouth before she can change her mind. 'Why will he go to prison, what's he done?'

'He hasn't done anything.' Her voice is harsher and louder than she means it to be. She sighs, stands up and goes over to the window. A group of boys have just met in the street, greeting each other with hugs and high fives. She wonders if they'll have to move and if so, where to? Surely they'd get to stay in London? Or maybe they'd live by the sea? That wouldn't be so bad. If you have to move from London, then the seaside is the best place to go.

She turns back to Jack and notices that he has eaten some of the brown sweets too now, the ones he says he doesn't like. She doesn't call him on it.

'Daddy – Dad – hasn't done anything, but the police obviously think he has. Someone has been telling lies about him.'

She thinks now about The Railway Children which

dad read to her last year, where the father is put in prison because everyone thinks he's a spy, and how the family learns to get along without him, and where the mother becomes strong and capable and how her mother is already strong and capable, so they are one up on the railway children, and she wishes she could remember their surname. It's something quite ordinary. That book ended happily and this will probably end happily too. Dad will come back and the police will write an apology. Mum will make them, and she'll make them pay for believing the stupid lies that someone has told. Then maybe they'll be proper rich and get to go to America and stuff.

She wishes she had a phone, so she could tell Emylia Nicholls about the police coming round. Of all her friends Emylia will react the best. She'll shriek and she'll scream then she'll tell everyone else. Every day Ella wishes she had a phone. She's the only girl in the class without one. She's probably the only girl in the whole school who doesn't have a phone. Even the kids in Year One have phones. Even the babies in *reception* have phones. If Dad does go to prison – or if her parents do split up – then she'd probably get a phone, a really good one.

She feels guilty for thinking like this. She's as bad as her brother.

'You can't tell anyone.' Jack is looking at her closely. It freaks her out that he seems to be able to read her mind. He's always doing it. It's weird.

'I'm not going to tell anyone dumb-ass. You're the blabbermouth round here.'

'I'm not!' Jack's face is outraged. Good.

'You are so. You can't keep a secret for toffee.'

'I can.' His voice sounds unhappy now. He can be so whingey.

'Shush for a minute will you.' Ella has heard a change in the texture of the murmurs that have been filtering up from downstairs. The steady drone of adult talk has changed in volume and pitch. She knows that the police are standing now, that they are moving towards the living room door. Then they're in the hall. The front door opens.

Jack joins her at the window, bony elbows digging into her as he wriggles in close beside her. Outside, the laughing boys grow sombre and disperse as they see the police emerge onto the driveway. Jack and Ella watch as the police walk to their car. They don't speak to each other. In fact, they seem lost in their own worlds. The man goes first, eyes straight ahead. The woman behind him. She pauses at the gate and looks back, her eyes flicker up to the window. Without thinking about it both Ella and Jack duck down so they can't be seen. Crouched beneath the window, Jack giggles. 'What did we do that for?'

Ella frowns. 'Don't know. Messed up.'

'Instinct.' Jack says.

Ella stands up. 'I'm going downstairs now,' she says.

'Listen,' says Jack. 'Mummy's on the phone.'

'Don't call her Mummy,' says Ella. 'It's babyish.' But Jack isn't listening, he's already on his way out of her bedroom heading down the landing. She follows. They'll sit at the top of the stairs and listen. Normally they like doing that, listening to their mum on the phone is fun usually, though she knows it might not be this time. Usually their mum is laughing or telling stories or working herself up about something. Sometimes she is serious and

quiet and comes off the phone shaking her head. When that happens, they know to leave her alone for a bit.

Ella thinks that nearly everything she knows about the adult world comes from hearing her mum on the phone. Jack likes to listen just as much as she does, but it's strange how he doesn't seem to learn anything.

3

Katy is cooking. Leeks and onions and garlic turning translucent in the frying pan. That's the trick with alliums. Give them lots of time, treat them gently, and they won't go bitter on you. A large dome of grated yellow gruyere is on a plate on the table. Fresh fusilli sits in a pan waiting for boiling water. With both the oven and the pot-bellied stove going the room is warm, cosy despite the size of it. This is a proper dining kitchen after all. A room built for noisy family dinners and supper parties. This room is the reason why – ten years ago now – we nearly bankrupted ourselves to buy the house.

The radio is on. Radio 4. The PM programme. A round-up of the news with Harriet Cass or Charlotte Green. One of the more comforting big-sisterly newsreaders anyway. There is war in the Middle East, earthquakes in South America, a multiple stabbing at a house in Manchester.

There is a government spokesman defending something, attacking something, or patiently explaining

something. Or maybe it is the opposition. I'm not really taking any of it in, but sometimes that is not the point of radio. Sometimes the point of radio is just to let us know that the world is still here, carrying on, that everything is pretty much the same as it was.

I watch her as she concentrates on making a roux. We're having a simple pasta au gratin. Perfect Friday night comfort food. God knows I'm in need of comfort. We both are. She doesn't look at me. Doesn't say anything. There is just the whisper of the onions frying in butter.

'Katy,' I say. 'Katy.'

She turns to look me full in the face. I am taken aback by how beautiful she is. I always am. Even now, after twenty-three years of being with her more or less every single day, it still catches me out, still makes me breathless. The frank stare, the serious eyes, the full lips, her rounded, ripened face, the face turned peachy by pregnancy. I want to touch the skin of her cheeks where two high spots of colour have appeared. I have a sudden urge to take her to bed.

'I'm so bloody angry Mark.'

'I know. Sorry.'

She turns back to the cooker, pushes her hair back from her face. 'Yeah,' she says. 'You said.'

It is rare that we fight. We have none of the stories that our friends do. The wounding public joke at a spouse's expense. The outraged confrontation about a too obvious flirtation at a Christmas do. The slanging match in the street, the discussion about who does more housework that escalates into the furious theatre of kicked doors, broken ornaments and hurled mugs. We have nothing like this in our history. We sometimes share a discreet

smile when we hear about this kind of thing from others.

When we were younger, we would marvel how great it was that we could have make up sex without all the tedious horror of quarrelling first.

When we disagree, we do it respectfully. Katy will always talk things through, try to consider the thing from all angles, while I retreat into quiet. But if we were ever going to fight, now would be the time to do it.

'Where are the children?' I say.

'Upstairs. Keeping out of the way. They're not stupid. They can sense there's something seriously the matter.'

My attention is snagged by the radio again. They are saying that in some superstore or other beer is now cheaper than water. I wonder what my dad would have said about that. Katy turns the radio off.

'Mark?'

The door bangs open and the kids are in. Before he even says hello, Jack tells me that carp have teeth in their throats and can I believe that there is no word for brother or sister in Korean?

Ella wants to play me the song they've been learning on guitar at school. As she weaves her tentative way through the melody to *Eight Days a Week*, she turns that peppy love song into a melancholy study in obsession. It becomes a stalker's anthem, ominous in its new slow tempo and uncertain changes. On another day it might have made me laugh. Not today.

There are tears in my eyes as I applaud. I can't help it. Jack makes sure he has his moment too as he tells us that he has been picked for the school football team.

'Really? That's great,' I say.

Jack is timid in social situations but a ferocious competitor in games. He's only in Year Four so the

school must think pretty highly of his skills. I decide that whatever happens I am going to see him play.

'When's the match?'

'Next Wednesday I think,' he says. 'We're playing St James's. They're proper good.'

'Yes, but Barton Street Academy have just signed a genius, a footballing wizard.'

'Have they?' Jack seems puzzled.

'He means you, you plank.'

I tell Ella not to call her brother a plank. I remind her that she's nearly eleven, that she's meant to be an example.

'Your face should be an example,' she says.

Ella flounces off and, after a minute or two, Jack follows her. The Chadwick kids, they squabble and they bicker but they don't like to be out of sight of each other. They're a team. How great it must be to know you've always got support in the playground, that your back is always covered.

In hurried whispers, before a child comes mooching back in wanting a drink, wanting to tell a joke, wanting to lodge a formal complaint about the other – before all that, I tell Katy the whole story. I do it quick but I try to leave nothing out. I spill it all from the first collision in Cambridge to the flight to Italy and all the madness in between. It's all there. I don't have to search my memory for details. No point, I know, in dwelling on the unfairness of it. Things just are.

Through it all Katy chops, slices, pares, stirs and grates. She ices the chocolate cake she made earlier.

When I've finished, her face is carefully neutral, impassive, impossible to read.

'I'm the same person you know Katy,' I say. 'I'm the same person I was this morning. The same person you've known all these years. Nothing's changed.'

16

'Mark,' she says. 'Oh Mark.'

I tell her what I'm not going to do. I'm not going to turn myself in. I'm not going to stand trial. I'm not going to have the whole mess of what happened raked over for the entertainment of tabloid readers. I'm not going away for years while Katy and Jack and Ella forget me. While the Bump gets itself born and all grown up without even knowing who I am.

'Because that's what I'd get Katy,' I say now. 'You know it. Even with one of your brilliant QC friends, even with mitigation, I'd be going away for years. I can't do that. You can't want that to happen.'

'Can you open the wine?' she says.

I pour two large glasses of a mid-range rioja. Katy has never really given much credence to the idea that a pregnant woman should stop drinking completely. She's always thought the odd glass did little harm to the baby, while being essential for the mental health of the mother.

If the medical opinion seems to be ambivalent on this, the Mumsnet opinion formers are definitely with Katy. If anyone gets too fingerwaggy about it, she can point to her lovely, healthy, high-achieving and more or less non-behaviourally challenged children. Wine and pregnancy, it's always worked for her and it works now. One swallow and she seems to come to a decision.

She tells me it all seems clear to her. 'Before we decide anything else, you need to have a word with Anne Sheldon,' she says. 'And you had better make it a pretty bloody persuasive one. *And* you had better stay away from the police until you've done it. Shall we eat?'

As easy and as matter of fact as that. So decisive. Weirdly subversive too. Katy has been a solicitor for over twenty

years. Shortlisted for the Law Society's Excellence Awards three times. She usually professes a lot of faith in the English legal system. She doesn't think it's perfect, just that it's better than all the alternatives. She is a fan of judges and juries. It's not that she doesn't believe that there are miscarriages of justice, but she does think they're incredibly rare and that they are always put right in the end. Almost always.

'Sort it with Anne,' she says again. 'I don't know where we'll be at the end of it all, but that's where you have to start. Isn't it?'

Put like that it does seem obvious. 'I love you,' I say. I kiss her neck. She tastes salty. I feel her spine stiffen.

'I'm trying to cook here,' she says.

We are eating the cake when the knock at the front door comes. It is unmistakeably official. It's angry, bullying, unignorable. A bailiff's knock. A social services knock. A policeman's knock. A sneaky trick to pretend to leave quietly and then to return at teatime when the quarry thinks there's a moment of reprieve. Believes he has time to collect his wits, to make plans. We should have guessed it was coming.

Katy is first to react. 'Fuck,' she says. 'Fuck, fuck, fuck.'

The children are startled. Both freeze, slices of rich chocolate sponge halfway to their mouths. Jack's face is clown-like, a smeared brown grin of icing and crumbs covering most of his chin. Ella, always tidier, has only a blob on the tip of her nose. Her eyes flash and I can see that she can't wait to use this powerful new weapon of a word wherever she thinks it will have most effect. Barbeques, parties, sleepovers, swimming, school – probably during assembly. Mummy says it, she'll say.

It is a word they've heard before – no one gets to the age of ten in London without hearing the f-bomb exploded several times an hour – but it's different in your own home. When it's your mother saying it.

The knock comes again, Katy puts her head in her hands, her hair making a tent over her face and I put a hand on her shoulder as I rise, feel the heat of her through her shirt. My big words about not giving myself up seem ridiculous now. She puts her hand up and over mine. I am surprised by how comforted I am by this. How much I need it. I start to move towards the kitchen door. It's over. I've told my story and now it's over. There's some relief there.

Ella is on her feet. 'No, Daddy. I do the door. You know that.'

'Oh, right.' I hesitate.

The knocking again. Raised voices too now. 'Mr Chadwick!'

'Daddy?' Jack says. His voice is barely there. 'Daddy, I don't think you should be here.'

'No you shouldn't.' Ella, emphatic.

Katy raises her head. Looks searchingly at each of her children. It's as if they have become brand new to her. As if they are wearing skins she doesn't recognise. Obviously they have picked up quite a lot of information while bickering and squabbling, while hovering around doorways. We should all think about this more. About how our children know everything. How they miss nothing. None of us ever have secrets from our children. Not ones that matter.

More knocking. The voices louder, on the borderline of proper shouting now. 'Mr Chadwick! Open the door please!'

'Daddy, go!' Ella sets off for the hallway. She sings out 'I'm coming!' Her voice is bright. It is pleasant, friendly and helpful. A voice that will keep the police in their place for a few moments longer, shuffling in their big boots rather than threatening to break down doors. Moments I can use to get out the back, get onto the bike, get through our garden and off into the alleyways that I know and the police don't.

Katy squeezes my hand. I squeeze back and already I know that it's the memory of that gesture that will keep me going through whatever comes next.

4

A quietish, civilised, back street Islington pub, The Castle Hotel, a sparkling Pellegrino in front of me. Ice and a slice. Safe amid the soft murmur of long-established middle-aged couples, treating themselves after a hard week. One of those places where food doesn't come on plates, but on little wooden chopping boards, fat chips in silver buckets.

I am disgusted. Furious. These people. Do they know how thin the ice is that they are skating on? How fragile their worlds are? One lie, one bad call and they're going under. There's no call for this smugness, for this easy confidence. I want to burn the place down. Chips in buckets, Jesus.

I swallow, take a breath. Close my eyes. I need to stay positive.

I phone Katy. She doesn't answer. I phone the landline too. No one picks up. The phone rings and rings until the

voicemail kicks in. I listen to it all the way through. Like the indulgent parents we are, we have let Ella and Jack do the voicemail message.

'The Chadwick family are not at home right now.' Ella. Her voice plummy, like a child of the 1950s. Like a swallow or an amazon. Like a member of the Famous Five.

Jack: 'But if you leave a message...' he collapses into breathless giggles.

Ella is cross. There's a whispered, whining, exasperated *Ja-ack!*

They do the final line in a ragged chorus. One of them will call you right back. Byeeeeee!

My stomach hurts.

My phone quivers. A text. Katy. *They've taken the address book and the laptops. They've taken the shoeboxes.*

Does passing on this information constitute assisting an offender, I wonder. Is she complicit now? An accessory? Somehow perverting the course of justice? Is she professionally compromised? I don't know how I feel about that.

My phone shivers again. It sounds loud to me. Like it's sawing through the table it rests on. I read the text. *Don't come back tonight. Don't call.* I swear I can feel my blood begin to thin. My heart begins to shrink. I pick up my glass. The bubbles in the water make me cough. I look down at the glass, notice some tiny, unidentifiable midge-like thing has dropped in. A black speck against the yellow of the lemon. But it's all right, fizzy water won't help me now. I need something else, something more, something that kicks hard. That is what pubs are for. For people to marinade their

anger in alcohol. Not for signature burgers on wooden platters.

'Hello, Sir. Remember me?'

Christ. The barman is Jake Skellow. He was one of those kids who make teaching a misery. A clown. A comedian without any decent material. A teenage Norman Wisdom – all pratfalls and gurning and silly voices. Bright enough when he wanted to be, which just made it worse. He was a right fucking pain in the arse. Yes, I remember him.

'Jake,' I say, 'good gracious. How are you? It must be what?'

'Five years, Sir.'

'You don't have to call me sir. Not after all this time. I'm not Mr Chadwick either. Mark, please.'

We shake hands. Jake has a firm, dry grip. He's taller than I remember. His hair cut into a classic rockabilly flat-top. His eyes are warm and brown as polished wood. I remember that when he was in my class he had a brace. His teeth look fine now.

He seems pleased to see his old teacher, cheerful. Keen to show me how well he's doing, because it turns out that he's not just the barman. He's only twenty-one and he's the manager here. I'm pleased to see him because it makes me get myself together a bit.

Something occurs to me. 'Jake, is this really a hotel?'

'We have a few rooms, yeah.'

'Do you have any vacancies?'

The police have got the laptop and the address books, so that means they know everywhere I might go to hide out. Because Katy is so good about Christmas and birthday cards and all that, and makes sure she has the

up to date address of everyone we know, they'll have the names of all our friends, all the relatives, even the distant cousins.

Worse, they've got the shoeboxes. The shoeboxes are where we file bills, bank statements, insurance stuff, house stuff, car stuff. All the hard copies of a life in half a dozen or so of the green Clarks boxes you get when you buy sensible hard-wearing, professionally fitted kids' shoes with three months' worth of growing room.

Getting these boxes means the authorities already have their fat thumbs on the artery that keeps the money going round. How long before they pinch that shut? I'll need to do something about that too.

Jakes clears his throat. It's very neatly done. A discreet tug at the sleeve of my attention. 'So, Sir, Mark I mean. How many nights?'

'Just the one for now.'

'Right. One night in the King George suite.'

'What's the King George suite?' I say.

Jake smiles. A dazzling flash of white. Yes, his teeth are fine. 'One of the Georges brought his mistresses here,' he says. 'We named our best room after him. The one with a balcony.'

I tell him that I don't want a suite, an ordinary basic bog standard room will be fine.

'Bollocks, Sir. You're getting the best room and it's free. Least I can do.' He pauses now and looks me straight in the eye. He's smiling, but his eyes are anxious. 'I need to apologise,' he says, 'for being such a dick in English.'

'That's okay,' I say.

'It isn't, Sir – Mark – not really. I was out of order. I'm surprised you never belted me.'

'I'm a consummate professional,' I say.

Jake smiles. 'I always liked your lessons, Sir. Mark, I mean. You never shouted at me. Never called my mum. Never even gave me a detention. You should have done all those things really. Reckon I owe you.'

I well up, eyes suddenly wet. But I think he doesn't see this. When you're desperate, random kindness can set you adrift, can unmoor you. I blink hard.

For all its royal name the room is nothing special. I don't think a king's mistress would have been all that impressed. A simple square box painted in a dusky grey. That famous painting of a butler dancing on a beach. It's true there's a balcony. It has a view of a street of estate agents.

But it's clean and there's a minibar. Ready mixed G&T in cans. Complimentary crisps. Jalapeño and cracked pepper, and something called poshcorn. A paper packet in pink and cream that claims its contents are light and fluffy butterfly-shaped morsels that are both savoury and sweet. Made by popcornnoisseurs, apparently. 119 calories per bag.

There are dinky bottles of kelp body wash in the bathroom. There are oatmeal cookies by the kettle. The kind of pointless luxuries designed to make you feel pampered and to forget you're paying £150 for a night in a bedroom half as nice as the one you've got at home. There are twin bathrobes as white and fresh as Jake's smile. As light and fluffy as a poshcorn morsel. It just makes me yearn for the cheerful mess of my house where there are fingerprints on the walls, dirt in the bath, and toys and books and clothes scattered everywhere.

I liberate a can of G&T and, lying on the big bed, I

google Anne Sheldons. There are thousands in the UK and narrowing my search down by age doesn't help much. There are still dozens and they are scattered across the country from the Shetlands to the Isle of Wight. There are none at all in Cambridge. So she has left there and she could have gone anywhere.

Tracking down Anne seems like it's going to be hard, but maybe I can find her through Bim. Finding Bim turns out to be easy. Once you have filtered out all the many millions of references to Building Information Modelling – the key free resource for the construction industry – there is only one contender.

The Bim I need is almost certainly the owner of the Orwell gallery in Felixstowe, but just to make sure I do some further digging. On the About Us section of the Orwell Gallery website there are pen portraits of the staff and yes, turns out that the Bim who runs this gallery is an acknowledged expert on the Vorticists.

Bingo.

I phone and listen to that unforgettable voice tell me that unfortunately the gallery is shut for staff holidays and will reopen on 1st October with an exciting new show by a Turkish abstract artist. I click off before I hear the name. First October. Bollocks. I take a breath. A week. Only a week, but still. Of course I should have known. Nothing is ever easy. Nothing is straight-forward. I shut my eyes. Take a breath. Count to ten slowly. But I have heard Bim speaking for the first time in over twenty years and it was okay. I didn't faint or anything. It didn't seem to touch me. That's something. A decent something.

I check where Felixstowe is and how to get there and then I'm left with the problem of how to stop myself

thinking. I open another can. It's actually quite hard to detect the gin in these drinks.

Katy has told me not to go back home tonight but I can't stay in this room either. I have to go somewhere. I have to do something.

I have a shower. I use up an entire bottle of kelp body wash and head off out of the Castle into the night, smelling like the sea.

I seem to cycle around most of North London, music loud, still trying hard not to think.

There's a breeze spiteful enough to keep people off the streets, but even so London seems freakishly quiet. Whatever the weather a London night should be raucous, should be mixed martial arts meets burlesque. It should be theatre. London at night should be all pissed up street-poets bobbing restlessly through the streets like discarded plastic bottles down the Thames. But not tonight. Tonight London is pensive, aloof and grown up. Things on her mind.

I stop once at an all-night cafe and the cabbies and the call girls and the foreign students chat together in a way that seems strangely small-talky. The weather, the football, the economy – how since the internet no one wants to pay the proper rate for anything. How we're all working harder for less, running to stand still. It reminds me of the staffroom. When did London get as banal as this?

Every half hour or so I make a stealthy return through the chill drizzle to the end of Haverstock Road but there is always that bloody police Astra outside the house.

I wonder what they think, the police. Sitting for hours

in the sweaty cubicle of the car, waiting to nick a guy who hasn't had so much as a parking ticket in twenty-odd years. Do they really believe this is a good use of police resources? They should be angry, they should be wanting to chase real criminals: muggers, burglars, rapists, terrorists. If they joined the force because of the hope of making a real difference to how things are, then they've been cheated.

Five times I come back, and the last time – at gone midnight – hanging back in the dark, I see our master bedroom light go off. I wait around another twenty minutes to see if the team in the panda car give up, but they seem pretty dug in. Not going anywhere. No getting past them.

I'm going to text Katy a last goodnight, only I realise I've left my phone back in the Castle. But at least I'm maybe tired enough now to sleep. Time to go back.

When I get back to the King George Suite I'm going to make the most of the facilities, I'm going to drink the minibar dry. I'm going to dive into the poshcorn. I'm going to warm up with a long bath. If I find myself crying, then a bath is the place to do it.

I wonder how safe it would be to email Katy from the hotel. Best not. It's not just mobiles they monitor these days. Funny, if a postie tampers with the snail mail then he goes to prison – but the electronic postmen, they seem immune. They get rewarded, even. These days you never know who is reading your stuff. Some googlenaut in Motherfuck Nebraska, some minimum wage Amazon drone hunched over his algorithms in Idaho, some spook in Murmansk, all of them getting a bonus for each piece of intel they extract. People forget: an email is not a private letter. It is a publication. It is the magazine of

you carelessly discarded in the waiting room of the world.

I am just outside the Castle about to swipe my key card when the door opens and Jake Skellow hurries out, takes me by the arm in a strong-fingered grip and hustles me into the shadows whispering urgently as he does so.

'None of my business Mr Chadwick, but the old bill. They're waiting for you. In your room.'

'Really?'

'Yeah, they came about twenty minutes ago. I've been looking out for you.'

'I wonder what that's all about?' I say. I'm trying to move my features into a frowning picture of professorial puzzlement. I'm cursing myself for not switching that bloody phone off, or for not throwing it away even. Jake straightens himself to his full height. This pretence has irritated him. He's lost a bit of respect for me maybe. He's come out from behind his desk into the cold night to give his old teacher a heads-up. I should be a little more honest. There's a pause. What do I do now?

'You know, Jake, I'm really not up to facing questioning by the police. Not tonight.'

Jake smiles. Another quick happy flash of those big white teeth. I have seen this before with kids at school, how they love to turn the tables, love to become the teacher themselves. The way they like to educate you about how the modern world works. About phones and computers. About pop or fashion. About how to escape from justice too it seems, because he has an idea.

'You could go to my place. Kip the night there. If you wanted.'

Now I remember some staffroom talk about the

troubled background Jake comes from. Some gossip about how his family were at war with the authorities, of the Skellows being involved in all sorts of dubious businesses – believable rumours of loan sharking, cigarette smuggling, buying and selling of knock-off goods, the breeding of banned dogs. It's fair to assume that Jake has not been brought up to respect the forces of law and order.

Obviously it is ridiculous to think of staying at Jake's, only I can't seem to think of any alternatives. Jake gives me the address. 'Key's under a pot by the front door,' he says. 'You'll need it 'cause Lulu won't be home. She's on nights.'

'Lulu?'

'My girlfriend.'

'Unusual name.'

'Yeah. It suits her too somehow. She's a bit bonkers but you'll like her. She's pretty sound. She's an artist, a photographer.' This said as an afterthought, with the studied casualness of someone who is very proud of the fact. He tells me she does shifts for security contractors, keeping an eye on empty buildings. He says it's easy work, good money and she finds lots of good locations for her photos that way.

I ask him if he's not coming back to his house with me and he tells me that he always stays in the Castle Friday nights. He is the manager after all. It's the biggest night of the week. Things go to shit if he's not properly hands-on. I ask him one more time if it's okay to stay at his. I need to be sure.

Jake shrugs. 'Just call it payback for not phoning my mum when I was pissing about in your class. She'd have battered me.'

He puts out his clenched fist. We fist bump, grinning awkwardly at the strangeness of it. Who'd have thought? Jake Skellow, class fuckwit of 2008 in cahoots with Mr Chadwick, Head of Year Eleven, both of them taking on the forces of law and order.

'If they ask – the police, I mean – I'll say you just didn't come back to the hotel.'

'Thanks again, Jake. I'm just.' I stop. I'm just what? I'm not sure how to finish the sentence. But Jake doesn't care.

'It's okay, Sir – nice to have a bit of excitement.'

'I think excitement is a tad over-rated actually, Jake.'

He smiles. It's exactly what a teacher should say. Something a bit jokey but a bit lame. I think he finds it reassuring.

5

You could say it began with a bike too. A bike, two boys, a girl, a butterfly, a fast car – a 1964 Daimler Dart – not that I knew that's what it was at the time. At the time, it was just an indigo blur. A panic of screaming brakes.

First week of the summer term 1990 and Katy, Danny and I were doing what students at Cambridge did in their first year. Certain students anyway. We were riding through the ancient streets with our college scarves streaming out behind us. It was also – though I wasn't thinking about it then – the first anniversary of the death of my sister.

Cambridge students have done this since forever and by 1990 it had become all very self-conscious and knowing. A kind of joke. Yeah, we still do this stuff, this bike stuff, this scarf stuff, but at least these days we're aware how ridiculous it looks.

It was especially ridiculous in my case. Me, with my stripy mohair jumpers, my distressed jeans, my battered converse high-tops. Me, who in those days sound-tracked

bike trips with noisy American alternative rock on the Walkman. Your Nirvana. Your Mudhoney. Your Sonic Youth.

But it wasn't just a joke. It wasn't just about irony. We wore those hornet-striped scarves with a complicated pride too. At least those of us who came from ordinary comprehensives did. God knows there were few enough of us who'd done that. We were a small group, though our lack of numbers did not give us special status in Cambridge. We were by no means an elite.

All around us the other kids seemed to consider it entirely normal to be there moving through all that venerated stonework, it's what they expected all along, whereas people like us were astonished at ourselves. Our eyes popped every time we passed Kings.

But I was dissatisfied somehow. It was like there was another Cambridge out there, one I hadn't got into, one whose selection criteria was nothing to do with exam grades, UCAS forms and personal statements.

Somewhere behind the colleges I could see, there was another secret university where the real stars gathered. In the festival of Cambridge some people had VIP wristbands and backstage passes and it wasn't me, Katy or Danny. Hence the trying too hard to belong. Hence the scarves. Hence the bikes.

A strange, sudden flicker of orange and I blinked, maybe wobbled slightly. The butterfly. A warning shout. Engine noise. A horn blaring. A fierce purple streak of metal. Close, too close. Way too close.

I saw a gawping face of a man on the pavement. A man in a pork-pie hat, his mouth a wide soundless O. A woman with a pushchair, her hand to her mouth. The incurious eyes of her baby.

There was a long second of silence where I was suspended between bike and road. That was the moment I remembered about my sister and that was also the only moment where I actually thought I was going to die too and it was not my past, but the near future that flashed before me. My parents being brave all over again, heads bowed as that useless vicar intoned something or other just as he did at Eve's funeral. I will lift up mine eyes to the hills from whence cometh my help.

Only there's no help, not really. Just another dead child, and dead children happen every day. Yea, though I walk through the shadow of. Then the old songs. *And did those feet in ancient times.* My father trying to form the words, though the shapes of them are as awkward as stones in his mouth.

Time zigzagged forward again and there was a series of sickening jolts – to my hip, my back, my elbows. I was rolling in the road, my bike turning a somersault in front of me. A long, low groan. My voice. Or a version of it. It faded out and I was trying for another breath but it wouldn't catch. I was drowning, my lungs were splitting.

But then – somehow – I could do it. I remembered the trick of breathing. I forced down shallow gulps of thick, petrolly air. There was the silence again. I relaxed into it. All I was conscious of was the hard road beneath my back and I knew I was going to be okay.

Sometime later – a second, a minute, a lifetime – I became aware of noise again. A high anxious hum, like a disturbed beehive might make. Above that, a keening, the strange foreign music of someone moving from anguish to anger.

There was a woman yelling obscenities, her voice familiar, but it took a while to place it. A young voice,

the words loud but incoherent. Choked and tearful. I was groping to fit a name to it. Finally, it swam out at me in waves of colour. Katy. Katy.

There was relief at being able to drag out the name that fitted that voice, but now, most of all, I wanted her to stop. The sound she made was jagged, raw, ugly. Somebody make her stop. Please. I opened my eyes. Coughed.

The shouting stopped. There was, unbelievably, a ragged round of applause and I became aware of faces – lots of faces – peering down at me, looming towards me. Faces loosening and relaxing. Lips, teeth, hair. Shining eyes. The man in the hat, his mouth shut now. Lips pursed. The woman with the pushchair, her baby waving red mittens, the fat moon-face all smiles now. Suddenly, I needed to be where all these faces weren't.

I stood up. Too quick. The world slipped sideways. All these people, they were sliding away. I put my head between my knees. There was a voice hot and sudden and too close to my ear. A woman. Her words popping.

'There's no air down there. You need your head up. Up. Stretch up. Like this.'

Anne. The first words she said to me and already she was showing me a way to live.

There was a hand on the small of my back now, another on my shoulder, gentle but determined. Irresistible, pulling me vertical, straightening me up. There was a little moan from somewhere. A long, whispery exhalation. I knew I was the source of it and I was embarrassed.

'I think you've done enough bloody damage, don't you?'

Katy, recovered and completely coherent now, her voice as hard and as icy as it had been watery and hot

before. Danny had his hand on her arm, pulling her away.

'Katy, come on. Don't make a scene.'

She didn't seem to hear him. 'I've got your number you know.'

'I'm all right,' I said. I was. All right covered it, more or less. The buildings were the right way up anyway. There was throbbing from my back. But it would be okay.

The people around us began to disperse, distant voices telling me to get checked by a doctor, telling me I was bloody lucky, telling the woman whose hand was still on my back that she was a bloody maniac, a menace, and should be in jail. I moved away from her, turned so I could see her properly. There was a long still moment. She moved her hand from my back, held it out for me to shake, just as if we were being introduced at some function. A village fete perhaps.

'Anne,' she said. 'Anne Sheldon.'

Anne Sheldon. The Lady Anne.

What did I see that first time? Was there any special radiance? Any inner light? Was I enchanted and lost instantly? Because that would be an excuse, wouldn't it? One a detective might get his head around. One a jury of twelve honest, averagely compassionate men and women might understand. I was bewitched. Beguiled by beauty. I didn't stand a chance, your honour. I couldn't help myself.

Only I didn't see beauty, not at first. In any case, Cambridge then – like Cambridge now and always – was full of beautiful girls. Beautiful boys too. Beauty in that late spring of 1990 when I was nineteen was utterly commonplace. Katy was beautiful. Her long blonde hair. Her serious grey eyes. Even Danny was beautiful too, in a way, with his floppy indie rock fringe, his big geometrical face.

Youth, optimism, hope – that stuff is always beautiful, isn't it? In Cambridge in 1990 there was more of all of that than in most places. Probably because we knew less about the world than people in most places. Nothing keeps you fresh-faced like ignorance of how the real world works.

So what I saw when I looked at Anne that first time was just a well-groomed woman on the verge of middle-age. She was, in fact, all of thirty-seven at the time, but I was nineteen – a kid, with a kid's ignorance of the gradations of age. At nineteen all proper adult ages are more or less the same. Thirty-seven, forty-five, sixty-two, a hundred and three. It hardly matters. They are all strange, faraway places you can't believe you'll ever visit.

She was short, compact. Heart-shaped face. Dark hair in a loose, artfully mussed bob. Cool wide-set eyes, the colour of bitter chocolate. Long drop earrings with some kind of green stone. Blue sweater. Nothing too out of the ordinary, nothing too beguiling. All that stuff came later.

One thing did stand out, however. Whenever I think of that moment I see her with an elusive smile playing around a generous mouth. But that can't be right, can it? She wouldn't have been giving me that characteristic amused look then, would she? The look that said: isn't this all just so utterly absurd? Not then. Not with everyone glowering and tutting at her. Not with Katy fierce in her face and threatening to sue, to take her to the cleaners.

'You'll live,' she said, and turned away. Then turned back. 'But your poor bike's probably had it. Give me your address and I'll send you a cheque. I'd do it now, only not sure where my cheque book is and I'm in a hurry.'

'We noticed.' Katy again.

'Katy.' Danny sounded exasperated. Danny and Katy

had been going out for less than a term and already they sounded married.

I mumbled my address and Anne produced a pen from somewhere and a scrap of paper from somewhere else, or maybe someone else produced them, Danny maybe, or someone among the diminishing group of onlookers. Much of the little crowd had by now drifted over to look at the car. It really was a beautiful thing.

Katy picked up on my haziness, how I wasn't following everything, how I was distracted.

'He's probably concussed,' she said. 'He could have a bleed on the brain.'

I don't think Katy really believed this was a possibility. I think she was trying, one last time, to make this woman understand what she'd done, or what she'd almost done. The hurt she might have caused.

Anne put the paper in the back pocket of her jeans. She squeezed my shoulder. She gave Katy a solemn, sympathetic look. Katy looked away. Anne moved past the group standing around her car, a vintage sports model I didn't recognise. Sleek. The shimmer of imperial colour. Even stationary that car was an event. It was unmarked by our collision as far as I could see.

We were silent until she'd gone. A snarl of bluish fumes. Going too fast.

'Nice car,' said Danny. Katy shot him a look.

'I hate people like that.'

'People like what?' He was frowning.

'People who think they can do what they bloody like.'

6

There were so many flowers I didn't know what to do with them. Fortunately, Mrs Boyd did. Mrs Boyd was the cleaner. My bedder, to give her official title. A large, boisterously cheerful lady who treated all the students as if they were neglected toddlers. She was affectionate, tolerant and very physical. Always ready to offer a hug. Coming from a family that never hugged, she scared me a bit.

'Give me a minute,' she said now. She was gone more than a minute, but not all that much more and when she came back she was clutching a box full of vases of all shapes, sizes and colours. 'Amazing what you can find in the porters' lodge. Who's the admirer anyway?'

'The porters gave you all these?'

The porters didn't even speak to me; I was lucky if I got a nod. They had their favourites and I was not one of them, though I was always scrupulously friendly and respectful.

I made tea for us both and as I did so I tried to tell the story of the collision. Mrs Boyd was impressed.

'Anne Sheldon? She's a one, isn't she? Well, she can afford it I suppose.'

'You know her?'

'Oh everyone knows Lady Anne, don't they? Married to Dr Philip Sheldon. A big medical science bod. They say he's brilliant. She's a sparky wee thing.'

'Why do you call her Lady Anne?'

Mrs Boyd shrugged happily. 'Everyone calls her that. She's just got that manner, hasn't she? Haughty like. Aristocratic. Extravagant too, clearly. Beautiful flowers though. Really brighten the place up.'

They did. It was a sign that I was getting better that I could acknowledge it. There was a time not too long before when I thought I'd never want to see a bouquet of flowers again. But these were not funeral parlour flowers. These were spring flowers. Light flowers. Life flowers. The flowers filled that small room with their rich ambrosiac scent. I felt light-headed.

'Look,' said Mrs Boyd, 'there's an envelope too.'

So there was. In the final bouquet was a stiff pale blue envelope, thick expensive stationery, my name across the front in a hurried, untidy hand. Inside there was creamy paper as soft as the envelope was stiff. 'Come on, then. Spill.' Mrs Boyd was looking at me with merry eyes.

'It's an invitation to a drinks party tonight. Just a few friends, it says. She thinks I might find it amusing.' I adopted a mocking tone for this last sentence, as if I were a disdainful aristocrat myself. As if I were a cartoon Queen Victoria.

'Well, I hope you're going,' said Mrs Boyd. 'Dr Sheldon's parties are legendary.'

'I don't know. I feel a bit weird.'

'Scrambled eggs, that's what you need.' Mrs Boyd proceeded to make some. She was right too. I felt a whole lot better after those eggs. I was just finishing them off when Katy called round.

There was the usual good-natured to and fro about whether Mrs Boyd should make more eggs. She was convinced Katy was in imminent danger of anorexia so was always trying to get her to eat. Katy laughed her off, protesting that she'd just had a pain au chocolat in Benet's. Mrs Boyd sniffed. She told her that wasn't proper food and she'd make herself ill if she wasn't careful and not to come running to her when she did.

Mrs Boyd mothered everyone but she mothered Katy more than most. She'd confided to me once that she was worried about her. Told me that Katy wasn't anywhere near as tough as she liked to think.

Finally, she accepted that she wouldn't win this time. 'You're sure I can't tempt you? Well, look, I'd best crack on. Have fun at the party. Make notes so you can tell me all about it.' Mrs Boyd bustled off with the porters' empty cardboard box in her hand.

Katy took a different view of the invite than Mrs Boyd. 'You're not going, are you?'

'I thought I might actually.'

She frowned. 'Really?'

I tried to explain, tried to say how this last year I'd been finding most things sort of pointless but that I was vaguely excited by the idea of this party. How I had the sense that this might lead to that other Cambridge. The one they'd been hiding from me.

Katy got up to go. She had an essay to plan. She was

just popping in to see how I was and she could see that I was fine. She collected her things. She told me Danny was waiting for her back at her room. I closed my eyes. Not her fault, but I felt physical hurt when she said things like this. It wasn't that I fancied her. I absolutely didn't. Not then. Good-looking as she was, smart as she was, thoughtful as she was, Katy was too much like the girls I'd known at sixth form college – but it must be nice to have someone waiting for you back at your room. Someone a bit special.

Katy and I had met during Freshers' Week. Literally bumped into each other on the stairs on the second day. We had failed to find the English literature reception together, had ended up wandering the corridors of the college, guided by a distant murmur of soft laughter that we never quite got to. I remember I was impressed by the fact that, uniquely among the new under-grads I had met so far, she didn't want to discuss her A-level results. Instead she was psyched about the Nine Inch Nails' *Pretty Hate Machine,* an album that we had both bought only that morning in Andy's Records in Mill Road. We were impressed by the coincidence.

'Of course I also bought Kate's album.' She gave me a funny sidelong look.

'*The Sensual World*? I didn't know it was out yet.'

'Just today. You don't like Kate Bush.'

'Yeah I do.'

'Blokes hate Kate Bush.'

'This bloke doesn't.' An audition passed and the first of a million discussions about what men and women like or don't like. Think or don't think. Do or don't do.

We saw each other every day, more or less, during those first few weeks. Coffee in Millie's, pints of dark beer in

The Eagle. I taught her how to play pool, she introduced me to great women poets. We played ferociously competitive games of scrabble. We made each other mixtapes. Eve had been the only other girl I'd known that had made mixtapes; it was a pretty exclusively male hobby otherwise.

Over time we became best mates, so people were used to seeing us together. They often assumed we were an item, though we were conscientious about denying it.

Then, out of nowhere, she got together with Danny.

'What's so special about him?' We were in The Eagle, deep into the third pint.

'He's clever, he's a second year, he's a half-blue in boxing. He's hung like a donkey. What do you want me to say, Mark?'

I didn't know, but probably not that.

'Look, Mark, clever and good at boxing doesn't matter. Even size doesn't matter all that much,' she laughed, and then grew solemn. She took my hand. 'The thing about Danny is that he desires me. Properly wants me. He doesn't just think I'm okay-looking or a good laugh. He doesn't care about my taste in music. He wants to fuck my brains out every time I see him. I see it in his eyes. He's obsessed and that's sort of exciting. I've never had that before. Do you get it, Mark?' She held my gaze.

Yeah, yeah. I got it. 'Do you want to play some pool?' I said.

Now, in my room, she paused as something occurred to her.

'So this Anne Sheldon sent flowers, which is all very lovely, all very *Brideshead* of her.' She gave it full sarcastic emphasis and paused again. It was theatrical in a lawyerly kind of a way. 'But was there, by any remote

chance, a cheque with her note? Money for a new bike maybe?'

I smiled. I couldn't help it. 'Now you come to mention it, no, there wasn't.'

'Typical. Bloody typical. It's not funny, Mark.'

'I expect she just forgot.'

'Well, you can ask her about it at the goddamn party, can't you?'

I could. But I didn't think I would.

7

6.30 p.m. prompt and I was at the Sheldon's front door carrying a £4.99 merlot. It was from Bulgaria or Romania or one of those places, and at least a quid more expensive than the wine I usually bought.

Dr and Mrs Sheldon lived in the heart of leafy North Cambridge. A substantial Victorian townhouse in Selwyn Gardens, backing right onto Wolfson College. The door was a rich pillar-box red, and at the moment I pushed the old-fashioned doorbell, I was convinced that I shouldn't be there. Talk about a fish out of water. I very nearly bottled it. Very nearly turned tail and went. Lots of better places I could be. I could go round to Katy's – hang out with her and Danny.

If I went round to Katy's we could listen to records. We could savour the extra-quidness of this wine. We could agree with each other about what selfish bloody wankers the likes of the Sheldons were. If people divide into drains and radiators then Katy has always been the

best of radiators, great at making the people around her feel good about themselves. Once she'd picked you for her team, you never got dropped. My friends right or wrong, that's always been her thing.

But it was too late. The door opened. Anne Sheldon was in the hallway, face perfectly smooth, mask-like, wearing a shiny, almost metallic-looking blue cocktail dress, smiling in that subtle, distracted way. Eyes the colour of smoke. Now I saw it. Now I began to be beguiled. Bewitched by something more than beauty. There I was, face-to-face with someone whose eyes seemed to have seen everything there is and found that none of it mattered much.

'Well, look at you,' she said. 'Look at jolly old you. You got the flowers then?'

'Yes,' I said, 'yes, I got the flowers.'

'Don't you scrub up well? I knew you would.'

I'd made an effort with my clothes. Clean black Levi's and a proper jacket. A good one in dark grey with the faintest of hunting pink stripes running through it. Saville Row via the Mill Road Oxfam shop. That was one thing about Cambridge, crammed with poshos like it was, the thrift shops were full of good quality threads. Under the jacket I was wearing a Dinosaur Jr t-shirt. I looked okay.

Turned out I was way early. Of course I was. Schoolboy error to take the time on the invitation as meaning the proper start time. But then, I was nineteen. I pretty much was a schoolboy. But it was all right. Anne found it sweet and, taking pity on me, immediately found me a job to do – she had me helping in the kitchen.

'Philip's upstairs working on his presentation for the conference in Stockholm. I expect he's just going to appear when things are in full swing. Make a big ta-dah about it. Here, you can make the punch.'

She handed me an old book, battered and water-marked. *THE RUDIMENTS OF ENTERTAINING: THE YOUNG HOUSEWIVES' GUIDE TO THE ART OF MODERN MANNERS.*

'The work of a Mrs Lamprey,' she said. 'Published in 1836 by Carey and Lea, Philadelphia and never bettered. Certainly a lot better than Mrs Beeton. Try the recipe on page 112. Never fails. Providing a good punch was part of modern manners back then. You should be good with alcohol. It must have been such fun growing up in a pub.'

These days everyone knows everything about everyone. Meet a new person in the day and you google them that evening. No one minds, it's expected. It's actually a bit weird not to, looks like you're not interested in them if you don't. In fact, many people don't even wait till the evening, they do all this casual stalking on their phone the next time they go to the toilet. Sometimes they look you up while you're stood next to them. There's no shame in it.

Not the case then. To find stuff out about people in 1990 took time and it took effort. In 1990 you waited for personal histories to be unveiled to you over weeks and months. To do any digging around on your own was considered sinister and weird.

Only, in this case, it was exciting somehow. I got a sudden kick inside, like someone had poked my heart with a stick.

Anne just laughed. 'I'm a researcher by profession. I know how to find things out. Now you do the booze while I do food. Don't stint with the spirits. With punch, as with love, you should always err on the side of recklessness.'

It occurred to me then that she probably knew about

47

my sister, but I was glad she hadn't mentioned it. I was sick of people being sorry about it, sick of the way they self-consciously adopted a solemn, sympathetic face when they talked about Eve. It wasn't really their fault – what else could they do? – but it still made me want to slap them.

I was left pouring, mixing and tasting. Chopping fruit, getting the punch to the colour and consistency of deep-vein blood. Two regal looking cats came in and stared at me with baleful eyes. Anne introduced them as her spoilt babies. Ophelia and Portia.

It was a good half an hour before there was another knock on the door. Anne was next to me at the time. She turned to me, dark eyes glittering in her pale, immaculate face.

'Now. I knew you'd be first here,' she said. 'But I wonder who'll be second. It'll either be the new muse or it'll be Bim.'

It was Bim.

'Bim. This is Mark. Mark this is Bim. My only friend. My rock.'

He was tall, as tall as me, and bigger built. A wrestler's shape. Bullet headed with the hair close cropped. Thick neck, bullish shoulders. Powerful arms, massive hands, legs like tree trunks. He looked like he could be a blue in several of the rougher sports. In his dark suit he looked like a gangland enforcer.

There were quite a few blokes who looked a bit like Bim at the university. Steak-fed men from minor public schools studying land economy and such like. Men who spent most of their time getting muddy on the sports field, flicking towels at one another in the showers and harassing girls in bars. Bim's looks were very deceiving. He had made no tackles, flicked no towels. He never

harassed girls. He had spent the last six years tinkering with a thesis on the Vorticists.

'Bim?' I said, as he took my proffered hand in both of his.

'A schoolboy thing. A whim of my chums at Marlborough, the entomology of which is lost in those mists where none of us shall ever travel again.'

'You mean etymology, surely?' Anne. Smiling.

'Do I, dear thing? Do I really? If you knew anything about boys' public schools you'd know they are absolute termites' nests. It's an insect life and no mistake.'

Bim's voice seemed to belong to another man altogether. A voice as milky and slight as his body was meaty and slab-like. Both chirpy and sibilant with a carefully cultivated lisp, his voice was like an inexpertly played flute, a thing that would fill all the gaps with its breathy music if you let it.

He paused now, my hand still in his, looked me up and down.

'Extraordinary,' he said.

I felt myself blushing, my face growing hot. I blushed easily then, it had been a curse in school where the smallest criticism – or compliment – could make me turn pink. Bim withdrew his hands from mine, clapped them together, laughed good-naturedly. The doorbell made its sorrowful clang.

'The new muse?' said Anne. Bim made a face.

'Bon courage,' he said. 'Come, my bright boy, lead me to booze immediately. Talk me through this beautiful punch. Our Mrs Lamprey's fabulous recipe perchance?'

'Of course,' said Anne. To me she said, 'It was Bim that got me Mrs Lamprey's shockingly neglected hostessing bible.'

49

'Yes, what a find that was. All the best bargains can be had at the Kings College Library damaged stock sale. Best £1.75 I ever spent.' Bim linked arms with me and walked me down the hall to the kitchen, while Anne went to the door. 'We don't want to be around when the muse makes her entrance,' he said.

But it wasn't the muse. Instead it was the first of the men in corduroy. There were a lot of these. A few were accompanied by wives with anxious eyes and too-stiff hair, but most were on their own. After a while there were also a couple of female academics. A chunky, frizzy-haired sociologist defiantly dressed down, jeans flapping around her ankles like the sixties had never ended. A thin historian, glamorous in a little black dress with her hair in a long grey plait. Mostly, though, it was just bespectacled men in brown clothes.

'Did we fight the punk rock wars for this?' said Bim.

There were some other students there, even one or two I recognised. Essayists for the student magazines. Politicos. Comedians. Poets. The convener of RockSoc.

Bim filled glasses with Mrs Lamprey's thickly gory drink, greeting each guest with fluty bonhomie, and after he'd done so and they'd moved away, he filled me in on their secret lives. The adulterers, the swingers, the S&M enthusiasts, the serial molesters of students, the collectors of Nazi regalia. Who knew that so much ill-fitting tailoring could conceal so much varied and transgressive passion? So much desperate heat. Though it was possible he was making it up. I had known him for less than an hour and already I knew Bim wasn't one for letting beige facts spoil a lurid story.

Every time he filled a glass for one of the guests, he refilled mine.

At one point, seeming put out, he said, 'All the while the new muse continues to fail to arrive.'

'Who is this muse?' I said.

'She's only the whole bloody point of this shindig. It's not so much a party as a launch,' he said. Sheldon's project. 'Oh, we can't skulk here anymore. We must circulate, dear boy. We must be bees.'

'Bees?'

'Bees. We must help pollinate this sorry meadow of ennui. Bring it to life, if that's possible. It is down to us.' He waved a hand. 'Or up to us. Whatever. Let the mingling begin.'

Together we excuse-me'd our way out of the kitchen and across the hall. The Victorians probably had salons and soirees in mind right from the moment they first started laying out the streets of North Cambridge, so it was a big house, several large reception rooms, but even so the place was filling up, beginning to sweat.

At the main living room – what back home we would have called the lounge - we paused for a moment on the edge of things. Then Bim was gone, moving into the clusters of conversations with bold confidence. Spine straight, broad shoulders back, generalised smile taking everyone in: the way a beauty on a crowded beach might wade into the sea, expecting admiration. Like Marilyn Monroe might have looked if she had been built like a brick shithouse.

I took a sip of my drink. Another. I had time to take in the look of the house. How it was dressed. The large pieces of abstract art on the walls, all blurred lines and bright squares of colour. The sculptures.

Yes, the sculptures. The biggest was in highly polished blackish stone, obsidian maybe, a good foot and a half

high. A lady holding a baby to her breast, both lady and baby fat bodied with perfectly round, perfectly faceless heads. The smaller pieces were simple cubes and spheres in bronze. No house I'd ever been in before had had sculptures. Ornaments, yes. Comical china donkeys brought back from Spanish holidays, yes. Collections of small ceramic hedgehogs, yes. Actual sculptures in bronze and in stone, no.

Mrs Boyd had said the parties hosted by the Sheldons were legendary, but I was getting discouraged. The drink was making my teeth ache and my stomach fizz. I'd smiled at Bim's stories, but they had left me depressed. So much dishonesty in the world.

I hadn't seen more than glimpses of Anne as she moved from group to group like a, well, like a shiny blue butterfly.

Once, on a trip back to the kitchen, she had looked over at Bim and me. She had raised an eyebrow and we had raised our glasses in salute.

I was properly alone now in that crowded room, wishing I hadn't come. Wishing I was in a pub or in my room having a laugh with Katy. Even Katy with Danny would be better than this. Even sitting on my own in a room thinking about Eve would be better than this. My instincts on the doorstep had been the right ones. You should always act on instinct, I thought now.

The minutes crawled by and still no one talked to me.

I got angry. Why would you invite someone and then leave them alone like this? By now Mrs fucking Lamprey's page 112 punch was kicking in and I was finding it harder to focus.

I retreated back to my spot in the corner of the kitchen by the punch bowl. Relieved to be back in that little

haven, I nursed a new drink. Vodka and coke this time, Mrs Lamprey's punch being long gone.

I decided to treat the whole event the way an anthropologist might treat unexpected access to the rituals of a secretive tribe deep in the jungles of the Amazon. This game worked for a bit, but not for long. Soon I was feeling properly shit. I was feeling like I'd become the most unattractive of wallflowers. Not even a wallflower actually, not even that – no, not even that. I was something drab, yes, but also something spiny, spiky and maybe slightly poisonous. A wallweed, a wallthistle. A wall fucking triffid.

I made up my mind to go. I'd been there nearly two hours and, courtesy of Bim, I did have some reasonably juicy gossip with which to regale Katy and Mrs Boyd, even if its provenance was doubtful.

Both of them would be disappointed at the absence of anything remotely legendary happening, though Katy would also be grimly pleased. Dr Sheldon hadn't even made an appearance at his own party. He'd stayed upstairs while his guests drank, argued and flirted in a heavy-handed, middle-aged, corduroyed way. Faceless intellectuals talking generalised bollocks.

With determination I began to make my way across the kitchen. I was going to find Lady Anne Sheldon and her shiny dress, and I was going to bid them both a courteous goodnight. I'd be polite but I would somehow convey that this has been two hours kind of wasted. Time I would never get back again. I would hint, in a way that was both veiled but unmistakeable, that she'd been unforgivably rude.

Only I found that my legs were slow in obeying commands from my brain. I walked two wobbly steps

and then had to stop and hold on to the kitchen worktop. That modern gentlewoman had known what she was about.

I straightened up. I made a new plan. I'd stay where I was. Exactly where I was. I'd nod and I'd smile and I'd try and look as normal as possible. I would sweat it out.

My whole body was in rebellion now, turning liquid on me. My guts were foaming. I had that slidey feeling again, the sense of the world slipping away from me that I'd had when I'd stood up after the accident. I looked for Bim and saw him laughing amid a group of pigeon-faced young men.

You bastard, I thought. You bastard. Get me pissed and then fuck off. Cheers for that. If I ever saw him again, we would have words. Like I would with Anne. Lady Anne and her shiny dress. Proper words not veiled hints after all. What was her game? Inviting me, and then ignoring me. Yes, proper words with her too. Definitely. And soon. But for now I would stay where I was. Here. A plan. Nod. Smile. I was fine. Fine. Don't move. Wait. Feel better. Leave. Never see these people again. Yes, a plan. A good plan.

Like the anthropologist game, this worked too, for a while. For a minute, maybe five minutes even, I just stood, not observing, not thinking, entirely focused on being upright, which was why it took me a while to notice when Anne was stood in front of me making introductions.

An older man with film star features, a Harrison Ford type. A man ageing well, crumbling in exactly that way that seems most attractive to both women and to movie producers. Just creased enough. Face craggy, skin rough

and weathered. Hair plentiful, steel-grey and unruly. Grizzled. Pale, haunted eyes. Yes, a very Hollywood idea of a successful academic.

'My husband – Dr Philip Sheldon.'

'Of course,' I said, as if I recognised him, though the truth was I didn't remember seeing him around Cambridge at all

Harrison Ford was genial. 'Ah, the kid my wife nearly killed.'

I didn't like this kid business. 'I'm fine. Really. No harm done.'

'Pleased to hear it. Actually, my fault anyway I suppose. Should never have bought her that damn car. Impossible to drive that thing at a sensible speed. More horsepower than anyone needs. I call it her beast.'

Dr Sheldon really did have a silver screen look. Even with my focusing problems I could see that he was definitely a big screen presence, even down to the teeth, which were surprisingly white and square amid the cinematic decay of his face.

'This is Dr Michelle Saker.'

I turned carefully towards Dr Sheldon's companion. If I moved slowly I would be all right.

I wasn't all right. I nearly fell over.

Dr Michelle Saker was something else. No ordinary Cambridge beauty, her. Even drunk, I felt her special allure. Dr Saker. Late twenties, black hair punkishly spiked, eyes a cat-like green behind heavy NHS specs. Madonna t-shirt. Red jeans. Expensive trainers. Jordans. Her stare defiant, as if she expected to be attacked and was keen to get her retaliation in first.

'Friends call me Mish,' she said. Her expression might have been fierce but her voice was fragile, shy. Colourless and accent-free. Small.

But I got it then. You didn't have to be a genius. The new muse. Dr Sheldon and Dr Saker. Philip and Mish. They were having, or would be having very soon, a thing. A fling. Maybe more than that. A proper love affair even. Though the professor was stood side-by-side with his wife while introducing his lover, it somehow didn't feel wrong.

Dr Saker and Dr Sheldon. On their own each of them was handsome, accomplished and very obviously super-brainy. But together they had a room-stilling quality. Together the two of them seemed lit by a kind of joint phosphorescence. A force that surely meant that no one could begrudge them coupling up. Not even a wife.

Of course I was wasted, possibly concussed too, so I was perhaps more susceptible to flights of fancy like this. Perhaps my brain was over-heating and I was beginning to see auras everywhere. And, then, from nowhere, I was puking. A geyser of Mrs Lamprey's blood-red punch, exploding from deep inside with sudden horror flick violence. I managed to step back one pace, and Dr Saker did a balletic twist and hop, so the puke mostly avoided her trousers, but her shoes were covered.

From somewhere far away, someone – Dr Sheldon, if I had to guess – muttered a bloody idiot, but whoever the voice belonged to it didn't sound angry, just tired. Mish Saker made no sound. I raised my head, looked right into her eyes. There was hurt there.

Somebody giggled and it might have been me, I put my hand over my mouth. It was slimy against my palm. A firm hand on my shoulder and another on my elbow and I was being steered through the kitchen, through the hallway and into a little cloakroom. I had never been arrested, but I imagined it might feel like this. A gentle but irresistible

movement. I hunched over the bowl waiting for further spasms. Behind me Anne locked the door.

'That was priceless. Absolutely bloody priceless,' she said. 'You should have seen her face.'

'I'm sorry,' I said. My voice disappearing into the toilet bowl.

'Don't be. I'm delighted. Now, get everything up and out, and then we'll pop you upstairs for a while. It's probably just the booze, but you've had a nasty bump on the head too. Best keep you under observation.'

Ten minutes later, all puked out, weak as a kitten and feverish, I was lying in a small dark room at the back of the house. A girl's room this, judging by the profusion of pink, the My Little Ponies and the posters. The double headed monster that was Bros sneering down at me. There's always something sinister about identical twins isn't there?

I lay there shivering and sweating and dozing, hearing the music and laughter coming up through the floor. After a while I felt comfortable, cosy. I was a child again. Ill but safe. I wondered when Anne would come and look in on me. Keep you under observation, she'd said. But time passed and no one came. I remained very much unobserved. Gradually I moved from warm, drowsy comfort back to the cold sweats of embarrassment. Sobriety returned with its hung head.

I got up, found my sneakers and padded along the landing. I stole down the stairs, halted briefly. I had to. Two boys were making out on the bottom steps. One of the poets and the man from RockSoc.

'Excuse me,' I said and stepped over them as they prised themselves apart without any hurry. One whispered to

the other and his companion sniggered. I had sounded comically prim maybe. I had never seen two men making out before and it made me feel a bit funny. Not aroused exactly but, well, funny. Definitely that.

Now I was in another hallway, not the one where I came in. This one was the servants entrance once upon a time. At one end I could hear the party and I was keen to get away before anyone came out and saw me.

I was mortified. Of course I was. But the worst thing was feeling that I'd somehow failed an audition. I'd had a shot at getting into that other Cambridge – the college behind the colleges – and I'd screwed it up. The wet breeze I had to push against now seemed to confirm it. The rustle in the trees seemed to whisper it as they shook their green heads at me.

Back home I remembered to nod to Ted, tonight's porter. Ted didn't nod back.

8

I didn't go to college the following morning. Or the morning after that. My head and stomach hurt. Instead I read without taking anything in, listened to records that suddenly seemed melodramatic and childish, let my room irritate me. The flowers were fine but everything else was wrong. My posters seemed quaint. Callow. They made my room seem adolescent somehow. Bands. Pictures of bloody bands on my wall. Like I was still fifteen. I suddenly saw myself as being no different from the girl who kept Bros on her walls. I would take them down.

Only thing I'd leave up was the picture of Eve singing with her group at her high school talent show. They were called 'The Good Terrorists' after the Doris Lessing book and they'd been okay actually, though they didn't win. Three boys and Eve. The lads all studious music nerds, Eve with her Edward Scissorhands hair and Cruella de Vil make-up. Wielding her guitar like a machine gun. My sister fighting capitalism through the medium of power

chords, feedback and songs about chocolate. Yeah, I'd leave that photo up.

Mainly I rolled ragged fags and smoked them, trying to ignore the stray strands of tobacco that ended up in my mouth, daydreamed and didn't move from my bed until Katy and Danny turned up after rowing practice – she was a cox for the college second eight, he rowed number seven, sitting just behind the stroke where you had to be both fit and skilled. Danny took pride in being the only state-educated student on the squad. Katy took pride in being fucking excellent.

'Look,' she said, 'we've brought beer and we've brought chips. Aren't we good?'

'Very good.'

'How was the party?'

'Oh, you know. Boring.'

'Who was there?'

'Oh, you know, people. Boring people.'

'So not legendary then?'

'Not legendary, no.'

She was delighted. 'See, told you. I knew it.'

9

Eve, at thirteen, was allowed to get the train from Colchester to Clacton with two friends. Dad needed persuading to let her go. But over days and weeks, she built her case: it wasn't far, only fifteen miles, thirty minutes on the train through the slow green countryside. They'll go on the pier, they'll eat ice cream, they'll go to the shops, a small adventure. A jolly day out by the sea. A lark. How did he expect her to learn to take responsibility for herself, if he never let her go anywhere or do anything? It's Clacton. Not Las Vegas. What does he think will happen? Mum. Tell him, please.

John Chadwick was surprised to find his wife taking her side. Come on, John. Don't be such an old stick in the mud. They're sensible girls. Let them have their little adventure.

So, early one Saturday, they took the 107 bus to the station and they arrived back more or less when they said they would and they seemed to have had a thoroughly

lovely time. The pier was great, the beach was great, the boys were great... joking, Dad. Keep your hair on. The shops in Clacton were surprisingly good too. They bought some things. Not much, just a couple of cheap t-shirts. Some tights. Some lipstick. Hair stuff.

The next morning, Sunday, when her dad was acting as linesman at The Blue Pig's home match versus The Greyhound, her mum brought her a cup of tea and sat watching her drinking it for a while. Calm eyes, a steady look, a funny sort of smile on her face.

After a bit, Eve started to get weirded out. 'What?' she said. 'What?' she sounded more aggressive than she meant to. Her mum's smile disappeared.

'So. London then. Find your way about all right? Manage the Tube?'

Eve's mouth opened and closed. Her mum explained. 'Last time I looked there wasn't a Miss Selfridge in Clacton.' They both looked towards the bags that Eve had left hanging off the knob of the door. So busted.

'Bollocks,' she said, and then clapped her hand to her mouth. 'Sorry.'

A long moment where things could go either way, but then her mum laughed. She lifted her forceful chin. Showed her strong teeth.

'It's all right,' she said. 'Don't worry. Just remember, whatever you do, whatever you're planning, I will find out about it. No more hiding things. No secrets.' She got up from the bed.

'Don't,' Eve began.

'Oh, don't worry, I'm not going to tell your dad.'

They both paused for a second, imagining the fuss that would take place if John Chadwick knew, not just the explosion here in the pub, which would be bad enough,

but also there would be the rows with the parents of the other girls to deal with, because he would be bound to assume his little girl had been led astray by her badly brought up friends. Would not believe that it had been Eve's idea, whatever she said. That would mean bad weather everywhere – at home, at school, in town on Saturdays, everywhere.

'Thanks, Mum. Sorry.'

'I'm serious. No more hiding things. No secrets. Drink your tea.'

Mum told me that story at the wake after Eve's funeral. 'I believed her you know, I thought we really would never have any more secrets. I thought she really would tell me everything. Absolutely everything.'

'She wasn't herself, Mum. She was ill.'

'But I should have seen that, shouldn't I?'

Of course she should, nothing I could say could change that. When it comes to your children, look hard, look close and listen. Listen more. Eve taught us that if nothing else.

I looked in my mother's eyes, eyes that were the colour of dust and clouds, and knew that our family was finished really, though none of us would ever say so.

We were quiet for a while, and around us the pointless noises grew: glasses slammed on the bar, people kissed and hugged and cried. The fruit machine paid out with a frantic rattle. Somebody laughed, somebody else shushed them.

'Don't tell your dad, will you?' Mum said.

'He won't care, Mum. Not now, not after all this time.' But I wasn't sure, maybe he would.

10

Of course I didn't really have to do it. Not actually go round. Maybe I couldn't afford to fill a room with flowers, but I could have sent a letter. I could have been gracefully abject on the kind of high end stationery I knew Anne appreciated. That would have done.

But I suppose I still had that sense that Anne and her professor had the key to a more vibrant life than the one I was living, and that with persistence they might still unlock it all for me. With patience, perseverance and charm I might just get a second shot. All hindsight of course, at the time I just acted without thinking too much.

If anything I was even more nervous standing on the doorstep this second time than I had been on the evening of the party, but then Anne was opening the door, welcoming me like we were old friends, like she had been thinking I might pop round. Like it was a completely natural thing for me to do.

She was dressed in a man's striped shirt, sleeves rolled

up to above the elbow on both arms. Designer jeans expensively ripped at the knees. She ushered me in, offered me tea.

As the kettle boiled she told me that she hoped I hadn't come round to apologise for my behaviour, that she hoped I wasn't one of those sensitive, hand-wringing types. She told me that she preferred men who were never sorry for anything. Men who never apologised. I didn't rise to it. I asked where the professor was and she said she didn't know but that she assumed he was with the new muse.

'This one does seem to have got her claws into him rather.'

'Oh. Right.'

'Oh. Right?' She was laughing at me. 'For a student of English literature you're not all that brilliant with words are you Marko?'

She put her cup down. Stood up quickly and yawned showing the neat white picket fence of her teeth. 'You know what? I'm all tea'd out. Do you fancy a spin?'

'What?'

'There you go with the razor-sharp repartee again. I'm asking if you fancy getting out of the town. I'm bloody bored of this house and it's a nice day, car's full of petrol and who knows how long I'll have it. Costs a bomb to run. But seeing as it was a present to atone for Phil's last little dalliance it seems fitting to try and get the most out of it while he's busy with this one. We could have a picnic.'

'So there are some kinds of apologies that you don't mind. Some ways of saying sorry are better than others?' I held my breath. I could feel the heat on my cheeks, knew that I was blushing. But Anne just laughed.

'That's it,' she said, 'that's the way. You mustn't let me

push you around. I'll just take advantage. Walk all over you. Yes, very expensive apologies are the most bearable I guess. So? You up for it? Do you have any other plans?'

No, I had no other plans.

The 1964 Daimler Dart. Anne Sheldon's car. Professor Sheldon's expensive apology. Fibreglass body, four-wheel Girling disc brakes, and a 2.5-litre hemi-head V8 engine designed by Edward Turner. The car that had almost killed me and the most beautiful mechanical object I had ever seen and, until that moment, I hadn't thought I was into cars.

Anne relaxed once we were moving. The driver's seat of that open-topped monster – that beast – was clearly a place where she felt at home.

'Gets a bit noisy, I'm afraid. We won't be able to chat much,' she said.

She was not wrong. We growled and belched our way out of the town. Every gear change accompanied by a bluish mist, the car snarling at being held up by the senseless irrelevancies like traffic lights, roundabouts and other drivers.

No, we didn't talk. Even if we'd have been able to hear each other over the noise of engine and rushing wind. I saw her lips move as she swore at fuckwits who kept to the speed limits, the morons who followed the highway code. I had to guess at the exact words but it wasn't difficult.

She got several hoots and it was impossible to tell whether she was being hooted at for her driving, which was ostentatiously reckless, or simply because she was a good-looking woman in a sports car.

Probably she got both kinds of hoot.

I couldn't tell you the route we took. I wasn't really concentrating on road signs. I was watching her hands. Anne had tiny hands with slender wrists that were nevertheless firm on the steering wheel. Her nails were a translucent cream. There were fine golden hairs standing up on her forearms.

She was wearing the same long drop earrings she had on the day we met, the day she knocked me down. They were swinging wildly in the wind as she drove. Like little green men doing the Tyburn jig. I reached out to touch the one nearest me. I felt the need to steady it, to stop its movement.

'Romeo Gigli,' she shouted. 'Four hundred pounds.'

I took my hand away. Those earrings cost as much as my term's rent. She laughed.

The grace of her throat. Her long, white neck. The necklace in coral and pearls. I wondered what that cost. And yes, I noticed the full swell of her breasts beneath her shirt. Of course I did. Yes, I noticed the way the sharp spice of her expensive scent slugged it out with the smell of old tobacco smoke. I noticed the way her small, pointed, pink tongue poked from between her lips as she concentrated on intimidating the other, lesser road users into getting out of her way. They did it too. Those yappy Fiestas, smug Saabs, arrogant Beamers – they might toot but they all moved over for Anne, her earrings, her throat, her necklace and her indigo Dart.

She must have noticed me staring, but she didn't turn my way once. She just maintained that subtle smile. It was as though she had been expecting this kind of examination and found it somehow quaint. Sweet, almost.

Once we had made it through the sweating metal of other traffic to the emptier B-roads outside the town,

Anne put her foot down a bit and frightened me sufficiently for me to stop looking at her, and instead sit back against the hot vintage leather bucket seat and look at the rare optimistic blue of the sky.

I closed my eyes. I could feel all the little bumps and ruts of the road just inches beneath me. The rattle of stones against the chassis.

I couldn't tell you now where we went. A large piece of elevated common land on the edge of the city. A stretch of green that had, in the distant past, been quarried. A place full of dips and holes where people spelled out their names and romances in large, butter-coloured rocks. JENNY LUVS HARRY. FRANK 4 JO. Or where boys used the rocks to name the male parts. BALLS. KNOB. COCK.

Maybe it's no longer common land. Maybe it's no longer all long grass and cow pats and benches commemorating people who always loved this view. Maybe it's a housing estate now, an eco-town perhaps, or a science park. But then, that day, it was everything good about England. There was an ice cream van. There were people flying kites, walking dogs. There were misshapen trees. There was a Saxon barrow, which ought to help pinpoint it, but doesn't really. The Saxon nobility seem to have littered the whole area with their dead.

We didn't speak while amid the noise of the car, but we didn't talk much once we were out of it either. I carried the plastic bag I was given, while Anne walked fast, always just a little ahead of me. It was clear that she knew exactly where she wanted to go.

There was a large tree under which she spread the blanket. I thought it was an oak but could have been an

ash, an elm or a beech. I didn't know about these things. But it was definitely ancient and substantial. A tree that had seen a lot.

Anne took the plastic bag and set out the picnic. In its entirety it consisted of two bottles of fizzy wine and some olives.

'All I've got I'm afraid. Maybe I should have made sandwiches or brought crisps or sausage rolls or something as well. I expect you're hungry,' she said. 'I hear teenage boys are always hungry.'

I laughed.

'What's so funny?' she said.

'Is that how you see me? As a teenage boy?'

'Well, aren't you?'

'I suppose. I mean I am, I guess, technically. But I don't think of myself as being one.'

'What, because you're at the University? Because you know who Hegel is? Because you've read Roland Barthes?'

I was embarrassed because I had only the vaguest idea who Hegel was and I hadn't read any Roland Barthes, though I intended to one day. But Anne didn't seem to notice. 'Anyway, there's nothing wrong with being a teenager,' she said. 'If I were you I'd stay one as long as you can. Men can, you know. Some men can spend years being nineteen. Or younger. They can be fifteen if they want. Hell, they can be thirteen forever. Harder for women. Open this, would you?'

She handed me a bottle and watched as I struggled to pop the cork. It was the first time I'd ever done this. The Blue Pig was not the kind of establishment where people routinely ordered bubbly. And, though I'd had plenty of champagne at Cambridge – some people drank nothing

else – others had always done the honours. So it took a while, the fat end of the bottle wedged in my groin while I sweated away at the cork, and then the foam shot from the angled neck all over my hand. It looked comically suggestive. Anne laughed and I blushed.

There was a charged moment, a stir in the air, while I filled glasses and we raised them to each other.

We talked about a lot of things that I couldn't really remember afterwards. I told some funny stories about growing up in a pub. I heard about her life as a child of the Empire, as the daughter of an army officer in Kenya, which she pronounced *Keenyah*.

I told her about discovering the library as a sanctuary from playground bullies in my first year of high school, about Mr Butterfield who saw a spark of something that no one else saw, the man who insisted I try for Cambridge. I asked her why we'd come here, to this particular spot.

'Because I was happiest here.'

She told me how, nearly twenty years before, an old boyfriend had brought her here to this tree and proposed and she'd said no, though up till that moment she had thought she might love him.

'That's when you were happiest? Turning down a marriage proposal?'

'Yes. Funny, huh?'

She explained that her suitor was a sweet boy – charming, clever, funny, good-looking, recently graduated with a first, a badminton blue, perfect really – but that she knew in the instant of his asking that he wasn't for her. That she needed something more. Something else, anyway.

'So it's here – in this very spot more or less – that I first

began to know who I am. Or rather, I began to know who I'm not.'

'How did he react, your boyfriend?'

'Oh, in the usual way. Shouted a bit. Called me names. Spread some disgusting rumours about me around the university, only one or two of which were true. Basically, he reacted how men always react to women who won't give them what they want. He threw a tantrum. Then he tried to punish me.'

She took an olive. Spat the stone on to the grass. 'He's married now. Three kids. He's ambassador to somewhere. Ecuador. Or Ethiopia. I forget which. Somewhere like that.'

'What a git.'

'Yes, funny to go from being adored to being reviled in the space of a few minutes. Quite an eye-opener. But even when he was yelling in my face, I was filled with a kind of happiness. Because I was finally, absolutely certain about something. To be certain of things is a total joy.'

I could imagine that, I who had so rarely been certain of anything.

'Anyway, it means this place – this tree – is special to me. The place where I discovered that sweet, charming, funny, badminton – all that – it's absolutely not my thing.'

'Sacred ground then. In a way.'

'I suppose so, yes.'

The day grew very warm, the sky remained that relentless blue. We had a competition to see who could spit an olive pit the furthest. I won, though not by much. Everything seemed to shimmer slightly, while around us was sculpted a soundscape of a romantic summer England. An insistent cuckoo, the drone of a biplane towing a glider high in the

sky, a distant dog barking. A farmer calling his sheep. A child laughing. Church bells. All we lacked was the sound of a village cricket team applauding a catch on the boundary.

She told me about meeting Professor Sheldon. About the merry dance they led each other.

'We had such fun at first,' she said. 'Still do now sometimes. He's so clever, so funny. Cruel as fuck of course, but that is a big part of his charm.'

I asked whether they had an open relationship and she laughed.

'Gosh, Mark. You do like to think in clichés, don't you? Open and closed are words to be used about shops, not about love.'

She told me their four simple rules for a happy marriage. No sneaking about. No germs. No bastards. No leaving.

'Maybe it's not for everyone but it works for us. Philip says that monogamy is a failed experiment and I think he's probably right,' she said. She drained her glass, refilled it. 'Tell me about your love life. Tell me about the fiery girl on the bike.'

'Katy? She's Danny's girlfriend.'

'Really? That cloddish fellow with the gigantic face? I think she'd rather be with you.'

'Bollocks.'

She laughed. We were quiet for a while. When we spoke again it was about things that didn't matter, about books we'd read and places in the world where we might like to live one day.

Anne drove us home, me clutching the bag with the blanket, the cups and the empty bottles tightly on my knees. If anything, she drove faster on the way back, throwing that car around with an even wilder grace.

She was quite pissed after all. We had drunk two bottles between us, and she had matched me plastic glass for plastic glass. Reckless. Stupid. Desperate. Insanely exciting.

When we reached Selwyn Gardens, she turned to me. She took a careful breath.

'Coming in?'

'All right. Yeah. Okay.'

'Oh, you honey-tongued seducer you. You Casanova.' She smiled and took my hand as she led the way up the drive.

Then we were in the hallway and somehow the space between us vanished. The air around us grew still and heavy. The house seemed to hold its breath. then her arms were round me. I was folded in the smoky-sweet spice of her.

'Oh Christ.' She was whispering against my chest. She sounded sad. Her face turned up towards mine and we were kissing, passionate, urgent, neither of us awkward or shy. Hands everywhere.

I couldn't tell you how long we were wrapped around each other before she pulled back, her hands on either side of my head. She was smiling up at me, close enough for me to see that the skin beneath her eyes was bruised looking with fatigue. It suited her.

She wiped her mouth with her hand. 'Crikey. You exquisite boy. You strange and exquisite boy.' She looked right at me now, eyes as dark and as infinite as a starless night. 'Fair warning, Marko. I love my husband. I won't leave him and he won't leave me. I fear I am going to be very bad for you. You should run.'

I could see that, yes, this woman was dangerous. Exactly the kind of dangerous, I realised now, that I had

been hoping for ever since I applied to Cambridge. I felt my heart cramp. Whatever was coming, I could take it.

'Have you got anything to drink?' I said.

She smiled. 'Yes. Yes, there's always lots to drink.'

11

Jake's place isn't far, Chaney Street in South Camden.
Ten minutes by bike. A redbrick Victorian terrace of the
kind half the population live in. It's like my own redbrick
terrace in fact, though half the size. At the front there's a
low wall and a garden of sorts, a scrubby patch of long
grass and dead leaves that provides a home for a wheelie
bin. There's a cracked and mossy concrete path to a cheap
PVC door with swirling frosted glass. By the door a big
brown pot containing a nondescript and dying plant.

It's the kind of plant pot that only exists to put the spare
key under. Lots of houses have one. Back in Haverstock
Road we do too. It's a wonder people aren't burgled
all the time. Except I have read somewhere that young
Britons are giving up on burglary as a profession. It's not
worth the candle. Goods are either too big to carry easily,
or not worth anything second hand. Or householders are
too likely to rise from their beds and batter you senseless
now that they have legal impunity to do that.

Every few weeks you read of junkies killed by professional types wielding cricket bats or golf clubs.

The house is cold and smells of chips, damp washing and cigarettes. The walls of the narrow hallway are an institutional pale green. The carpet a worn beige. The lightshade one of those cheap paper orbs you see everywhere. A couple of quid from Wilkos.

The small kitchen is tidy though, no dirty dishes piled up in the sink. Just a few cups on the draining board. There are three flying ducks above the gas fire where, in a more gentrified terrace, there would be a contemporary art print above a wood burning stove. Who put the ducks there? The landlord? Or is it an ironic homemaking statement by Jake and his artist girlfriend?

Most of the kitchen is taken up by a battered but sturdy-looking table on which sits a fat, half-melted church candle in a plain white saucer. There's not much worktop space for peeling and chopping, but there's room for a vivid Moroccan blue earthenware bowl containing a lemon, a pear, a greenish banana. There's a fat butternut squash, a bag of nuts, a not quite empty wine bottle. A heavy Chilean red, 14.5 per cent. The kind of wine Katy and I never touch now. These days our criteria for choosing wine is that it costs more than eight quid a bottle, but less than twelve. That it's no more than 12.5 per cent.

The only really odd thing is that everything is labelled. There are yellow post-it notes on every item giving the name of that thing in Italian. *Tavolo* on the table, *frigo* on the fridge, even a post-it with *la anatre* attached to the back of the leading duck. Even the wine bottle – *bottiglia di vino* – is labelled in this way, even the pears – *pera*, even the butternut squash – *zucca violina*.

Suddenly, I'm ravenous. There's not much in the fridge. Five cherry tomatoes on a vine. A cucumber. Some half-used up jars of posh jam. Plum. Damson and bramble. Two cans of cheap lager. A large bar of vegan chocolate. Half a carton of soya milk. Both of which explain the lack of meat and cheese. A hard kitchen to categorise. Kind of studenty, but not madly so. Grad-studenty maybe.

I scout around the cupboards. Doesn't take long and yes, in the last cupboard I find a packet of Frosties about a third full. Perfect. Turns out that Frosties are exactly what I fancy, the complete very thing, even with soya milk.

We do have fancy cereals in the Chadwick house but they are only ever for during the holidays. School days it's porridge, occasionally it's scrambled eggs. Sometimes it's Weetabix or Shredded Wheat with the absolute minimum sprinkling of sugar. Frosties are the sort of thing that Ella and Jack only ever get the first week of the summer holidays and not always then.

I am in the cupboards getting a bowl and a spoon when something stops me. It's only Frosties, but even so, it's pretty much the only food in the place and if it wasn't for Jake and his partner then I'd be in some squalid London nick for days of questioning. I should leave their food alone.

I put the cereal and the bowl back in the cupboard. The soya milk back in the fridge. For the same reason, I leave the beer, despite cheap lager being suddenly another thing I fancy. Frosties and lager, that would have been great but I can't do it, can't help myself – I need permission. I open the fridge, take out a can, feel the heft of it in my hand. The beer is something called Steinbrau Blonde. A nonsensical mangling of languages that shouts crappy

bargain booze. It's not a G&T but it'll do the same job more or less. Can I? No, I can't. I just can't.

Tea though, I can have tea. People who have given you the keys to their house expect you to make yourself a brew.

I make tea in one of those mugs that replicate those classic orange Penguin book covers. This one is *The Invisible Man*. I take the tea upstairs, taking care not to splosh any on the carpet as I go. It means it is slow going. My hands are shaking. My nerves are gone.

At the top of the short, steep, narrow flight of stairs is a tiny landing with three closed doors. I open the first one. Jake and Lulu's room. Male and female clothes strewn any old how. A king-size bed, red and black duvet half on the bed, half on the floor. The room smells sweaty, gamey almost. I guess that this is where Jake and Lulu spend most of their time.

An old dressing table with bowed legs painted a vivid cricket pitch green is the only furniture, though there are photographic prints on the wall. Studies of faces and places in sombre black and white. Old warehouses coming down. New skyscrapers going up. A close-up of a laughing Jake. A mosque in some desert town. Dignified old ladies hurrying past East End betting shops. Babies.

I click the light off and open the next door. A small bathroom and it's exactly what you would expect. Not disgusting, but not clean either. A variety of his and her potions, a pair of scales. And, like everything in the kitchen, all labelled with their Italian names. *Crema idratante*, *bilancia*. There are books stacked by the bog. Some heavyweight academic books, political books. *The Case for Animal Rights*. *The Mathematical Principles of Natural Philosophy*. Pierre-Joseph Proudhon's *What Is*

Property? Not really toilet reading. Unless he's changed a lot, I can't believe they are Jake's choices either. More predictably there's also a well-thumbed *Teach Yourself Italian.*

I sit on the toilet taking swallows of hot tea and trying, not very successfully, to think about what to do until Bim's gallery re-opens in a week. Trying, also without success, not to think about what will happen if either Bim or Anne refuse to see reason. Wondering now if it might just be best to hand myself in, to take my chances in the courts after all. But I take another slug of tea and find I have the strength to think no, fuck that.

When I've finished my drink my mouth feels icky, I'd love to clean my teeth, but using someone else's *dentrificio,* even more than eating their Frosties and drinking their beer, seems like an abuse of hospitality, so I content myself with smearing toothpaste along my teeth and gums and rinsing with water. Rinse and spit. Rinse and spit. So much of life comes down to this: small repetitive actions done without thinking. Habits and impulses. So little that human beings do needs real concentration. We are animals really, and not majestic ones. Not lions. We are insects. We are insects who just happen to be cursed with self-consciousness, with the knowledge that we'll die soon, probably in pain, and then we'll leave everything we love behind us for ever. And, how do we deal with that? By distracting ourselves, by anaesthetising ourselves, by only thinking when we absolutely have to.

In the tiny second bedroom there's a single bed with a sleeping bag, but the rest of the space is filled with boxes. Books and clothes. There's just one picture on the wall. A close-up of a toddler, mouth smeared in jam, but face

closed and hard, giving a very deliberate finger to the photographer and so to the whole world.

It's even colder in here than it is in the rest of the house and I guess Jake and Lulu hardly ever come in here. They dragged in the boxes of stuff they didn't immediately need, hung the picture and shut the door on it all.

I take my shoes and my jacket off, lay them on a box and climb into the sleeping bag. It feels dampish, smells musty and it's very nylony and chill. Nevertheless, I sleep, in a troubled, restless sort of way.

12

There is someone in the room. Someone standing a pace in by the door, at the foot of the bed, backlit by the light in the hallway. A prickly nest of hair, the face just a vaguely pointy grey shape beneath.

'Eve?'

As soon as I've taken in that she's there, she's gone and I hear the click of another light going on. The emphatic sound of a door being shut. Someone pissing. Taps running, the toilet flushing. The brushing of teeth. The click of the light going off again. The rattle and wobble of the door being opened again. All of it sounding as though it was taking place right next to my head.

People who bang on about old houses being best should remember that using the cheapest materials to construct the thinnest of walls was a Victorian value. Funny how you can tell someone is not in the best of moods just by the way they open and close doors. Now that I'm properly awake I feel foolish for having said my sister's name.

I watch as the blurry wraith that must be Lulu moves past the open doorway of my room again. She doesn't look my way this time.

I think about getting up, introducing myself. But I don't. Instead I lie staring at the ceiling trying really hard – and failing – not to feel sorry for myself. Distracting myself by thinking about what has made the police act now, what do they have? What have they been told?

A memory comes to me. A solemn child's face at an upstairs window. A child with a thin pale hand raised in salute.

The TV goes on so there is then the murmur of voices, occasional bursts of laughter. Applause. Whoops and cheers. No sense lying here now. No chance of getting back to sleep.

As I walk down the stairs, I am blinded by a flash of a camera.

'Sorry.' A voice that doesn't sound all that sorry. As my eyes recover, I can start to take her in properly. Jake's girlfriend is sitting on one of the utilitarian chairs, smoking. She must be at least ten years older than him, and as casual as he was businesslike. She wears a baggy black sweater over a thin frame, faded jeans, battered white trainers. Non-branded as far as I can see. She looks at me with a frank stare. Eyes the slow grey-green of a waveless sea.

In the unflattering 100 watt light of the kitchen she looks knackered. Skin pouched with shadows. Hair cut short as short as a schoolboy's and dyed a coppery red. Wide mouth. Long, sharp nose, with a discreet silver stud winking from her left nostril. She also looks fiercely

irritated, brows knitted and frowning. She nibbles on the nail of the little finger of her right hand.

'You got Jake's text,' I say.

'Yes, apparently we are harbouring a fugitive.'

Her voice is sharp, while her accent speaks of an expensive education, of tennis clubs and winters spent skiing. Reminds me of the voices I heard all around me every day at Cambridge.

'Well, sort of I guess. I appreciate it anyway. I'm Mark by the way. I was Jake's teacher. Ridiculously.'

She waves her cigarette impatiently. Yes, yes, her gesture says. I know all that. I'm not interested in names or any of this how do you do shit. She looks at me for a long moment. It's unnerving, uncomfortably forensic and also kind of sensual somehow. Hardly anyone ever looks at us closely, do they? Glances fall onto us then slide away, drift incuriously towards other faces, other scenes. But this woman looks properly, like she's hunting for something she's lost.

'Bit of a coincidence bumping into Jake at The Castle,' she says now.

'You'd be surprised,' I say. I tell her that if you add up everyone in my classes it means that every year I teach about two hundred students and I've been doing it for over twenty years. That's more than four thousand ex-students out in the world, and they get around. I bumped into a whole hen party of ex-students once. In Bratislava of all places.

'What's your crime?'

I am taken aback by her directness, by her lack of ordinary social graces, by the way she keeps her gaze on me.

'Well, it's complicated.'

'I'm very smart. Try me.'

I'm at a loss. I open and close my mouth. I must look like a simpleton. The silence seems to last for minutes. Lulu waits. And waits. Her dark eyes don't leave my face. I'm going to have to say something. Somewhere church bells begin to sound, doleful and muffled as if coming through miles of fog. I count the clangs. Six. Lulu sighs now. She seems, finally, to lose interest in her question.

'I hate night shifts,' she says. She stands and stretches theatrically. 'Do you want something to eat? I have to warn you we've only got Frosties in the house.'

'You know, Frosties would be bloody great.'

She raises an eyebrow at my eagerness, but doesn't say anything. She gets the packet from the cupboard, she fetches the milk, bowls and spoons. I notice that she walks a little stiffly, a little carefully, as if the floor might give way.

While we eat I confess that I nearly helped myself to the cereal when I first came in. I'm nervous and it makes me gabble a bit. I'm just making conversation, but Lulu's face clouds over.

'I think that would have been a very bad move. I was a bit dubious about having you here at all, even for one night and if I'd come back and found you'd nicked my Frosties – well, let's just say there would have been consequences. It's my favourite thing after a long shift. A bit of crap telly, some Frosties and a beer before I get my head down.'

I'm a bit thrown by this, unsettled by her mood changes. Would she really have turned me in if I'd eaten her cereal? It makes me realise all over again just how precarious things are. How small things need thinking about. How even tiny decisions can have big consequences. Lulu,

meanwhile, heads to the fridge and fetches the Steinbrau. She passes me a can.

'Your last beer,' I say. 'I'll get you some more before I go. More cereal too.'

'You don't have to,' she says. 'Cheers.' She takes a long swallow.

'I will though. Least I can do.'

She shrugs. We sip in silence for a moment.

Lulu says, 'So I'm thinking not theft then.'

I am baffled. 'What?'

'Your big crime – probably not theft, what with you being so scrupulous about not helping yourself to our food and everything.'

She's not going to let up.

'No, it wasn't theft.'

'You're really not going to tell me, are you?'

'I can't. Sorry.'

'How frustrating.' She pulls at her lip. 'Tell me what Jake was like at school then. That's not a big state secret, is it?'

I smile. Try to relax. Maybe it'll be okay. I think about the young Jake Skellow. What should I say? I begin cautiously. 'I suppose you'd call him high-spirited.'

Lulu snorts into her beer. 'High-spirited. Yeah, right. I bet he was a terror. A little sod.'

'He had his moments,' I say.

'I can imagine.'

So I tell her some classic Jake stories. The time he jumped from the first floor window in form period. The time he brought in a baby owl he'd found on the way to school, hoping he could keep it alive in his locker. The times I'd caught him listening to some terrible hip-hop on his headphones when we were meant to be reading

Of Mice and Men. Other stories like this too, all of them about attempts to needle authority figures, to derail lessons, to discombobulate the teachers.

But there are stories I don't tell. For instance, I don't tell her about the time I saw Kayleigh Harbinson touching him up under the desk while they were meant to be watching Baz Luhrman's *Romeo and Juliet.* It had been quite blatant, but I had been sure it was much more to do with challenging the teacher than with pleasuring her boyfriend. Which is why I had refused to be challenged. Why I had let it go.

As I talk Lulu allows herself a flicker of a smile every now and again. It lands on her face for an instant then it's gone. When I'm done, she asks if I think Jake will make a good dad. I am taken aback.

'Why – you're not?'

She smiles, shakes her head. 'No, no but we're thinking about it. That is, we talk about it sometimes when we're feeling especially loved up.'

I give it some thought – will Jake Skellow make a good dad? Impulsive but kind. Will jump out of a window to get a laugh. Will offer shelter to strays of all kinds. Has an endless supply of fart gags and funny faces. Yes, actually I think he'll be great.

'You don't think he's too young?'

'Everyone is too young to have children,' I say.

She frowns. I just mean that everybody struggles as a parent – the fifteen-year-old schoolgirl living on alcopops and snapchat, yes, obviously, but also the forty-year-old fully zero-balanced, all yoga-ed up solicitor – doesn't matter who you are, or how sorted you think you are, children knock you sideways in ways you can't predict. I tell her this.

'Yes, but that's why you have them isn't it?' she says.

Of course I think of Ella and Jack. They'll be up by now. If this was a normal Saturday, I'd be making them a cooked breakfast. They'd be squabbling loudly – one of them would probably be crying or complaining about the other. Afterwards Jack and I would be off to judo while Katy gets Ella to ballet. I close my eyes. I could cry. Lulu sees. She chews on the nail of her little finger. She frowns again.

'You got kids yourself then?' she says.

I just nod, I can't do any more than that. I am too full of grieving to do anything else. We sit in silence for a minute.

'There's a 24-hour shop near here, isn't there?' I say, finally. I'd noticed it on the way over. 'I'll get those bits of shopping.'

Lulu doesn't protest. She can see I want to be on my own. Anyway, she seems lost in her thoughts. She doesn't look at me as I pass her on the way out of the kitchen and into the hall. She just scratches at her freckled arms, sips her drink, nibbles on her fingernail.

I walk slowly to the shop. I am trying to think clearly. What to do now? Now I'm awake and up, should I just take off again? Again I'm thinking I should just hand myself in. I'm just not suited for life on the run. I haven't got the tradecraft to be a fugitive. Even for a week. Too soft, too polite. Too many staffroom flapjacks, too many 6 p.m. merlots.

I'm away – what, twenty minutes? When I'm back Lulu is showered and changed. With wet hair combed down she is more boyish than ever. The jumper and the

jeans have been replaced by an old and comfortable-looking wine-coloured dressing gown, loose over tartan pyjamas. Dressed for bed you can tell just how skinny she is, her collar bones delicate and fragile. She's wearing one surprisingly old-ladyish beige slipper. She's wearing one slipper, because she's only got one foot. From the left knee down the pyjama leg hangs empty.

I stare. Of course I do. As I'm probably meant to. Lulu arches an eyebrow, gives a frowning smile and exhales wearily.

'Shark,' she says. 'Surfing in Australia ten years ago. All very dramatic at the time. Fine now, but yes, I can still feel the leg sometimes, as if it was still there.'

This explains the careful movement up and down the stairs, the stiffness as she had fetched and carried things in the kitchen.

'You'd never know,' I say. I wonder why Jake thought it was important to tell me that his girl was an artist, but not about this.

Lulu shrugs. 'Good prosthesis,' she says. 'I have microchips in my patella and in my plastic ankle. I am bionic. I am the six-million-dollar woman. But a whole shift and it gets sore.'

'It must do,' I say.

'So that's my big secret. Now you should tell me yours.' She smiles at the transparency of her own ruse. How can I refuse her now?

I take a breath.

'When I was eighteen my sister killed herself,' I begin. I wait for the eyes to widen, for the murmured sympathy. Only it doesn't happen. She simply nods. Her eyes drift to the ceiling and around the room and then settle back on mine. She frowns slightly.

My mouth is dry. I begin again but stop. There is fumbling at the door.

'Typical Jake,' Lulu says, 'blundering in at just the wrong moment.' She shakes her head, bites her fingernail.

Jake is all good cheer.

'Brrr,' he says, rubbing his hands and blowing on them as he moves into the kitchen that feels suddenly crowded now. 'Brass monkeys in here. Hey babe.'

He kisses Lulu and she wraps her arms around him to pull him into a deeper kiss. A public display of affection from which Jake emerges breathless.

'Steady on,' he says, embarrassed. He catches my eye. 'And, Mr Chadwick, Sir. Mark. How are you doing?'

'I'm okay.'

'He's fine, Jakey, he's had cereal. He's had beer. He's told me all about Young Jake – you wee rascal, you. You scallywag.'

Jake does a theatrical surprised face, hands to his cheeks in mock-horror.

'You didn't tell her about Kayleigh Harbinson?' he says. I tell him I concentrated more on the baby owl story.

'What's the Kayleigh whatshername story?' Lulu's eyes glitter. She can clearly guess what kind of story it is.

'Kayleigh Harbinson,' says Jake. 'She was a right goer. I'll tell you all about her later.'

He doesn't seem discomfited at all. In fact, Lulu and Jake seem very easy with each other. No stretch to believe that they are in love, that they are ready to become parents. That the ages they are might turn out to be the very best ages for it.

Jake makes more tea and as he does so he tells us about the irritated detectives who appeared down in the bar

fifteen minutes after I had headed off. The detectives who had left the hotel scowling and muttering to each other.

'Proper pissed off they were,' says Jake as he hands us mugs of strong tea. 'Gutted.'

'They don't have you on CCTV giving Mark a warning?' Lulu says.

'Nah. They did take our tapes but we don't have any cameras covering
where we were talking. It's a blind spot, it's why I picked it.'

'You're sure? Because this blinking country has cameras everywhere these days.'

'Yeah, but most of them are bust,' says Jake.

Blinking? I think. Blinking? It must be obvious that this thought is flickering across my face.

'Lu doesn't like to curse,' says Jake. 'Not properly.'

'It's unimaginative,' she says, her eyes moving over me with an off-centre look that makes me wonder if I have done any unimaginative cursing in front of her. I don't think I have. Just the one bloody that I can recall. She smiles suddenly as if she can read my mind.

'You worry too much Mr Chadwick,' she says.

'I swear a lot,' Jake says. 'She's always telling me off.' They share a look. Both of them smiling again. They really do seem like a great young couple. Lulu's tiredness seems to have gone. She cups both hands round her mug. Takes a sip. Looks at me.

I can see that she's actually got a very striking face. Disquieting with its surprising planes and angles. Now that Jake is back the shadows have vanished and her face has electricity in it, quick and agile, strong cheekbones. Long eyelashes. The red in her hair catches the light and gives her a strange halo. She reminds me of someone,

though I can't think who. She looks like an indie movie star. That French one that's getting all the press at the moment. Or maybe she looks like a singer I've seen profiled recently.

'Of course I don't know much about it,' she says, 'but my feeling is that successful fugitives need money. Quite a lot of money. Money and a place to go.'

'I'll get going soon.' I say. 'Get out of your hair.'

'No need to rush,' says Jake.

'Where are you going to go anyway?' says Lulu. 'I'm curious. You have somewhere to hide out that doesn't cost? You have friends and family?'

Not that I can trust, I think. Not that the police don't know about. But I don't need long. Only a week and then I can concentrate on the real work of repairing the torn fabric of my life.

'I'll be okay,' I say. I'm really hoping this is true.

There is silence now. I wonder what time it is. The grey light outside seems to be getting stronger. Maybe it is time to get going.

'Anyone want a proper drink?' I say. 'Not Steinbrau Blonde – couldn't bring myself to replace like with like. I got proper beer. Adnams.'

Jake laughs. 'It's seven in the morning, Sir.'

Lulu raises her head. 'I'll have one.' She opens it with a bottle opener she has on her key ring, takes a swallow. 'Hm, very nice. Normally you can only get Special Brew there. Maybe even the dossers drink craft beers now. Oh, and here's a thought. You should stay here.'

'Yeah, right,' says Jake. He forces a laugh as if trying to make us think Lulu might be joking. Her lips twitch. She raises an eyebrow. That's all it takes to get Jake to subside into silence. There's a pause.

'I'm not sure,' I say.

'You have a better plan, Mark? What were you going to do? Exactly?'

Of course I don't really know. Maybe the universe would provide, send a sign.

'There are lots of cheap hotels,' I say.

'They'll want ID,' Lulu says. 'And the police can use TripAdvisor too. Simple thing to have some poor community support officers knocking on hotel doors.'

'Might take a while to track me down.'

'It might. But then again they might get lucky on day one.'

'I could get a tent,' I say.

Lulu laughs, Jake snorts and I find I'm smiling too. It does sound pathetic I guess. I think about a tent. About finding a suitable pitch, somewhere that avoids the ID problem. Could I even put a put the tent up on my own? Last few years we have taken the kids to those child-friendly festivals like Wilderness or Latitude, and it's always Katy who takes the lead in tent construction. I am very much restricted to an assistant role. An ineffectual holder of poles, a banger in of the metal pegs when the real work is almost done.

'You should definitely stay here,' says Lulu. Another pause. The selection of another cigarette. The lighting of it. A deep pull. Smoke coiling and rising around the cheap yellowish sphere of the kitchen light.

She turns to me again. 'Don't forget you'll also be getting some eyes out in the outside world. People looking out for you.'

That is true. And it's important: no one can do anything on their own. You need a team for everything. For little things and big things. We live in a world of partnerships,

of networks, of groups and gangs and teams. No world for lone wolves.

I look at Jake. He's looking at the floor, hands clasped in front of him, apparently deep in thought.

'Jake?' I say.

'I think Lulu always gets what she wants.'

'It's true I do,' she says. Her dark eyes gleam. I wonder why she's so keen to get me to stay.

She shrugs. 'You've got an interesting face,' she says, 'perhaps I'll take your picture.'

13

Later, in the bank: waiting. It's agonising, though my impatience is shared by all the others in the line. Everyone is sighing at the slowness of the one cashier, rolling their eyes at the way people take their time over a simple thing like paying in or taking out money. All of them wishing they'd done whatever they have to do online.

It's funny though, each huffing customer, so fidgety in the queue, becomes a dawdler themselves when called forward to cashier number one please. It's as if they have somehow earned the right for a long heart-to-heart with the bank guy just because they have been kept waiting. As if taking ages in their turn will somehow make up for the lost time. Illogical and infuriating.

According to the name badge hanging slack from his schoolboyish white shirt, the bank guy is called Ian. Ian is chubby-faced, in his early thirties, with an uneven goatee in which small flecks of grey are already visible. He has

the soft, defeated, eager-to-please look of someone still living with his mum. Worried eyes that widen when I tell him I want all £3,212 of my savings out in cash there and then.

'I'll be half a sec,' he says.

I feel the pressure of the people behind me shift, a silent, disapproving sigh seems to escape from them all in unison. I have become a dawdler myself, an idler, another man abusing his time at the till. Someone stopping the weekend getting started. Spoiling things for everyone.

Where is this Ian going? I try not to worry. I imagine conversations with line managers. Ian is just a clerk after all. There'll be permission to be sought from somewhere. Doesn't mean anything sinister. Not necessarily.

I try to slow down my heart rate, to control the urge to bolt. Surely there will be no stops on my money quite yet? Next week it could be different, but right now this £3,212 is still mine to use as I see fit. If I want to take it all out I can. If I want to burn it all I can. No one can stop me.

I check my watch.

Ian's half a sec turns out to be seven long minutes. I fight the urge to apologise personally to those behind me, but I can feel their eyes boring into my back.

Ian is all smiles when he comes back, but offers no explanation for his absence. Just gives a quick, cheerful 'sorry about that' as he slides back into his seat. I think how Ella would have responded. I'm sorry about your face, she would have said. Everything is your face at the moment. You tell Ella her room needs a bit of a tidy, she tells you your face needs a bit of a tidy. You tell her she's being a

bit childish, she tells you your face is a bit childish. Then she thinks for a moment and says yes, you've got her on that one, she is childish. But maybe, Dad, that's because she is, after all, an actual child. Which is when you tell her she's a strange kid and that it's a good job she makes you laugh. She tells you your face is strange, that it's a good job your face makes her laugh. It should annoy me, but it doesn't.

I sign the forms and stuff thirty-three bundles of the Queen's face into my rucksack.

I always meant to be more prudent. I meant to put away 10 per cent of my earnings ever since I first got a proper job. I meant to tithe myself in order to ensure some cushion against exactly this moment. But there'd always been something to spend money on. A broken boiler, a dying car, a dead dishwasher. A storm-damaged roof. An emergency holiday. An urgent sofa. A vital bathroom upgrade. A baby.

So the saving thing never really happened. Not properly. Instead I just have this 3K. It is something though. It is definitely that. Shouldn't need this money to last long. It should be plenty. I had even wondered about just taking out enough for a week, but in the end had decided that I might as well gather all the resources I could while I could. Because you never know.

Takes me a while but in the end I find a call box and phone Katy. She doesn't pick up. I spend a pound to listen to Ella and Jack do the voicemail message again. As I twist the payphone's cord around my wrist, as my children's voices come through that obsolete wire, I'm aware of faces outside turning my way, of some gum-chewing and hoodied pre-teens pointing through the glass at me. This is clearly no good. I need a proper phone.

So coming out of the call box I go in search of the cheapest phone on the market. I find it in Cash Converters and these dumb phones are so cheap that on a whim I buy seven of them. One for every day of the week. I can use one, throw it away, unwrap another.

The salesman, a skinny teenager with an astonishing black and bushy woodcutter's beard, is quite impressed I think.

Cashcon has to be the saddest shop in any town. Tablets, phones, laptops, mountain bikes. The massive flat slabs of home cinema systems. You find all of that in there, but that's not the sad thing. The sad thing is to see just how much musical equipment is on offer. Guitars, keyboards, drums, violins, saxophones. This shop even has a fine Irish harp for sale. A hundred and nineteen pounds, or fifteen quid a week for ten weeks if you buy it that way.

A lot of creativity ends up stockpiled in the contemporary pawnbrokers – pre-loved dreams offered for sale at a few quid a week. Dreams given up to buy food, pay the rent and get the kids some nappies.

Outside again and heading for Superdrug, I think how weird is to be doing errands, to be getting stuff, to be poking about in Cash Converters, to be shopping almost as if it were any normal Saturday. I'm drifting. I need to do something more than this. Take control.

In Superdrug I buy razors, toothpaste and top-end aftershave. The bank clerk – Ian – had smelled of cheap scent. Lot of Lynx going on, depressing in a grown man. Like bottled under-achievement. Distilled essence of low self-esteem. However bad things get I don't want to smell like that.

From there I go to M&S and make the menswear department very happy by buying a cheap suit that more or less fits. I also buy two pairs of jeans, half a dozen nondescript shirts, some t-shirts, socks, underwear. Pyjamas. A pair of anonymous shoes.

Despite being a Saturday morning it is so quiet in there that all three of the sales guys in menswear are serving me. Three tall young lads with well-moisturised faces and shockwaved hair. They do the business of de-tagging and bagging and taking cash as if they were constrained by the rules of some ancient guild, each taking one part of the task. They take almost no notice of me because one of them – the shortest and the blondest – is regaling the others with a story of sexual conquest. A tale of some shit he's in with the missus because of a piece of accidental adultery.

'One mistake should be allowed, shouldn't it?' he says. He has an impish face, and a scruffy five-day beard that makes him look like a bonobo or some other excitable primate.

'Yeah, should be, like, three strikes and you're out kind of thing,' says the second guy, smiling.

'Wasn't with one of her mates, was it?' This is the third guy, the one who hands the bags to me. He is pulling at his top lip, growing unexpectedly and darkly pensive. Clearly this is his personal line that can't be crossed. Cheating is okay as long as you leave your missus's contact list out of it. His buddy is quick to reassure him.

'No. Girl what works in Housing Advice. One of the graduate trainees.'

'Girl from the council? You want to be careful. Playing with fire there matey. Housing Advice sheesh,' says the

second guy. He is obviously impressed though.

'There you go, my friend.' He hands me the bags. He doesn't even look at me.

'You just have to deny it and keeping denying it,' says bonobo-face.

'Yeah. Never apologise, never explain,' says his mate.

All three of them are grinning at each other. A conspiracy of cheating bastard men. I want to bang their heads together.

I am in the store's cafe when the police arrive. Shocking how suddenly the torpid atmosphere of the shop is ruptured by a shouting swarm of bulky black stab vests moving with surprising grace through the womenswear department, knocking aside racks of lingerie, pushing their way through the LBDs and the yoga pants as they head towards me.

I take a panicked look around. There's nowhere to go. I stand, ready for rough hands to seize me, ready for my head to be shoved onto the table amid the scone crumbs, ready for the cuffs.

Only the police run past me, dodging between the tightly packed tables like side-stepping rugby players. It's not me they're after. On one of the cafe's two faux leather sofas a bloke rises, runs his hands through his hair resignedly. He looks kind of relieved. He's in his mid-thirties maybe, slight build, clothes just a bit too young for him. Skinny jeans, scarlet hoodie, Converse trainers.

A girl next to him starts to weep silently, shoulders heaving, as the police surround the two of them. She's fifteen at a guess. Seventeen at most. I teach several

year nines who look older than her. The two of them are led away, as docile as well-trained labradors.

As I sit again, feeling foolish but with my heart thumping, I hear the man at the next table telling his wife that it's that RE teacher, the one that run away with that girl. Remember? The one that has been in the papers? That bloke has ruined his life for a shag, he says. What a berk.

Jake and Lulu are still upstairs when I get back to their place. I know they're in because, as I lock the bike in the hallway – better to be safe than sorry – I can hear the murmur of voices, the creak of weight shifting in the bed, canned laughter from some TV show.

I clear away the beer cans and put the cereal bowls in the sink. I can't wash them because there is no washing-up liquid. Jake and Lulu need to do a big shop. Maybe I can do it for them. I'll think about that.

I pick up the post-it notes that have fallen from their perches and are scattered on the floor like yellow petals. I put them back in their rightful places, only they have lost their stickiness and immediately flutter to the floor again. I write out new ones from the pack that sits by the kettle. *Frigo*, *forno*, *radiatore* and I put them on the fridge, the oven, the radiator respectively.

I make a cup of tea and settle myself at the kitchen table, and crack on with setting cover work. I know it's sort of ridiculous, that I have more on my mind than worrying about whether the students of Parkside have enough to do, but that's how teaching gets you. You have to be a little in love with your kids or you wouldn't do it. You want the best for them. If you can't be with them for any reason you don't want them to be fobbed off with

worksheets or DVDs, you want them to do something meaningful. Something that might help them progress. So I spend time writing lesson plans that are achievable, stretching, entertaining and are at the same time easy to deliver by whichever poor sap ends up taking my classes. It feels important to do this. I find it soothing, it's a way of tricking myself into thinking that things are still normal.

Jake appears just as I finish. He is immaculate in white shirt, black trousers and thin knitted tie in chocolate brown, the exact same shade as his eyes.

'All right, Sir? Mark I mean.' He smiles, but you can tell his heart isn't in it. He opens and shuts cupboards. Sighs. I tell him I'll go and get more shopping, get some proper food in.

'It's all right.' He asks me what I've been doing, where I've been.

'Oh, you know. Had some things to sort out. Listen, Jake, I really appreciate you giving me a place to stay.'

'That's okay,' he says. But this morning he is giving out every sign of a man who thinks that it isn't really. A man who has changed his mind about having me here. He makes tea for us both. I ask him if he's working tonight and he nods glumly. Tells me that he's got to be at The Castle for five. 'But at least I don't have to stay over tonight. I'll be back about midnight.'

He gives me a long look over the top of his mug, a look that seems to me to be somehow significant. He looks away. 'Lulu will be at home,' he says.

His chin tilts up, his shoulders are back, he looks kind of defiant. Like a nervous amateur boxer. 'Actually, Sir, Mark. Sundays. Lulu and me. It's sort of quality time for us.'

Oh right. Of course.

'Message understood, Jake. I'll take myself off for the day.'

'You don't have to.' This is Lulu, coming into the kitchen heading for the kettle with her steady, cautious steps.

'It's okay.'

'Mark. You really don't have to.' She looks a bit pissed off, though she keeps her voice breezy. I'm not sure of the dynamic here but there's clearly some domestic power struggle going on.

'Tell you what,' I say, 'I'll be out most of the day – I have stuff to sort out anyway – and maybe I'll come back about six, do us all a big Sunday dinner for about eight o'clock?'

I didn't actually know I was going to offer that until the moment the words spilled out.

'That sounds like a decent compromise,' Lulu says. 'You know I'm mostly a vegan, right? And, Jake, I hope you're going to show me an exceptionally good time tomorrow seeing as you've kicked our guest out especially.'

I take myself off upstairs then, lay on my bed, thinking – of course – about what Katy is doing with the kids. Where I might be able to find them. One or other often has a party on a Saturday afternoon, or there'll be a play date of some kind. It occurs to me that maybe now that Jack is getting into football we might spend future Saturdays watching the Arsenal.

I was never into football much myself as a kid, though as a boy growing up you have to know a bit just to fit in in the playground. Of course you hear a lot of sport chat in a pub, opinions you can parrot back to your mates and so sound authoritative.

I keep up with soccer now for much the same reason I did as a child. It helps with relationships in the classroom. The kids at school think I'm a passionate Arsenal fan. At first it was quite hard to pretend to be elated or downcast on a Monday morning, depending on what the result required. But I faked it till I made it and now I do genuinely feel cheered when Arsenal win, feel a real pang when they don't. Even though I couldn't name more than three players. Even though I've never seen them play except on the telly. Nevertheless, I realise now that I've become enough of a fan to be miffed if Jack chooses to support one of the other London teams.

Even these inconsequential thoughts drift into a kind of nausea as I think about how there might actually be no Saturdays at the football, ever. Like there might be no more Saturdays watching judo competitions or dance shows. Like there might be no more Sundays at museums or galleries. No more festivals, no more holidays, no more hiking and biking.

None of the other parental rites of passage either. No collecting the kids from discos or nightclubs. No clearing up sick from their first morning after the first night before. No helping them through break-ups, no going to any graduations, no nothing. It's like a wound inside, blood leaking, going where it shouldn't, grief pooling around my heart. But grief doesn't ever help. Grief paralyses. Anger does help though. I realise now how angry I am. One lie, one stupid mistake a lifetime ago when I was someone else entirely and they think they can humiliate you, take you away from the people you love, the people who need you. They think they can destroy you. Well, I'm sorry, but I'm not going to be destroyed. I won't be taken from the people who need me, the people I love. I

refuse. I won't have it. I thump the wall with my balled first. And again. And again. And then again.

Lulu's face appears at the door. 'Cup of tea?' she says.

'Thanks,' I say. There's a pause. I feel foolish. My hand hurts. 'I'm sorry about —'

She cuts me off. 'It's fine,' she says, and she hands me a mug. This one replicates the jacket of *Bonjour Tristresse*. I see her eyes flicker to the tattoo on my forearm, but she doesn't say anything.

She manoeuvres around the boxes to sit on the edge of the bed. She looks tired. She apologises for the way Jake was with me.

'He was all right,' I say.

'No, he was being an arsehole,' she says. 'He was moody because of you staying I think.'

'Should I go then?'

'No, he needs to get over it. He brought you here after all.' She sips her tea. 'I used to think it was flattering, this jealousy thing – now it gets on my tits. Anyway, this morning's performance has put me off project baby so that's something.'

I wonder aloud how they met, how they first got together.

'You really want to know?'

I find I do. Find that I'm sick of thinking about my own stupid self. Anything that takes me away from myself for a few minutes is worth it.

Eurocamp, summer before last, Italy. Firenze, or just outside. Lulu had been a manager and Jake what the company called an apprentice – a euphemistic term for a grunt on less than minimum wage. He'd been sent over by some uncle with connections in a desperate

attempt to get him to shape up, get him out of every-body's hair.

'It's obvious he fancies me straight away. I make it very clear I'm out of his league.'

Jake gives it a go anyway. Puts the hours in. He finds out Lulu's a photographer and so surreptitiously down-loads some stuff, does some learning, engages her in conversations about David Bailey and Terence Donovan and Trude Fleischmann. Finds out she's a vegetarian and so gives up meat himself.

He makes the effort to learn some Italian which none of the other English blokes ever bother to do. Lulu finds this impressive.

He helps her with allocating pitches to the visitors. It's a simple software system but Lulu seems to struggle with it. One night they go out for a few beers and at the end of the evening she suggests he kisses her goodnight. He gives her a respectful peck on the cheek.

'I'm like – not like that. A proper kiss. Thing is I had decided I was going to get off with him the very day he arrived at the site. Decided it even while I was being all cool with him. It was very nice that he tried so hard to impress me, but he needn't have bothered. He just had to wait.'

I'm thinking about how it was with Katy and with Anne, how it's always the women who decide these things.

'Of course it is,' Lulu says. 'Men might think they're making all the moves but usually the girls have decided one way or another right at the start. We don't give you lot much say in things really. Probably better that way, don't you think?'

'I'm not sure about that.'

'It is, definitely.' She grows thoughtful. 'When I met Jake he was a virgin with smelly feet. He was a bit of a prat. He's better now. Though clearly there's still work to do.'

She changes the subject, asks me what I fancy doing tonight and I can't think of anything. What the hell does it matter?

Lulu sighs. 'What is wrong with us all today?' she says. She gets up. 'Più tè?' she says.

'Mi piacerebbe,' I say, even though I haven't finished this mug.

'Parla Italiano?' She is surprised and delighted.

'Sì, un po'. We lived in Italy for a while. I'm out of practice now though.'

I think about the year we had in Italy. The year of recovery. The space that Katy had negotiated with the dean so that we didn't have to go back to Cambridge at the end of that mad summer. The year of cheap wine, of reading nothing but science fiction, of riding temperamental scooters through narrow, cobbled streets, of lying naked in Katy's single bed for hour upon hour, trying to figure out how to sleep again.

'I'm trying to learn it properly. We're planning to go back, Jake and I, find a little bar to run, get away from this damp little rock. If he grows up a bit, we might think again about maybe bringing up some bambinos in the sunshine. Hey, maybe you could give me a lesson? In lieu of rent. That's what we'll do tonight. We'll stay in, talking shit in *Italiano*. Got to be better than punching walls.'

'Maybe.' I tell her I've got some money now actually. I could do rent for real if she wanted. That would be fair. She waves her cigarette-holding hand in that irritated

way she has. I see her wonder whether to get offended or not and decide that, in the end, it's not worth it.

'I noticed the new clothes,' she says and laughs. 'Exceptionally ordinary, extraordinarily unmemorable. Well done you.'

14

Ella has to do her homework. She has to find an animal she likes and research it and write about it. She has decided to write about dolphins. She's annoyed that her mum won't let her use Wikipedia.

'Why not?' she says, her eyes flashing. 'Everyone else will be using it.'

'I think you've just answered your own question, haven't you?' says Katy, keeping her tone light. She doesn't want to fall out with her daughter right now. But she knows she can't give in either. That way madness lies. Give in once and you are your children's bitch for ever.

'Have I? Have I really?' And, shoulders back, head up, her hair tossed dramatically, Ella stalks from the living room.

Amanda Campbell laughs. 'Well that's reassuring,' she says.

'What, you're reassured that my eleven-year-old

daughter seems to be sprinting towards hormonal adolescence way too fast?'

'Sweetie, she's slow. I'm reassured because I don't usually see any signs of attitude from your kids. I've always thought they were way too polite. Nice to know they're normal.'

Katy sips at her wine, wriggles to get comfortable. She wonders if her parenting skills have just been judged and found to be lacking. She can see why Amanda is relieved though. Her own kids are pretty feral after all. They do lip and backchat more or less constantly, in a way that would drive Katy mental. Mark and Katy have often talked about it. A night round at the Campbells' can be quite frustrating as Amanda and Nick battle – and fail – to get their kids to bed.

'What is wrong with using Wikipedia anyway?' says Amanda. 'I find it invaluable in my practice.'

In her room Ella flicks through the library books she got out that morning. She can't think why she chose such a boring mammal, so they live in the sea, so what? She wishes she'd stuck with rats, which were her first choice anyway, till her mum talked her out of it.

Then – on practically the last page of the last book – she finds it. Something interesting. She calls Jack in to tell him.

She tells him about how dolphins kill each other. They do it in groups of four. Two swim alongside the victim and hold it down. Two swim on the surface. When the two holding the victim need to come up for air, the two on the surface swim down and take their places and they repeat the process as often as necessary until the victim drowns.

Turns out dolphins aren't just cute, smiley, brainy

circus performers who will somersault for fish, turns out they are evil killers.

'Is that really true?' says Jack.

'Of course it is dum-dum,' says Ella. 'It's in a book.'

15

I get it. I really do. They are performing for me, turning me into a voyeur for their own amusement. Or they are trying to get me out of the house. Or both. Whatever, Jake and Lulu are having the noisiest sex. It begins as whispers stealing into my dreams and moves through distinct movements like a musical score or a choreographed wrestling match.

I get up and scurry to the bathroom and as I pass their room I can hear sleepy laughs and the soft wet explosions of kisses given and taken. I have a piss and a wash and then I'm followed back to my own room by a kind of low growling. As I pull on my clothes, the growls are already turning into languid groans, surprised gasps.

By the time I am downstairs and boiling the kettle and putting toast in the toaster, there is the percussion of the headboard hitting the wall, the see-sawing string section of bed springs creaking, the guttural duet of need, the slap of sweating flesh against sweating flesh.

At which point there is an unexpected silence. I imagine a hand on a chest. A silent command to wait. Not yet. Not yet.

Wait. Wait some more.

Here it comes now, the gradual swelling of that ancient melody again, the picking up of pace, the drawn-out moans, the wordless coaxing and urging. The bed springs squeaking. The renewed thump of cheap bed against thin wall. Quality time indeed.

As I unlock the bike, toast gripped between my teeth, plum and damson jam dripping onto my chin, I think how it all seems a bit put on. Not faked exactly, but a bit theatrical, a bit Hollywood, but maybe I'm wrong about this, maybe they are just young and uninhibited. Of course they are not in the habit of keeping things quiet so as not to be disturbed by a child.

It is uncanny how sensitive kids can be to the sounds of their parents having a bit of a cuddle. How the very first moves of a hand around a breast in a marital bed, the first gentle placing of lips to neck, can call a child from sleep and send them trip-trapping sleepily down the corridor to Mummy and Daddy's room.

I cycle up towards Haverstock Street, and need only the briefest of glances to see that the fucking Astra – or one just like it – is still there.

I have a sudden vision of trashing the car, a brick through a windscreen, a lighted rag in a petrol tank. If they're going to get you eventually, why not go down fighting? Why not give them a proper crime to deal with?

I need to fight this, fight the urge to fight back. I need to let discretion be the better part of valour, however angry I am, however tempting the vision of a burning panda

car. I get back on my bike and away before any copper can nudge his colleague to say hey, isn't that our guy?

The South Bank, I decide. We often spend Sundays there. There's a chance I'll see Katy and the kids. A remote chance, but better than none.

Pushing my bike through the meandering crowds I can't escape the feeling that I'm being watched. My skin itches. I find I keep looking over my shoulders, or looking up, scanning the windows of office blocks.

Not only that, but the faces of my fellow Sunday moochers start to seem familiar. I see colleagues, kids I've taught, people I grew up with, schoolmates. Ella and Jack of course, and every pregnant woman becomes Katy for a second, but I also see several Annes, Eves, a couple of Bims.

It's a kind of reverse prosopagnosia. Instead of being blind to faces I should know, I am convinced that every passer-by is someone I've met, someone I've spent time with. Too many people and all of them morphing into people I know as they come close, only turning back into strangers at the last moment. Even the *Big Issue* sellers and the beggars begin to take on the features of forgotten uni friends.

'Mark? Mark Chadwick?'

A pavement artist, lips chapped and crusty, deep eyes, grey hair chopped into a very 1990s bowl cut. 'Mark Chadwick. I can't believe it.'

'Danny?' Because I can see it now. The face has lost its geometry, the skin has reddened, and there's the black and yellow of a fading bruise on his left cheek, but he is still in there somewhere. God, when did I last see him? It's got to be well over twenty years. Basically, it went like this: I got to Italy, told Katy we needed to be together, she

called her boyfriend from a payphone that night and that was it, that was all she wrote. Danny was history. There was a bit more to it than that, but not much more.

I saw Danny around Cambridge a few times when we finally came back but we never acknowledged each other. Why would we?

If I'd had to guess how Danny would turn out, I'd have said a lawyer like Katy, or something in the City, a corporate hatchet man of some description.

I ask how he's been keeping.

'How does it look like I've been keeping?'

I look at his work, chalked out on the floor in front of him. It's all right. He's halfway through a decent reproduction of Manet's *Le Dejeuner sur l'herbe*. Funny, but I can't remember Danny ever showing any interest in art when I knew him. At his feet, a large polystyrene McDonald's cup is two-thirds full of loose change.

We don't talk for long. I buy coffee and a Danish for each of us from one of the nearby stalls. He tells me that he started out as I would have predicted – law school, prestigious firm, some stuff to do with intellectual copyright – before it all went pear-shaped.

'A problem with El Boozo. But hey, at least I'm not begging.' I think he means it as a joke, but it's hard to be sure.

He tells me that on a fine day, if he's working particularly well, during the holidays or at weekends, if no scrote has set up in competition nearby, he can make nearly ten quid an hour.

'What do you do if someone does set up close to you?'

'You move on or you have a word. Depends on how big they are,' he says, and he points to the bruise on his cheek. 'You should see the other guy.'

Unprompted he gives me an insight into the uncertain income stream of a pavement artist. He says mostly people will try to ignore him, though if they do, accidentally, make eye contact, they give loads, guiltily stuffing fivers into his cup. But it doesn't happen often. As a nation we are pretty good eye contact avoiders, we've pretty much got it down.

He doesn't mind that, the people he can't stand are the ones that try to enrol him on some programme, the ones who want to help. The vicars and their ilk, all the soft cops of the charity sector. The tightwads who give food instead of money.

I feel I'm in the clear. I always meet the eyes of the homeless, always give proper money. It's a point of principle, though of course there's always more you can do.

He asks about me and I say that I'm okay, that I'm teaching actually, that I've got two kids with another on the way. Strangely, I don't tell him that I'm wanted to help police with their enquiries, that I've found myself in the world of warrants, court orders. In the realm of the real cops. The hard cops.

'I've got a son,' he says. 'He'll be sixteen now, I think. About that anyway. I don't see him of course.'

Of course. How can men bear it when they don't see their kids?

Then he asks the one question that he really wants to ask. 'Hey, do you ever hear from Katy at all?'

'You could say that. We're still together. We're married, Danny, she's the mother of my children.'

For a moment he looks amazed, his eyes widen. He can't help it, he looks stricken. His face darkens. Only takes a fraction of a second before he regains control of his expression, makes himself smile, and I notice how his gums are receding, how he is missing an incisor.

'That's great. That's really great.' There's a pause and he looks up at the sky, as if assessing the chances of rain coming along to put a stop to his earning potential for the day. His eyes flicker back to me, and then away again peering up the river. 'I suppose it means it was fate, the two of you getting together. That you were soulmates, that there was nothing I could have done to hang on to her. That's good because it did mess me up. Her chucking me.' Now he looks at me. His eyes are wet. 'She's really bloody special, Mark.'

'I know mate.'

We shake hands, his grip is weak and I remember how I read once that a weak handshake is an indicator of a possible stroke to come. I pull a crumpled tenner out of my back pocket.

'Don't you fucking dare,' he says.

'Sorry.'

'It's okay. When you see Katy, say hello,' he says.

'I will,' I say. I won't though. It would make her too sad.

I spend half an hour on the London Eye, looking at the frantic jumble of the city spread out before me, the muscled thrust of glittering chrome and glass. That foreign-backed newness, those shiny steel beanstalks pushing a way through the grubby brickwork of the past. All those cranes. There's been talk about how London should become a city-state like Singapore or Hong Kong. How it should leave the rest of the country behind, the way an old-style spacecraft jettisoned the worn out parts of itself as it headed for the stars. We're in orbit now, the city might say. We can make it on our own. We're gone. See ya, don't wanna be ya.

Or maybe it would be a kinder farewell. London telling

the country chin up, don't cry. It's not you, England, it's me. Left behind, England would turn to El Boozo big style and end up like Danny, scraping by on making people feel guilty. Getting into fights with the scrotes trying to nick his pitch.

I have been on the Eye before. We took the ride the night we decided to have children. How audacious is that? To look down at a city of eight million striving souls and think that we could add to it. That, actually, we had a duty to add to it. That there was room for a couple more, that preserving our DNA really mattered.

I remember we spent most of the ride snogging in a way that we hadn't for years.

16

When I get back to Chaney Street the house is throbbing to modern RnB. Which is okay, I don't mind contemporary dance music, though left to myself I never seek it out. It's certainly a whole better than what I had feared I might be listening to. I was convinced they'd be at it again. That I'd be cooking to a complete symphony of ostentatious sexual vocalisation. Better by far to be cooking to a soundtrack of Usher and Alicia Keys.

I'm keeping it simple in the kitchen. A thick spicy lentil dahl and a bean stew with herb dumplings. Something Eastern, something Western, you could call it a fusion dinner. To go with it I'm doing rice cooked with garden vegetables, spices and nuts. All the ingredients from Borough Sunday Market where I also got amazing wholemeal bread and fancy condiments. Various chutneys and a demon chilli sauce so Jake and Lulu can sweeten or fire up the dishes depending on taste. Always tricky knowing how far to go with the spices when cooking for new people.

For dessert we're having a plain apple pie. Who doesn't like apple pie?

I know I'm doing all this to distract myself from the reality of things, of course I know that. But what am I meant to do? There's only so much crying and fretting and worrying you can do. I think human beings are programmed to get on with things, to keep going, to put one foot in front of another and keep trudging on. Most of us anyway.

It's what we all did after Eve died – except my father couldn't – and it's what I've done since my parents went. Just kept going. Because if you can't keep on keeping on then you just cause more pain to those around you. Too much grief is selfish, it's like deliberately infecting yourself over and over with some horrible disease and then seeking out your closest friends to pass it on to them. Getting on, cooking dinners, doing chit-chat. It is better than giving your sickness to those closest to you.

'Smells good, Sir.'

Jake. Dressed in grey sweatpants and a pink t-shirt that carries the logo of the 1972 Munich Olympics. Fashionably retro. The Olympics where a dozen athletes got murdered. Interesting that something like this has become acceptable vintage wear.

This 'sir' business is beginning to annoy me, because I don't think it's accidental now. I think it's somehow satirical, but I decide not to correct him. That's what years of teaching do for you: they show you the value of not rising to small provocations.

Jake has a sleek, self-satisfied look – a roguish glint in his eye. This annoys me too. Well done you, Jake, I think. But we can all have sex you know, it's not really that big a deal.

I ask him if he wants wine or beer because I bought both.

'Awesome. Let's get proper arseholed,' he says.

We're onto the second bottle and have demolished quite a bit of the bread before Lulu joins us. She is as subdued as Jake has been loquacious. He's been giving me his thoughts on everything from cars, to business, to schools, to video gaming, to how to solve the problems of the Middle East.

I paraphrase, but Jake's views on these things are essentially that the Bugatti Veyron is the best car ever made, that British business needs to get its act together otherwise we'll find we're going to be left behind by the rest of the world.

'Not just by big boys like China and India, but by Brazil and Nigeria and Vietnam, places like that.'

Jake thinks that high schools should be much smaller, five hundred kids each, max., so that teachers can properly get to know all the students. He thinks they should teach video gaming which should be taken more seriously as an art form. He tells me that it is bigger than the movie industry and the music industry combined and has still only really just got started. He says the problems in the Middle East could be solved by the judicious application of a nuclear warhead or two.

'We need to bang heads together down there,' he says.

He talks fast and confidently, as if everything he says is just good plain common sense and he hops from subject to subject unpredictably without noticing that I don't say anything much except aha and yeah and really? Everything he says gets on my wick. It's not just what

he says, it's how he says it. His bullish, authoritative, doubt-free manner. I'm not a big fan of certainty. I don't trust it.

He is in the midst of a detailed explanation of how the drinks trade could be reformed – which is obviously something I know quite a bit about, not that he bothers to ask – when Lulu comes in.

She comes over and puts a finger on his lips. Strokes his cheek. Kisses him.

'Hush,' she says. 'Shush now.'

Jake becomes much quieter when Lulu is with us, lets her take the conversational lead – not that she seems inclined to converse all that much. She praises the food, she asks about my day. I say I bumped into an old friend – which is true enough I guess.

'We had a good day,' says Jake. He grins. Lulu frowns. I pour more wine. 'I popped the question.'

Lulu sighs. 'Oh, Jake.'

'We're going to get married, we're going to be Mr and Mrs Skellow. What do you think of that, Sir?' His smooth face is shining, his teeth gleam, his eyes glow.

What do I think of that?

'Congratulations,' I say, and it sounds hollow and forced. Entirely inadequate. I need to amplify my response. I stand and shake Jake's hand. I hug Lulu. She smells of soap, the skin of her cheek soft against mine. Her body firm and warm. 'Bloody well done both of you,' I say.

'Thanks, Sir,' says Jake.

Lulu leans back to look me in the eyes, one hand around my waist, the other on my shoulder. 'Whenever you're asked to do something by someone close to you, you should always say yes, don't you think?'

No, no I don't think that. Who could think that? It's a mad way to live a life.

'Yes,' I say. 'Yes, of course. I'm sure you'll be happy together. Marriage is a good thing.'

'A good excuse for a knees-up anyway,' says Lulu. 'A bit of a do.'

I break away from her to return to my seat.

Yes, Jake, I think. Let's get proper arseholed.

17

Anne liked sex best at twilight, in what she called the hour between dog and wolf when it's hard to tell friend from enemy. Dr Sheldon would be at college still, in his lab, or with Mish. He'd be somewhere else anyway, and we would be exploring each other in Selwyn Gardens. We could be in almost any room, we weren't fussy. Though we didn't go into the kid's room obviously.

It wasn't just that we were respecting her space, it was also that we both had the feeling that the *Mein Kampf* look of the severely pouting pop stars on the wall might be off-putting. Who can think of sex when being watched by a glittery herd of My Little Ponies?

Sometimes we would be in my cramped college bed, on expensive all Egyptian cotton sheets that Anne had brought round the second time she came to my room. 'From Beaumont and Brown.' She'd said, 'Good quality bed linen impresses a lady, Marko. A useful life lesson for you.'

Or we might be in the countryside out near Great Chesterton and Whittlesford or one of the other villages around Cambridge, the murmurations of starlings wheeling and tilting above us. Both indifferent and somehow watchful. The bald miles of the fields stretching flat into the distance.

Once or twice we even contorted ourselves so that we could do it in the Dart, laughing at the delicate, careful manoeuvring that was necessary to avoid getting a gear stick up the jacksie.

Yes, we'd do it more or less anywhere, at more or less anytime, but twilight was definitely Anne's favourite time, with the greedy dark closing in on the last of the day, the light thinning, bleeding away into dreams and shadow.

I took to skipping lectures. This was my real education, this crepuscular cartography, these hours where Anne showed me all her hills and curves, her hollows and forests.

She turned out to have so many secret places to introduce me to. I journeyed to her ankles, navigated her collar bones. I discovered her toes, battered out of shape by years of childhood ballet. I found her elbows, the kissing of which made her shiver. I found her hips, the kissing of which made her gasp or sigh or growl, depending on her mood. Her ears, the backs of her knees. The scars on her stomach.

She had two, an appendix scar and a caesarean scar. They intersected in a ragged cross like someone in a hurry was marking where to find treasure on a map drawn on the back of a handsome envelope.

One night, eight in the evening, naked, lightly sheened

in sweat, we lay watching a moth trying to find a hole in the bedroom glass, both of us too heavy and sticky with love to get up and shoo it out in the night. My fingers traced a slow route from Anne's neck to her thighs. When she spoke, she was thoughtful.

'You know, when I had my appendix out I was worried about what boys would think of it.'

'Think of what?' I was only half-listening.

'My enormous great scar, you idiot.'

'It's beautiful. They both are.'

'Yeah, yeah.' She took a breath, shifted against me. 'But you know what the doctor said once, when he came round to check that I was healing up properly?'

'He said that you would grow up to be the best-looking woman in Cambridge? That you would become the wife of a top professor, that you would become a woman whose cruel beauty was notorious?'

'Not quite. He said a scar is stronger than skin. I've always remembered that.'

'Very profound.'

'Yes, it is actually. A lesson for life. By the time I got the other scar I didn't care what anyone thought. People should have scars. It's how you know they've done some living.'

But then she didn't want to talk any more. And, gentle but insistent, she pushed my head lower. She had other lessons she wanted me to learn besides geography, and I was a good student. Diligent. Conscientious. I was, after all, a self-starter – in charge of my own learning. It's how I got to Cambridge in the first place.

Later – quite a bit later – she asked me if I had any scars.

'Not that I know of, but you are very welcome to look.'

125

She did. She moved over me an inch at a time. She inspected me very thoroughly but she didn't find any scars. This was before the tattoo of course. I told her my scars were all on the inside. I meant it flippantly, as a kind of joke. But I found that I was suddenly short of breath, that my eyes were hot with unexpected tears. Anne didn't comment. She refilled my glass. I started to do something I never did, I started to talk about Eve, the sister that never really got started, the funniest, sharpest, brightest of us all, but she stopped me. She put a cool finger to my lips.

'She was a brave girl,' she said.

I'd never thought of what she'd done in that way before. That it wasn't something out of the blue. That instead it was an action that fitted the story she was writing for herself.

As a little girl, Eve had always been a tree climber, a risk taker. Her death maybe did come from the same impulse. She had been an adventurer, an explorer, from the beginning to the end of her life. Just someone running ahead of the rest of us, sprinting into the dark without fear, eyes open.

We drank in silence for a while. Then Anne told me of her husband's own cry for help.

'At least I assume that's what it was,' she said. 'Anyway, help came running. That is, I came running. I've kept the note. Not his best work, it has to be said.'

I didn't know what to say. Who keeps suicide notes? I hadn't kept Eve's though I could remember nearly every word, despite only reading it once all the way through.

She wrote that she felt half-submerged, that her days were like walking in a fog that would never lift, through rain that would never stop. How she thought about

running away but that the trouble was this: wherever you go, there you are.

She wrote that she had a sickness – a leukaemia of the soul she called it. But her last lines had been swollen with a dumb kind of hope: *don't worry I'll be there, I'll be watching over you all. Expect me when you least expect me. I'll be the voice in the wind, the bird on your window sill that seems strangely tame. I'll be sending you signs from the universe. I'll be that black cat that comes out of nowhere to cross your path. I'll be a spider, a butterfly, a moth, a wasp. I'll be the annoying insect that won't leave you alone. Think of that when you reach for a heavy book to swat me with. I plan to be many kinds of ghost.*

Idiot girl.

I picked up the bottle. It was empty. I went to the rack in the kitchen, selected another. I went for a heavy Malbec. Anne was teaching me about wine and I'd learned enough to know we needed something with a kick. When I came back I asked Anne why she thought her husband had made his cry for help.

'Oh who knows? I think I said I'd leave him. Maybe his work wasn't going so well. It was way before Mish anyway.' She was quiet for a while, then she said, 'Tell you what, Marko, let's have a rule. Let's not tell each other any sad stories ever again.'

I agreed to this and we toasted our resolution.

Later she said, 'Mark, do you think we should be absolutely stinko absolutely all the time?'

'Yes. Yes I do.'

'Good. Because I think so too.'

18

But it wasn't just sex and drinking. There was sex, drinking and art. Fast first class trains to London to private views. A show called *Ghost* at the Chisenhale Gallery, a show called *Meaning and Location* at the Slade and a show in an old biscuit factory in Bermondsey where the major piece was real maggots feeding on a real pig's head.

'The guy who did this is such a charlatan,' said Anne.

'Yeah, but a good one,' said Bim, who usually came with us. 'His phoniness is so well crafted it's almost beautiful. It might even last.' I never caught the artist's name.

There was sex, drink and the theatre. *Dancing at Lughnasa* at the National, *Death by Beheading* at the Royal Court. First nights and press nights and after-show parties, Bim discovering who was doing what to whom, or making a guess at it anyway.

There was sex, drink and music. Opera. Gerald Barry's *Intelligence Park*. Azio Gorghi's *Blimunda*. There was also sex, drink and food. Fast drives to country

pub-restaurants. Slow food joints with names like the Green Man and the John Barleycorn. Places that often challenged my right to buy or consume alcohol, which Anne and Bim thought was hilarious given that I had worked in a pub more or less since I was old enough to walk. I'd been asked for ID a lot since I'd been in Cambridge and my solution was to keep my passport on me at all times just in case.

'You know what makes me sad?' said Bim, the first time I had to produce it. 'I bet that passport, battered as it is, has never been used for its real purpose. I bet Babyface Chadwick here has never actually left this sceptred isle.'

'Fuck off,' I said. He was right of course.

'We'll go places,' said Anne. 'There's so much I want to show you, Marko. Berlin. Paris. Venice. Wouldn't he suit Venice, Bim?'

'He'd need some new clothes,' said Bim.

So there was sex, drink and clothes. Anne bought shirts and shoes at places she knew just off Saville Row. She made me have my hair cut at Blow on Vauxhall Bridge Road and then she whispered that she had a room booked at the Langham Hotel and she'd like to be in there and naked by sunset if I didn't mind.

It was in that room that she taught me to roll spectacular joints.

'I thought all young people knew how to do this,' she said. 'I thought you were taught it at all comprehensive schools.'

'Not me,' I said. 'Not at my comprehensive school.' Until that moment I had been pretty much just-say-no about drugs of any kind.

The art and the plays, the music, the food and the clothes. The drink, the joints. All of it helped sharpen the

appetite for the unwrapping of each other, the journey towards the centre of each other.

It was Katy who attempted to bring mundane reality back into my life. I hadn't really seen her or Danny for weeks, I had left them behind the way I'd removed those band pictures from my walls. One minute they were there, the background to every day – the next they were gone, binned without sentiment. Yet here she was, appearing in all her wholesome sixth-formy beauty at my room, telling me that the exams were almost here and what was I going to do about it?

She was breathless with her news. It was as if she were predicting the imminent end of the world, as if she'd had advance notice of Armageddon, that we were on a collision course with an asteroid.

'Chill, Katy. It'll be fine.'

'Really? So you're all prepared, you feel confident? Because this is Cambridge, you know Mark. These examinations might be quite hard.'

'Well, I haven't got a revision timetable if that's what you mean by prepared, but I think I'll be okay.'

'Good. So that's all right. Silly of me to worry.'

There was a pause and to be honest I was sort of hoping she'd just go home but instead she told me her exam dream. A hundred frowning girls in a sports hall, all of them writing. Except her. None of the others even pause to think. But she can't get started. The gym is full of the frantic scratch of cheap biros, the brisk reverbed click of the teacher's shoes hurrying up and down the rows giving out sheets of A4. It's an essay on the end of the slave trade and the minutes are ticking by, but in the dream all she can do is stare at her lucky Pippa doll, paralysed. Her

head filled with the roar of the ocean, the crying children, the whips cracking. All the desperate seasick mothers trying to soothe their babies right up until the moment they are wrenched from their arms and thrown into the freezing sea. She can't breathe. She can't write anything because her heart's too full. She wakes in a panic. Her face wet. Sick with the sense that everything – all these drowned kids – it was all her fault somehow.

I thought of Eve. I could imagine her having a dream like this and not just at exam time. Could imagine her crying about it for days. Could imagine her leaving school because of it. When Katy finished telling her dream I wanted to hold her, but I didn't. Instead, like a prick, I just told her that dreams don't mean anything. Told her that other people's dreams are always boring.

She didn't stay long after that. When she left her body was clenched like she had an ache somewhere.

I told the story of Katy's visit to Anne. We were listening to *La Traversee de Paris*. We were in the biggest of the living rooms, wrapped around each other, sort of watching a black and white film with the sound down, something to do with a spy plot in wartime France. John Mills as the lead.

'But you were completely correct – other people's dreams *are* boring. They *don't* mean anything. She's right about the need for study though, isn't she?' said Anne.

'I'll be okay.'

Anne sat up. I reached for her but she put a firm hand on my chest to keep me down and away. She was frowning.

'How long till the exams?'

'I don't know. Couple of weeks. Three maybe.'

'Fuck, really? Well, this won't do.' She stood up, zapped off the film.

'What?'

'You have to go.'

'What?'

'Oh do stop saying what like that, you know I hate it. It makes you sound retarded. You need to go because you need to be with your books.'

'I'll be okay, really.'

'Yes you will, because you'll be studying every breathing second of the next two – maybe three – weeks. You're not to come here, Marko. Oh don't look like that.'

Anne explained that she wanted me back in Cambridge come the autumn. She wasn't going to be the cause of my being sent down. 'So I don't want to see your sweet, heart-breaking face until the day the exams are over and then...' she tailed off.

'And then?'

She closed her eyes as she thought for a moment, inspiration seemed to strike and she smiled happily.

'And then we'll have a party.'

'A party, like the one you had before?' I said.

'Yes, a party like that one only much better. I think you'll be able to hold your liquor now for a start. Now, get your pants on and scoot. We're taking no chances.'

At the door, Anne's briskness faded and she seemed uncharacteristically smoochy. She could hardly let go of me. Kept covering my face in kisses.

'I know. I'm being stupidly bloody sentimental. It's only three weeks. But you had better pass, Mark Chadwick. You had better bloody pass.'

I was amazed to see her eyes were glistening with the beginning of tears.

'Now, listen,' she said, 'I have the mother of all house parties to plan so I'm going to go inside. I'm going to shut the door and you are going to walk away without looking back.'

I was nearly at the end of the drive when I heard my name being called.

'Mark! Marko!'

I turned and was rewarded by the sight of Anne on the doorstep, jumper pulled up, no bra, showing her breasts. Flashing me for a full five beautiful seconds. She pulled the jumper down again.

'Three weeks!' she called. 'Just three weeks!'

I started back towards her. She was smiling, but still she held up a warning finger. I stopped.

'Or less!' I shouted. 'Three weeks or less!'

But she was already closing the door.

19

Eve had a thing about people talking a lot less and listening a lot more. She was especially keen on men talking less. She thought that men should mostly just shut up for a change. By shutting up she meant not just that they should stop blethering on about stuff all the time in places like the Blue Pig, but that they should stop writing books, stop making records or films or TV shows. They should stop writing articles or plays, they should stop performing comedy. They should stop exhibiting their art. They should refrain from making speeches and getting themselves elected. They should stop putting their opinions forward in any forum whatsoever.

'It needn't be forever,' she said. 'Just ten years or so. Twenty maybe.' Her thing was that this would be good for women and men. It would be good for art.

'Think about the stuff you lot would have to say after a decade of silence,' she said to her brother, her father, her teachers. 'There would be some proper amazing work.'

Sometimes some reckless bloke in the public bar or at school would try and argue with her, would try and say that it didn't seem right that they should have to shut up just because other more privileged men had taken up more than their share of airtime in the past.

Eve would just smile and shrug. 'Can't make an omelette without breaking eggs.'

Of course it was about herself really, not about men at all. Eve was full of things to say and was worried no one would get to hear them. She also worried that she herself was too self-absorbed, that she was too selfish, that she took up too much airtime. It annoyed her that the men and boys she knew never seemed to struggle with this. Not the boys at school, not the regulars in the pub, not her dad, not her brother.

She always said that she was going to get a tattoo on her forearm of a heart with an arrow through, with the initials LM in the middle of it. People would wonder who LM was, but it wouldn't be anyone. It would stand for Listen More and it would remind her to shut up occasionally.

She also said that all men should have this tattooed on them when they were babies. 'Less painful than circumcision and more useful,' she said.

20

The exams weren't that bad in the end. They didn't really touch us and why would they? Exams were, after all, what we knew. They were what we did. We had aced exams all our lives.

We were children who had walked early, talked early, who had finished the Biff, Chip and Kipper books before anyone else. We had always been in top sets for everything. We had kicked the living shit out of GCSEs, given the A-levels a right slap. We had taken RE and General Studies and Latin in our spare time just a little while ago. In our lunch breaks. We were not going to let these ugly little first year college exam bastards trip us up. Even if they were 'quite hard'. No sir.

It got so I was almost enjoying them. I'd look at a question and be all oh *puh-lease,* not that old chestnut. Is that all you got? Is that really all you got? I went and tore the very arse out of that paper. Across town, Katy

and Danny did the same. We were on fire. Yeah, we had superpowers. We could do magic.

That's what it felt like, only it wasn't really magic. It was hard work and organisation. We were well planned. We drew up study schedules – even me – and we stuck to them. We were as disciplined as athletes. As focused as ballet dancers.

Part of the discipline for me was that I really did keep completely away from Anne for three weeks.

Instead I sent postcards. One every day on the back of which I scrawled any inspirational quotations that I came across while cramming. Sometimes I sent whole poems. Lines from Keats, Shelley, Coleridge. Marvell. Donne. Yeats. The big guys. The real heavy hitters. If we had world enough and time. Tread softly lest you tread upon my dreams. The liquefaction of her clothes – all that. I missed her way more than I'd expected to. Missed her with a fierce and ever-present ache. Missing Anne was a thirst.

I got just the one reply. On the same lavish blue paper as before, a note came telling me to be at Selwyn Gardens for 6.30 p.m. for drinks on the day of my final exam. There was no poetry, but there was a little sketch in Chinese ink of a tall skinny boy and a full-breasted woman naked and embracing, each with a bottle in their hand. I smiled when I saw that. It was going to be a hell of a party. It was going to be legendary.

After that it would be May Week, the ten days of officially sanctioned misrule. In June of course, not May – oh, that Oxbridge sense of humour – a time when it was officially okay for everyone in Cambridge to go mental, when every college and department had balls and parties and drinks and croquet and stuff like that, and I felt the

time had maybe come for Anne and I to be seen together amongst the students, to be at least a bit semi-official about the fact that we were an item. Dr Sheldon had his muse and now his wife had hers and the world should see that and take notice.

21

I was in my room changing from the jeans and t-shirt into the new suit when from my window I saw a battered fawn Sierra nosing its way into the courtyard. I was startled for a moment because it looked like the battered fawn Sierra my dad drove, only it couldn't be. It was a fact that there were lots of battered fawn Sierras in the world. But I kept watching.

The driver's door opened as a serious-faced porter approached the vehicle. Ted. His very bald spot seemed to be quivering pinkly with indignation. Whoever was in this car would be left in no doubt that they couldn't park here. Even the Vice-bloody-Chancellor wouldn't be allowed to park here.

A middle-aged woman got out. My mum. My mum who never drove anywhere if she could avoid it. The porter and my mother exchanged a few words and began to walk towards the entrance to the college, by which time I was out of my room and running down to meet

them, taking the ancient stone steps two at a time. A wonder I didn't break my neck.

Mum looked like she hadn't slept for a week. Her face seemed all bones, her skin somehow dusty and dry. Flaky. She had grey roots showing. My mother never let her roots show. Her smile flared briefly when she clocked me, lighting her up for a second, but it faded just as quick.

'Mark, your dad's in hospital. His heart. Went in last night. It's – he's very poorly, Mark.'

'Shit. You should have called.'

'We did, left a message with the porters. Did you not get it?'

'No. No I didn't.'

'I'm afraid it's not going to be a great holiday for you.' She peered at me, seemed to see me properly for the first time. 'My goodness, you look very smart.' Then she was in tears. I was suddenly furious. I wanted to belt someone. I wanted to punch the person to blame for breaking my dad's heart. I wanted to punch Eve.

We had never fought as kids but right now I wanted to slap her hard and over and over. When I was too tired to slap her any more, I wanted to ask her what she thought she was doing. But I couldn't. She'd cheated me. She'd cheated us all. Right then I couldn't see her as a risk-taker, or a pathfinder, or a strange mix of sass and sensitivity, right then she was just a selfish brat. Spoiled rotten.

'I'll get my things.'

As I packed my cases, as I loaded the Sierra, I thought about how I was going to tell Anne about missing her party, should I run round to Selwyn Gardens, take a precious hour to say goodbye? Should I just swing by as we drove out of Cambridge, drop a note round? Either

of those things would mean explanations to my mother, explanations I was too frazzled to make.

Lucky, then, that Danny and Katy should choose this moment to come round on their bikes. They murmured sympathy. Katy hugged my mum – the first of thousands of hugs she would give her over the years. And yes, yes of course they would pop round to Selwyn Gardens. They might not stop for tea and a chat, but they'd certainly put a note through the door. Of course they would.

'I'm sorry to make you miss your party, Mark.'

'Don't worry about it Mum. Just a party. Let's get going, shall we?'

'And that girl, Katy, she's very considerate. Very lovely too.'

'Yes, I suppose.'

'She's crazy about you. That's obvious.''

'Bollocks.'

She sighed. 'You're your own worst enemy, you know that, don't you?'

'Whatever. Now, can we get going? Please?'

22

What sort of people run pubs? Desperate dreamers, that's who. Those who want to be their own boss. Those who can't hack nine-to-five jobs. Those who like being in pubs basically. Drinkers. Or drinkists as Eve had called them. She said it implied a kind of devotion to their art. Anyone could be a simple drinker, but you had to have dedication to be a drinkist.

My dad and people like him.

My dad didn't drink the profits of the Blue Pig. But only because there weren't really any profits. He drank the losses. He drank the overdraft. He did it while working ninety hours a week, always with a fag on the go. If he ate anything it was a bacon sandwich. The only exercise he took was changing barrels and he even smoked while he did that.

Of course the fact that one night while he was wiping tables and collecting glasses, his daughter was bleeding to death in the bathroom, having first medicated herself

with brandy she'd half-inched from behind the bar, well that didn't help his health any either. Didn't curb the need for a drink.

It was no surprise that he'd got sick. The surprise was that it hadn't happened before this.

We went to the hospital before we got home. I was shocked. The wheezing, snuffling little bloke in the bed seemed not to have anything at all in common with the shouty man I'd known just a few months ago. My father had always been burly, overweight but carrying it well. The bloke impersonating him in this narrow bed seemed insubstantial, the only noticeable thing about him was the yellowish skin loose on his face.

He was asleep when we got to his bedside, the racing chuntering away on a telly high up in one corner of the room he shared with an octogenarian who was altogether more sprightly than Dad. A man who introduced himself as Harold Thorne, lungs.

We didn't wake Dad. We just stood and stared. Mum squeezed Dad's hand, and he made a sound halfway between a sigh and a snort, but didn't stir otherwise.

'Funny, he's usually livelier when it's not visiting hours,' said Harold Thorne. The old man seemed surprised to find that this didn't cheer us up.

23

One thing was clear: May Week was out. I would be in Colchester all summer. The Chadwick family would be struggling together to keep the Blue Pig going. There was no spare cash to pay for additional bar staff, so it would have to be me that stepped up.

The Blue Pig was a classic traditional boozer. Small saloon bar. Even smaller public bar. Tiny snug. A group of regulars, men who could be any age from thirty-five to sixty-five, red-faced and paunchy in puckered apologetic shirts. Men who knew a lot of facts. Men who laughed a lot at not very much. Men who were deeply unhappy. Brave men in a way. At least they kept going. At least they never gave in. They didn't, as a rule, cry for help, though perhaps they should have done.

They were all dead proud of me too. I was like a mascot in the Blue Pig. They were prouder of me than my dad was.

My dad would tell the regulars about anything I did, but he took care to do it as a piss-take not a boast.

'He can speak Anglo-Saxon you know. He's done it on the phone for me just now. A whole poem in Anglo-bloody-Saxon. What's the use of that?'

The ketchup-faced men who made up our clientele, they'd be working hard to convince him that a son who can recite Anglo-Saxon verse was a miraculous thing. Something worth celebrating. Well done, mate, they'd say, as if it was him who got the scholarship not me. As if I was John Chadwick's own glittering prize. Bloody well done. Their congratulations all the more forceful because their friend and host would never see his daughter graduate and they knew how much he had loved her.

They had loved her too. Eve with her quick smile and her gentle way of teasing that somehow never caused offence. You lot, she would say, you saddoes. Don't you have homes to go to? Isn't there anything better you could be doing? You've heard there are these things called books, right? The regulars would blush and smile all sheepish into their ale. They didn't even seem to mind being told that they shouldn't speak when women were around. Not if it was Eve telling them. Not that it ever did stop them talking.

We were busy. There were darts teams for both men and ladies. There was a pool team and a quiz team and we were always raising money for something too. If there was a bed to be pushed through town for charity, then the drinkists from the Blue Pig were there to push it in their PJs or dressed as giant babies.

We did food. Of a sort. Ham, egg and chips. Pie and chips. Scampi. Nuked lasagne. Cheese and onion sandwiches on white bread.

The Pig was a real community hub for the streets of terraced houses that hemmed it in. Yet somehow we were more or less skint more or less all the time, and always had been. When I was a kid there were always notes coming home from school about unpaid dinner money, requests for contributions to trips would be met by frowns and the sucking of teeth. Anything needing doing to the car caused a grim silence to fall over the private areas of the pub. Gloom was, of course, barred from the public spaces, there a relentless jollity had to reign at all times, and had to rule even now.

Like all half-decent publicans my mum and dad were counsellors, psychologists, comedians, chat show hosts and impresarios. But still, in the mornings, before the doors opened, you could smell resignation. The sense of futility inadequately disguised by banter, as inescapable as damp.

One odd consequence of my sister's death and now my dad's illness was that the pub became more popular. Everyone wanted to do their bit to help. They wanted to support us, to help us through.

So we were all run off our feet, and what with the serving of beer and crisps, the barrel-changing, the cleaning of toilets, the making of cheese and onion sandwiches, the frying of chips, the paperwork, the listening to sad men tell bad jokes, the collecting and washing of glasses, the visiting of dad – with all of that to do, Cambridge and all that had happened there took on the aspect of a half-remembered dream.

My least favourite job was the emptying of the Eazyzap, the UV insect killer. 1990 was a bad summer for insects generally. They were everywhere. We had already had the invasions of flying ants and hoverflies and German

ladybirds, and now in September we had the wasps. Councils had set up special helplines for those who had discovered nests in attics and gardens, the local news was full of stories of small children being stung and having to be airlifted to hospital with their faces swelling like balloons. We had a bloke swallow a wasp at a barbecue in the beer garden.

My phone calls to Anne went unanswered. The letters and the cards went unanswered too.

Sometimes I thought of her in Cambridge or London, imagined her sniggering with Bim at a book launch or a private view. I had to assume our thing – whatever it was – was over now. Maybe Mish was in the past too now, and Dr Sheldon and Anne were at the stage of comparing notes about their most recent lovers as they flicked through the papers, as they listened to Radio Three, while they argued about books and music and architecture or whatever they did to get themselves through the days. After a couple of weeks I made the decision not to write or call again. I would suffer, but I wouldn't let anyone see I was suffering.

Sometimes I got a letter from Katy who was teaching English out in Italy over the summer. Living what she called *La Dolce Vita*. My replies were brief. Distracted. I was living a real life not the dream of one. Real life was the clack of pool balls, the tragic heartiness of men who didn't want to go home to their wives or children. It wasn't philosophy or feminism or socialism or long-dead poets. Real life was talking close of season signings with the fat men who drank the IPA.

The Eazyzap – that was real life.

Real life was also listening to my dad as he recovered – because John Chadwick had found a new culprit for

what Eve did. Found it in a conversation with Harold Thorne of all places. Harold Thorne-Lungs as mum and I had taken to calling Dad's roomie.

Harold Thorne-Lungs was one of those old men who lived on their own and spent way too much time in the public library. He was a type I recognised from the pub quiz league. A man who was fundamentally none too bright but who had decided to fill himself up with facts and theories which he then poured into anyone who found themselves next to him for more than half a minute.

But in all his stream of chatter Dad had latched on to a few words, the way a desperate prospector might seize on some tiny yellow specks glinting amid the river dirt when panning for gold.

It was something to do with known side effects of the supposedly mild depressants Eve was taking for her anxiety. A certain percentage – a decent percentage – of people responded badly to this drug. A percentage whose worry about something daft and ordinary like GCSEs, or spots, or the situation in Palestine could turn fatally dark under their influence.

It sounded mad to me, and my dad could be very, very boring about it but at least he seemed animated when discussing the theory and if it helped get him on his feet again, helped him on his way back to his rightful place behind the bar, well it couldn't be a bad thing, could it?

Six weeks into my life as de facto pub landlord – heir to the whole desperate kingdom of *what'll you have, mate?* – Bim walked in to the Blue Pig and told me that there was a life that needed saving.

24

'She doesn't want to see me.'

'She doesn't know what she wants.'

We were sitting in the snug, the only two in there at that time. Just gone eleven and the pub had only been open a few minutes. I liked this time usually. It was a day-dreamy space in the day. Time to flick through the *Daily Mirror*, get my head together. Think about my dad. Think about Anne. Think about Eve. Get as much of the quiet grieving done before the day proper began.

But now, today, I saw the pub through Bim's eyes. Saw the scruffiness of it, the mediocrity of it. The smell of it too. Stale. All of it. Stale beer, stale cigarettes, stale lives – that slow reek seemed more pervasive than ever today.

Bim was quite at home however. He had a pint of ruby mild and, though his suit was too well-tailored to be typical of the 11 a.m. drinkist, he didn't actually seem out of place. A casual observer might think he was a

dynamic young sales rep from the brewery outlining a new promotional strategy to one of the tenants.

He was telling me about the mess Anne was in and I was telling him that it wasn't my problem, though I knew already that I would do what I was asked to do. Whatever it was.

In the day I only thought about Anne in the gaps when I wasn't busy with the beer and the pork scratchings and all that, but in the nights she came to me with her fast car, her sharp scent, her deft hands and her enigmatic smile. In the nights she never left me alone.

'All day she sits watching TV and drinking. She doesn't get dressed. She doesn't see friends. She can't be bothered with Dorcas, let alone Ophelia and Portia.'

Ophelia and Portia I'd met often. Dorcas I'd forgotten about. The girl with Bros on her wall. The keeper of the My Little Ponies.

'Poor kid's only nine. She's been away at school and has come home to find the fairy tale has gone very brothers Grimm. Come back from Mallory Towers into a war zone. Incredibly messy. Philip's going for custody you know. He'll get it too, the way Anne is now.'

'Maybe that's the best thing.'

'If you knew Philip at all you wouldn't say that. Luckily the kid is now safely at Grandma's so she's spared the worst of the horror for the time being.'

I had been down from college for all of seven weeks. It was hard to believe that the poised, sports-car driving woman of not quite two months ago had gone to pieces so dramatically. I said as much.

'It's true, believe me. The car's gone by the way. Trashed. Ended up in a ditch near Royston. Silly cow was pissed of course. Then there are the men.'

'The men?'

'Men. Boys. Winos. Basically anyone she happens to be sat next to in the local Dog and Duck come last orders. She's getting quite a reputation amongst the demi-monde.'

I sipped my coke. Kept my face blank. Told myself that it probably wasn't true. Reminded myself of how Bim liked all his stories to be melodramatic and splashy.

'But what can I do?'

'I don't know. But she's clearly taken with you. You could take her out of herself.'

'What does that even mean Bim?'

'Not too sure, but it's what people say isn't it?'

I asked if friends or family would not be better placed to intervene but Bim assured me there was no family that mattered. Especially as Anne's own mum had her hands full looking after Dorcas at the minute.

'Besides there are issues there,' he said, rolling his eyes.

'What about you Bim? Can't you help her?'

'I've tried Mark, I've tried, but we've fallen out rather. She's not listening to me now. Anything I say seems to be unhelpful, seems to encourage her to further outrages. She can be quite childish you know.'

'What about this place? I can't up and leave it.' I explained about my father, knowing even as I put down this obstacle, Bim must know all about my dad's heart attack and would have no trouble brushing it aside. He had clearly been giving the problem of Anne a lot of thought and, for whatever reason, had decided I was the man who could help. I didn't even know why I was arguing about it really.

Bim said, 'I could help you out running the pub.'

'You?'

'Yes, why not me? I used to work in bars as an

undergrad. I don't suppose it's changed all that much. Tell you what, audition me this evening. Let me do tonight's shift and if it goes okay you can shoot off up to Cambridge tomorrow morning, help Anne get her head straight, let her know what's what and come back the following day.'

'You reckon I can sort it in a day?'

'You can make a start, dear thing, you can make a start. Let her know she's not alone, that brighter days are on their way. She needs a friend, Mark.'

The first of the day's customers drifted in soon after that, and Bim went off to take in the delights of Colchester – the castle, the clock museum, St Mary's church from where, it was popularly believed, the rhyme Humpty Dumpty had originated.

'According to my handy tourist guide Humpty Dumpty was a Royalist civil war cannon perched atop the church tower and was shelled by the besieging parliamentarians until tower cannon and, presumably, cannoneer were no more. Until they were beyond the help of the king's men and, indeed, horses. I will go there and mourn the death of handsome cavaliers and curse the memory of Cromwell and his repulsive roundheads. And yes, I know the roundheads were the good guys.'

I stayed in the bar through a quiet lunchtime and a slow afternoon. I ran the idea of a relief Friday night barman past my mother who had seen Bim when he came to the pub asking for me. She wasn't keen on the idea, though she agreed to see how he got on, to give him a chance.

He got on fine. Bim – the regulars loved his ridiculous name – vamped the camp, did outrageous and outspoken in the way only gay men are allowed. Did banter that

veered pretty close to the borderland of flirtation in my opinion, and the customers lapped it up.

I'd noticed before how, when a group of straight men were in the company of an openly gay man, one they liked, they all became just a little bit ooh-la-la themselves. It seems the English working class adore a bit of camp. Look at the success of Larry Grayson, Liberace, Julian Clary, Graham Norton, Dick Emery. A bit of *you are awful, but I like you*. A bit of *shut that door*. All goes down an absolute storm with the masses. The same masses who can be brutal if they so much as catch a glimpse of a gentle male goth in make-up on the street.

But Bim didn't just do the chat. He also did the basics properly: served the right drinks, charged everyone the right money. And at the end of the night he beat the shit out of an obnoxious drunk.

It's fair to say he passed the audition.

The drunk was a guy called Andy Hemingway. Ham-faced, late twenties, solidly muscled at one time, but already running to flab. A nuisance well known to most of the local pubs, not to mention the probation service. Nice enough when sober, he was an evil sod with a few beers in him. So why did the pubs serve him? Because serving people intoxicating liquor was our business and people like Andy Hemingway are just an occupational hazard. Collateral damage. The unfortunate by-product of what pubs do to make a living. Toxic waste yes, but also an important revenue stream.

Anyway, quite often we didn't have to serve him. Someone like Andy H spread himself about. He went out of a night, had a few of jars in various different boozers, moving on when they stopped serving him. Each pub

got unlucky enough to be his last port of call every now and again, and then he had to be humoured, while the pub's nicer regulars supped up and left. Had to be nursed through the door and gently pointed the right way home and the publican had to ignore the nasty little remarks he made, the vicious racism, the squaring up to any strangers that might be in.

The night Bim was working, Hemingway was already loaded when he arrived at the Blue Pig. Only we didn't know it at first. He drank one pint quietly, listening to the fruity chat between Bim and the regulars. Then, just as we'd rung last orders, he started telling the bar how queers should be treated. Not well, it's fair to say. Not in Andy Hemingway world.

Bim ignored him.

I called time. Bim asked everyone to drink up now ladies and gentleman. Asked if they hadn't got homes to go to. Cheery stuff. Quite like how Eve would have done it actually. With panache. With charm.

Hemingway refused to surrender his glass, said he was still drinking. Called Bim a fat faggot. Bim just smiled. Hemingway stood up asking him what he thought he was smiling at. Bim raised his hands in the universal gesture of I don't want no trouble mate. He looked like a weary soldier surrendering. Hemingway sneered.

Bim jabbed both forefingers fast and sudden into Hemingway's eyes.

As Hemingway doubled over, squealing, hands to his face, Bim hit him – hard – right in the solar plexus. Twice.

Hemingway sprawled on the carpet, coughing and gasping, trying to clutch his stomach and claw at his wounded eyes simultaneously. He was writhing on the floor, thrashing like a landed fish.

Bim knelt over him, pulled his head up by his hair and – gently, reasonably – explained that if he ever saw him again he would really, *really* hurt him. Furthermore, he continued, still gentle, still reasonable, if there was any future damage or vandalism to the pub, if there was any comeback to the staff or patrons of the Blue Pig, then he, Bim, would assume, rightly or wrongly, that it was Hemingway's responsibility and he would burn his house down. 'Regardless of who is in it at the time. Of course, you might feel that I wouldn't have the balls to actually do that, just being an old faggot and everything, but are you going to test me, old son? I mean, are you?'

With that he hauled the whimpering Hemingway to his feet and sent him out into the night with a sharp cuff to the side of the head and a well-aimed boot to his arse.

'Fucking hell,' said a regular.

'No swearing at the bar please,' said Mum automatically. 'He had that coming a long time, mind. Might do him good.'

Her eyes were shining.

'Welcome to the team, Bim,' I said.

25

They are there by the side of the pitch, buttoned up against the chill breeze and squally rain. Katy and Ella. Katy's mum and dad, Claude and Alice. All there to watch Jack's debut for Barton Street. I imagine Ella's loud complaints about being made to stand out in the cold and the wet and the adults taking different approaches to dealing with her moaning – Claude will tell her that there's no such thing as bad weather, only inappropriate clothing. Alice will have brought sweets to bribe her into silence.

Katy's mum spoils the kids with the treats Katy and I don't allow them. For a while we tried to persuade her not to, tried to tell her she was undermining our authority, told her that as far as we were concerned she was poisoning her own grandkids. She just smiled and took absolutely no notice whatsoever. We gave up in the end. We had no choice, her will so obviously less wavering than our own.

My own mum would no doubt have been the same had

she got the chance to be a granny, had liver cancer not got her fifteen years ago, just months after that second heart attack got my dad. I remember her funeral, Colchester cemetery on a day just like this one. I didn't feel particularly orphaned. Didn't feel anything much. The family had died years before. When Eve killed herself she took the whole family with her. Mission accomplished because isn't that what every suicide really wants if they're honest? To wipe out everyone close to them.

Eve. The best of us. The one we all looked up to. And, it turns out, the cruellest of us all. Though it was Eve who taught me you could live without those you love. Maybe I should be grateful.

The game is also watched by a scattering of other parents, other grandparents, other siblings all standing, similarly hunched against the weather, watching the boys run after a ball that looks too big for them. Some dads can't help themselves, can't stop themselves shouting frustrated encouragement and advice. Mark up. Find some space. Make the tackle. Look for someone to pass to. Man on. Pass. Shoot. Get stuck in. Break his legs. Break his flipping legs.

I can't hear the actual words, they are lost in the wind, but I can imagine them. Get rid. If in doubt, put it out. All that.

It's advice they sorely need too. Barton Street are all over the place. Even watching the game through binoculars from four hundred yards away I can see this. Barton Street aren't really playing football at all. They are simply chasing the ball the way puppies would, and not athletic puppies either. No greyhound pups these. They look like a breathless pack of mongrel terriers. Up for it but incapable of keeping any kind of shape.

Jack is having a particularly bad game. He's covering a lot of ground, yes, but he's doing it running alongside the opposition players when they have the ball. He's not challenging the beefy forwards so much as pacemaking for them. Keeping them company as they make an uncontested journey towards the goal he's meant to be defending.

It's like he's suffering from a sudden and inappropriate excess of politeness. After you, he seems to be saying – do go ahead old man. I watch as a burly lad from St James's trundles past my son, unhindered, the ball at his feet. It's weird because Jack is not like this at the Saturday morning judo. He gets stuck right in there, often felling much bigger boys in seconds.

I wish I was down there, wish I could shout with the other dads. Not that it would do much good. The shouts from the other parents don't seem to be working after all. It's painful to watch. But at least I am here. It's the first I've seen of my kids for five days. It's the longest I've ever gone without seeing them.

I move my binoculars across now to take another look at Katy. She's just chatting with the other parents and she looks completely comfortable and at ease. And very pregnant. She looks as if she could pop any minute.

She looks well too, though it's hard to tell things like skin tone from all the way up here, even with these ex-army field glasses that Jake found for me. They were his dad's apparently, he was a corporal in the Royal Artillery and they still have real live Gulf War desert dust on the lenses.

As I watch, I see a chunky lad thump a ball from midway in the Barton Street half. Jack jumps out of the way, the unsighted goalie fumbles it and the boys from

St James's have scored again. I make that five with three minutes of the first-half remaining. It is even possible I missed a goal or two. Depressing.

I am watching the game from a car park that conveniently overlooks the football field, well beyond the boundary of the school. I'm hidden by a screen of mature trees.

I am taking a risk I know, but it had all seemed worth it when I'd seen little Jack run out with his teammates. They'd looked good too. In what now seems like astonishing hubris Barton Street Academy are wearing the golden shirts, sky blue shorts and white socks of Brazil.

From here I can see Claude, gesticulating madly. Even from this distance I can see he is incandescent. Katy's dad is a retired PE teacher, and in his day school football meant an introduction into an adult world, no concessions made to the delicate bones of children. No taking care of their fragile hearts. If they're playing rubbish they come off. No messing. Didn't do him any harm, that's what he'd say.

There's at least one police officer here watching the game too, with a panda car parked close to the touchline, and at first I'm irritated. Can't you even let my boy play soccer without spying on him? Then it makes me think.

Anyway, I have seen enough, time to go. I move out from under my cover and cycle off towards Haverstock Road. Where, just as I'd hoped, there is, for once, no police issue Astra outside my house. No resources to watch two places at once. Not these days.

26

When I am as sure as I can be that the coast really is clear, I wheel the bike briskly to the back door, keeping my head down. I am so nervous and in so much of a hurry that as soon as I retrieve the spare keys from under the pot, I drop them again. I take a slow, deliberate breath. Steady myself. Remind myself how I'm going to play this. It's just going to be in then out. Do the thing, then go. A surgical strike. No more than two minutes.

I've psyched myself up for this, but still I'm unprepared for how the house spooks me, how much it hurts to be back after five days away. The dishwasher full of plates and bowls inefficiently stacked, the washing machine full of clothes. I get a cramp in my stomach. A sudden pain in my chest. I move through the house, touching cushions and prints. I go to look at the kids' rooms.

Jack's curtains are closed and in the watery light that filters through, it takes a few moments to make out all the figures on the floor. Legolas and Aragorn, Gandalf

and the Goblin King, various Doctor Whos. A couple of Luke Skywalkers, a moodily youthful five-inch-high Indiana Jones. Knights, wizards, dragons, wolves, but also, incongruously, some innocuous farm animals. A jersey cow, a sheep, a goat. Some 00 scale chickens.

Jack's games are always epic, a never-ending story of quests and battles and magic. Warriors striding clear-eyed into forests and fires. Heroes battling ancient curses, fighting fate, creating myths. Going to their doom fearlessly with swords drawn. Dungeons. Dragons. Blood.

A peep into Ella's room which is as ordered as Jack's is chaotic. A place for everything and everything in its place. A good girl. Nothing on the floor. No clutter. Nothing to put away. No dolls here. Ella has never been one for dolls.

Here's her guitar in its case in the corner. Here are all her books in the bookcase. Jacqueline Wilson, Malorie Blackman. *Noughts and Crosses*. Her mother's old Judy Blumes. Eve's Pippi Longstockings. Her Moomin books.

No sorcerers for Ella. She likes her miracles to be the everyday kind. Ella's heroes – usually heroines actually – win out with wisecracks not wizardry. They have backbone and they have gumption and they don't really do quests.

She has a bookcase full of Eve's old Ladybird books too. Everyone loves Ladybird books and here are thirty-six including all the ones about the kings and queens of England, as well as other classics such as the People at Work series and the Peter and Jane books.

Everyone gets wistful when they see these books. Even if you never had any Ladybird books as a kid – even if you never had any books at all – you can feel a pang for the kind of childhood they represent. Dad back from the

office and putting his feet up with a pipe. Mum placing a home-baked Victoria sponge on the table. Cheery postmen, smiling policemen on bicycles. Men fixing things with spanners and wrenches. Look and Learn arriving on a Saturday. Peter doesn't surf the internet for porn. Jane doesn't get arseholed on WKD.

Eve was obsessive about collecting these books. Right up to her last year she was bringing them back from boot sales and thrift shops, even if she already had them. In that bookshelf now there are at least three copies of the *Ladybird Book of Pirates* in various stages of disintegration. The picture of Ann Bonney and Mary Read fighting the Royal Navy on the deck of a burning ship was practically a manifesto for her life. How her life should have been.

There is dust on the guitar case and I worry about Ella not doing her practice. Has Katy been strict enough with it this week? Once you've started kids on music lessons you can't ever stop. The world is full of adults who resent their parents for not forcing them to keep going with an instrument.

Even with the traffic and then the sitting outside and now this painful nostalgic tour through my old dead life, I have still only been away from the match for maybe twenty-five minutes. Half an hour tops. Ages before they're all due back. Time to empty the dishwasher, to put everything away. Time to unload the washing machine and hang all the clothes around the radiators.

The relief in stacking plates in their proper places, of putting away cutlery. The potency of holding the children's damp clothes, of smoothing and untangling them so they'll dry properly. The complicated sorrow involved in finding a place for Katy's knickers and bras to dry. Her socks. All her t-shirts and leggings.

I do these simple tasks in a daze. It reminds me of another clean up in another time. I shudder. I can't help it.

And, after that, I take five minutes to put some basics into a carrier bag. My clothes are still in the drawers, my work suits still in the wardrobe, and my toiletries still in the bathroom, all of which is a relief, even though they seem like relics from the distant past. A life impossible to imagine anyone living any more.

I put one of my Cash Converters phones on each of the kid's beds, a yellow post-it note on each one.

Just for you love Daddy. Will call you later xxx.

Katy's phone I leave on the bed and spend ages thinking of what to write on her post-it, but can't think of anything. Everything seems trite, sentimental, inauthentic somehow.

These will be the first ever phones for Ella and Jack. Because we are one of those families: the kind where the children are protected from electronic devices. It goes with not letting them have fizzy drinks or eat processed food. It goes with trying, however ineffectually, to stop their grandmother buying them sweets.

No, our children don't have mobiles. Like they don't have tablets, PCs or TVs. Like neither of them has a DS. Like they don't have an Xbox or a PlayStation. If they need a computer for homework, then they borrow my laptop. When they've done it – plus their piano and guitar practice – then they can watch a TV programme on the iPlayer. But we monitor what they watch or what they play and we never let them do it for more than an hour at a time, unless it's a good documentary or a classic movie.

Everyone we know thinks we're unbelievably

puritanical, but then everyone we know also compliments us on how nice our children are, how imaginative, how polite, how resourceful – how they seem to be able to entertain themselves, how astonishing their vocabulary and their general knowledge.

We are aware of the risk that when our kids are older and running their own households, well, maybe they'll gorge on gadgetry to make up for their childhood deprivation. Maybe they'll become the earliest of adopters, live in houses where the TV never ever goes off, where there's one in every room, where they sit, morbidly obese, curtains drawn, stuffing down Snack Pots, their only ambitions being to add to their Minecraft worlds. They might do that, but somehow I doubt it.

We had decided originally that Jack and Ella would each get a cheap phone on starting secondary school, just so they could tell us if they were going to be late home because of an over-running drama club or whatever. You could argue that I am just bringing things forward a bit, and these are, after all, emphatically entry-level phones, designed for six-year-olds really. Absolutely minimum spec.

I am taking a last look round the living room, when I hear the car pull into the driveway. For a panicky second I make a move towards the kitchen and the French doors that lead to the garden. But I stop. I am not a burglar here. This is my home. This is where I should be.

27

'Daddy!'

Ella throws herself into me, knocking me back into the armchair. I gather her into me, wrap her up in my arms. She smells of fresh rain. Jack hovers by the door, looking up at Katy. I see her tiny nod and Jack moves over towards me, slowly, almost reluctantly.

'Hey there, big man,' I say and suddenly my son is squirming into me too. He also smells of rain but of other things too. Mud and sweat. Both my children smell delicious. 'How did the football go?'

'I don't know,' Jack says. I throw a questioning glance towards Katy, who comes and lowers herself carefully on the sofa across from me. She winces. She may have looked fine through the binoculars, but close-up she looks knackered. In all three of her pregnancies her back has given her trouble more or less from day one.

She says, 'It was eight-nil when we left. Jack got himself subbed.'

'I asked to come off. We were rubbish,' he says. 'It was embarrassing.'

'Yeah, I saw some of the first-half. Did look a bit one-sided.'

'We had no tactics at all. Mr Hopkins is useless. He doesn't know anything about football.'

Mr Hopkins is the teaching assistant who also runs the football team, a man whose distinguishing feature is that he is always smiling. Not a typical attribute of the successful football manager I guess.

Katy says, 'Only a game you know. It's meant to be fun, Jack.'

'Losing is never fun,' he says.

Sensing that he is properly upset, I try and keep things light. 'You know what Samuel Beckett says – Fail. Fail again. Fail better.'

Jack is annoyed. 'What does that even mean?'

'Well, I guess it's about the importance of learning from defeat. About persevering.'

Jack sighs. 'Yeah well, who does this Beckett guy play for anyway? Accrington Stanley?'

Ella chimes in, 'Are you back properly now, Daddy? Forever?'

She's always the good student, always looking straight to the heart of the question. What should I say?

But I don't have to say anything because Katy says it for me.

'I'm afraid Daddy will have to go away again, sweetheart. For a bit anyway. He can't stay long.'

Ella doesn't say anything, just frowns.

Jack says, 'I'm going to go and play in my room.'

'You need to run the bath,' Katy says, 'have a quick dip before tea.'

After Jack has gone, Ella seizes her chance to have my undivided attention and tells me about school, about her friends – some complicated story about someone who did something to someone else and no one was talking to the first someone but it turned out that they hadn't really done it and it was another someone who was just causing trouble and that she, Ella, has only tried to sort everything out but now some of her friends are angry with her and people are sitting next to different people in class and some people are not talking to some other people at playtimes and it is all generally terrible and what does Daddy think?

'I think it's always best to leave well alone, to not try and sort out other people's problems for them,' I say.

'Oh Daddy,' she says. 'You just don't get it, do you?' She flounces off towards the door. She pauses when she reaches it. 'It's still nice to see you though.' Then she's gone and it's just Katy and me in the room. The silence stretches out between us.

Eventually, I say, 'Cup of tea?'

Katy just sighs. She sounds just like Jack. 'You know the police will be sitting outside again now. They follow me everywhere.'

I make some quick plans. So I'll have to go down our garden, over the fence, through Mrs Oksanen's vegetable patch and out into the streets that way. Which will be a pain with the bike, but perfectly doable. I'll just have to wait till it's dark.

'They're called Alex and Syima by the way. The police. I'm getting to know the regulars. He's a Chelsea fan, she's got a boy the same age as Jack.' Katy arches her back in her chair.

Then Ella and Jack are both back in the room holding

their phones and throwing themselves back into my arms, telling me that I'm amazing and wonderful and the greatest dad in the world ever ever ever.

'Dad's got us phones, Mum!' says Ella. 'Proper phones.'

'Great,' says Katy, flatly. 'Just great.'

'Come on, kids,' I say. 'Mummy's tired. Let's go and make tea. You two can lay the table.' I stand up.

'I've got to have a bath,' says Jack.

'I've got guitar practice to do,' says Ella. They scoot out the door, giggling at their own audacity. I look at Katy. But she's looking at the floor. I keep looking at her. She keeps looking at the floor.

'They're just cheap ones,' I say. 'They don't do anything flash. No internet or anything. It was quite hard to find phones that limited to be honest.'

She doesn't say anything. I go to the kitchen, fill the kettle. Put the oven on. I'm thinking chicken nuggets. I'm thinking chips. Peas.

We have chicken nuggets a couple of times a week but they are good ones, not mechanically recovered meat scraped from the feet of hens, not squares of random protein and water in a rectangular box. No, instead we get good pieces of diced free range chicken from Harold Naylor's butcher shop in Cumberland Street and breadcrumb them at home. I do big batches every couple of weekends and freeze them.

We defrost them in the microwave, whack them in the oven and hey presto, good, nutritious, easy-to-cook food that kids love and which is also good for them. The chips aren't home-made obviously but they are chunky and low-fat, and resemble the hand-cut jenga chips you get at the better sort of gastro-pub.

When I go back in Katy is no longer staring at the floor. Instead, she's staring out of the window. She doesn't turn my way as I come over with her tea. Even when I'm just centimetres away, blatantly in her space, she doesn't look at me. I put the mug carefully on the floor next to her.

'Don't kick it over,' I say and I move back to my own chair. Maybe this is it. Maybe we will never say anything meaningful to one another again.

'I'm making the kids some nuggets,' I say now. She doesn't reply, but I'm absurdly gratified when she bends forward and takes the tea from the floor, sips at it, settles back in the sofa, wriggles a bit to ease her back.

I am not giving up. I will have something resembling a conversation with my wife however much she tries to block me.

'I've got you another phone too,' I say. 'Just couldn't stand not being able to talk to my family.'

Katy sips her tea. Her face is all flushed hollows. Shadows and bone. At last, she speaks. Her voice is tap-water thin, but at least we're talking, that's the main thing.

'You know the thing I loved most about you was how normal you were. How sensible and kind. How decent and how ordinary. Just goes to show, doesn't it?'

What? What, exactly, does it go to show? She's a smart, well-read, observant woman, surely she knows that there's no such thing as normal? What about when I rocked up in Italy out of my bloody mind? Did she think I was normal then?

But I don't say this. Now's not the time. I drink my own tea. I'm thinking that I need to let her have her say. I need to let her get all the anger out of her system. Only then can I start with how it all was a long time ago. How

I was a different person, completely fucked up and mad. Then I can try and explain how things were. Remind her about my sister.

I can tell her that if I really am decent, normal and kind, well that is all down to her actually. Her and the kids. The whole conversation is one I have rehearsed several times in my chilly box room in Chaney Street.

'Let me make the kids their dinner. Let me put them to bed. Then let's talk. Properly.'

She looks away again, chin resting on her hand. Now she rubs at her nose, something she often does when under pressure or thinking deeply. We played a lot of Scrabble when we were first together, and this gesture was how I could tell when she had a rack full of useless consonants. A fistful of high-scoring but unusable Ks, Qs and Ws. It's lucky she never got into poker I suppose.

'They've had nuggets twice already this week,' she says. 'I need the toilet.' She heaves herself up from her chair and leaves the room. I hear the door to the downstairs toilet close, and I shut my eyes.

28

Some of the things Eve was worried about in April 1989, the things that stopped her sleeping and sent her to the doctor asking for help: the Exxon Valdez oil spill; the approach of asteroid 4581 Asclepius; the collapse of Communism; the new local government tax; the protests in Tiananmen Square; the gang rape of a jogger in Central Park, New York; the shooting of eight trans-sexuals in Peru; NATO's modernising of its short-range nuclear missiles; the tornado in Bangladesh that killed two thousand people and the way the news didn't really report it; her GCSEs, especially maths; how hard her parents worked in the pub; the feeling that maybe her friends weren't really her friends; the sending into space of Global Positioning System satellites. Beyond all this there was a generalised sense of dread. An anxiety that something really bad was going to happen – something worse than all these things put together.

She worried about worrying. She worried that it was

a kind of narcissism to fret like this about things she couldn't control.

Her GP, Dr Miriam Clark, had a kind nature and had known Eve since she was a baby. She wanted to help, though she also found these hypersensitive girls a little bit annoying. She definitely thought it *was* a kind of narcissism, though she was too nice to say so. She saw so many girls like this. Still, she would try to help. There were some new products to help, products the medical press had been enthusiastic about.

29

We have tea and the kids don't moan at all about having chicken nuggets again. They'd have them every day. As they eat Jack relaxes enough to tell us some interesting facts: black-lace weaver spiders eat their mother before leaving the nest. Starfish don't have brains. Honking your car horn is illegal in New York City. Human body odour is irresistible to goats on heat.

'What does on heat mean?' says Ella.

'I don't know. Dad?' says Jack.

'I don't know either,' I say. A typical teatime. God, I've missed all this. I could cry.

Katy has a bath. Jack and Ella play reasonably nicely together upstairs. Not too much squabbling. Not even all that much 'your-facing'.

I read to them and for much longer than I usually do. I've always enjoyed this part of the day. Kids cuddled up to me, warm and smelling of toothpaste and soap. Both of them with their moppets. Ella holding her battered

stuffed rabbit, Fluffy. Jack with his favourite bear, Benji. All of us, including me, especially me actually, getting lost in the stories. Today both kids are practically asleep before I stop.

As I tiptoe out of Jack's room, there's a rustle from the bed. 'You haven't said it Daddy.'

I haven't. I've forgotten. I feel a sudden flush of shame.

We have this thing Jack and I where, as I leave the room and put my son's light out, I say 'Love you to the moon and back', and Jack replies with 'Love you to the furthest thing in the universe and back'. It's a thing we adopted from lines in that children's book *Guess How Much I Love You* and we've been doing it for years now. More or less since Jack could talk.

We'll have to stop some time – we can't still be doing it when Jack is twenty – but I hope we've got a year or two left.

We say our lines now and Jack puts his head down with a drawn-out sigh.

Downstairs, Katy seems in a better mood. Wine is open and she's poured two glasses. She asks about where I've been staying, and I hesitate.

'Don't worry. I won't grass.'

'It's not that,' I say. Except it is. A bit. It'll be accidental but if she's getting into the habit of cosy chats with Syima and Alex and their colleagues, it could slip out. Anyway, it's best she doesn't know in case there's some Law Society disciplinary thing waiting down the line.

Katy smiles grimly and takes a swallow. I watch her long neck flex. Then I tell her about my dark little nest at Jake and Lulu's house.

I tell her about how my last few days have been split,

bizarrely, between leading informal Italian conversation lessons while also using all the resources of the internet to try and find out where Anne Sheldon is. Trying and failing.

But she's not listening.

So I stop there. I could tell her more about Jake and about Lulu. About Lulu's leg and about their ridiculous plan to get married and have children. I could tell Katy about the fights they've had. Three in the last three days. Humdingers too and how I've had to listen to them make-up afterwards, which they've done very noisily, and how I now know for sure that the least erotic thing in the world is listening to other people have sex.

But I really don't think she's in the mood. So we have a long silence instead. I reach for my glass. The wine is citrusy and subtle. Hints of gooseberry. More than decent. More than ten quid a bottle if I had to guess.

I try to get eye contact with Katy, but she won't look at me. Instead her gaze travels around the room as if she's surprised to find herself here. She pushes her hand through her wash-and-go bob. I think it's time to talk properly.

'You know, I don't think there are many people who would like to be judged by the things they did when they were nineteen, when they were at college.'

Her eyes widen and she laughs. Only it's not really a proper laugh. There's no humour in it. Just a short dry bark. Almost a cough. It sounds unlike any noise I've ever heard her make before. It's disturbing actually.

I stop talking. Just look at her. At the beautiful full moon of her face. She eases back, wriggles a bit, stretches, her back clearly giving her more gyp. She takes another hit of the wine, places her glass carefully back on the coffee

table that fills the space between us. Wriggles again.

'Do you want a cushion? Or a pillow?' I say. This fidgeting is getting on my nerves.

'It's okay,' she says. She takes a breath and she looks right at me, fire in her eyes. 'Mark, listen, when I was at college I drank too much lots of times. And yeah, I did stuff I wish I hadn't. I snogged some inappropriate men and once I woke up with someone I wished – really wished – I hadn't.'

I'm about to ask who but she holds up her hand to stop me.

'I got the stupid tattoo on my arse.'

'I love that tattoo.' I do, too. A wonky, brick-coloured rose she got done in Italy after an afternoon on the prosecco and I love it. I think it's fun, a sign of a secret silly side of Katy that only I know about. My own silly tattoo itches in the way that it does.

'It's stupid. Childish.' A pause. 'They told me how he died, you know.'

'Katy—' I begin, but she holds up her hand again. The internationally recognised sign for just shut up for a goddam minute. I take a slug of wine.

'Mark, how long have we been together?'

'Twenty-three years, more or less.'

'Twenty-three years,' she repeats and she's looking down at the floor now as if amazed to find it carpeted. As if carpets were an extraordinary invention. She looks up and holds my gaze. 'Twenty-three years. More or less. A long time to keep a secret. Especially one like that.' She takes a deep, deliberate swallow of her drink. Looks back at that fascinating carpet.

'Mark, you need to know I've slept with three other men since I've been with you.'

This is absolutely not what I'm expecting her to say

and it's so unlikely, so impossible, that I laugh. Actually laugh.

In a cold, dead, wholly new voice she tells me who, where, and how. She counts the fucking ways. I want to interrupt, to shut her up. But I don't. Because somehow I find I also want every sordid little detail. So I just sit there as she gives me all the becauses. Because she was bored. Because she was lonely. Because these men, they were really fucking keen. Because why the hell not? Because the days are long but life itself is pretty bloody short. Because the idea of waking up to my face every day for the rest of her life filled her with mortal fucking dread.

She tells me that the bike she bought for my birthday was chosen for me by one of her lovers, a cycling enthusiast. A guy who followed the Tour de France every year, a guy who knew his stuff when it came to wheels and frames and gears.

'I got him to tell me what bike he would buy for himself if money was no object and then I got that. Two thousand pounds.' She says this last bit with a sort of wonder.

'And the baby?' I say at last.

'Oh don't worry, the Bump is definitely yours. Is that really what you care about most?'

I get up and, taking great care not to yell or shout or slam any doors, I make my way out of the lounge, through the kitchen doors, down through the damp gloom of the garden and over the fence into the Oksanens.

I have to leave the bike, but I don't care about that. Not now.

30

The first thing I noticed was the For Sale board. Houses usually look at their best when they're for sale. They present shining faces to the world, stand to attention like primary school children desperate to be picked to be some kind of monitor. Not this one. The Sheldon's house looked like it was dying. It might as well have said 'Do Not Resuscitate' on the board instead of the agent's name.

This house didn't look like it had ever been well loved. It looked neglected. Tatty. Like it had been sick for some time. There were soda cans in the garden, stray plastic bags, cat shit. All the curtains were closed. In the afternoon. This was a house beginning to rot.

I'd phoned earlier, but there hadn't been an answer. I'd left a message, but Bim had seemed very certain that Anne would neither pick up the phone when it rang nor would she listen to any messages.

'I'm telling you Mark old chum, she's lost the plot big

time. She's in a right two and eight. Just try and keep the shock off your face when you see her.'

Now there was no answer to my ringing at the front door. Deep in the house that bell sounded dully. It reflected how I felt somehow. The whole atmosphere was unsettling in a dreary kind of way. I felt exposed, like there were hidden eyes watching and I could swear, right at that moment I couldn't hear any birdsong. Nor was there wind in the trees. But at least there was the steady rumble of traffic blithely progressing down the road as it always did. Traffic, I thought, was like a river. Always changing, never changing. Timeless. Going on forever in its blind way, something beyond the comprehension of the individual humans sat listening to the radio in their individual cars. Traffic, the eddy of it. The eternal reassuring ebb and flow of it. Very occasionally deadly. Traffic did the job that God was meant to do.

I was still unsure why I'd come. It was nothing to do with Bim's feeling that I could work a positive transformation, that was certain. The truth was, I just couldn't help myself. I needed to see Anne again. I knew I was courting scorn and humiliation but I had to anyway.

I went around the side of the house, down the passage between it and the garage and tried the door there that lead straight to the kitchen. It was open.

I hesitated. It would be the first time I'd ever gone into a house uninvited. I was also growing nervous about what I might find. A conviction was building that inside this house I might find something terrible. A dread of something I couldn't name.

Still, I went in. All keyed up and ready to explain myself. No need. What did I see? Nothing really.

The kitchen was messy, but not outrageously so. A box

of Alpen on the kitchen table. A pot of jam with no lid but a knife poking from the top. A baccy tin, a packet of Rizlas, a bottle of milk. Two flies doing a crazy game of kiss chase with each other around the light fitting. A sink full of crockery.

The floor was coated in generalised crud it was true – breadcrumbs, mud, stray peas, bits of onion skin – and the air was slightly rancid and damp. In other words, it was in the state millions of other kitchens were in on any given Saturday morning. But here at least was something I could deal with straight away.

I didn't go any further into the house. I put the lid on the jam, added the sticky knife to the cold, grey and stinking puddle in the sink, which I emptied and filled again with fresh scalding water.

I opened a window. Let the air stumble in. I washed up. With the determined application of what my dad would call elbow grease I got rid of all the many indeterminate stickinesses that were dotted like tiny mountainous islands on every surface. I found some furniture polish and soon the air no longer smelled like the inside of a mouldy tent, but instead of synthetic pine needles, the scent of the respectable world in 1990. As if the collective dream home of the nation was a Finnish plastics factory.

I was not quiet. I deliberately banged and clattered, sloshed and sploshed and even sung a bit but Anne didn't appear and I was forced to conclude she was out; I didn't want to think too hard about where she might be.

Going from the kitchen to the hallway, I found the hoover and got rid of the detritus from the floor. I thought about doing a full mop, but I was knackered now. The after-hours ales Bim and I had sunk just a few hours previously were kicking in and the kitchen looked good

enough anyway, a million times better than it did when I had walked in. I allowed myself to smile for a moment at the bafflement Anne might feel if I didn't get to see her and she came back to find this room suddenly spick and span, as if the cleaning elves had been in.

How cool to be an elf. To go through life doing random acts of kindness for poor mortals with no expectation of applause or reward.

I tried to remember the climax of the story of the elves and the shoemaker. I thought that the story ended quite tamely, even quite happily by Hans Christian Anderson standards. Did the shoemaker and his tailoress wife end up making little bespoke suits for their faery visitors? Did the elves stop coming after that? I thought that was how it ended.

It was a fairly right-wing fairy tale when you thought about it. A small business, a family firm, falls on hard times due to the necessary vagaries of the market place, and is saved by some private philanthropy, some individual giving by kind-hearted pointy-eared donors. And, when the business is back on its feet again, the recipients happily repay their benefactors with interest.

It was a conservative fantasy of how an ideal benefits system should work. I wondered what Katy would think of this theory. Perhaps I should put it in a letter for her.

It was then that I realised that Katy and Danny never gave my message to Anne, never told her why I had to miss her party. So actually, fuck telling Katy about the bloody elves. I'd love to know her reasons for not doing that simple little job.

But as quickly as my anger came, it evaporated. What did it really matter now?

Coffee. I'd make myself some coffee. I put the kettle on and I was looking for the Nescafe when I heard a noise behind me. A wet cough.

It wasn't Anne. No, it was some middle-aged short-arse baldy beardy ginger fuck wearing bottle-green corduroy trousers and a faded denim shirt, cringing his way into the kitchen on Argyll patterned socks, a cricket bat held loosely in his right hand like it was a stick of dynamite that might go off. Whatever else he might be, this guy wasn't really vigilante material.

What was most annoying was how he seemed to very quickly decide I was no threat to him either. As I was taking in the corduroy mildness of him, the guy was simultaneously relaxing, breaking into a relieved smile that revealed sharp grey teeth.

'I, er, we, er, thought you might be an intruder.'

'I am an intruder.'

He bared his ratty teeth again. 'Yes, well, granted, but we, er, thought you might be dangerous. A burglar, or even, Doctor, you know, Sheldon.'

'You were going to try and batter Dr Sheldon with a cricket bat in his own home?'

'Well, no, but, there has been some unpleasantness... Anyway, who are you exactly?'

'A friend of Anne's.'

'Good. Good. Ah, me too.' He strode towards me, suddenly resolute, hand outstretched, as if he had decided to act the part of a man being decisive and taking charge. 'I'm Dr Masterson. James.'

I shook his hand. It was predictably limp. This bloke was really getting under my skin for some reason. Under my skin and on my tits.

'Mark Chadwick.'

Masterson smiled again. 'Ah yes. Anne's mentioned you. She was hoping you'd make an appearance.'

'Where is she?'

'Sleeping. Well, not, ah, sleeping, exactly, not any more, not with all your, ah, activity, down here – but resting. We had rather a late one last night. You know how it is.' He gestured towards his tobacco tin. 'Fact is I, ah, really came down for that. It is my shameful addiction to the dreaded weed that finally drove me from our refuge to, ah, confront, whoever was in here.'

The thought that this creature had been cuddling up with Anne Sheldon all this time – while I had been down here cleaning the kitchen – filled me with a hot and sudden rage. I had a dim sense that this might be irrational so I tried to contain it. Tried and failed.

'Well, Mr Masterson. I think you should, ah, take your tobacco and, ah, fuck the fuck off.'

Masterson's face darkened. The rodent smile vanished. 'There's no need to be uncivil. We're on the same side you and I.' He stopped, licked his lips. 'And it's Doctor Masterson.'

'James has been very kind.'

Anne. Finally. She stood in the doorway, a diminished version of the woman who had hurled her Dart around the country lanes of Cambridgeshire. The woman who had lain belly to belly with me in the soft dusk at the end of a long summer's day. The woman who had shown me everything. 'He's even lent me his car.'

She was whey-faced and frail, shrouded in a grubby towelling dressing gown, goose pimply legs beneath the hem. Eyes rimmed red. Mascara traces in the lines beneath them. Skin puffy. Moving with the careful steps of the convalescent.

She was in a state right enough. In a bad way. Objectively, I could see she looked terrible. Nevertheless, my heart turned over at the sight of her. The faint trace of a smile still glistened at the edge of her mouth. My skin prickled suddenly. There was heat in my face. My body remembered the way we had moved together. The way we had tumbled and sweated in all the rooms of this house.

'Mark,' she said, 'my exquisite boy.' Her voice was languid, no heat in it. It made me feel constrained, nervous, paralysed. Mocked. Maybe she was still angry about how I had left Cambridge without a word, missing the party that was in my honour. Well, I could explain that at least.

'I take it I'm, ah, surplus to requirements now then?' Masterson. Sulky.

'Yes, James. Yes, I think you probably are. For the nonce. You're a brick to let me have the car. An absolute sweetie. I won't forget.'

He looked gutted. As well he might. No proper man wants to be called a sweetie. Might as well call him a eunuch. As Anne well knew. Cruel. Not that I cared. Masterson's presence was a profound insult to me at this moment. A weeping sore.

There was a ripple of awkward silence as Masterson went to pull his Timberlands on and tie his laces. Timberlands. In red. The idiot.

When he stood up, he shook my hand again. He gave Anne a moist kiss on her proffered cheek.

After he'd gone – Christ, he took his time with those laces – Anne sighed and answered the question I absolutely didn't ask. The question I wouldn't dream of asking.

'Not that it's any of your business, darling, but I

didn't fuck him. Credit me with a little taste. But I did need someone round last night for... well, for reasons. Mostly we played backgammon. Now, you were making coffee I think.' She nodded to the jar of Nescafe. 'Not instant, please. Let's try and maintain some standards even while the barbarians are at the gates. While you're doing that I'll go and get decent. Oh, and could you get some paracetamol? I think there's some in that drawer.' She indicated the drawer she meant and smiled. I got the full wattage of it this time. The whole wide laughing brightness of her teeth and lips. I found I was smiling too. Maybe I should kiss her now.

'I'm very pleased you're here you know,' she said.

'You've got Bim to thank.'

'Good old Bim.'

'He said you were shagging winos.'

'How silly. A dear man, but what a vulgar imagination he has.' She went, stepping lightly down the parqueted hall. She seemed stronger with every moment.

I opened the drawer and there was paracetamol in there all right. Boxes and boxes and boxes of it. Someone had been buying in bulk. Someone was in a lot of pain a lot of the time. Someone's life was more or less all headache.

I kept two packets. Threw the rest away. You didn't keep live ammunition in the house. Spray cans of air freshener should be all the toxic danger you had in a home.

31

Ella and Jack watch one police car leave and another one arrive. It's like a baton change in a relay race at sports day, thinks Jack. He doesn't say this because he is afraid of whatever nasty thing Ella will say back. She's been angry nearly all the time these last few days and so has his mum. You have to be so careful what you say in this house now.

Keeping her eye on the car, Ella is speaking. Jack isn't sure whether it's to him or to herself. He's not sure if she even knows the difference.

'You know what happened yesterday?' she says. 'Three policemen watched a little boy drown. He'd broken a window with his football and they were chasing him and he ran into a canal. The police wouldn't go in and get him. Said it was dangerous. Said there were weeds under the water and that they weren't allowed to go in after him.'

'That's horrible,' he says. He pulls at her arm. He wishes she would look at him.

Ella says, 'But that's not the worst thing.'

Jack wonders what could be worse than this. Thinks this might be the worst thing he has ever been told.

'The worst thing is they wouldn't let anyone else dive in either. There was a crowd of about a hundred people and the police wouldn't let anyone go in for him. They all watched him die right in front of them.'

'Is that really true, Ella?'

'Really, really true. Cross my heart. Emmy told me. She was there. She saw it all.'

Now she looks at Jack.

'How old was the boy?' he says, his voice just more than a breath.

'I don't know.' She looks at him for a long beat. 'About eight I think.'

'I don't believe you,' he says.

'I swear,' she says. 'They can't rescue children who are drowning but they can sit outside our house munching all day long.'

Jack is happier now that he's pretty sure Ella is making the story up, thinks she was just trying to frighten him. That's okay. He's used to that. Jack thinks that maybe there was a boy that fell in the canal but he probably didn't drown and the police probably didn't just stand and watch. How could they?

He peers hard at the shapes in the police car. Sure enough the man police officer is eating some kind of bun. 'That's Alex,' he says, 'he's always eating.'

'It's disgusting,' says Ella.

32

I didn't know if I was meant to follow Anne up the stairs. It was what my blood and muscles wanted, but she was so coolly detached it made me hesitant. I would take nothing for granted. I would wait for an unmistakeable invitation, maybe see how things were at dusk, when the hour between dog and wolf came around. See if we were friends or enemies then.

In the meantime, I opened windows and gathered up cups, plates, glasses and bottles and took them all through to the kitchen. Soon the sink was full again and there was a platoon of empty wine bottles by the back door.

By the time Anne came back down the stairs I had thoroughly Mr Sheened the cloakroom and was making a start on the downstairs study. So absorbed in this task was I that I didn't hear Anne come in and I jumped when she put a gentle hand on my shoulder.

She was showered, smelling of expensive apricoty cleansers, face immaculate, dressed in jeans and a grey

sweater. She looked round the room, her eyes grave. Then she brightened.

'Well, aren't you the miracle worker?' she said. 'You'll make someone a lovely wife one day. But, please, please, please stop it. You're making me feel inadequate. That coffee now? Or shall we be terribly decadent and have wine?'

'You decide.'

'Oh good. I was afraid you'd insist on coffee. Surprisingly puritanical, the young I find. And, actually, I know exactly what we should drink at a time like this.'

Still no reference to the way we had been with each other just a few short weeks ago. I wondered if maybe it was possible that she was feeling shy too and was relying on alcohol to dissolve this wall that had somehow sprung up between us. It was just about possible.

We drank a powerful red wine from New Zealand – 'they're really getting their shit together over there' – and Anne smoked and I tried to explain about missing the party but she just flapped her hand in a way that made it clear that we weren't going to talk about that kind of ancient history.

I asked her about the car crash. She told the story in a few curt sentences. It was a simple one. An angry woman driving too fast in the rain. An S bend on a country road. A tractor. A hedge. A ditch. A write-off.

'I've always been an emotional driver. How I'm feeling in my head is reflected in what happens on the road. But everyone walked away unharmed. And, you know, at the time it was somehow quite exhilarating.'

'Bim says you were over the limit.'

'Four times over, they say. Which leads me to think the limit must be quite shockingly low. God, what a boring

little nation of milk-sops we're becoming. Scared of drink, scared of smoking, scared of every damned thing.'

She took a deep pull on her fag, and I noticed how her fingers shook as she took it from her mouth. 'Scared of sex too,' she said. 'Have you seen those adverts? The ones with the tombstones on? Everything's getting very Victorian. Worse, because at least the Victorians had the guts to be hypocrites. This lot, the arseholes in power now, I'm very much afraid they actually believe they're saving us from ourselves. They genuinely want to Do Good. The self-righteous bastards.'

'You'll lose your licence. Automatic ban for a year.'

'Frankly, my dear, that's the least of my worries.'

'Tell me the big worries then. Perhaps I can help.'

'I very much doubt it.'

'Try me.'

She thought about this. She kept her eyes on the ceiling, on the thin blanket of smoke that hung there, as if it was the most fascinating thing she'd ever seen. When she spoke, it was in a resigned, faraway voice.

'Do you remember how to roll a joint?'

I did. Like riding a bike it's not something you forget, and, as I skinned up, Anne told me about Philip Sheldon standing here, in this room, straight-backed, voice even, announcing that not only was he leaving her, he intended to marry Mish Saker, that they were going to start a family.

'That's how he put it. They were going to start a family. Pompous arse.'

He'd told her that not only was he having a child with Mish, he hoped to have many more with her, three at least. He told Anne that he would, of course, have to sell both this house and the cottage in France. A shame but

there it was. Oh and he'd told her that he'd never been happier. In fact, he believed he'd never been happy at all until he met Mish.

He'd told her that once the child was born, Mish and he were going to move to the USA, to California, to make a fresh start. To be near the research facilities of the American chemical giant that was going to pay him the insane mega-bucks to work for them.

They'd found a lovely place. Perfect. Five bedrooms, studies for both Mish and himself. Room to entertain. Oranges, figs and almonds growing wild. Furthermore, and he hoped that Anne would see the sense in this and not make a damn fuss, he intended to stop paying the school fees for Dorcas. But it was entirely reasonable because they wanted to take her with them.

It'd be perfect for her. She'd go to a local school. Be with her new brother or sister. Have a warm, Californian Disneyland life rather than the chilly, damp Enid Blyton life they had inflicted on her up to now. She'd love it. Anyway, she could always come back for holidays if she wanted. If Anne felt that she could cope.

Dr Sheldon hoped Anne wouldn't be selfish enough to stand in their way, but if she did try he was certain that he'd emerge victorious in court, especially given Anne's recent contretemps with the law. Given her drinking. Given what he was sure any decent judge would see as an unacceptably chaotic lifestyle, her lack of any means of support.

That was the gist of it.

'He's going to take everything, you know. Really, I'll be left with nothing.'

'People get divorced all the time. It's no big deal these days.'

'Yes. And the women end up broke while the men end up with their new bits of stuff living the life of bloody riley in the California sunshine. I think that is a biggish deal actually. Not to mention, when couples get divorced at least the women usually get the children, but he's right, he's going to get Dorcas too. I know he is.'

She sounded bitter and she gave me a hard, cold look. For that moment it was as though she hated me. But of course it wasn't me she hated. It was only all men. All women too for that matter. All young women anyway. Then she sighed and her body, which had become tight and hunched, seemed to unfurl slightly. She took a pull on the spliff, offered it to me. I shook my head. I couldn't have said why, but at that moment, I just didn't fancy it.

'Suit yourself,' she said, and I felt like I was flunking some crucial test. 'But at least have some more wine,' she said. 'I'll go and get some.'

She was gone for a good fifteen minutes. Fifteen minutes where I tried to distract myself from wondering what was going on here exactly by prowling around the room, taking books off the shelves, stroking the smooth curves of the sculptures, picking up the photo of an anxious-looking, gap-toothed girl in plaits, Dorcas, I supposed.

Fifteen minutes during which I saw a long medical word on the top letter of a tottering pile of unopened post. It was a word that rang a bell somewhere in the back of my mind. Reminded me I must remember to call home, get the latest on my dad.

'You know, people hate nosy parkers.' She didn't really sound annoyed, she actually sounded like she'd got herself together a bit. There was light back in her voice. A kind of quiet music.

'You were a long time.'

'Yes. I went to the cellar and I had trouble deciding. But I think this should hit the spot.' She poured us each a glass. We toasted one another silently. It was easily the best wine I'd ever tasted. I was only really used to cheap stuff admittedly, but this was a revelation.

Anne smiled again. She had clocked my startled look.

'Yes, it's a bit special. I'm glad you can appreciate it. A lot of boys your age wouldn't. It's a 1973 Margaux. Philip's of course. I'm drinking my way through his collection. I'm aware that some will find this petty, but I find that knowing I'm drinking his pension makes each mouthful taste better. Really brings out the fruity, oaky notes I find.'

She held her glass up, eyeing it critically. The wine was dark, almost inky. 'Do you think it's small-minded of me Marko?'

'No.'

'Well, you should because it is. But I don't care.'

She finished her wine, poured herself another. Offered the bottle to me and I topped up my own glass. It really was bloody lovely. Anne made a deliberate effort now to stretch and relax. She smiled. She said, 'So, Mark, what am I going to do? Any bright ideas? No? Well, do give it some thought. Set me right.'

She went on to say how frightened she was, not just of losing her daughter, her home, of being broke. But how she felt physically threatened too.

'It's why I had poor old Jimmy Masterson round last night. Philip is vicious when he's crossed. He's capable of anything.' She paused for a second. 'I'm sure he's got rid of the cats.'

'By got rid of you mean...?'

'Yes. At least they've not been around for a while

and you've met them. Portia and Ophelia aren't exactly hunter material, are they? Not the type to run off and try their luck in the wild. Soft as butter the pair of them.' She seemed to come to a decision, straightened up in her chair. Looked me straight in the eye.

'Do you play backgammon, Mark?'

I shook my head. No backgammon in the Blue Pig when I was growing up – bar billiards, yes. Shove ha'penny, even – but no backgammon.

'Pity. We'll have to think of something else to do, won't we?'

33

The something else turned out to be a walk. My idea. Anne was resistant at first.

'But what's the point?' she said, petulant.

'Fresh air is good for you. Walking is a proven mood enhancer.'

'I'm not sure I want my moods enhanced. I think my moods are fine as they are.'

But in the end she fetched a coat, pulled on knee high Cuban-heeled boots in green leather. Not really boots for walking, but they'd do. We set off out of Selwyn Gardens into Grange Road.

We ambled past Wolfson College and past Newnham College. We stopped to look at the ducks from the Fen Causeway. We went past the Scott Polar Research Institute with its sculpture by the explorer's mother in the garden. The sculpture that was titled Youth, and had uncalled-for optimism in every chisel stroke.

All the time we talked quietly of nothing very much.

We pointed out things of interest to each other. Oddly-shaped houses that were surely too narrow to live in. Blue plaques commemorating forgotten architects, forgotten inventors, forgotten poets.

We imagined what might be going on behind the windows of college rooms. Anne spun detailed and believable stories of lonely mathematicians composing love letters to waif-like beauties. Letters they would never send to girls that would never know these forlorn numbersmiths even existed.

I imagined a foreign tourist staying in the room where Cromwell had once slept, initial awe fading into prosaic irritation with the ancient plumbing and the mysterious coughing of an old college that made sleep impossible. Noises that could be the heat pipes, but could also be ghosts.

We made our way up Hills Road to where it became Lenfield Road. We found ourselves in Silver Street and wandered to the Backs, where we watched some pretty Japanese kids attempting to negotiate a punt.

Those kids were having a lovely time. The girls were shrieking with panicked laughter, as if they were on some scream-if-you-want-to-go-faster fairground waltzer, the boys were trying to be reassuring, commanding. Little admirals. They were having fun. The kind of innocent fun that might end in kisses later. You couldn't help smiling watching that joyful vignette. I couldn't anyway. Anne could. This whole scene annoyed her somehow.

'Bloody tourists,' she said. I pointed out that complaining about tourists in Cambridge in the summer was like complaining about penguins in the Antarctic, sand in the desert. It was like moaning about the chemical composition of the atmosphere. Plus those bloody tourists

she was so dismissive of were also bloody brilliant for the local economy. They probably spent way more than the bloody students for a start.

'Yes, yes, I know. You're right,' she said. 'But let's go somewhere else, get away from the colleges. Let's see the real Cambridge. Let's go where the tourists don't.'

So we walked along Chesterton Road towards Newmarket Road where the charmingly lop-sided houses gave way to fast food outlets and places to get your tyres changed. We walked past the football ground all the way out towards the park and ride. By the time we had got near the perimeter of the town's dinky airport, rain had come on, skittering down the gutters like spiders, and so we sat in a pub called The Fox and had pints of dark beer.

It was a barn of a place, unlike the Blue Pig in every respect except for the sense of a defiantly cheery struggle to make ends meet. We had steak and chips and I told Anne about Bim's first shift in my parents' pub.

'Isn't he a marvel?' she said. 'Bim the warrior. Bim the avenging angel. I would've liked to have seen that.'

The pub had a collection of board games in one corner, one of which was backgammon and for the next couple of hours we drank slowly, while Anne taught me the game. She was a good teacher: patient, good-humoured, tolerant. I was, as ever, a good student. A quick study. I didn't fall in love with backgammon there and then, but I began to see how it could become addictive, how I might one day, with practise, fall in love with it.

I was already in love with the idea of being taught things by Anne of course. Anne knew it. She even tested its limits.

'How's that lovely girl? The delectable Katy,' she said at one point.

I shrugged. 'She's all right I think. She's teaching English to kids in Italy.'

Anne nodded. 'Of course she is. She's one of those young women who are never knowingly under-employed. She's the future, Mark.'

I thought she was probably right. The 1990s would be the decade of women after all. That was what the UN had decided. An unlikely coalition of allies had been agreeing with them all year. The Secretary of State for Employment, the guy who ran the Confederation of British Industry, the Trade Union Congress. The EEC, the Army. All of them saying women were where it was at. By the new millennium they'd be running everything.

It was another thing Eve would miss. The girl who was a singer, a writer, an artist. A girl who could have been anything – now just a box of ashes, unbelievably small. You wouldn't believe what a small heap of dust a person becomes in the end.

'I was very surprised when you said Katy wasn't your girlfriend. Very surprised indeed. You missed a trick there I think, Mark.'

I was confused by this. I hadn't ever wanted to be with Katy. I had wanted to be with Anne, but now she seemed to want to pretend that nothing much had happened between us.

'Who's LM?' she said.

She had noticed the tattoo. I told her how I'd had it done on a day when I was more than usually oppressed by memories of Eve. She was everywhere in the Blue Pig after all. She'd made up dances with her friends in the cellar at thirteen, The Good Terrorists had rehearsed in

the function room, had played their first three gigs there too. There was a wonky watercolour of a blue pig on the wall, a painting she'd done at ten.

Of course I thought of her every time I spotted a Daddy long legs, a ladybird, a wasp, a butterfly. Every time I went to the Eazyzap. *I'll be the annoying insect that won't leave you alone.*

So one slow afternoon, in search of pain I think now, I went out and had a big scarlet love heart tattooed on my arm, the initials LM written in the centre, a bit wonky because it was the first real tattoo inked by a seventeen-year-old apprentice who was shaky with performance anxiety.

It was okay though, the pain was distracting enough but bearable, and the owner of the tattoo parlour, embarrassed by the shoddy workmanship, let me off paying.

There was a short silence after I told this story, and for something to say I asked something that had been nagging at me.

'What is parflutretoline?'

Anne told me it was Dr Sheldon's project. The active ingredient in something sold as Fluxin. He led the team on it. A real breakthrough worth literally billions.

'Of course it's not actually the money he wants. He thinks he deserves a Nobel prize. You know he is genuinely enraged when another year goes past and he's not in the running.' Her mouth twisted. 'What kind of planet are you on when you actually start thinking like that – thinking it outrageous that those Nobel bastards are ignoring you again – are you all right?'

I nodded, though I wasn't all right. I could feel something beginning to boil inside me. A sickness rising. But I checked myself. It would turn out to be nothing.

I changed the subject and we talked of other things, unimportant things. Later, Anne said, 'You know what I'd like to do now?'

I had no idea.

'I'd like to watch a film. Before I met Philip I used to go to the pictures all the time, but he hates films. He can't sit in silence for two hours. He doesn't have the concentration for films. He has a very TV mind you know. He loves those game shows. Things like *The Generation Game* and *Play Your Cards Right*. He is a fan of all that. Funny, isn't it?'

It sounded like carefully cultivated eccentricity to me, but I didn't say anything. Instead I went and fetched a paper from the bar. It was now 7 p.m. The ABC was showing *Pretty Woman* at seven forty-five. If we got our skates on we could make it.

'Well, let's get those jolly old skates on then,' Anne said. 'A romantic comedy about a tart with a heart. Perfect. It'll be like a date and we've never actually had one of those, have we?'

We hurried back into town and had time to buy tubs of Häagen-Dazs and a bag of wine gums, and in the dark of the ABC we sat with arms resting against each other.

By the time Richard Gere had got himself lost on Hollywood Boulevard our legs were pressed against each other too. I could hear the blood rushing in my ears. The air seemed to be growing more solid. I was finding it hard to concentrate on the back and forth of the dialogue.

By the time Richard Gere and Julia Roberts were making love on the grand piano our hands were linked. By the time the Jason Alexander character, the villain, was attacking Julia in her hotel room, Anne's hand was on my thigh, stroking gently. My hand moved so that

it was doing the same to her. I moved my fingers up towards the hot centre of her and she grabbed my wrist to stop me. It was like being fourteen again, like being on one of my first dates, unbearably exciting. I moved my hand back to her knee.

There in the dark, chewing wine gums, Anne's hand on my thigh, Richard Gere renouncing the cold ways of business in order to have a better work-life balance, I wondered how the evening would end. Who would start things when we were back in the house? Anne, I decided. Obviously it would be up to Anne to start things. Unless it wasn't. Unless it was up to me. Whatever, I knew that within minutes of getting in we would be sprawling across her bed, or maybe we wouldn't even get that far. Maybe we would do it in the hallway, the kitchen, on the stairs. We were back. We were an item again. A thing.

When we reached Selwyn Gardens, when Anne had the key in the front door, she stopped a moment and said. 'It was a good idea. The walk. My mood is definitely enhanced. Well done.'

She kissed me lightly on the lips and I followed her down the hall. A drink, then bed. It looked like we would restrain ourselves until we reached the bedroom. At the entrance to the living room she stopped, abruptly. Behind her I could see her shoulders tense.

'Hello, dear. Had a nice time?'

A cool, deep, sarcastic voice from the darkness beyond. Sheldon. Anne put her shoulders back and took a determined step into the room. I followed her as a lamp clicked on and Philip Sheldon was revealed, sitting in one of their over-stuffed armchairs as if entirely at ease. Long legs stretched out, crossed at the ankles. He was in

shirtsleeves, hands steepled together, a pose that suggested a serious man quietly contemplating the events of a busy but rewarding day. He had a large glass of wine on the table next to him. He was every inch the relaxed *pater familias* at home. A man enjoying some much-deserved downtime. He was even wearing slippers for fuck's sake.

34

'Philip.' Anne's voice was stony.

'Anne. Anne. Anne.' He seemed to be tasting her name, chewing it, savouring it, turning it over in his mouth as though it was new and exotic and lovely to say. As if each syllable kept surprising him with sweetness. There was a chill silence afterwards. Sheldon broke it, his head turned towards me.

'And you, you young scamp, a surprise to see you here I must say.'

I couldn't think of anything to say and Sheldon smirked.

Anne spoke, her voice tired. 'I'm sorry, Philip.'

I was taken aback. Anne sounded utterly abject.

'You don't have to say sorry to him.'

'Oh, but she does. You do, don't you Anne?'

'I'm going to have a bath.' Anne turned and walked back past me and towards the stairs. I took a step after her. Caught her by the shoulder. She stopped.

From the room behind us Sheldon called out, 'Offering

to scrub her back? Nice. Good for you. She's not bad in the sack, is she? I'll give her that. A decent screw when she feels like it. When she can be bothered to put the effort in.'

'Get rid of him, please. Just get rid of him.'

One clear task to focus on. One straightforward job to do. Anne ran up the stairs, her head down and I watched her. She looked shrunken somehow.

I took a second to think and headed off into the living room. If he'd got any sense Sheldon would take one look at me and he'd take off of his own accord, but if not, well, he'd be gone in ten minutes anyway. Or less even.

I rubbed my knuckles. Decided to treat the professor as just another unruly Saturday night customer, just another drunken fuckwit punter needing bouncing.

'Come in then, boy. Don't skulk out there. Come in, take a pew, have a drink. Let's have a wee chat you and I.'

'Anne wants you out.'

Sheldon ignored me. 'Just sit down,' he said. For some reason – a lifetime of obedience to teachers probably – I found myself doing it.

Sheldon said, 'You're in over your head you know.'

I said nothing. Five minutes, that's all I was giving him. Five minutes, and then Sheldon was out. The professor put his hands behind his head, regarded me with studied cool. Flexed his slippered feet. Then he told me where he'd been, what he had been doing while Anne and I were walking the streets of Cambridge, while we were watching Richard Gere and Julia Roberts do their thing.

While we'd been doing all that, Sheldon had been in a windowless room in the basement of a Cambridge nick answering the viciously invasive questions of hostile detectives.

'Because you know what she did, don't you?'

I stayed silent. I wasn't getting into a discussion with him. Couple more minutes and then Sheldon really was out on his ear. 'She accused me of interfering with our daughter.'

So I heard how Dr Sheldon was arrested at home and questioned for hour upon humiliating hour by grim-faced policemen who had no time for academics anyway and hot-shot scientist is kiddie-fiddler, well, that's a story they understood – that played right into their prejudices. The rage with which he denied it also seemed to them to be a kind of supporting evidence of course. Why are you getting so het up, Sir? Touched a nerve have we, Sir?

After questioning, he was left to sit for several hours while a team was despatched to Hampshire to talk to Dorcas where, in a child-friendly lilac room with pictures of bunnies on the wall, a baffled and distressed kid frustrated a sympathetic lady from social services by plainly having no idea what the hell she was talking about. In my head I could picture that poor girl, anxious even on a normal day, struggling to get her head round the implications of what was being said to her. Wondering how to pass this latest test she'd been set by the incomprehensible adult world.

'Eventually it was clear even to the goons from her majesty's constabulary that the dates and times didn't add up. For several of them Dorcas was at school, for others I'd been a thousand miles away on a bloody lecture tour. I will be suing of course; I'll be having their guts for bloody garters. Anne's too, if I can.'

Through all this, he didn't actually seem angry or outraged. He didn't look like a man out to turn guts into bloody garters. He didn't look like a man who'd been

through a gruelling ordeal at the hands of the police. He looked like a man replete. A man with a glutted look, full of smug self-satisfaction. Bloated with triumph.

'Just thought I should let you know what you're dealing with.'

'I think you should go now, Dr Sheldon.'

'Leave my own house?' He stared at me, challenge giving a glowing heat to his eyes. Then he relaxed. 'Yes, don't worry. I'm going to go. I'm going to go back to my very beautiful, very passionate, very sane partner. Tomorrow Mish and I will spend a happy day discussing names for babies. While you try and deal with the fallout here.'

'What fallout?'

'Well, I imagine that even our dozy constabulary won't leave matters where they are. I think that tomorrow Anne can expect a knock from one or more disgruntled boys in blue. I don't know what the penalties are for wasting police time in the way that she has, but they are probably reasonably punitive wouldn't you say?'

With that he finished his drink, heaved himself from the armchair and crossed the room with the confident strides of the righteous drunk. He stopped right in front of me, ran a hand through his unruly grey mop.

There was something I needed to ask him.

'Parflutretoline – Fluxin – is it as dangerous as they say?' By they, I meant my dad and Mr Harold Thorne-Lungs but Sheldon reacted as if I were talking about the propaganda of an organised conspiracy. A terror cell. He stiffened, his fists clenched, his lip curled.

'That is a vile, disgusting libel.' He made a very visible effort to get himself under control. He exhaled noisily. 'In a very few individuals, in the first weeks of taking it,

there is some slight risk that our product might exacerbate symptoms before it relieves them. We are talking about very, very few people – mostly adolescents – and nearly all of those few affected in this way are successfully moved on to alternative and more suitable forms of medication. Our drug is a major contribution to curing one of the greatest epidemics of the modern age, that of anxiety and psychological distress. Who have you been talking to?'

It was true then. Harold Thorne-Lungs and my dad, they'd got him bang to rights.

There was a long silence. Dr Sheldon looking at me with a pitying contempt, while I thought about the psychological distress my sister's death caused to quite a lot of people.

'And you, sunny Jim,' the professor was talking again, his voice granite hard, 'you may not have the glorious Cambridge career you were hoping for. No starred firsts for you. No, you may well find your academic studies become a great deal tougher from now on. You might find your final degree is undistinguished I'm afraid. No BBC afterwards, no becoming a QC or an MP or forensic accountant or whatever you were hoping for. A shame but there it is.'

'You're pissed.'

'Yes, but to paraphrase Winston Churchill, in the morning I will be sober while you will still be a tragic tale of potential that somehow failed to flower. Expectations that never quite blossomed into successes. A mind that turned out to be third rate after all.'

I stood up. Sheldon moved back a step, wobbled. Just about kept himself upright. 'You going to hit me then, boy? Good because then you really will be finished.'

I eyeballed him hard. Sheldon held my gaze. Even in the thin light cast by the lamp I could see how sallow and liverish the skin of the professor's face might become in the not too distant future. How even now rumours of thread veins were making themselves known on those chiselled cheekbones. His new love seemed to be taking its toll. Again I could think of nothing to say. Sheldon grinned in triumph, I could see inflammation of his gums in the gaps between his large square teeth. Yes, love seemed to be doing him in. Someone needed to take him in hand or the medical science career would be down the toilet; there would be a new, younger, less blemished scientist to take his place. A woman probably, in this decade of women.

'Good night, old bean,' Sheldon said. 'Enjoy the wine.'

After he'd gone I sat for a while in the growing chill of the house, just thinking. I headed off up the stairs with two glasses of that dark wine. I knocked gently on the bathroom door and then went in without waiting for her to reply.

'He's gone.'

'Did he tell you what I did? Am I a terrible person? Do you hate me now?'

Her eyes were shadowed and deep, skin marble white. For a second I saw someone else there instead. A girl much younger, lying in water cooled and coloured by her own blood. I shut my eyes. Eve, you fucking idiot.

'I don't hate you.'

She smiled, and she looked suddenly shy, suddenly young. 'Why don't you have a bath?' she said. 'Use my water, it's quite clean.'

I didn't spend long in the bath, just long enough to wash myself thoroughly. The water was tepid and since Eve's

death I found I didn't really enjoy baths anyway. Lying still, with nothing to do except think and remember and speculate about how we could have stopped her – that was too much. These days I just had a quick shower in the morning and another in the evening. You don't think much under hot showers.

When I got out, I wrapped myself in a large white towel and when I opened the bathroom door I found Anne had put my rucksack just outside. I put on clean boxers and a fresh t-shirt and padded back down the landing towards the master bedroom.

'Hey you,' she said, softly, fondly. She took her glasses off and dropped them on the floor. She did the same with her book.

Anne wriggled under the covers, she turned towards me as I climbed onto the bed and her face was full of shifting shadow. Her eyes gleaming with black light. She looked at me for a slow minute, while I struggled – and failed – to think of something to say.

'Well,' Anne breathed. 'Here we are.' Her voice was low, full of heat.

It was gone midnight and the house grew expectant somehow. Like it was keeping quiet, trying hard not to disturb us.

We lay in silence for a few minutes, our arms just touching, ghost touches, until we were startled by anguished screeching nearby. We both jumped, then we both laughed. Outside in the garden, in the flower bed beyond the bay windows, beyond the blinds, something was killing something else. Killing it or fucking it. The tamest and tidiest of gardens is a warzone at night, where kill or be killed, fuck or be fucked is the whole of the law. Where nature feeds herself just like she always has.

Anne wrapped herself around me. I breathed in the smoky heat of her.

She said, 'Last night poor old Jimmy's little chipolata was pressing into me all night and I felt no temptation at all. Not even any curiosity. I was just irritated. And, you know, when he did finally fall asleep, he snored.'

In our weeks together I had only once stayed with Anne the whole night. That was that time at Langhams and neither of us had really slept at all that night. Sleeping hadn't been what we were there for.

'I might snore,' I said now.

'You won't. Somehow I know you won't.' We kissed. It was strange because we were clumsy now, whereas when we had been new lovers we had been pretty graceful. Now our teeth clashed. Now our mouths – hungry, greedy, ardent – didn't quite fit. Anne tasted of toothpaste, but she hadn't managed to rid herself completely of that enticing undertow of cigarettes, wine and whisky. We kissed more and touched, she reached for me, squeezed me none too gentle and then she broke away.

'Phew,' she breathed. She raised herself up, clicked off the lamp. Turned away on her side. I listened to her breathing, to my own heart pumping, to the blood pulsing around my body, to the house, which was holding its breath again. 'Thank you Mark,' she said. 'I'm glad you're here. I know everything is going to be fine.'

We lay together like that for a while. In the dark, me pressed into her back, holding her shoulders. It took me a while to realise she was crying.

'What can I do?' I whispered at last.

'You're so sweet,' she said.

This was too much. I gripped her shoulders, dug my nails right in. 'I'm really not,' I said. 'You have to know that.'

She was startled by my vehemence. I heard her sucking at the thickening air. 'No, you're not sweet. Not at all. I don't know why I said it.'

Minutes passed. The wood-smoke scent of her seemed to fill the room. It seemed to be getting warmer too. Then, in a low flat voice she began to tell me what she wanted to do to Dr Sheldon. Told me how she had been dwelling on it while I was in the bath. Told me he needed teaching a lesson, a painful lesson.

Was she serious? Was I meant to offer to help, volunteer to be her enforcer? I didn't really think I was enforcer material, didn't think it was in my skill set. Bim was her man for that stuff. Best to say nothing.

There was quiet again. She sighed, a long desperate exhalation, and when she spoke it was as if to herself.

'Forget it. It's all right. I'll be all right. Honestly. Don't worry.' A pause, another sigh. She squirmed against me. 'That's not going away, is it?'

She reached back, grabbed me with her hand. 'No chipolata either.'

35

I woke early, my head thick, my throat dry, my bones aching. It was like I was coming down with something, but more than this I had a feeling that there was something profoundly wrong with the world. Anne lay with her back to me. I put my hand on her shoulder, tentative. She growled, shook it off.

Despite it being summer, the house was chilly. I dragged my clothes on. Anne didn't stir. I had a piss, splashed cold water on my face, went downstairs, drank three mugs of water. It tasted metallic, faintly rusty. I went through the rituals of making coffee – another thing Anne had shown me – Ethiopian beans in the grinder, the ground coffee in the little tray in the stovetop coffee pot, the water in the reservoir at the bottom, the whole thing screwed together and placed on the hob to begin its magic.

I clicked the radio on, found I was listening to a recording of a piano concerto recorded live in New

York in 1956. It occurred to me that to be a DJ on a classical station was surely to have the easiest job in the media. You read out the sleeve notes from the back of the record cover. You dropped the needle on the disc. You then had twenty minutes or so to read the paper or whatever, before it was time to cue up the next thing. What a great job. Maybe I could do that after Cambridge. Become the hip young gunslinger of Radio Three.

After I'd had coffee, I went down the road to the Spar. I got bread, eggs, orange juice, *The Times*. Croissants. I paid with a twenty and so had half a ton of loose change given back to me. I stopped at a phone box and called home. Bim answered: everything was fine, everything was great and, no, he didn't mind staying on for a few more days.

'Absolutely not. I'm having a ball. I find the role of mine host surprisingly congenial. How's everything where you are?'

I told him everything was fine, everything was great in Cambridge too. Anne was getting herself sorted.

'Good-o, knew you'd be just the ticket.'

'But I might need a few more days here.'

'As long as you like. I'm having fun and I've nowhere special to be. The Vorticists will wait forever if they have to. Here, have a word with your gorgeous mother.'

Mum told me how nice it was to have Bim around, how popular he was with the customers. How they hadn't seen Andy Hemingway since Bim had a quiet word. I laughed at that and Mum did too. Some quiet. Some word.

I asked about Dad and she said that he seemed to be improving slowly, though he was driving everyone nuts with this drug thing. It seemed everything was getting

better. So why did I feel so hollow when I put the phone down?

When I got back Anne was sitting at the kitchen table, smoking and coldly furious.

'Where have you been?'

I lifted the bag of shopping. 'Breakfast.'

'Aw. Isn't that nice? Isn't that sweet?' Ugly sarcasm, a nastily deliberate deployment of the word sweet.

I didn't say anything. I was baffled, uncertain about what I'd done wrong, but clearly there was something.

'You left me on my own.'

'For five minutes.'

'Twenty-five minutes. And it could have been hours for all I knew. It could have been forever. No goodbye. No note. I thought you'd left without telling me. Again.'

'I wouldn't do that. You were sleeping. I was being considerate.'

'Fuck that.'

'Fuck considerate?'

'Yes. Fuck considerate. Fuck nice. Fuck breakfast too actually.' She flapped her wrist at me. 'I have coffee and I have a cigarette. Sets me up for the day quite nicely.'

'Not very healthy,' I said. It was lame but I was trying to keep things light.

'Fuck healthy.'

'Okay, okay someone's clearly got out of bed the wrong side today.'

'No someone just wants to be informed if her lover is leaving the house.'

She rose from her chair, back very straight and moved from the room with exaggerated grace. Head high. Imperious. Careful not to stomp, careful not to hurry.

I swallowed two paracetamols. Made toast. I loved toast. It was my favourite thing. Left to myself it would be more or less all I'd eat. I found butter and jam, made more coffee, poured juice into whisky tumblers. I found a tray and took it all upstairs, a packet of pills perched on the side like an exotic condiment.

Anne was back in bed, curled up under the covers, the only part of her visible a copse of dark hair. I put the tray down on the bedside table. She didn't stir.

It was gone ten already, maybe I should make a start getting back to Essex after all. Maybe Anne needed time on her own. Maybe I was getting on her tits.

She sat up now. She wouldn't look at me. Took the pills, washed them down with juice. Nibbled the corner of a piece of toast.

'This is it, isn't it?' she said, mouth full of crumbs. 'I won't see you again.'

'Bollocks.'

'You just want to have sex with me.'

'No I don't.'

'You don't want to have sex with me?' She was smiling now, and I thought the clouds might be passing, that things might be okay.

'No. No. I mean. Yes, of course I want to... do that. I just meant that's not all I want to do.'

'What else do you want to do, Marko?'

'I want...' I stopped. What did I want? 'I want... I want to, you know, hang out. To watch films, go to plays, exhibitions. To see bands. To go to dinner. To talk. You know, all the usual things.'

'You want to be my boyfriend? A proper boyfriend?' She smiled. She was definitely cheering up now. She might even be laughing at me, though not in a horrible

215

way. 'You know, I haven't seen a band since 1973,' she said. 'Not since I met Philip.'

'Oh. Who was it? The last band you saw?'

'T. Rex.'

'You saw T. Rex in 1973? I'd have loved to see them.'

'They weren't so special. I prefer music you can dance to. Philip only likes classical music of course. But you see Mark, there's a bit of an age gap here isn't there? I'm nearly forty. I'm a mother. I'm someone who saw T. Rex on the Electric Warrior tour and you're... Well, you're just a boy.'

She drank more juice. Her hands were shaking again. She saw me looking and held her hands up. 'I'm in a bad way, aren't I? I told you right at the start that you don't want to be mixed up with me. I've become old, Mark. I've become properly old and I'm going to become invisible the way old people do.'

She looked inexpressibly sad. Her eyes filled with tears. I couldn't bear it.

'But last night,' I began. 'Last night...'

'Last night was... last night. This is this morning. That was then and this is now.'

I thought about going back to the Blue Pig, about Bim asking how Anne was and having to say that I thought I might actually have made things worse.

I wanted to hold her but I didn't know how. There was silence. Then she said, with exaggerated casualness, 'My mother is bringing Dorcas back today.'

So that was it. The return of the kid.

'Do you want me to go?'

Her eyes widened. 'No! Really no. But I assumed you'd want to go home. I mean, nine-year-olds aren't the most interesting company, are they? Women are at their

least attractive when they're with their children. All that nagging, all that nose-wiping.'

'It'll be fine. Really. It might even be a laugh.'

'You think we can play happy families, Marko? Go to the park? Eat ice cream and jelly?'

'I love jelly.'

'Of course you do.'

'What about Dr Sheldon? He won't like me being around while Dorcas is here, will he?'

'No. Philip will hate it. It'll make him crazy. So there's the bonus of that I suppose.'

'You know...' I stopped. Perhaps I shouldn't say what I was going to say. Perhaps it wasn't my place. But she was ahead of me as ever.

'Yeah I do know. I need to sort things out with my husband. Properly sort things out. I will, very soon I promise. Guide's honour.'

'Maybe I could help. Be a sounding board or something.' It was definitely more my thing than beating the shit out of him was.

'Mediate between Philip and I? You think you're up to that? You're very ambitious all of a sudden Mark Chadwick.' A thoughtful pause. A steady look that was making me blush. I knew it. I could feel the heat in my cheeks. 'Just be here, Mark. That's all I need. You can't stay in my actual boudoir any more of course. You'll have to have one of the attic rooms. We'll tell Dorcas that I've had to resort to taking in lodgers since her daddy is spending all his money on his bit of fluff. Might mean we have to do some tip-toeing around in the night of course. Some creeping up and down stairs. But that'll be all right, won't it? Might even be exciting.'

Our eyes met. The exact same thought struck us at the same moment.

'How long till she gets here?'

'An hour at least. Could be two. Could be three. What do you think? A properly noisy fuck in the living room? Shall we make hay while the sun shines? Seize the carp and all that?'

'What?'

She laughed. 'That's my boy.'

36

10 p.m. and I'm back in Chaney Street. As I approach Jake and Lulu's house I decide I can't face them. Tonight, whatever the risk, I can't be watching TV or lying on my bed in that tiny damp cave of a bedroom. I need to be out and I need to be drinking.

In the little shop I buy a half-bottle of value scotch. It's a brand called Claymore and sure enough it chops at the guts like the rusty blade of an unwieldy sword. Fact it's not really a brand as such, it's what you might more accurately call an unbrand, and it tastes the way I imagine plumbing chemicals might. Sink unblocker, something like that. It's perfect. The first swallow makes me splutter and spit, and a passing dog-walker asks if I'm all right.

At first I just mean to walk and think and drink on my own, but it's a cold night and worse than this it is unbearable to see the lights behind the curtains and imagine all those people happily doing nothing important.

Curtains drawn or not, I can see it all so clearly: the watching of box sets. The buying of crap on eBay or Amazon. The Facebooking, tweeting, emailing, snap-chatting, texting. The skyping of loved ones overseas. The instagramming. The placing of logs into the wood burning stove.

I see homework and the ordering of the weekly shop. Couples arguing with each other, some bickering good-naturedly, others squabbling nastily, trading spite. Others, well, maybe they're making love or at least thinking about it.

I see flowers in cheap vases. Late suppers. Ham and Branston Pickle. Slices of shop-bought cake. Battenberg. Fondant fancies. I see coats hung up in hallways, umbrellas propped up ready for use if necessary.

I see animated conversation in rooms where ornamental plates are displayed on old-fashioned dressers. Photos of graduations. Framed certificates.

I see a young woman in a tracksuit with her head on her boyfriend's shoulder as they sit close together on a sofa. Maybe she's just back from her spinning class, maybe he's moaning about the restructure at work. She's making sympathetic noises, barely listening. Maybe they've just moved in together and are still learning how to get along. Enjoying the grown-up novelty of a shared dishwasher.

All of this mocking echoes my life with Katy, and it makes me want to smash my fist into someone's face over and over and over.

I'm not an idiot. I know that there is also real pain among the muddy shadows that flit behind these curtains. There must be children who can't sleep, who call out for their

mummies, who can't find their moppets - their Benjis or their Fluffys. Kids who need a cuddle, or who have wet the bed.

Yes, not everyone is sitting in the wood burner glow of human warmth. Behind some of these curtains sit the lost and the lonely, the suicidal and the heartbroken, the weary and the sick. Someone is sitting there with no one to text, email, skype. There are people in these houses for whom even music means nothing. People that even alcohol no longer helps.

But tonight I have no sympathy for them. They should buck up. Pull themselves up by their bootstraps. Just get it together. Are they looking at fifteen to twenty years in jail? Have they lost Katy? Ella? Jack? The Bump? A sister? No? Well, then. Fuck them. They don't know they're born. It's in this mood of truculent self-pity, with my stomach fizzing with bad bargain booze, that I somehow find myself in the Neptune.

37

The Neptune is a kind of Blue Pig. A pub like the one my parents ran in Colchester a lifetime ago. A pub of the kind that is dying out. Two bars, neither of them huge. A quick glance into the one with a brass sign reading 'saloon' on the heavy oak door reveals a modestly proportioned room with a viciously acrylic carpet.

The walls are painted cream over woodchip and there are paintings of animals. Disappointingly there are none of those pub classics – the ones of dogs playing cards or snooker, instead there are merely faithful representations of woebegone spaniels, dignified black labradors. Sly cats. Horses. A seventeenth century sheep cuddled by a moon-faced boy in a smock. On a shelf that runs all around the room close to the ceiling are dozens of dusty china water jugs.

There is no one in this room. No one behind the bar either come to that.

I go to the other, equally heavy door, the one where the brass plate reads simply 'BAR'.

There's a bit more life in here. If two young blokes playing pool count as more life. If a fat geezer on a stool, steadily munching crisps while watching the rolling news on the TV high in the corner counts as life. If the stutter and blink of a fruit machine counts as life. For me, for now, it will do. It's all the life there is. All the life I want. I stumble into a stray chair on the way to the bar and only then do I realise that the Claymore at least has done what it was meant to do. I am actually already quite drunk.

Now I order a pint of London Pride. A good, bog-standard working beer. The fat man on the stool next to me turns and gives me a long look. He seems to be thinking about saying something, but then thinks better of it and turns back to the telly. The lads playing pool laugh at something. It is probably nothing to do with me. I worry that my situation has made me paranoid. It's only been a few days. What will I be like after a year? After ten years?

The pint is £3.90. Cheap for round here. I give the barmaid a fiver. I take my change across to the pool table, put the quid on the edge.

'I'll play the winner, shall I?' I say.

The lads are finishing up their own game. They look at each other uncertain, wrong-footed. These boys must be in their early twenties, hard-looking with their severely cropped hair, their Maori style tattoos that snake around powerful biceps, the names inked in Gothic script on the forearms of the lad nearest me. Brandon, Elona. His children presumably.

They're tall too. All young guys seem tall now – that eighties and nineties diet has been much derided but it has

produced big, big lads that's for sure. All that mechanically recovered red meat, all those hormones – it will kill them off eventually, but first it turns them into giants.

But, despite their size, despite the aggressively decorated skin and the shorn hair, despite the unblinking eyes, I feel quite safe. It isn't just the confidence cheap whisky will give you either. Any halfway decent high school teacher knows that young men are mostly sweethearts really. The little boys they once were are close to the surface. You don't need to dig down very far to find them.

'No, you're all right,' says the nearest lad softly. 'We're going in a minute.'

Across the table, his mate pots the black with a tricky shot from one end of the table to another.

'Get in,' he says, then straightens up. 'I'll give you a game, mate. If we make it a little interesting.'

So suddenly we're playing pool for money. Twenty quid. I am on fire. I haven't played pool for years, but I played hours every day when I was young and it's one of those things you don't forget how to do.

I pot a yellow from the break and almost clear up from there. By the time I only have the black to put down, my opponent still has five balls on the table. None of them in easy positions either. Truth is, either he isn't very good at this game, or the prospect of real actual money has made him tense up and in pool, like in any game, like in life, you need to stay loose if you want to succeed. You need to be fearless. You can only win if you don't care that much about losing.

I am lining up the black when it occurs to me that I don't actually want to win. Getting twenty quid from this lad absolutely isn't the point. Winning isn't what I'm

playing the game for. This is meant to be about a kind of companionship. Yet I've raced to a winning position and haven't exchanged any words with these lads except, 'Good shot.' And, more often, 'Bad luck.'

I look at the faces of the lad I'm playing and his mate. Both of them are closed and hard. Yes, young men are simple. They just need to be loved unconditionally by everyone they meet. That's all. They need to be joshed and joked with and given attention. Not too much to ask really.

But they've learned that the world doesn't want them, instead it fears them. The world views young blokes in the same way it views dangerous dogs, as creatures needing muzzling and neutering. The world crosses the street when it sees them coming. No surprise it makes boys want to destroy things. To break their toys. I get it. Tonight, of all nights, I get that.

I haven't given them any of that joshing and joking. Any of that love. Instead I've unthinkingly set about crushing them. Destroying them. I've done what the old always want to do to the young.

I decide to miss.

For the next fifteen minutes or so I bang the black ball about, while my opponent painstakingly reduces the disparity between us. While we play our parts I find out that he's called Baz, that he's a landscape gardener, that he plays guitar in a metal band but he doesn't have as much time for that now what with the kids and that.

'Family life is more important to me than music,' he says.

His mate is called Darren and he works in Sainsbury's and it's okay for now. He'll probably give it up to go travelling quite soon. Not much to stay here for now he's

225

split up with his girlfriend. He suddenly looks like he's going to cry.

Baz covers the embarrassment of his mate getting all choked up by asking about me, and I tell them I'm a teacher on sick leave with stress. I invent a recent divorce. Baz says he's sorry. I tell him there's no need to be.

'No, it was the best thing,' I say. I look over at Darren. 'It gets easier, mate. Time heals. It really does.' I wonder about how easily this imagined life is coming to me.

Then Baz pots his last red and then the black, we shake hands and the barmaid calls time and rings the bell as I fork over a twenty. Money well spent. Baz and Darren get their coats. I get the feeling that they are both happier now than they were at the start of the evening. So I guess I've done a decent thing. Hurray for me. Hurray for Baz and Daz.

People – women – often say that one of the problems with men is that they don't talk about their feelings with one another. That they don't share their worries, their hurt. In some way it seems to suit women to believe that. Seems to provide a kind of comfort. But it's wrong. My experience is that, when it's safe, men talk all the time about the same stuff women talk about. Only they like to do that confessional stuff with something in their hands. They like to open up while they're doing something else.

When men open up to one another they do it while playing games. They like to multitask, if you like. Men talk to each other in rooms with dartboards or with pool tables. The darts, the pool cues, they are not always the surrogate weapons they appear to be – sometimes they are simple props designed to encourage intimacy. Sometimes a pool game is just a prolonged hug for people who don't get enough of them.

Before he heads out into the night Baz says 'You had me beat right up until the end. You need to work on your killer instinct mate.'

Then the barmaid is calling last orders and the fat man, now the only person in the pub besides me, lumbers off his stool. He nods at the barmaid.

'Mind how you go, Rodney,' she says.

The fat man grins so wide he suddenly looks like the cheerful child he must once have been. He has just two teeth. Both top incisors. The rest of his mouth is a dark wet cave and his tongue pops out briefly, a small, blind, pink creature coming out from its nest to sniff the air.

I know with the sudden clarity of the drunk that the barmaid is the only person that ever tells Rodney to mind how he goes. I know that he loves her. He is old and ugly and lonely and yet he loves with the same ache with which the young and handsome and popular love one another. Think about that, amazing isn't it?

When all the corner pubs are finally gone, when all that's left are vast warehouses for the curation of vertical drinking, or gastro-pubs selling roast dinners at forty quid a head – who will bring light into the worlds of all the Rodneys then? Who will make them smile? Who will suggest that they mind how they go?

It occurs to me that pub games are being squeezed out to make space for diners. By the time my children are old enough to order pints in bars maybe pool tables will seem as quaint as skittle alleys. Lots of pubs have got rid of them already. Soon there'll be nowhere left for lonely men to talk or play.

Men who like to pass the time in games and chat, they take up too much goddam room. It's no longer a country for them.

Ten minutes after Rodney leaves, I am also drinking up, am also advised to mind how I go. My God, am I on the way to becoming Rodney? Twenty minutes after that, without remembering anything of the walk back, I am fumbling for borrowed keys in Chaney Street.

38

In the kitchen Lulu cracks open a beer – she's back on the Steinbrau Blonde, I notice. She must actually like it – and she silently hands me one. She gets out a beef Pot Noodle from one of the cupboards.

'I've just got in myself,' she says.

'That stuff will kill you,' I say. 'I thought you were a vegan.'

She smiles briefly. 'I am. There's no animal products in a Pot Noodle, not in this flavour anyway. I am, however, probably the wrong sex to be eating this stuff really.'

'How come?'

She reads out the cooking instructions and it is funny the way that Pot Noodles are blatantly aimed at the hunter presumed to lurk inside every red-blooded man. Consumers are urged to RIP the tinfoil of the lid, TEAR at the little sachet of soy sauce, and GRAB a fork to DIG in. Ripping, tearing, grabbing and digging. Eating this concoction of dried soya becomes the very essence of a manly life.

Lulu says, 'Isn't that mad?'

She rips the lid, pours boiling water into the container. Pouring is not mentioned as a step, I note. Pouring water clearly not male enough to be included in the instructions. Ripping is for men, but pouring is for ladies. Lulu meanwhile gets on with the tearing of the sauce sachet with her teeth. 'Grrr,' she says.

We move into the tiny living room and she puts on the gas fire, plonks herself down on the sofa, switches on the TV and pats the space next to her. There are no other places to sit in this room in any case. So I go and sit down. I feel oddly shy.

The telly is showing the results from yet another talent competition. There's a boy – maybe ten years old – murdering *In the Midnight Hour*. This kid should be sleeping in the midnight hour and doing nothing else. This kid has school in the morning.

Lulu picks her phone up off the coffee table and taps at the screen.

'What are you doing?' I say.

'I'm tweeting what you just said.'

'You're tweeting about this show?'

'Yeah, look. *Bloke next to me thinks only place #Marlon should be at midnight hour is in bed asleep. He has school in morn.* I've tweeted that.'

Fucked up as I am, I start a bit of a row. A pointless one. I find myself saying that all these programmes they should be banned, that I am amazed she thinks they're worth talking about. That I thought she was a serious, intelligent girl. A photographer. An artist. Can't she see what a waste of time these shows are? And to tweet about it, well how inane is that?

Lulu gives me a hard look. There is a flush creeping

into her neck. She says that it is funny how it's only ever men who try to shut women up about these programmes. She says that men's leisure interests – football, say – well, they are talent contests just as unimportant – and much more boring – than this one, and they're on the bloody news for chrissake. She says that no woman who was a guest in the house of someone they hardly knew, would accept their host's hospitality and then slag off how they like to spend their time. Only a man would do that. Only a man would be that disrespectful.

'I'm tired,' she says. 'I'm hungry. My leg hurts. The house is cold. I have been working my blinking butt off. I'm skint. Tonight I want to forget all that by watching crap TV with a beer and a Pot Noodle. And for your information I am thirty-two. I am a serious, intelligent woman. Not a girl.'

Without looking at me, keeping her eyes on the screen where little Marlon is now in tears and being hugged by a gaggle of toothy kids – fellow competitors at a guess – she says that right now social media provide places where women feel free, where they can be vocal, where they can have a laugh with their mates, and so of course men try and say it's a waste of time.

Then she asks me why my hand is on her thigh.

I move it quickly into my lap. 'Shit. Sorry. Sorry.' Because it's true, my hand was on her right thigh, sort of. Lying alongside her leg anyway, definitely touching it. I can feel the heat in my face, feel myself blushing.

She laughs. 'It's okay.'

'It's a small sofa,' I say.

She turns her eyes away from the screen now. Looks right at me. But her look is not hard now, it's soft. I could

imagine it's fond almost. It's shockingly intimate, she seems to be seeing right into my head.

'Not that small,' she says. She keeps her eyes on mine. There is a long pause, a silence that begins to grow almost tangible, clammy, like mist. She keeps looking at me, eyes the colour of bark. A wet and muddy brown.

'Do you fancy me, Marko? Do you want to shag me?' Her voice is conversational, bland. For a moment I wonder if she's said it at all, wonder if I have maybe imagined it. But she waits patiently for an answer.

No, no is the answer. I don't want to go to bed with Lulu. I want to go to bed with Katy. I want to go to bed with my wife. Want to feel her hands around my shoulders, on my back, in my hair, her shallow breaths in my ear. Her legs wrapped around me, heels on the backs of my thighs, urging me into her. More than this, I want to wake up with Katy. To bring her coffee and while she drinks it I want to have her tell me that there were no other men, that it had been a story made up to hurt me and that she was sorry she'd done it. Maybe I wouldn't even mind if it was the apology that was the lie. Whatever, we'd never mention it again. I'd eBay the bloody bike.

But also yes. Yes, of course I want to go to bed with Lulu. Christ, I don't know what I want. I am drunk and lost. I am a man with no place in the world. A man that can't see straight. A man who has found out there are no certainties in the world and no one you can rely on. I feel like dying. I feel impossibly old.

'You don't mind about the leg?'

No. I don't mind about the leg. I haven't even thought about the leg.

She chuckles deep in her throat. She sounds genuinely delighted. Now she puts her hands on each side of my

face. They feel hot and dry. She rests her forehead on mine. Her smiling eyes are on mine. I can smell the Steinbrau on her breath.

'You know what you really need is toast,' she says. She releases my face and moves back away from me.

'Toast. Yes. Great.' I say, my voice hoarse. I feel a sudden relief. Yes. Toast. Toast is exactly what I need. The very thing. Toast and tea. Not sex. While Lulu goes to the kitchen to make it, I stumble upstairs for a piss and remember that the last person to call me Marko was Anne, a lifetime ago. No one else has ever done it. Not Katy, not Eve, not anyone.

The fire warms the small room and it grows cosy as we munch toast with damson jam and Lulu tells me about the trip Jake has booked for them. They're going to Majorca. I tell her they should make sure they go to Deia. It's where Robert Graves lived. The poet who believed that men were in thrall to the Goddess. That they were at the mercy of witches. Turns out Lulu knows this already. Lulu knows about *The White Goddess* and *The Golden Ass*, knows all about *Good-Bye to All That*.

'Well, we might visit his house I suppose, if we have a cloudy day, but you know, we might also just stay on the beach getting ripped on sangria if that's all right with you. We need to reconnect I think, me and Jake.'

The buttered toast works its magic and we grow easier with one another. She tells me about her childhood in Cheltenham. About her mum the social worker and her dad whom she hasn't seen since she was nine, but who did at least buy her first camera. Her dad, the man who ran off with his wife's sister, her aunt. People, eh? The things they do.

She tells me about her work, about how she sits sketching or reading or practising her Italian while watching CCTV screens of empty warehouses that are destined one day to become luxury apartments for foreign billionaires to leave empty.

She tells me about her life before she lost her leg. How she used to be a good girl, how she once needed to get merits, smiley faces, A stars. How, a lifetime ago, she cried when she failed to get a distinction in her grade 8 cello. Imagine that, she says.

She tells me how nothing makes her cry these days. She tells me she doesn't need a career, a pension, a mortgage or any of that bollocks. She doesn't care about gold stars or good marks. These days she wants to have experiences not smiley faces.

'People worry about security,' she says, 'when there's no such thing. Not really.'

We clink mugs. I can drink to that.

We drink more tea, and the telly provides a chirruping soundtrack of nonsense while she talks about her new project which will be a photographic study of siblings.

'That's a good idea,' I say.

'Well it was that or a study of hot guys with baby animals and I think someone might have done that already.'

Now I find that I am telling her about my own sister, Eve, everyone's favourite. Telling her how Eve devised a whole language for all of us to speak when she was seven. Insisted we used it all the time for several weeks and how it drove our parents mad. I tell of the little handmade books she made, clumsily stitched but full of stories about a family of blind children who lived without adults on an island beyond the edge of the map.

I tell of the way she always stood up to bullies, how if she saw someone throwing their weight around in the playground then that person was going to get a smack, or, at the very least, get a verbal hammering that would reduce them to tears. I tell Lulu about Eve's song writing, about her painting, about the way she loved to wear hats. How she always looked great and how the camera always loved her.

'Sounds like we'd get on,' she says.

Yeah, I think they would.

Without warning, the room is filled with the looming presence of Jake. Neither of us heard him come in, and I see him take in how we're sitting, the toast, the beer, how snug we are. How the air is heavy with confidences and shared stories. I see the hurt flash across his face, the same look I saw years ago when I told him that the wounded and abandoned owlet wouldn't survive in his school locker.

'Jake,' I say.

'Hey, babe,' says Lulu.

Jake has his phone in his hand. 'I'm going upstairs to the bog,' he says and his voice is thick and choked. 'Then I'm going to call the police. I think you'll have about five minutes.'

'Jake,' I say again. I stop. What can I say?

'Don't be a plonker, Jake,' says Lulu. She is chewing on her fingernail.

'Five minutes,' Jake says. 'Tops.'

He swallows, making a furry noise in his throat. And, without looking at either of us again, he crosses the room in a couple of steps and takes the stairs two at a time.

Lulu stands up. 'Come on then,' she says. Her voice is a fierce whisper. I follow her down the hall, I feel dazed,

though I remember to pick up my bag. As she opens the front door she yells at the top of her voice.

'You heard Jake! Just get lost!'

I'm confused because now she steps outside pulling me with her, slamming the door shut behind us. 'He'll think I'm chucking you out. Might give us an extra minute. Come on, car's round the corner.'

She sets off down the path and into the street. As we move away from the house she says, 'I'm always going to go where the action is, you should know that.'

It seems to me that we are going painfully slowly. I want to break into a run, but we can't of course. I am conscious of the spitting rain and the stinging wind whipping around my ears. The moon is smudged by racing clouds and lights the wet street intermittently, turning the sky itself into a spinning light of the kind you find on police cars. Somewhere, not too far away, a siren wails. Doesn't have to be for me. London is a city of sirens. Could be going anywhere and it's probably an ambulance anyway. I force myself to keep calm.

As we reach the car, I can hear a dog barking and I imagine that soon there will be deep voices shouting orders at me, the firefly glimmers of torches in the hands of burly men. It'll all be over soon.

I'm almost relieved.

Lulu is in the driver's seat, the engine is on. She looks across at me. Her face is shining.

'Well, this is all jolly exciting, isn't it?'

39

Ella wakes suddenly from confused dreams. There's the dull throb of a diesel engine outside her window. An unfamiliar light. She slips from her bed and crosses to the window. The police car across the street is manoeuvring its way out of the tight parking space. She watches until it is finally free and away from the cars that hemmed it in. As it moves down Haverstock Street, she sees the flashing lights come on. The siren pulls the night apart.

Her heart beats wild in her chest, the panicked wings of a trapped bird. She pads down the landing to her brother's room.

Jack twitches in his sleep. She shakes him awake. Pinches him.

'Ow. That really hurt me.'

'Your face really hurts me.'

She hisses at him that the police have gone, that they are not being watched anymore and what does he think

that means? Jack rubs his eyes, makes her say it all again slower this time. 'Means the police have gone. It means they know where dad is.'

'We should tell mum.'

But when they go to their parents' room, they find that mummy already knows, she was woken by the siren and looked outside and clocked the empty space in the street. But it's okay, she seems sad, but not too sad, just kind of quiet and she'll make them both warm milk and honey if they promise to go straight back to bed afterwards.

'What about our teeth?' says Jack.

Ella rolls her eyes.

'After you've cleaned your teeth again obviously.'

They sit in Ella's room playing the game of dreaming up good names for the baby. Jack does the boys' names, Ella does the girls'.

'Paul David Chadwick.'

'Quorra Moon Chadwick.'

'Caleb Liam Chadwick.'

'Rhythm Nixon Chadwick.'

'William Edward Chadwick.'

'Sea Pixie Chadwick.'

'Wyatt Jesse Chadwick.'

'Sparrow Chia Chadwick.'

'You're not doing it right, they're not real names.'

'They are so. They are all better than *Paul.* Better than *William,* better than *Edward.*' She twists her face as she says these names, makes it like the sound of them hurts her mouth.

'Well, I'm not playing anymore.'

Ella makes him go back to his own bed and so, when their mum hauls herself upstairs – it's really getting to be

an effort to carry this bloody baby around now – with two mugs of warm milk sweetened with locally grown honey, the children are in separate rooms, both of them crying, both of them pretending not to be.

40

Lulu has got us clear of the tightly packed streets of South Camden and out on to the Euston Road. My heart rate is returning to normal after the shock of almost running Jake down. We had just turned out of Inkerman Close when we'd seen him standing in the middle of the road, shouting words I couldn't hear, but not nice words that's for sure. Words Lulu would definitely think were unimaginative. She had gunned the engine and headed straight for him. Jake held his nerve pretty well, only throwing himself out of the way at the last possible moment, banging on the side of the car as we went past, howling with impotent rage, like he was some kind of crazed matador and the car was a blind and desperate bull.

'Would you really have run Jake over?'

Her voice is airy, light. There's fizz in it. 'Oh I knew he'd move. He knows better than to play a game of chicken with me. Anyway, where to?'

'Felixstowe.'

'Seriously? I don't even know where that is.'

'Suffolk.'

'What? You mean beyond zone five? Out in the actual country? Jesus.'

It might be the early hours of a Thursday morning but it's slow going even after we get out of London and onto the A12 heading east. There are cones, narrow lanes, temporary speed restrictions, lorries aiming for the port and the continent, overtaking each other while going exactly the same fucking speed. Lumbering towards the boats that will take them to the Hoek van Holland and beyond. Plus there's the rain and the spray on the road. It's like driving through a cheerless – endless – car wash.

Lulu needs to concentrate and so do I because I could easily throw up if I wasn't mindful about my breathing – in-and-out, slow, slower, there we go, nice and steady – and if I wasn't keeping my eyes closed against the flicker of halogen lights through water. So we don't talk much.

Round about Romford, Lulu says, 'Well, I think that's Jake and I done. No wedding bells I fear.'

I think for a moment about all the morning sex and the late at night sex I've been forced to hear over the last few days, the grunting and the crying out, the thud of headboard against wall. How desperate it had seemed.

'A shame I guess. But there it is,' she says now.

'I'm sorry.'

'Don't be. I think we'd reached the end of our rainbow or whatever. I'd taken him as far as I could.' As if she were a CEO and he a company she was leaving.

It is a long, straight drive to Felixstowe. After Romford

there's nothing much. The anaemic lights of commuter towns – Brentwood, Shenfield, Ingatestone, Chelmsford, Witham, Ipswich – flicker beside the road like clusters of faintly glittery midges as we follow the HGVs to the coast. And, as the rain finally stops, we're climbing the almost defiantly unspectacular concrete bridge over the River Orwell and then, under impassive moonlight, we see the cranes of Felixstowe docks. Massive Meccano structures that belong in some much bigger place. Shanghai maybe or Rotterdam. They look alive and menacing, blind metal dinosaurs black against the velvet midnight blue of the night, striding through the sea like some Victorian imagining of an alien invasion – like a scene from *War of the Worlds*.

We drive through the empty streets of the town before stopping in a car park down by the seafront, where we use the public toilets.

'Hey, we really are in the country,' Lulu says. 'It's only 20p for a piss here.'

We have breakfast in Ken's Koffee Kabin in the town's main shopping street. A very old school caff. Lulu places an order for two veggie breakfasts. The fat bloke in charge – Ken I guess – turns to the nervy looking girl working alongside him.

'Told you,' he says, smiling, triumphant. Turns out he'd had a friendly bet with his cook that we'd be vegetarians. Said that he'd known the second we'd come through his door. Said that he could always tell.

He's wrong of course. I'm not actually a vegetarian, just can't take the idea of bacon, sausage and black pudding right now. But I don't tell him this. Let him have his small victory, everyone needs those from time to

time. In fact, that's what a successful life is: tiny victories strung together.

The actual breakfast is a decent one and very good value at £3.95.

'You forget, don't you?' says Lulu, 'that there's a world outside London where things don't have to cost a fortune. I wonder what the house prices are like?'

So now she is googling Felixstowe. While she's doing this her phone quivers again. It's gone off dozens of times this morning. It makes an outraged buzz. A desperate hornet caught in a small boy's jam jar. A meat-crazed bluebottle. I'm guessing it's Jake, though she doesn't say. She ignores it anyway.

'Did you know the suffix stowe marks a holy place?' she says.

She goes on to tell me about the town's founder. It seems St Felix was one of the less interesting saints. A quiet kind of bloke as saints go. Set up a school, did a bit of writing, did some sitting around contemplating eternal mysteries. No one was raised from the dead. No snakes were cast out from the kingdom. No martyrdom even. Felix trundled to his threescore and ten years before dying quietly at home surrounded by old friends. The patron saint of keeping your head down and getting on with it. A far better saint for modern England than George with his dragon-slaying and maiden-rescuing.

'You need to get rid of your phone,' I say.

'What?'

'Your phone. You need to get rid of it. They can trace it. Even when it's off it's like a homing beacon.'

She doesn't protest and so we walk from the cafe down to the sea and Lulu throws it as far as she can into the swell of brooding water.

'Freedom!' she shouts as it arcs and plummets into the wet murk, a thin silver seagull diving for a fish.

We find the gallery easily enough. A double-fronted shop in what seems to be the main shopping street with a large canvas in the window. It's a bucolic scene of cows grazing in a field and so faithfully rendered as to be almost photorealist, only the cows are neon pink and toothpaste white, the sky is a metallic green, the grass is a stinging yellow. It's a fun idea. The painting is priced at £12,000. In the bottom right-hand corner of the window there's a small poster advertising the fact that tonight there's a private view.

'Ooh, I do like a private view,' says Lulu.

'Really?'

'Free wine, free snacks, good-looking people flirting, what's not to like?'

There are two buttons beside the door of the shop, one for the gallery itself and one for the flat above and I ring the one belonging to the flat and wait.

Somewhere a baby starts crying.

'I actually don't think this is such a great idea,' says Lulu. 'It's seven-thirty in the morning and you look like shit. Your eyes are all red and you have a bit of a mad look to be honest. Is it the right time to have serious conversations?'

I press the bell again. And again. And again. I knock. Hard. Harder. The baby cries get louder and then the door is opened by a hard-eyed teenage girl in a piebald onesie with a fat, red-faced and very angry baby on her hip. The girl is not happy. She is almost as pissed off as her kid.

'What the actual fuck?' she says.

'Sorry to disturb you,' I say. 'I'm looking for Bim.'

'What the fuck is that?' says the girl.

'It's a person,' says Lulu. 'It's his name.'

'Fucking stupid name. Do you know what time it is?'

'He doesn't live here then?'

'No he doesn't fucking live here. It's just me and Jezebel.'

'Now that is a great name,' says Lulu. The girl doesn't reply though her eyes maybe narrow slightly. She's suspicious. She shifts Jezebel's weight on her hip. The baby stops crying. She hiccups and then stares at Lulu with an intense curiosity. Seems to be drinking her in. Maybe she's surprised to see someone react to her name with such genuine enthusiasm. Lulu waggles her little finger in front of the baby who buries her face into her mother's shoulder.

'Aw, she's feeling shy.'

'No, she's fucking mad because she's been woken up. Is that it? Can I go back in now?'

Afterwards, Lulu says it's probably a good thing we haven't found Bim yet, means we can get ourselves a bit presentable because it looks like we'll be going to this private view, doesn't it?

41

When men and women first get together they often revert to childhood. The first stages of a romance are a deliberate return to innocence. A couple just starting out play all sorts of chasing games. Tig among the trees as they stroll through parks. Hide and seek. Every game a kind of kiss-chase. They are as giddy as hares in March.

They giggle at silly jokes. They tickle one another. They imagine exotic future lives for themselves in the same way that children do. They plan dangerous adventures they will never have, but that are thrilling to think about. Dangerous adventures like setting up home and being together for ever. To make this seem real they might play house, have a go at being mummies and daddies.

This is one reason why new lovers are often surprisingly happy to babysit, or to take young nieces and nephews to the cinema. This is why they go to the zoo, not just to laugh at the antics of the monkeys, but to see the eager faces of toddlers light up as they see those monkeys for the first time.

This is the sort of thing Anne and I begin to do once Dorcas is dropped off in Selwyn Gardens by her grandmother.

It was me that drove it. I got the poster paint and the glitter. I bought the Airfix kits and the frisbee. I made meals that were also faces. The sausages were thick lips, upturned into a superior smile. Oven chips were sandy-blonde hair, button mushrooms were serious grey eyes, a juicy half of a grilled tomato was a drinkist's nose.

'It looks like my dad,' said Dorcas and I laughed because it did actually. Kind of.

I took her to galleries and was unnerved by the girl's sophisticated understanding of the tubercular glamour of the pre-Raphaelites. Her frank delight in the sick, pale, dying faces of market girls dressed up as medieval queens and biblical temptresses.

We went to the local museum where Dorcas was fascinated by the way there was room after room of stuffed wildlife. The foxes and martens, the owls and the badgers. The bears and the reindeer. The entire aviary of stuffed birds, some of them looking decidedly threadbare and dusty. She stared agog at all the unseeing eyes staring blackly back at her.

We played bowls and French cricket in the garden. Dorcas and Anne tried to teach me how to do handstands and cartwheels. We made swords from sticks, and I had us all pretending we were the three musketeers training to take on the cardinal's men.

I thought we were all enjoying this time, but on about the fourth day, just after Dorcas had gone to bed, Anne reached for her wine and sighed.

'Not long now, thank God.'

'Not long till what?'

'Till the little princess is back at school. I don't know about you but I'm finding all this hands-on parenting bloody exhausting.' I asked what they usually did during school holidays and Anne had to think for a long time before she shrugged and said, 'I don't know. She has her sketchbooks and her dolls and there is always television isn't there? Television is a pretty good babysitter I find. Pretty educational. Sometimes Philip takes her with him to the lab. She seems to like that.'

I had to admit that Anne had more on her plate than I did however. A lot more stress. There was, for example, the daily row on the phone with her husband. The daily row had to be followed by the daily post-mortem on the row with her solicitor. This in turn was followed by time spent working out how much that second phone call had cost her. The numbers were astonishing. A single fifteen-minute conversation represented the entire profits of a busy Friday night in the Blue Pig.

No wonder she sometimes found it hard to concentrate on Lego, or to properly appreciate the dress designs her daughter was sketching.

I was in the children's playground spinning a shrieking Dorcas on the roundabout when I had the unnerving sense I was being watched and turned to see – of all people – Professor Sheldon's paramour, Mish.

She looked utterly out of place here. She was dressed neutrally enough in jeans and sweatshirt, her pregnancy just beginning to be obvious, but she had that curious stillness about her that set her apart from the other adults, the tired mums and the restless dads. That was before you properly took in her freakish Hollywood looks. Looks the glasses did nothing to hide.

Those cheekbones, those lips.

As I walked towards her I wondered about her heritage. What collisions of DNA gave skin that particular buttermilk sheen, gave eyes the subtle grey-green of a field under frost? Helsinki by way of Tehran maybe? Or was she the descendent of both Irish kings and Pathan warrior princesses?

'This is a coincidence,' I said.

'Isn't it?' she said.

She nodded towards Dorcas who had now moved from the roundabout to the swings. 'She seems like a happy little girl.' I followed Mish's gaze and actually I thought Dorcas didn't look entirely happy now. Instead, she looked both watchful and wild, kicking herself up as high as she could, but keeping her eyes fixed on where Mish and I were talking. I waved and then sat down on the bench.

'How are you anyway?'

'I'm fine. Mostly fine. Not too sick.' I had forgotten how thin her voice was. I strained to hear her. There was another pause before she smiled suddenly. Those teeth, the way the light shone from them. Plainly she remembered the last time we had met, remembered her little jump away from me as I was overcome by punch. As I fell puking at her feet.

'How long is there to go now?'

'Till the baby? About twenty weeks.'

'You're looking forward to it? And the move to the States and everything? To the ranch with the lovely fig trees or whatever.'

'I'm okay with it. Look, there's no need to be so hostile.'

'I'm not being hostile.' Except that maybe I was. I hadn't meant to be but maybe there was a spikiness to my questions that I hadn't been aware of.

We sat in silence, both of us watching the hypnotic back and forth of Dorcas on the swings. Mish didn't look at me as she spoke again in that hesitant papery voice.

'It's inconvenient that Phil and I fell for each other so hard, I know that. I almost wish it hadn't happened. I never meant it to happen. I worked hard at not letting it happen but in the end...' she tailed off into a sigh. Now she did turn towards me, perfect brow crinkled into a frown. Eyes searching mine for some sympathetic warmth. I was careful to keep my face blank. 'You know, he'd been miserable for years. And Anne, well, she's quite nuts you know. You must know that.'

'How's Dr Sheldon's work going?'

She seemed surprised by the question. She frowned. 'It's very stressful at the moment actually.'

Yes, I could imagine that it would be. What with the world beginning to acknowledge that his precious drug was lighting the blue touch-paper of suicidal thoughts in the minds of the very people it's meant to help. Yes, I could see that work might be a bit on the stressful side.

Mish finished by saying that she was just wondering if there was some way that she and I could help somehow. Get the two of them round a table, stop them destroying each other.

'There are children to think about.'

'If you're thinking about the children, why do you have to take Dorcas with you to America?'

'Maybe we don't. Maybe we can work it out. I do think that, as a general rule, children should be with their mothers. But it's for Phil and Anne to talk about. They need to speak to each other properly.'

'They speak to each other every day.'

'No, they don't. Not really. They try to score points off each other for twenty minutes and then they swap abuse for an hour and a half and come away wanting to smash up the furniture.'

I smiled at this. It was a spot-on analysis of the way Anne and Sheldon's phone conversations went. I'd remarked on it himself.

'Afterwards they spend another hour on the phone to solicitors,' I said.

Mish clapped gloved hands together. 'Yes! Yes, that's right! All those heart-to-hearts with lawyers. As if your solicitors can ever be your friend. We're all going to end up in the poorhouse at this rate. All going very *Jarndyce v. Jarndyce.*'

This is what life should be about, I thought, conversations where people just drop in Dickens references expecting you to get them.

It was then that Dorcas leapt from her swing while at the highest point of her arc. She landed on her feet. She bowed in our direction, every inch the regal ballet lead, and headed off to the slide.

'Impressive balance,' said Mish. 'I wonder where she gets that from?'

In the ten minutes it took Dorcas to finally tire of the delights of the playground, by the time she had come over and said a shy hello to Mish and asked me for an ice cream, I had agreed that we would try and arrange a face-to-face meeting between the Sheldons which we would referee if necessary.

'When it happens maybe we should lock away the booze?' I said.

'Good luck with that,' she said.

I watched her as she walked away. She had a loose easy

stride, strong, confident. Too late I realised I'd forgotten to ask her where she was from.

Dorcas was tugging at me.

'Let's go home, Mark. Let's go home and do something fun.'

'You big bully. Oh, and Dorcas, do you happen to know where Mish comes from? What her background is?'

'Yes. I do.' She recites, 'She grew up in Crawley in Sussex but her dad is from Kettering. He is an accountant. Her mum is from Redditch and is a primary school teacher. Mish says she is as ordinary and as dull as it's possible for anyone to be. But I don't believe her. Anyway, is that enough information? Why do you want to know?'

'No reason.'

'Daddy says Mish is living proof of the galvanising effects of boredom on the young.'

'He says that does he? What do you think he means?'

She looked at me scornfully. 'He means that she was so desperate to get away from home that she worked really really hard at school. That's obvious isn't it?' Sometimes it was very easy to see that Dorcas was her father's daughter. 'Can we play Monopoly when we get back?' she said. Mish was apparently forgotten already.

'Okay.' I reminded her that I wouldn't go easy on her. No allowances just because she was eight. No letting her off parking fines or jail sentences. I'd made that mistake before.

'Excellent. I'll be the banker,' she said.

42

Getting Anne to agree to a sit down with her husband was surprisingly easy. I had expected a battle, but there just wasn't one. I brought her coffee and croissants and scrambled eggs the following morning, told her Mish was going to try and coax the professor into agreeing to hash things out in a grown-up way. I was all prepared for fury, and she did go quiet for a few moments, glowered into her coffee. But when she looked up she was smiling.

'Come here,' she said. 'You're my own diplomatic corps, my very own Kissinger – you've heard of him, right?'

I had, of course, but decided to play along. It always delighted Anne when I affected not to know the basic stuff of recent history. I asked her if he was a Russian General-Secretary. The first West German Chancellor after the war? That composer who did a concert for peace in Tel Aviv recently?

'Stop it,' she said. 'Come back to bed.' And, with her

hands deft and busy beneath the covers, she explained, unnecessarily, that Kissinger was the US Secretary of State who brokered peace between the US and China, and also the man who first said power was an aphrodisiac. 'So are croissants of course,' she said. 'Or at least they are in this house.'

Which is when Dorcas stumbled in rubbing the sleep from her eyes.

'Hello, munchkin,' she said.

'Don't call me that,' muttered Dorcas.

I could see her point. Who would want to be a munchkin? Tiny, squeaky, powerless and living under an unnecessarily bureaucratic and ineffective system of government. That's before you got to thinking about the worry of wicked witches.

It wasn't long before I realised that she'd agreed to meet up with Professor Sheldon so quickly because she had been certain that he wouldn't countenance the idea.

I spoke to Mish on the phone.

'He won't do it.' Her thin voice was tinier than ever, I had to strain to hear it. 'I thought I could persuade him but I can't. He's adamant.'

'Right,' I said.

'Right, indeed,' she said.

'I'll sort it out,' I said.

She laughed. I hung up.

43

Cromwell College was not among the finest examples of university architecture. By 1990 it was already looking very tired, very much in need of a makeover. It was on no guided walks, no bus tours. It was on the indistinct edge of the city, its windows looking out across the car park, past plasticky fencing to the salty green of the fields where a few dust-coloured cows flicked their tails in a desultory attempt to keep the flies away. In another town there would have been light industrial units here, or one of the malls which were then beginning to plonk themselves beyond the final hedges of home counties towns.

Unlike the more historic colleges there were no ex-police service porters guarding Cromwell. I simply strolled in, consulted a list blu-tacked to the wall of who occupied which office, and set off up the stairs to find him. Inside, the college building reminded me of my high school. It had that smell that is part cheap sausage, part industrial Shake n' Vac and part sweat which so many

schools share. The older colleges didn't smell like this. Their hushed hallways were rich with the pungency of flaunted history. Maybe they had special plug-ins ensuring that the reassuring and woody notes of power permeated all areas at all times. A gadget set to somehow evoke the piney coffins of all those junior officer alumni killed while forging the Empire or fighting the Kaiser.

Professor Sheldon's door was closed, but I didn't knock. Just turned the handle and walked in. I think I had assumed that he'd be out, that the door would be locked but it opened and there he was, sat at a utilitarian desk in a creased white linen shirt writing in what looked like a school exercise book. He looked up, made a big thing of rolling his eyes.

'Well, well, well,' he said, determinedly unfazed. 'If it isn't Kid Galahad. Annie's young white knight. Drink?'

'You're all right.'

'Am I indeed? I'm all right? Well, that's nice to know.'

He took a half-empty bottle of Glenfiddich from a drawer of his desk, unscrewed the cap and half-filled a tumbler that was next to a neat stack of exercise books just like the one he was writing in.

Other things on his desk. A copy of *New Scientist*, an old jam jar full of cheap biros and pencils, a calculator, an anglepoise lamp, a box of tissues. That was it.

The rest of the room was just as drearily ascetic. Heavy books in uniform brown spines on solid shelves. Just the one print on the wall. A standard issue Rothko print like you see in offices everywhere. Art for people who can't really see the point of art.

Often a tutor's room at Cambridge was like an extension of their home, full of knick-knacks. Comfortable mess everywhere. Saggy armchairs, sweet wrappers, a

record player, over-flowing ashtrays, pictures of gap-toothed children or grandchildren, their drawings even – colourful pictures of grinning stickmen sellotaped to walls between posters chosen to demonstrate the breadth of the occupants' interests. Something from the Spanish Civil War maybe, or an advertisement for a long-gone free festival. Dylan. Ginsberg. Country Joe Macdonald And The Fish.

Maybe there would be ethnic instruments leaning in corners. A ginbri. A djembe. A worn but vibrantly patterned rug on the floor. Tea. Sherry.

None of that nonsense here. This was the opposite of the professor's erstwhile home. The complete rejection of it. No sculptures, no anything. The only thing that wasn't grey or brown in this room was the egg-yolk yellow body of the fat and sluggish wasp crawling up the closed window behind the professor's head.

'What can I do for you then boy? Because whatever it is I suspect the answer is no.'

I looked down at him and I saw the fear that was creeping up on him like water rising on a man trapped in a cave, saw that there were shadows at the edge of his vision. He wasn't afraid of me, but he was growing afraid of life and this was a new thing for him. Meanwhile I was sharp, strong. I could feel my blood and muscles singing, ready to do whatever I wanted. I felt light as sunshine. Just as fear was a new thing for Sheldon, so this confidence in my body was a new thing for me. Exhilarating and strange.

This man becoming old in front of me, I felt some sort of compassion for him. He was just like a regular in the Blue Pig. He was just another sad middle-aged man wondering where all the years went. I didn't like him, but I understood him.

I opened my mouth to ask him – nicely I swear – if he couldn't consider having a rational, sensible, business-like conference with his ex-wife? If maybe they could just sit down, have a cup of tea. Or wine even, if it would help. On neutral territory, with Misha and I there as seconds if need be.

But I didn't say any of that.

'You killed my sister,' I said.

It was only as I said the words that I knew that it was true. I don't think I had really believed this until it just spilled out like that, thoughtlessly, almost accidentally. But the professor's reaction confirmed it. I could see the hard truth of it in the way he flinched as if slapped, the way he blinked, the way his eyes widened. I saw it in the curl of his lip, in the exasperated sigh he gave, in the way he didn't yell or shout or try and physically hurl me from his office. In that moment it had the force of revelation. A moment where I saw all the shoddy research, the hidden results, the massaged figures, the sloppy hurry of the whole process.

Then and there I saw the way my sister – and God knows how many others – had been sacrificed. And for what? Not for anything real. Not even for money, not really – though someone would have been making proper money somewhere. Someone always is – but Sheldon had been driven by something more nebulous, something less honest than avarice. By a desire for reputation, for prizes, by a need to win some sort of competition with himself.

I didn't feel compassionate any more.

When he found his voice it was quiet, without heat.

'I'm sorry you feel that way.'

He didn't ask why I was accusing him like this. He didn't need to. He believed it too.

I said nothing, kept my eyes on his face while he looked anywhere but at me. Eventually he stood, turned to look out across the fields, out to where the cows grazed amid the drowsy late summer sunshine. I watched that wasp crawl up the glass, its buzzing suddenly loud.

The professor moved to pick a book from the shelf and squashed the insect between it and the glass with careful, deliberate force. He took a tissue from the box on his desk and wiped the book carefully before putting it back on the shelf. Then he rubbed away the small smear of gore from the window.

'Sorry, old girl,' he said, addressing himself to the tissue. 'But had to be done.' He dropped the tissue into the small wastepaper bin. He looked at me. 'Fascinating creatures, wasps, but that doesn't mean you want them around. Only crazed females at this time of year of course. The males will be mostly goners by now, fucked to death by the women.'

He turned back to face me. He licked his lips.

'So. What do we do now?' he said, 'because from I've seen I don't think you've got it in you to be one of those dogged campaigners who keep after big corporations for years and years. I can't see you popping up at shareholders' meetings, making a fuss, shouting your infantile accusations and then being carried kicking and shouting from the hall. I can't see you delivering leaflets, smashing the windows of pharmacies. Maybe you'd write letters to your MP? Or the newspapers? Is that your plan? Because I have to tell you Fluxin passed all the tests set for it. Not just for the UK, but over most of the world. Maybe you think the tests should have been more rigorous, and maybe I even half-agree with you, but also, Mark, here's the thing: it's doing real good. For most people it really

works. Maybe if you're looking for villains you should look somewhere else, maybe at the doctor who proscribed Fluxin for your sister, and maybe even closer to home than that. Maybe you or your family should have noticed your sister's distress? Have you considered that?'

Listen more.

This speech seemed to have taken what energy he had right out of him. He sat down heavily, his face flushed.

My arm itched. The teenage apprentice and her shaky hand. But I hadn't known what to do before and now the professor had just given me the plan. All the things he'd said I wasn't up to doing, they would be exactly the things I would do. I should thank him.

It wouldn't just be me, either, my dad would be on the case too. He'd make quite an impression on television I think, all that passion, all that publican charisma and I'd like to see them carry him out of a conference hall when he was back to his fighting weight. My mum, with the quiet sorrow in her eyes, up against a shifty weasel-wordy PR man in a too-sharp suit. The regulars would help find any necessary money. They'd love that. Always up for an excuse to launch a fundraising campaign are the good old boys from the Blue Pig. Justice for Eve would be something we all could get behind, as a family, as a community. Had a ring to it.

At the very least we could irritate and needle and annoy. We could make the executives and shareholders of drug companies and their backers twitchy and nervous. We could have them looking over their shoulders. We could be like a mosquito in a tent, almost invisible but a powerful nuisance all the same. We could give quite a few people the sleepless nights they deserve. We could be wasps too.

Maybe the campaign would take the rest of my working life, but that would be okay. It would be better than whoring myself out in the City, or doing some pointless doctorate on some rightly forgotten minor poet. It would be a useful life. As useful as anything else anyway. What else are our days for, if not to upset the powerful and avenge the weak?

So I gave him the essence of this. How maybe he was right, maybe I wasn't the type yet, but maybe I would be. I was up for giving it a go anyway. Maybe that's how you build a life: you decide who you are then you become that person.

I said all this and then I found I had one more thing to say.

'Does Mish know?'

He looked up at that. 'Does Mish know what?'

'About the dodgy research.'

I was that certain. Technically, I suppose, it was a guess – but not really. If you look hard enough at how a man sits in his chair, you can learn everything you want to about a person and how they've lived their life. Doesn't take long. Another thing you learn from formative years spent standing behind a bar watching men sitting over pints.

Sheldon sighed again, took another swallow of his drink. I looked at the window, I could just see a mark where the wasp had been. A grubby smudge where there had once been a spirit that was focused, tenacious, mean... He took another heavy breath. The man looked so tired, all ominous shadows around the eyes. I wondered about the state of his vital organs. I was, after all, very used to the signs of poor liver and kidney function. He bowed his head, everything about him seemed to sag. He may not

have been sure if I was up for the fight, but we were both certain that he wasn't.

'For God's sake, sit down man.'

'I'm all right standing thanks.'

He finished his drink and poured another, resting the neck of the bottle on the glass in an effort to disguise the shake in his hands. So transparent. Might not be alcoholism of course, not entirely. Might be early stage Parkinson's, something like that.

'What do you actually want, Mark? What are your achievable goals here?'

'Getting you to apologise for a start.'

'I could do that.' A deliberate pause, a slow swallow. 'But I wouldn't mean it. I mean, I am sorry for your sister's death but...'

Yeah, I got it. He meant that he was sorry the way a soldier might be who'd blown up a kid while blowing away the enemy. From Sheldon's point of view Eve was collateral damage. A kid caught in the crossfire.

He meant he wasn't sorry at all.

But it was a good question, what were my achievable goals?

It was then that another wasp appeared. Smaller, lighter, far livelier than the bloated semi-hornet Sheldon had squashed a moment ago, it – she I suppose, if Sheldon was right – hummed insistently against the window. Sheldon started but made no move towards it. I walked around the desk, yanked the latch of the window to open it, guided the wasp towards the shimmer of fresh air with a waving hand. For a second she looked like she'd go, but then she took a sudden swerve up towards the ceiling. Maybe she'd find a nook up there, a safe place to hibernate. Oh well.

I returned to my side of the desk, and now I sat down.

'You can meet with Anne and you can be reasonable about the divorce, you can leave Dorcas here with her for example, not go for custody.'

'Really? You're deciding what's best for my child now?'

'I'm not arguing.'

'You think I don't really want her with me. You think I'm just trying to hurt Anne.'

I said nothing.

'You're right of course.' Another swallow. How many units has he had now? At least eight I reckon. These are not pub measures he's pouring. 'I do love her though.' He looked at me with a look both defiant and pleading.

'Yeah, I know.'

There was silence. The breeze outside the open window murmured to itself. You could hear the endless whoosh of traffic in the distance. Somewhere a pigeon cooed.

'Sometimes I think that going to America, it's not about the opportunities there, it's about just getting away. And about escaping the person I've become here, but...' He paused again, took another deep swallow. Nine units now. At least.

Wherever you go, there you are.

'You know there's nothing I can do about Fluxin. It's nothing to do with me now. It's out there with potential side effects pointed out on the user instructions in bold type.'

'Meet with Anne.'

'If I do, you'll leave me alone, there won't be any crusade following us across the Atlantic?'

'I didn't say that. I'm not promising anything. Just do the right thing as far as she's concerned.'

'Right thing. Wrong thing. Things are so very black

and white when you're young aren't they? Must be lovely to be so goddamn righteous.'

I said nothing.

'I'll do it, okay. I'll do it. Dorcas will stay here with Anne. She can even keep the frigging house. If she wants.'

I stood up. He had one last parting shot. Of course he did.

'You and Anne, you look ridiculous together, you should know that.'

Which is when I left him, standing to close the window, rolling the *New Scientist* to act as a swat as the wasp circled the room.

44

The summit was arranged for the following evening and neither Mish nor I would be around when it happened. Getting the parties to agree to Mish and me being there as referees had been impossible. In fact, the ridiculousness of us being anywhere near while they thrashed out who got what, this was something Anne and Sheldon could agree on. Yes, they'd meet dammit, they'd even share a meal, but only if their respective lovers were well out of the way.

For the whole day Anne was fretful and anxious which made her snappy with Dorcas and me.

Neither of us could say or do anything right. In the end I took the kid into town, and when we returned we went into the kitchen and shut the door and together the two of us worked methodically on making a shepherd's pie and apple and blackberry crumble with vanilla custard, Dorcas having first assured me that these were dishes both her parents liked.

From buying the ingredients to laying the table Dorcas was in charge of the preparations for the meal. We were,

after all, using tried and tested recipes that she had learned that term at school.

I hadn't really cooked much before. Working in the pub had meant I was a master of the microwave. I could tell you instantly the power setting you needed for a potato to bake, how long you should nuke a pizza for, how many minutes a chicken pie took. What I'd never had to do was follow a recipe that wasn't printed on the packaging of a frozen ready meal.

I found I liked this proper cooking lark. It was soothing and – as Dorcas pointed out – there really wasn't much that was difficult about it. You bought the right ingredients, you used the right tools – the knife that was sharp enough, the measuring jug that had both imperial measures and metric on a helpful conversion table down the side – and you followed the steps carefully. You didn't skip any steps or try to guess any measures.

You made sure the oven was properly pre-heated, you used a timer, you didn't allow yourself to get distracted by something on the radio or by reading an article in the newspaper you'd bought earlier in town. You washed up as you went along so that the surfaces were always clear and ready for action.

If you did all that, then cooking was easy, idiot-proof. Just like making an Airfix fighter plane really. Easier than that. The hardest dish to cook is easier than making a moderately tricky 1:72 scale model of a Sopwith Camel with all its bastard struts.

Yes, I found I liked cooking. I found it was relaxing. I decided I was definitely going to do more of it.

Dorcas and I ate early and Dorcas took herself off for a bath before going straight to bed, wisely keeping out of

her mother's way. As the day had worn on the fretful snappiness had become a brooding, charged silence that was a bit scary actually. I was glad I was going out.

Earlier Anne had wondered what I was going to do.

'I thought I might go down the rub-a-dub. Play some pool.'

'An excellent plan.'

'I'll phone you though. About ten? Just to check things are going all right.'

Anne said 'I wonder what "all right" will mean in this context. You know I used to be able to get almost any male to do what I wanted? It's true. You should have seen me as a schoolgirl, Marko. Always so many boys queuing up to carry my books for me. Frustrating how Philip has always been immune. Now you can sod off into town if you like. And don't worry too much. If you're near a phone and you remember to call me that'll be great but I won't expect it.'

She kissed my nose. Smoothed the hair back from my face. Kissed me again. 'The main thing is – don't get too wasted. I don't want to have to contend with brewer's droop tonight on top of everything else. I suspect I'll need some physical comfort after Philip has gone back to the pneumatic Mish. Not fair if he gets a post-negotiation shag and I miss out.'

'You don't have to worry about that.'

'No. I don't suppose I do. I sometimes forget just how young and vigorous you are. I could bloody love you, you know. If I let myself.' Her voice dropped. She moved her hands from my hair to my cheek. Her touch was light, her hand cool. 'But I won't let myself.'

'You're sure you don't want me to stay?'

'No. You go and have fun. Have you got ID?'

'Oh right, thanks.'

Anne tousled my hair. 'You'd forget your head, if it weren't screwed on,' and then, almost blushing at her uncharacteristic mumsiness, 'What a stupid thing to say. Sorry. Go on get out of here.'

I went to the Albion, a backstreet pub that I was quite fond of, and played pool. It was winner stays on and I stayed on for the whole evening.

I was good at pool – let's not forget I was brought up in a pub – and I even won some money. Fifty quid. I had a pint after every game, but it didn't seem to affect my ability to play. As the evening progressed, calculating the angles got easier if anything. I couldn't miss. Another message from the universe maybe. A small sign. A minor wonder. I just couldn't work out what it meant.

At ten I rang Anne from the payphone in the pub. She picked up but the bar was too noisy and I couldn't hear what she was saying, and the bloke I had to play next was impatiently banging his cue on the floor in time to the music from the juke box, but at least she'd know I had called to check on her even if we didn't have an actual conversation.

At closing time I walked back through quiet streets, my stomach fizzy with cheap beer and my head woolly. I felt pretty chipper though. It was a dry night. Wind whispering and sniggering in the trees, but otherwise the weather kept its trap shut. The weather steered well clear. Even the traffic disappeared for a while.

45

Lulu and I are walking slowly through the neatly planned, mostly well-kept Victorian streets of the town looking for a hotel or a guest house where we can rest up and it takes a while because Lulu has to stop at the windows of all the estate agents of which there are a surprising number. She gasps at what you can get for your money here and her mood seems to darken. By the time we've looked in the windows of the fifth agency she's as angry as Jezebel's mum.

'You can get a six-bed mansion here for the price of a garage in London. You get a garden and you get to live by the sea. It's mental.'

She falls into a brooding silence.

Just off the main drag I spot a likely place. It's a guest house called The Limes, though there is only one tree in the garden and it's a dead elm anyway.

'Let's try this one,' I say.

Lulu is still thinking about houses. 'You know what they should do?'

'No, Lulu what should they do?'

'They should offer the right-to-buy to private tenants. If you've been living in a private house for a while, three years say, you should be able to buy the house at a massive discount.'

'Won't that mean that people just stop renting out their houses? They'll just leave them empty.'

She thinks about this. 'Well, in that case we'll just take the blinking houses. We'll say to landlords, look you've got spare property so decide which one you want to live in and we'll have the rest – and we'll give them to people who need them. Simple as.'

I think maybe she's right. Maybe it is that simple. Take what you need. No argument.

The lady at the reception of The Limes looks at us dubiously and she gets more suspicious when I ask if she's got two rooms. She says she has just one room.

'Oh, for God's sake,' says Lulu. 'We'll take that one. How much is it?'

'Forty-five pounds including breakfast.'

'Forty-five pounds each?'

The receptionist is baffled. 'No dear, forty-five pounds for the room.'

'And there's an en-suite?'

'Yes. All our rooms are en-suite. There are tea and coffee making facilities and satellite TV. Free Wi-Fi of course.'

'Of course,' says Lulu. 'We'll take it.'

As the receptionist gets us to fill out a form – she doesn't ask for ID I notice – she asks if we really don't have any bags.

'Oh we both have baggage,' says Lulu. 'Don't you worry about that.'

'In the car, is it?'

Lulu doesn't answer and the receptionist doesn't push it.

As we walk to the room. Lulu says, 'Forty-five pounds a night.' There is wonder in her voice. 'That works out less than our rent.'

'Don't forget the free tea and coffee making facilities,' I say. 'The satellite TV, the free Wi-Fi.'

'The someone else doing your cleaning every day.'

'That too. And the breakfast.'

'Yes, let's not forget the breakfast. Come and sit by the window.'

'You're not taking my picture.'

'Yeah, I am.'

She does. I don't even argue about it all that much. Like Jake said, Lulu is a girl who gets what she wants. You don't have to be with her very long to realise that.

As a portrait photographer she's professional and she's quick, radiates competence. Turns my head this way and that with firm fingers, makes adjustments to my posture. Gives instructions in a precise, clipped tone.

'Photo probably won't come out anyway,' I say.

'Why, you a vampire?' she says.

I go onto the landing, unwrap another of my Cashcon phones and call the children. I call Jack first. I refuse to get my hopes up. Their phones will have been confiscated, there will be another police hand ready to answer for them, or they'll simply be out of charge, so I'm not surprised when there's no response. Still, I call Ella anyway but I'm just going through the motions really, so when her excited hello bubbles into my ear I am almost too surprised to speak.

271

'Daddy? Daddy? Is that you?'

I shut my eyes against the sudden tears welling there.

'Yes, sweetheart. Yes, it's me.'

I ask her what she's doing right now and she says she's not doing anything, she's just chilling and so I say well, maybe she could use the time productively, play the guitar or draw a picture, read a book or something and she is instantly cross.

'Oh for God's sake, Dad.'

She's right to be irritated. I'm irritated myself. I can't believe I've opened with this pompous teachery stuff. I don't even mean it, I was just feeling my way into the conversation. I try to row back. 'I'm sorry, darling. I can't help myself.'

'I know,' she says. 'It's not your fault, it's just who you are.' There's warmth back in her voice. Is it? I think. Is that who I am? I need to make some changes. Do some work on myself.

I ask how Mum is and she sighs. 'She's okay. Bit mardy. On the phone a lot.'

Is she now? And mardy is a new word.

I tell Ella that this is a difficult time for Mummy and she's got to be grown up and helpful. I ask if she's excited about the new baby coming. 'You know it'll be soon now,' I say.

I can practically hear her eyes rolling down the phone.

'Yeah. I'm ecstatic,' she says. She sounds every inch the adolescent wearied by the stupidity of the parental world.

'Is your brother there?'

'Yeah. Of course he's here. He's always here.'

'Can you put him on please?'

A pause. Then Ella is back. 'He says he doesn't want to speak to you.'

'Tell him he's got to.'

There's a pause full of frantic whispering. I can't hear the actual words though I can get the sense of it.

'Dad?'

'Jack. You didn't answer your phone, bud.'

'I know.'

I ask him what's new in his life. I ask about football and school and his friends and am answered in grunts. In desperation I ask if he's got any got new facts for me. I tell him one of my own. I tell him that when a town has -stowe on the end it means holy place.

'Dad, I said I didn't want to speak to you and I meant it.'

The phone goes dead.

I phone the landline. I'm just going to leave a message, just going to say that I'm still their dad, that wherever I am, whatever I'm doing, whatever they hear, I'm still on their side, that they are still the most important people in my life, and that they must never forget how beautiful they are. Really, they must never forget that.

Only, I can't say any of this because someone picks up.

'Mark?'

'Katy?'

The last time we spoke we said horrible things to each other. Awful things. Things that you would imagine would kill any relationship. Words dipped in poison and all the more venomous for being delivered in bitter whispers so as not to disturb the children. Katy had closed the door on me with a terrible cold finality and I had left Haverstock Road blinded by a searing rage. Almost walking into the path of a passing van and not caring.

But twenty-three years steeped in the steady routines and shared responsibilities of a more or less happy family

life means that we can absorb a lot of damage. Take a lot of punishment. That's the hope anyway.

Katy's voice is low and scratchy and she tells me why. She's got the beginnings of a heavy fucking cold and not only that, she's going mad, the kids are driving her nuts.

'Acting up, are they?'

'You could say that.'

Turns out that over the last few days our lovely well-mannered kids have taken to answering back, to complaining about the food that's offered to them, to making a fuss about judo and guitar and homework. They've been late to get ready for things, they've been losing things, they've been fighting, they've been fractious and tearful.

I know better than to say that this is because they're missing me. Know better than to remind her that until now I've not spent more than a single night away from them since they were born. That I've always been around.

'You didn't say any of this yesterday,' I say.

'I had other things I wanted to talk about.'

'I'm sorting it, Katy.'

There's a long silence. I can hear her awkward, mucusy breathing.

'I'm afraid I'm not sure you can, Mark.' She tells me that maybe I shouldn't call again. She tells me that she'll need to report that I've phoned her to the police.

'I have to play it absolutely safe. You know that, don't you?'

'I know.'

'Goodbye, Mark. Take care.'

'No wait. Katy!' I want to keep her on the line. It feels really important that I do that.

'What is it Mark?' She waits, though I can feel the impatience.

I can think of absolutely nothing to say. 'Don't worry, it'll keep.'

She sighs. 'I've really got to go now. Kids need their tea.'

After she hangs up. I check the time. It's gone eight. Eight o'clock and the kids haven't had their tea yet?

As I walk back into the room Lulu asks if everything is okay at home.

'Yeah, fine. Why wouldn't it be?' I say. 'Shall we get going?'

46

Anne was out on the driveway, no coat, rubbing at her bare arms. She was furious, spitting with frustration.

'That fucker,' she said as I reached her. 'That fucker.'

She was in my arms sobbing, hot tears on my neck. I'd never seen her like this. Frantic, crying, out of control. I stroked her hair, breathed her in. She was rigid with tension. Clenched and shivering with rage. A fair guess that negotiations had not gone well. That the professor wasn't playing ball.

'You told me it would be okay. You said he'd be *emollient*, I think that was your word.'

Calmer now, she stepped back from me, took a breath, wiped the backs of her hands across her face. She told me that he had been utterly unreasonable about the house, about custody, about money, about every fucking thing. He'd reneged on everything.

'Now he won't even leave. He's up there pissed out of his mind, saying he'll go when he bloody well feels like it.'

'We'll see about that.'

'You going to duff him up for me then, Marko? You going to be my hero? Bravo.' She sounded sarcastic and I was stung. She saw I was hurt and sighed. 'Why are men always so bloody sensitive?'

Dr Sheldon was lying full length on one of the sofas. He was spark out, his face gentle in slumber. He stirred as we came into the room and struggled to a sitting position. Squinted up at us.

'Aha,' he said. 'She's back, and oh, look who she's brought with her ladies and gentleman. It's Sid Vicious, the apprentice back scrubber.'

He closed his eyes again, his head lolled.

'How much has he had?' I asked.

Anne shrugged. 'Couple of bottles while he's been here and he was already half cut when he arrived.'

I moved to the sofa, got my arms around him and attempted to heave him upright. It was hard to get a decent grip on him. He was unresisting but he wasn't exactly cooperative either, and he was a big man. By the time I got him onto swaying feet I was sweating. I was also unprepared for the sudden shove which sent me sprawling across the coffee table knocking wine glasses and bottles to the floor. There was a loud, discordant glissando of glass breaking.

'Fucking great.' Anne turned and hurried out.

Sheldon was delighted. He clapped his hands together, laughed loud and theatrical, gave himself the voice of an excited sports commentator.

'Oh my word. He's down! Kid Galahad is down! What a shocker for the fans.'

He really was a nasty piece of work. A fucker right

enough. As I got to my feet, Sheldon held his hands up.

'Okay, okay. I'll go quietly.' He looked to the door where Anne was bustling in with a dustpan and brush. 'Dearest. You all right to give me a lift home?' He sat down again heavily.

Anne looked at him. Her eyes narrowed and hard. Her face flushed. She bent to the floor sweeping the glass into the pan. 'Anne?'

She didn't look towards him as she said, 'Yes. Yes, all right. God.'

I started to speak, started to tell her it wasn't a good idea. But she cut me off. 'Don't just stand there, Mark. Go and get a cloth. There's fucking wine everywhere.'

When I came back with kitchen roll, Sheldon was on his feet again, Anne had her arm round him. He was leaning all over her.

'Come on, Mark. Help me get him into the car.'

Halfway down the tiled hallway Sheldon changed his mind again, became truculent and bullish.

'My house,' he said, his voice gluey and indistinct. 'My bloody house.' Sheldon tried to fight us as we pushed and pulled him towards the door, but his feet had no grip on the floor, his fingers got no purchase on the walls though he did manage to knock pictures skew-whiff. But it was hard work. Christ, he was heavy. Sheldon lumbering and stumbling and weighing at least two hundred pounds. So hard to keep hold of him as he lurched into explosive spasms every couple of steps, jerking backwards and upright and almost breaking free.

I had to adjust my grip on him several times. Had to pull him tighter into my body. Nostrils full of the smell of him. Cologne. Whisky. Arrogance. Privilege. Easy to focus on how much I hated this man. I gave him a dig

in the kidneys with my balled fist. And another. Sheldon gave a satisfying gasp.

Anne was ahead of us, moving tables, umbrellas, coats, shoes, anything we might stumble over, or that Sheldon might anchor himself to.

'Come on,' she breathed. 'Quick.'

'My house. My bloody house.'

Then the door was open and we staggered into the cold wet air. 'My house!' Sheldon's voice, still slurred but more forceful now. I put my hand over his fat sausagey mouth, felt him slobber against my palm. Almost stopped. Almost let him go. Almost.

Around the corner, the frantic percussion of our boots on the gravel. From somewhere I could hear music. Thirties dance music. Clarinets. Who listened to that stuff these days? Of course it was like we were dancing to it, Sheldon and me. Like we were doing some kind of crazy waltz. One. Two. Three. One. Two. Three. Anne had the side door to the garage open and then she had the back door of the Masterson's old Volvo open. Quick now. Get the bloody man inside. Get him in the back of the car.

Sheldon seemed to surrender. To decide to give up fighting, to just accept things. About fucking time. He allowed himself to be pushed into the back seat where he did a little pantomime of making himself comfortable. It was with relief that I slammed the door shut on him.

Anne and I stood in that garage, both of us panting.

'I don't think you should drive him back.'

'What do you think I should do then clever-clogs?'

I shrugged. 'Get him a cab?'

'I don't think a taxi driver will take him, not the state he's in.'

A thought struck me. 'Hey, are you over the limit?'

Anne laughed. 'Hey, you know what? I just might be.'

'You can't drive then. You're in enough trouble.'

'I think I'll decide how much trouble is enough, thank you very much.'

She told me that Sheldon only lived a mile away, that she'd be careful, that if I could just go and finish clearing up the mess in the living room she'd be grateful and oh could I check on Dorcas. She's normally a heavy sleeper but, well, we've been making something of a racket, haven't we?

We stood staring at one another. Should I forcibly take the keys off her? Anne's dark eyes flashed. I dare you, they seemed to be saying. Just try it. I fucking dare you.

'Go on, dear. Please.' She smiled at me and my heart twitched.

47

I knew exactly what to do about the wine. Dab tonic water on the stains, be liberal with it and then add a lot of salt, really a lot, wait a couple of moments and then scoop the soggy mixture up with kitchen roll and bin it. Do it quick, don't skimp on the salt and use good quality kitchen roll and you'll find the stain will have vanished in minutes. A little miracle, an everyday kind of magic. Something to do with the chemical interaction between the main elements. You don't grow up in a pub without learning a few cleaning shortcuts.

Working in a pub you find a vital part of the job is clearing up the messes made by various fluids. Beer and wine, yes, gravy, yes, but also blood and piss. Faeces of many different constituencies. Spunk too, because there's not a pub toilet in the country, no matter how rank, that people haven't tried to have sex in. Growing up in a pub is like growing up on a farm – the basic facts of life, the truths about humanity's primal urges, well, they're pretty inescapable.

The important thing is to try and get to the stains, whatever they are, while they're still fresh if you can, otherwise you'll just have to apply a lot more of the other important ingredient besides the quinine and the salt – elbow grease.

The wine came up easily enough but there was so much of it and in such hard-to-get-at places. It really had gone everywhere. It was amazing, there were only dregs in the glasses but still flecks and drops of wine had managed to get on all four walls, on both sofas, even on the sodding ceiling.

It was while I was bringing a chair from the kitchen into the living room – something to stand on to try and reach the ceiling – that I heard a noise behind me. A breath. A world-weary sigh.

Dorcas standing in the doorway and watching me with serious eyes. She was holding a large, battered, old fashioned teddy bear by the ear.

'What are you doing?' she said. I got down off the chair.

'Cleaning,' I said.

'Oh,' she said. She seemed to think this was a reasonable enough answer. She didn't express any further curiosity, didn't ask why I needed to be cleaning the ceiling. The two of us looked at each other. God, she looked exactly like her dad. It was weird. Dr Sheldon's face reconfigured in the form of a rather sad little girl. I couldn't think of anything to say.

Finally, Dorcas said, 'Where's Mummy?'

'I'm here poppet.' Anne appeared in the doorway behind her and folded her into an embrace. 'You should be in bed. What are you doing up?'

'Something woke me up. Were you and Daddy fighting again?'

The voice was precise, clipped, accusing, the voice of a future minister, a future judge, a future ambassador to the UN.

'No, sweetheart we weren't.'

'Where's Daddy now?'

'Let's get you back to bed, shall we?' Anne scooped the kid up and vanished.

I took the chair back to the kitchen. On the way back to the living room I took a few moments to straighten the pictures. The posters for exhibitions and theatre shows they had seen: Kazimir Malevich at the Stedelijk Museum Amsterdam, Theatre De Complicite at the ICA, the Leipzig biennial.

I arrived back in the living room just moments before Anne reappeared.

'Didn't take long.'

'She's wiped out poor thing. She went off in seconds.'

'No, I meant it didn't take long to get your husband back to his new home and then get back here.'

Anne sat down heavily on the sofa. She got up again, she rubbed both her arms as though she was cold. She moved around the room, touching the sculptures, picking up books. It was as if she hadn't seen it before. As if she had woken from a sleepwalking dream to find herself in a stranger's room. I didn't like it. She hadn't been away anything like long enough to get Sheldon to his house, get him inside and then get back.

'Anne?'

She looked at me. I saw how fierce her eyes were. The stare of a hungry cat. A desperate wildcat with nowhere left to run to.

'I didn't take him home.'

'What?'

'What? What?' she mimicked me cruelly, capturing perfectly my flat Essex voice, my baffled tone. 'That's your bloody catchphrase.'

We held each other's gaze for long seconds before I made a move towards the door. She sprang towards me, clutched at me. 'No, Mark. No. Please. Stay here.' But both her voice and her hold on me were weak, uncertain.

I shook her off and hurried down the hall, fumbled at the catch on the heavy front door. Anne followed as I crunched across the gravel in a few short strides to the side door of the garage, noticing as I did so that the main door was closed and that the room stank of petrol. I gagged. Stopped. Behind me Anne said softly, 'Don't look. Please, Mark don't look.'

But I had to look, of course I did.

Professor Sheldon was lying across the back seat, hands beneath his head, long legs folded. For a moment I was confused. He looked almost exactly as he had looked when I had left the garage to return to the house to start cleaning up. He looked like a man sleeping. A man with no worries and a clear conscience.

Then I wasn't confused. Then I knew.

In seconds I had that old car door open and was pulling at Sheldon's legs, heaving him out onto the concrete of the garage floor where he lay cherry-cheeked and absurdly healthy-looking. Eyes open but unseeing. That's when I felt my blood surge in my veins. A sudden wonder.

I looked at Anne.

'Fuck,' I breathed. 'Fuck.'

Now that the truth was out, now that I knew the worst, Anne seemed to have composed herself.

'Indeed,' she said.

'What happened?'

'Don't be dense, Mark. You know what happened.'

I did. It was astonishing. It was unbelievable. But it was also very simple. There was the professor nodding off in the back seat, and Anne – about to lose her child, her husband, her home – had decided that no, actually she wasn't going to drive this man back to his new place, back to lovely Mish. Why the hell should she have to do that?

This bastard man, this man who had broken all the rules, who had torn up the contract between them. He'd forfeited any rights to any help at all.

So instead she was going to attach a hosepipe from the exhaust of Masterson's old Volvo, feed it through a tiny gap in the back window and then she was going to turn on the engine before getting out of the car and waiting the ten minutes or so it would take for Sheldon to move from drunken nap to endless sleep. At the moment she was doing it, it seemed right. It made sense. It seemed like justice.

Horrifying maybe, but easy to grasp at least.

I allowed myself to be taken by the hand to the house where Anne gave me whisky, made me swallow it. I coughed as it seared my throat.

'You have to help me, Mark. If you tell me there's no other option, that I have to call the police and that I have to tell them everything, then I'll do that. But there must be something else we can do. There must be.'

Her small hands twisting round each other, her face flushed, her eyes glittering.

Of course, yes, actually there was something we could

do. She saw it, saw that I'd glimpsed a solution, a possible way out. She saw it in my face almost the very second it came to me.

'What is it, Mark? You have to tell me.'

Christ. I sat down and took another swallow of the whisky. I didn't cough this time, instead I could appreciate the satisfying fire of it. I looked up at her. She came close to me, put her hands on my shoulders. Kissed my head. Then went back to twisting her hands in front of her, agitated and scared-looking, and beautiful too with that flushed skin, those flashing eyes.

I knew I shouldn't do this. Knew it was a bad idea. But then, with shocking clarity, I saw my sister lying in pink-tinged water a year ago and remembered who put her there.

People die all the time. People are killed all the time. How many poets died in Nagasaki? How many potential philosophers were burned to death as children in Dresden? Every wartime bombing raid killed teachers, nurses, doctors. Murdered binmen and milkmen. Shop assistants and salesmen. Window cleaners and chimney sweeps. Babies. All of them killed by young men who were welcomed home as heroes. Men who were given medals by a grateful nation. Had sculptures to their sacred memory unveiled by the Queen.

'It might not work. Probably won't... but... But have you still got his old note, the one from before, from when he... ?'

I tailed off, but I'd said enough. She got it.

'His cry for help you mean? Yes, yes, I have.' She hurried out of the room, while I sat and sipped whisky and tried to think about nothing.

She was back in minutes, a page of A4 notepaper in her

hand. Sheldon's scrawl all over it. She was secretary-brisk.

'We haven't got long, Mark. We need to work out between us exactly what happened. We need to get the story right and then you need to go.'

She was right. I needed to get out of there anyway.

'We'll be okay, Mark. A couple of weeks and we can see each other again. This is the best thing. It is. Doesn't help anyone to tell the truth. Doesn't help anyone for Dorcas to lose both parents.'

I needed her to stop talking. I couldn't concentrate. My head ached. My stomach fizzed and cramped. I needed to get to a toilet.

'In a little while we'll be able to see each other again. We can do things properly. Go and see those bands. Go out to dinner and to the pictures. We can do all of that. I'll be all yours, Marko.'

48

I was standing on the driveway again. It was a clear, cold night. The music had stopped. No more clarinets, no more pulsing swing beat double bass. There was a harmless breeze. There were cars coming at regular intervals down the road. I looked at the sky, there were a million dead stars up there sending out light from aeons ago. Light from back when humanity was still a clump of unlikely cells in the first ooze. Nothing had changed. Not really.

A movement at an upstairs window caught my eye. I looked up. A solemn face staring down. A child's face. Dorcas. She lifted her hand. Then she was gone.

There was something at my feet now. I looked down. A cat rubbing up against my leg. Ophelia. Or Portia.

'I thought you'd been got rid of,' I told her.

I stood on that driveway and listened to the night. Traffic. The air in the trees. A distant fox. Something squealing in terror. Nature feeding itself.

I looked back up at the window. No one there now.

No newly fatherless child waving all unknowing. I was walking away briskly, out of the driveway, dimly taking in the presence of another cat watching me impassively from the wall. Portia. Or Ophelia. I was thinking what this might mean.

I'll be watching you. I'll be that black cat that comes out of nowhere to cross your path but my head was really hurting now.

Then I was heading into town, walking a mile down Trumpington Road. Our plan meant I had to spend these hours just walking. Walking meant thinking, there was no avoiding that. It would be easier when it got light. There would be a cafe - Benet's maybe or Carrington's – eggs, toast, noise. All of Cambridge's most pointlessly lovely faces laughing at nothing. All of that might help me not to think.

About lunchtime I would phone Anne, check that everything was okay, that it was all right to go back round there. That the investigating authorities had bought our story. Once upon a time the beautiful Lady Anne had argued with a drunken and a violently intimidating Dr Sheldon, that – upset and scared – she had left to clear her head and had returned an hour or so later to find that he had gassed himself in the car, that he had left an untidy note saying everything had got too much, that he had never meant to cause so much pain to those he loved, that he was too cowardly to bear it. That he was sorry, so sorry.

Like she had told me once, it wasn't the professor's best work, nothing the Nobel judges would take seriously. But definitely his writing, his own words. It would do. It was good enough.

After about ten minutes it began to rain, and I cursed

myself for not bringing an umbrella. Apparently, that can happen. Turns out a man can be killed just yards away from you, that he can be turned into so much meat, while you dab at wine stains with tonic water and salt. Just a few minutes later, you can be worried about a spot of rain. A touch of drizzle.

Somewhere not far away an owl cried out. Along the roadside the neat trees shook like fists. The breeze whispered curses. I knew then that I was in the wrong place. While the rain slicked my hair with its cold dead hand, it came to me with absolute clarity that I needed to be somewhere else. There was someone I needed to see, and I was amazed that I had only just realised it.

I needed to find the girl who was haunted in her dreams by murdered children. I needed to find her and never leave her. Katy had been showing me the promise of something ever since we'd met and I'd been too blind to even see it, never mind recognise its value.

The owl called again. That too-human screech.

I hailed the next cab that came swishing down the glistening road.

I pulled open the door. 'London,' I said, as I climbed in. 'Heathrow Airport.'

The taxi driver was determinedly unsurprised. 'Sixty quid,' he said.

'That's okay.'

It wasn't like it was even my money really. It was money won from the hopeless pool players. The poor saps who had the misfortune not to be brought up in pubs. I put my hand in my back pocket. Felt the solid rectangle of my passport.

The cabbie didn't ask, but I felt the urge to tell him anyway. I was going to Italy. That I was leaving the

country for the first time. I was going to Rome. To tell a girl I loved her. That I couldn't live without her. That I didn't care what trouble it caused. And, as I said it, I knew it was true.

'Like Romeo and Juliet,' the cabbie said. 'Beautiful.'

49

Brutally lit, severely white, as wipe-clean sterile as a butcher's or a path lab. It's just another shop from the outside, but once you get in, the Orwell gallery is a classic contemporary art space. Light without warmth. Light without life.

But then our weekend family trips to well-reviewed exhibitions have taught me that much contemporary art seems to be about the treatment of wounds, psychic or otherwise, so it's no surprise that galleries look like little clinics. No surprise too that so many visitors to these galleries look as lost and as helpless as visitors to hospices – unsure of how to behave. Should they frown or smile? Are they allowed to laugh? Should they feel guilty that their minds drift away from the work on the walls to what they'll have for tea?

The private view is almost over when we get there, just half a dozen baffled white-haired types clutching glasses of wine, like they were lifebelts in freezing seas. No sign of any good-looking people flirting.

I recognise Bim at once. He hasn't changed. Bit heavier maybe, but then he was never exactly svelte before. He's wearing the same kind of dark suit, same bouncer's haircut. He is nodding and smiling at a sharp-faced older lady in front of a large canvas of a deep purple sheep in a scarlet field. All the work around the walls is like the painting in the window. Painstakingly realistic scenes rendered surreal by the simple use of inappropriate colours. They're all right actually. I mean, you wouldn't want one in your living room or anything, but still, they are very well done.

When Bim sees us, he waves us over, utterly unfazed by my presence here. It's like we'd last met just a week or two before.

'I was waiting for you to get here,' he says. He clocks my expression. 'Amber, my charming tenant,' he explains. 'Mother of the delightful Jezebel. Never gives my whereabouts away, always lets me know if people come looking. Very useful.'

His voice is still that startling descant. He puts a big hand on my shoulder, lets it lie there. 'You look good. Maybe not quite the young Apollo of the old days, a bit squidgy round the edges perhaps, but not completely gone to seed.'

I find that, despite everything, I'm happy to see him. I force myself to think coolly. Anne's friend. Not yours, Mark. Anne's. Her rock.

'I was never that good-looking,' I say.

'Oh but you so were, dear chap. Completely ravishing. Clean-limbed and golden-eyed, like someone from myth, definitely.'

Lulu chimes in, 'I'd have liked to have seen that.'

'Oh, he was really something, my dear.'

I introduce them. 'Lulu's a photographer.'

'Really? Any good?'

'I'm not bad.'

'My dear, not bad is the worst thing to be. Not bad is horrid. Bad art is fine, there's a place for bad art like there is for good art. But not-bad art? That's just landfill. There should be a charity dedicated to the incineration of not-bad art. They'd have my standing order in a jiffy.'

'Well, then. My photos are flipping amazing.'

'Much better.' He claps his hands. 'Send me some of your work. Any friend of Mark's is etcetera. Let me get rid of this rabble and we'll go back to our gaff and have soup and a glass of something lovely.'

As we walk through the town Bim tells us about his love for Felixstowe.

'This is where the real England is Mark – not in the cities and not in the rolling hills. Neither London nor the Cotswolds. Neither satanic mill nor brooding moor. Not Cambridge either. England is in the coastal market towns. England will finally die when its market town high streets do, when the sea rises enough to drown the amusement arcades. Ah, here we are.'

Here is a honey-coloured bungalow with a neat square of lawn between it and the road. Bim fiddles with keys.

'How's the gorgeous Katy?'

'Good. She's good.'

'Excellent. Now you'll have to excuse the mess.'

The bungalow is as warm and as cluttered as the gallery was chilly and antiseptic. It smells of roasting vegetables. There's a coal-effect gas fire, a densely patterned three-piece suite that's just a bit too large for the room. Knick-knacks everywhere. The paintings on the wall

are seascapes, landscapes, watercolours. The kind of unthreatening not bad art you see everywhere.

There are holiday photos on every surface. Bim on crowded beaches, Bim in front of ruined castles, Bim shaking hands with Mickey Mouse at Disneyland. In nearly every photo he is accompanied by a chubby, balding man with soft, smudged features. In most of them there is also a skinny, smiling blonde kid. Turns out this is Grace, their adopted daughter.

'She's at Max's mum's for a week.'

'Max?' I say.

'That's me.' It's the man from the photos. Plumper in the flesh than in the pictures, his eyes flicker and dance as they take me in. He is smiling, but he looks wary. He nods towards the photos. 'She's a handful. Could start a fight in a phone box, but we love her. We wouldn't have her any other way. You have children?'

I just nod. I can't speak, there's a lump in my throat as solid as a golf ball. But it reminds me what I'm there for. Max fills the gap in conversation with polite questions to Lulu. What did she think of the exhibition? Has she been to Felixstowe before? And I get that this is sensitivity rather than curiosity. He has spotted that the talk of children has upset me. He wants to give me time to recover.

I look at the photos again. We have never taken our children to Disneyland, and we've always sort of sneered when our friends went – but if I ever get the chance then I am going to make sure we go. I'll buy a TV, the biggest they sell, and I'll get an Xbox, a Nintendo, a PS4. The highest spec tablet. And, yeah, from now on, given the chance, the Chadwicks may spend whole mornings in their PJs. Whole weekends in front of the screen. We're

going to slob out big time. The new kid babysat by Nickelodeon.

Of course it might be too late for all of that.

Max is back in the kitchen making soup and in the living room Bim tells us how he saved his life. 'Max made me see that life didn't have to be an adventure all the time. You didn't have to boldly go, seeking out new worlds or whatever. You could just stand and stare, it was okay to do that.'

I find myself struggling to respond. My conversational skills have atrophied over the last week. I feel all wrong, feel that my arms and legs are sticking out at awkward angles. I run my tongue over my teeth. My mouth feels furred.

Lulu says, 'You have Grace and that's an adventure surely? That's boldly going.'

'She is. It is. But I hope to goodness she doesn't ever see it like that that. I hope she sees growing up with two dads as the most unadventurous thing there is. If, when she's fifteen, she throws things, stamps her foot and shouts that we are the most boring parents in the world and that we have ruined her life with our petit bourgeoisie conservative stick-in-the-mud values, if she does that, well, I'll be a very happy man.'

I smile at this. I know where Bim is coming from and I say so. This is something I can talk about. I begin to sketch out my own beautifully placid family life. After a minute or two, I stop. He's not exactly yawning but he might as well be.

'Dreams, farts and families,' says Lulu.

'What?' I say.

'Your own are endlessly fascinating, other peoples... well, not so much.'

'I was listening,' says Bim. 'I was rapt.'

'Yeah, yeah. Course you were.' They both smile.

Max pops his head back into the room. 'I need to nip out. A cumin seed crisis. I've turned everything off. Don't touch anything.'

Lulu is standing looking out at the streets.

'There's absolutely no traffic,' she says. 'None.'

'Another good thing about living here. And it's not too quiet. Not usually. Felixstowe hasn't quite escaped the endemic sadness shared by all the former resort towns of England, but the presence of an active deep-water port and its proximity to bigger places like Ipswich and Colchester means it isn't entirely desolate. The town still has some sort of purpose. A dock town, a dormitory town and a retirement town. Three pretty good uses for a town in the modern era. Rents are inexpensive, there are decent schools and people here are surprisingly up for buying art.'

Lulu turns from the window and sits in the armchair opposite. Bim looks at me expectantly, gives me the signal that it's time for business.

'Bim. Do you know where Anne lives?' I say.

'I do.' There is a long pause. 'But to be honest Mark, I'm reluctant to give her address to you.'

'I need it, Bim.'

'Well, yes, if you're to escape justice, then you probably do. But thing is – Anne has at least faced up to her responsibility.'

'It's not about me, Bim. It's about being able to watch my kids grow up. About being a part of their lives.'

'I would say that's still about you, Mark. The kids will manage.'

I can hear Katy's voice telling me the same thing, that everyone will be fine without me.

Now Bim sits silent, his back resting against the wall, his eyes closed as if he is listening to far off music.

'You can really hear the sea from here,' says Lulu.

Bim raises his head, sits forward, rests his fleshy face on his lumberjack hands. He drinks his wine, puts big arms on his big, square rugby players' knees. 'Philip wasn't a good man, I know that,' Bim says. 'Unkind, unreliable, utterly self-absorbed, all that. But neither was he especially monstrous. Didn't deserve what happened to him.'

'I know. I know. I'm sorry. It shouldn't have happened.'

There might not be traffic but there's still the sea, and above that eternal murmur I can hear teenagers shrieking. Could be theatrical laughter or it could be an assault. Hard to tell.

Bim sighs now. 'For what it's worth I tried to talk Anne out of confessing. Couldn't see the point.'

I seize on this. 'That night. It was – it was disgusting. Horrible. I'm not denying my part in it but I was just...'

I stop.

'You were just what? An innocent bystander?'

I want to say yes, yes I was. It would be almost true. But I know it would be the wrong thing to say.

'I'm not saying that. But I was trying to help Anne. I kept quiet – I helped her keep it quiet – for her, for Dorcas, like you would have.' Bim's face is impassive. 'What bloody good does it do anyone for us to go to prison now?'

There's a long silence. Bim looks down at those massive hands. Turns them over. There seems to be something he can read there. 'Anne thinks it'll do her some good.' A pause. 'You know she's dying? No, of course you don't.'

Okay. Finally, I get it now. 'She wants to put her house in order?'

'Something like that.'

'Don't tell me she's got religion?'

'I don't know. It's possible.'

Shit. It's hard to fight faith. Eve was the only real believer I've ever known well. And look how that ended.

Eve had always thought there was something bigger than this world. She was convinced of it. Once, at ten, helping Mum prepare a Sunday roast, she had held out the green brain of a cabbage and said simply 'Look at this. How can anyone say there's no God?' It was true when you looked at something closely, saw it in all its intricacy – and when you heard the belief in Eve's voice – then it did seem hard not to think there was some divine intelligence behind it all. You stepped back into the real world in all its randomness and the idea of a divine plan seemed ridiculous again.

'Just let me talk to her, Bim.'

'That's all you're going to do? Talk?'

I can feel sour heat rising in me. 'Yes, of course that's all I'll do.'

But I know that I will do more if I have to. I'll talk to her, yes, but if necessary I'll also beg her. Beseech her. What else can I do? What does Bim think I'll do? Bim's expression is calm. Steady.

'I won't hurt her,' I say.

Still Bim says nothing. Keeps his eyes on me. What else does he want? I can't say anything more. If he doesn't believe me, he doesn't believe me. Anyway, is it true? What if Anne is determined to refuse my talking, my begging, my beseeching? What will I do? I don't know exactly, but I know I can't trust myself to stay rational. Bim might be right to be hesitant.

Lulu says, 'I won't let Mark do anything bad.'

'You think you could stop him? He can be quite determined can our Mark.'

'Not as determined as me.'

Bim looks at her for a long minute. He looks back at me. 'But Anne – she's still in my gang too, you know. Like you are, Mark. I want her to prosper.'

He seems to come to a sudden decision. He sighs again, passes his big bouncers' hands over his eyes, and he gives an address. It's an impossible one.

'Cambridge, eh?' says Lulu. 'You know I've never been there.'

It's like a fist to the gut. I feel rage building, a physical force inside me, the first stirrings of a hurricane. I force it down. Swallow, breathe, count to ten slowly in my head. I get to three.

'Bim. Why are you doing this to me? She's not still in Cambridge. She sold that house years ago.'

Bim shrugs. 'That's where she is. She did try to sell the house but it was 1990, the year boom became bust if you remember. Sale fell through. She went abroad for a few years, like you did funnily enough, rented the house out. Then she came back.'

'But I checked. I googled her.' I can hear the whine in my voice.

'Oh well, if you googled her…' says Lulu.

'But you probably didn't use her married name, did you?' says Bim. 'Anne Sheldon is Anne Thibaud now. Monsieur Thibaud was some kind of French advertising executive I believe, but anyway he hasn't been on the scene for years.'

Now we hear the sound of someone at the door. Max is back. He goes straight down the hall towards the kitchen. He is singing something vaguely operatic but which I don't recognise.

'What have you told Max about me?' I say.

Bim smiles. 'Oh just that you're a friend from Cambridge days down on your luck, needing money to take your hot new girlfriend on holiday somewhere nice. You're worried she'll chuck you otherwise, being, you know, so much younger and prettier than you are.'

'I like this story,' says Lulu. 'But you should know, how realistic is it, really? I'm way out of Mark's league. He'd never get a bird like me.'

Bim smiles. 'No, princess, it's possible. Love makes blind fucking idiots out of everyone.'

Lulu frowns. Bim is handing me something. The key to Anne's house.

'In case she won't open up voluntarily,' he says. 'Which is definitely a possibility. Hung onto it twenty-odd years. God knows why.'

I don't say anything, just slip it into my pocket. There is a brief moment of heavy silence before Max is back in the room.

'Grub's up,' he says.

50

We are back at The Limes, under the covers and back making good use of the facilities. We are showered, we are drinking tea and we are watching live poker on the TV. We are getting the maximum bang for our forty-five bucks. We are still full of the roast vegetable soup Max had made. We are quite drunk on very decent wine. If I am careful not to think about anything – anything at all – then I could be content, at least for this moment.

Lulu's leg is under the bed. Taking her prosthesis off had been the first thing on her mind when we'd got in. She'd told me how she was only meant to wear it for six hours at a stretch and she'd gone more like twenty-eight hours and it was bloody agony now. But she'd bathed her leg, and rubbed some special ointment into the knee with its neatly stitched scar. I'd told her the thing Anne had told me about a scar being stronger than skin. Lulu had smiled.

'That, Mr Chadwick, is a very true thing,' she'd said.

So now we are watching TV. We are both in t-shirts and underwear, bodies not touching, though I'm very aware that Lulu is only centimetres away. The heat of her. The pulsing energy of her.

With her eyes still on the screen, she says, 'I wonder what Jake is up to now?'

It's not a real question, she doesn't need me to answer. I don't say anything, but if I had to guess I'd say he would be trying to fuck someone or fight someone.

She says, 'When I was young I was so flattered when men approached me, when they desired me, but then...' She drifts into silence. On the screen a young woman wins fifty grand and receives it with the merest ghost of a rueful smile.

'But then?'

'But then you find men are led by their cocks and that those cocks are blind with no morals or discernment whatsoever. So you have to be fastidious about the cocks you let into your life. You have to apply high standards, stringent checks. You have to make them work hard for everything.'

I think it's interesting that the word 'cocks' doesn't qualify as an unimaginative swear word. We let another hand go by.

'It's okay. I won't make a pass at you, Lulu.'

'You see that's what I've come to know about you, Mark. You're lazy. You rein yourself in. Hold yourself back. You don't throw yourself into life. There's not enough fire in your belly. Because, actually, old chum, you should make a pass at me. I'm a passionate woman. I'm a passionate, attractive, newly single woman. We're on a bed in a cheap hotel. We're drunk, we're clean, we're not wearing many clothes. You should be trying to snog me, you should be trying to get into my knickers.'

'Oh, right.'

'We'd kiss for a bit, touch each other up for a bit and after a while I'd decide if I wanted to take things further. I probably would, knowing me.'

'I'm very tired, Lulu. I'd like to get going early tomorrow.'

'And you're very much in love with your wife.'

'Yes, yes I think I am. Sorry.'

'Don't be sorry. It's nice. I guess. Though I don't think being with one person forever is going to be my thing.'

'You think monogamy is a failed experiment?'

She turns towards me. Christ, she's stunning. 'I think that's it exactly. A failed experiment.'

We watch another poker hand. The young woman is on fire, she scoops the pool. A million quid. Still she hardly reacts. A brief smile, a wink to someone in the crowd, handshakes for her opponents, all of them men in early middle age. They smile, but they want to murder her. They must do.

'My name's not Lulu by the way.'

'No?'

'No. It's Lorraine.' She takes a slow breath. 'The leg wasn't a shark: it was cancer. Just boring old cancer.' Her voice is stretched, tight. 'After the op I decided that cancer would be the last boring thing that I ever allowed to happen to me. Now tell me about the terrible thing you did.'

But I can't. I'm still not ready for that story. But there's another story I can tell. I take a long breath of the room's antiseptic, lemony air. I wet my throat with tepid tea.

'It was a stupid row,' I say. 'Eve was sick and we didn't know.'

51

Eve in her room playing the same two chords over and over on her electric guitar. It's a Gibson Les Paul Junior with a P-90 pickup. The same guitar the bloke from The Clash used, bought for her by her dad for twenty-five quid off a bloke that came in the pub. She is driving everyone mad as she tries to write a song about how the whole world is weighing her down. But it's just a song, just teenage angst in minor chords – not worth taking seriously.

Her mum was shouting. Eve should be helping in the pub. She should be doing banter with the sad fat men. She didn't want to, she thought her brother should take a turn.

'He's studying!' hollered their Mum. 'He's got exams. He's going to Cambridge.'

'Yeah, right,' said Eve.

Along the landing from all the yelling, her brother felt bad for a second. Because he was not studying. He was reading *The Day of the Triffids* – for maybe the fourth time – and it was on no exam syllabus, just a good, fun

read, but he was into it and didn't feel like moving and if his mum believed he was working, well why should he enlighten her? He felt lazy and for once he was going to give in to it.

Outside his room, the row between mother and daughter escalates until Eve is NOT going to that party she was so desperate to go to and her mother DOESN'T CARE if all her mates are going. It's TOUGH. She should have THOUGHT OF THAT before she started getting so BLOODY LIPPY.

The shouting gets so annoying that the brother can't stand it and puts the book away – he can't concentrate on it any more anyway – and comes out onto the landing to shout that it's okay, he'll do Eve's shift but his mum tells him it's TOO LATE, Eve has MADE HER BED and NOW SHE CAN BLOODY LIE ON IT.

So the brother – Mark – went out instead, and by the Rec he met Ali Beswick, a pretty, tiny pixie of a girl, one of Eve's best mates. He explained the situation to her.

'That's crap,' said Ali.

'Parents. What can you do?' he said.

'Yeah, they're all mad. All beyond help,' said Ali and they smiled at each other and now somehow the brother was going to the party and he spent a few hours there, drinking warm cider from big plastic bottles and going through the record collection of the people whose house it is. They had pretty good taste.

He was quite happy doing that. He didn't need to talk to anyone. He pulled out a copy of the second Scott Walker album, the subject of a retrospective in *The Sunday Times magazine* only that week. They called it a seminal work, made him feel he should seek it out. He wondered if they'd miss it.

Ali introduced him to a skinny, beaky kid called Andy Shreeve and after he'd drifted away she told him that he was brilliant at chess, played in a league, and oh, also, his sister had a massive crush on him.

Really? Mark looked harder at this Andy Shreeve as he danced with rather too much concentration and vigour to some generic indie pop – Ride? Inspiral Carpets? – he seemed all elbows and knees to Mark. He looked like some kind of wading bird. A chess-playing flamingo maybe.

Time passed and when he decided to go, he looked for Ali Beswick to say goodbye. When he couldn't find her he was told by one of the other kids that she was last seen disappearing together with Andy Shreeve into one of the bedrooms.

The kid leered, 'Do you think he's passing on some tips about the classic openings.'

This kid was a short-arse in an ugly grey jumper that made him look like he was wearing school uniform. He had a very punchable face. Mark thought about lumping him. Didn't. Instead he walked out of the house without saying anything else.

He felt no surprise at Andy Shreeve's behaviour and he knew it was dumb to feel pissed off at him. It was hardly the boy's fault if Eve had a thing for him. But he was depressed by Ali, though he knew he shouldn't be. These kids were only fifteen – babies really – and all's fair when it comes to making out. Why should you be all hands off just because you know your best mate fancies the same chess prodigy that you do?

When he got home the pub was quiet. The last of the regulars had rolled off home and his mum was wiping tables. She looked weary, defeated, bloody knackered.

She was wearing the face that the punters never saw. He asked how the battle with Eve ended.

'Oh she piped down in the end. I think she put her headphones on.'

'Maybe you were a bit harsh Mum.'

'I know. But she's maddening, that girl.'

'She's at a difficult age.'

'We're all at difficult ages, son. That doesn't ever stop.'

Mark popped his head into Eve's room. She wasn't there. He sniffed the air which was a pungent syrup of tobacco, joss sticks and booze. On the table next to the bed squatted a half-empty bottle of three-star Napoleon brandy. It made him smile. She'd gone for the good stuff, the stuff no customer in the Blue Pig ever asked for.

He could see the notebook on her desk, a couple of verses of her song. It wasn't finished, being mostly crossings-out and scrawled second thoughts. He read a few lines. It was all blood and darkness. Rain on flayed skin. Hearts and bones and tombstones. He couldn't decide whether it was any good or not. Anyway, lyrics without music are always half-formed things. Limbless creatures. Flightless birds.

He didn't notice the letter under the notebook. That mad letter that talked about becoming a bird, a cat, a butterfly. Of watching over them all.

He walked the few steps to the bathroom. Knocked softly.

'Hey, hey Sis.'

There was no answer. He knocked again and still there was no reply. Still sulking, or maybe she had her phones

on even in the bathroom. It was possible. No one loved music as much as Eve.

I find I have to stop then. There's a pain in my heart, another in my head and sudden liquid heat behind my eyelids.

'You don't have to tell me any more if you don't want to,' says Lulu.

But I do. I tell her about going back to my room, about listening to the stolen album of songs of Scott Walker.

I tell her about the panicked banging on my bedroom door just as side one comes to a finish. I tell her about joining forces with my red-faced and yelling father to knock the bathroom door in. I tell her about my sister's pale body lying in cool pinkish water. I tell her about my mother's unbearable screaming, a sound no one should ever have to hear.

I tell her about my own unnatural calm. The calm I still can't forgive myself for.

I tell her how I made the redundant call for the ambulance, how I went back into Eve's room, found the fucking stupid letter and also the little bottles of the pills that no one knew she was taking, the pills that were meant to keep her afloat through those teenage years when the news commits violence to your heart, when the small betrayals of friends cut deep, when everyday pressures can feel like they are crushing the very life out of you.

'What the bloody hell are those?' said my dad, his voice shaking.

I tell Lulu about the strange limbo afterwards, about life picking itself up after a fashion, dusting itself down in a dazed kind of way and dragging itself forward towards

the old rhythm of opening times and closing times and barrels that need changing. Crisps. The Eazyzap.

I tell her how I somehow staggered on zombie-like, lurching towards exams and towards Cambridge. How, once I was there, I discovered love at the same time as I discovered someone to blame for my sister's death. Actually met the guy who was responsible. Who might have been responsible anyway. Sort of. Maybe she could imagine how that did my brain in.

After a moment I tell her about how I see Eve now, see her all the time, every day in the faces of my children. Sometimes in the faces of other people's children, and sometimes in the look of any bright-eyed girl on the streets. That I see her in the faces of schoolgirls and prostitutes and policewomen and in the defiant eyes of those rare office workers who will meet your eyes on the Tube. The ones you know are fighting hard not to be ground down by admin systems and senior management.

I tell her how, even when there's no one around, I can still sometimes feel her presence in the air. The crushed petal smell of the hair gel she used, the sudden song of a laugh just like hers, that these things can have me staring round me, wondering where she might be hiding. That sometimes, I see her in the birds, in the cats, in the fucking squirrels. *I'll be the voice in the wind, the bird on your window sill that seems strangely tame.*

I tell her all of that. Then I stop and listen to the dark.

'Hey,' she says. 'Hey, you're allowed to be heartbroken. Everyone's allowed that.'

52

We don't talk much on the way to Cambridge. At Lulu's request, I'm doing the driving today, sticking to B-roads because we are fairly certain Jake will have given the car's registration number to the police.

We have the radio on. Radio One. It's comforting. The DJs are inane in a peculiarly English way. I don't know any of their names – I haven't listened to Radio One since the days of Simon Bates and DLT – but they are in the tradition I recognise from when I was a nipper. A bit flirty, a bit saucily hyperactive, a bit laddish – especially the women – but sweet really, somehow kid-next-doorish. Unthreatening is what they are, and the music is easy enough to daydream over.

Lulu is restless however. 'How can you stand driving on these mickey mouse roads?' she says. And later, 'Flip, the places some people get to live.'

She means places like Boxford and Cavendish and Clare – places that radiate a sense of quiet superiority,

with their ancient pink-washed houses, their farmers' markets, their cheese shops. Their smug signs welcoming us to their village and asking us to drive carefully.

Stebbing Bardfield has a sign reading '500 years of creativity' as you drive in.

'I bet that is such a lie,' says Lulu. 'I bet it's 480 years of growing turnips and twenty years of artisan bread and designing websites. And all that please drive carefully through our village stuff. What's so special about their blinking village? What are we meant to say "Oh, gee, thanks for reminding me, I was about to put my foot down, but now I won't"? Are we allowed to drive as fast as we like through shitty places? Makes me sick.'

'There are some nice houses around here, huh?'

She laughs. 'Yes there are. And yes, I'm quite jealous. I must be getting old. I didn't used to care about houses.'

The miles crawl by. Hedges and fields and roadkill. We let the DJ burble to the nation about her hangover for a while, before Lulu reaches forward and snaps her off, replacing her with some hardcore hip-hop. At least I assume it's hardcore. It feels like it to me. It's like being assaulted. It's like being in the centre of a riot in a Bronx nightclub. Like being beaten round the head by baseball bats made from the bones of dead jazz drummers. I quite like it. Or at least, I like the contrast between the sounds inside the car and the feudal agrarian world outside the windows.

Just audible under the music, the satnav's chilly, vaguely S&M schoolmarm tone is directing me to bear left and then bear right on the B1179.

Lulu is asleep. She has the experienced traveller's knack

of falling asleep anywhere at any time and I think about maybe not going back to Selwyn Gardens. Maybe I don't have to do that.

I think about a room in a shared house, a cash-in-hand job in a pub in a big city. Not London obviously but somewhere an ordinary person could afford to live. Birmingham maybe. It's coming up in the world. Or Manchester, Sheffield, Leeds, Newcastle, Glasgow. Somewhere like that.

Or maybe I could get an old camper van and simply drift from lay-by to campsite to car park. I could make a living doing the gardens of old ladies in villages like the ones we're driving through. Maybe I could keep up with the kids on the net, through emails, through digital files of all kinds. Some careful skyping. Surely it's never been easier to be an absent father and still be a presence in the lives of your children?

Or maybe it would actually be kinder to vanish altogether. Maybe, in time, I could have a new wife, new children even. It's not an unattractive notion, is it? Just rip everything up and start again.

I think now about all the times I meant to sit down and work out a proper plan. To get myself a refuge, somewhere to run to should the need arise. To quietly rent a static caravan in a part of the world where I'm not known. Didn't even have to be a caravan, could have been a garage even. An allotment with a shed on would have been something.

I could have got a false ID. I'd actually researched it once. Found out how you get the birth certificate of a baby that's died, how you present it as your own, use it to open bank accounts, get passports, driving licences, mortgages. There was even an easy way to get a new

national insurance number though I can't remember the details.

Somehow I just didn't get around to it and the years passed the way years do, as did the terrifying dreams. Italy helped with that of course. And Katy.

Italy and Katy worked on me together until I recovered enough to come back and finish my degree. Little things at first: cheap wine, slow sex. Days spent talking about nothing important. Lots of laughing at Italian soap operas. The days when Katy knew I couldn't laugh, when the TV had to go off. The way she knew when a row about politics was exactly what we needed. The day she showed me you could cook omelettes without oil and still get them out of the pan intact if you were quick and skilful. The time she took off all her clothes at midnight on a Tuscan beach. The day I realised she only cried at the happy parts of movies: the lover returns, the family is mended, the abandoned boy/girl/alien doesn't die, but gets to go home instead.

Later, back in England, there were the miracles of our children of course, but Katy's qualities hit me at other, more unexpected times too. When Jack challenged her to bottle flip and she did it first time. The parents' evening when, bored with waiting for Mrs Baptiste to finish with the family before us, she climbed the rope that hung in the primary school hall. So many moments like this. Katy, Jack, Ella, I owe them everything. Then I wonder if maybe I owe them leaving them alone

From Kedington to Great Wratting. From Little Bradley to Brinkley and on through Balsham, all the ghosts of possible future lives crowd in and jostle me and are only dispelled by the outraged bellow of a car horn. I'd been drifting into the path of a tractor. Shit.

I straighten up, get the car back on the right side of the narrow road.

I look across at Lulu. She's awake now and watching me carefully, as if she's been reading my thoughts. She turns down the music.

'This is Jake's thing really. I'm more of a Fleetwood Mac kind of a girl.'

A voice cuts in. That voice you don't argue with.

'In three hundred yards take the first exit and enter the roundabout.'

There's a moment of quiet.

Lulu says, 'Are you one of those men who think the satnav lady's voice is hot?'

I blush. I know I do. I can't help it. Beside me Lulu chuckles. Chortles even. I've only ever heard one other person laugh like that. Eve. My heart turns over.

'Why are blokes always so blinking obvious?' she says cheerily, and settles down to kip again.

53

Jack is woken by the sound of shellfire. He scurries down the corridor holding Benji by the ear. Mum watching the news on her laptop. Warships blasting a pirate base on the East African coast. He is disappointed to find Ella is already in the bed next to her, he'd thought he might be first for once. But no.

He looks at his mum. She is in tears.

'Just kids trying to make a buck,' she says. 'No one told them they could be blown to bits.'

Jack watches as a missile sends a cloud of dust into the sky. He knows what that dust is made of. It is bits of the bricks of houses, but it's also bits of people. Bones and skin and hair.

There's a shot of the ship now. Tanned men in white t-shirts cheering as the rockets whoosh away into the sky. He's excited because he knows about all this.

'That's a Type 23 Frigate,' he says. 'Duke class. Fires

missiles called harpoons that can hit places eighty miles away.'

'You complete spoon,' says Ella.

His mum is giving him a hard look, and he is concerned that she hasn't tried to wipe away the wet on her cheeks, though she has a box of tissues next to the bed. 'Jack, you worry me sometimes. Where did you learn that?'

His heart sinks. He's done something wrong, though he can't think what it is. It's good to know stuff, right?

'At the library. They have a book there called *Jane's Fighting Ships*. Dad told me about it once. It tells you about every warship there is.'

'See, Mum, I've always said we shouldn't go to the library. It's dangerous. It'll give Jack ideas. It'll turn him into a freak like Dad.'

'Hush now.' Mum is frowning but she doesn't look really cross. The news has changed too. It's football now, which means Mum will switch it off soon, which is okay. Jack has decided he doesn't care about football. He's just going to concentrate on the judo.

'Kids,' Mum says. 'How do you fancy a great big massive huge adventure?'

'Yay!' says Ella.

'Before school?' says Jack.

'Instead of school,' says Mum.

'Double yay!' says Ella.

'All right,' says Jack.

'Well, don't get too excited,' says Mum. 'Trust me it'll be fun, now we got to get ready. Wesley is coming to pick us up in two hours.'

Wesley? Wesley? Who is Wesley? They don't know anyone called Wesley, do they?

'You'll like him,' says Mum. 'He knows a lot of facts

too. Mostly about cycling, it's true, but I'm sure you'll get on.'

'Is it like a holiday, Mum?'

'Like a holiday, yes.'

Jack wants to say that it's not right to go for holidays in school time, and shouldn't they wait for Daddy to come home? What if they're away when the baby decides to come? But he knows this is the wrong thing to say right now. No point saying things that no one wants to hear.

Ella is already out of the bed and heading for her room. She calls from the landing. 'Mum, will I need my guitar and should I bring my swimming costume?'

Mum gives it some quick thought.

'Leave the guitar, bring your cossie,' she says.

54

An hour before dawn. A brick through a window. A fire in the garden of an empty house three streets away from Selwyn Gardens. A young woman makes a 999 call from a phone box. She says there's suspicious characters breaking in. The call handler asks her to stay on the line, but she lets the receiver drop. Walks away.

It's an old ploy, one Lulu heard about from Jake but, as she says, that doesn't necessarily mean it won't work. Lulu's theory is that when they get the call they'll send the nearest car and that will be our guys.

'They'll be wanting action. They'll love the chance to put out a fire, to see if there are any vandals around to give a clip around the ear to, any tramps to bollock.'

When they go to deal with this non-incident we'll get in to where we need to be. When she suggests this as a plan I try to argue against it. It sounds flimsy to me, way too simple for a start. But what is the alternative? It is a relief to decide to do something.

Anyway, she's right. I see them go past me, the woman driving, her male companion rubbing his hands. Her serious, him gleeful, desperate to get stuck in. My fist closes tight around the key Bim gave me.

I'm back in that garage. I'm fine. Really. It doesn't unnerve me that much. Probably not as much as it should. It's just another storeroom, a place that smells of rust and damp. A place to keep shovels and rope.

It doesn't even smell of exhaust fumes. Not really. A slight tang of petrol maybe, but all garages have that. No, it's just a space full of junk like any other garage anywhere in the world. Old paint tins. A muddy mountain bike entangled with a girl's shopper in shiny pink complete with basket. A broken chair, some plastic boxes of yellowing newspapers. An old washing machine. A stunt kite. A tent untidily crammed into its bag after some long-forgotten family holiday. A large bucket. Garden forks and spades. A hover-mower. A wheelbarrow. A chest freezer. A set of golf clubs in a battered tan bag. A cricket bat.

Just stuff. Ordinary stuff. No ghosts.

I am startled by a whisper in the darkness.

'Now, switch off the electrics.' I do as Lulu asks and we move into the kitchen, where I locate the landline handset by means of the pinprick of green light. A simple job to snip the wire.

This James Bond routine is Lulu's idea too. She'd told me I had to cut off the power to stop Anne alerting the police by switching lights on, and we sure as hell don't want her making any calls. We want to be able to talk to her properly, really make sure she's listening.

It all makes me very, very tense. I am fighting to control

my rising panic. It is lucky that Lulu had insisted I go to the bathroom before we began.

'The one thing I know for certain about breaking into houses is that you always want to go for a dump the moment you're inside,' she'd said.

Another gem from Jake, I guess.

She'd shrugged. 'No, actually. Got it from TV. Which is where everyone learns these things. Where even blinking spies learn them.'

We move down the spacious hallway. Twenty-three years since I was last in this house. But I know my way around it seems. Don't have to think too hard. Which is good.

Lulu whispers, 'You go upstairs. I'll have a poke around down here.'

I'm at the foot of Anne's bed watching her sleeping. Again, I am surprised by how little I feel. Yes, it's probably wrong that I'm here, that I didn't find a way to ring the doorbell and just announce myself honestly. It's reckless too. But I had to do something and, actually, reckless feels good right now. Feels right anyway.

My sense is that the room is pretty much unaltered, though in this dark it's hard to tell. I find I can't really remember the colour of the walls or the carpet, like I can't recall where the wardrobe was, the chest of drawers, the mirror. I remember the bed though. This big bed, surely this is the same one.

In this curtained pre-dawn gloom Anne's hardly there. She's not really recognisable as a person. She's just a small, indistinct shape under the covers. The room is cool, like a chapel of rest. She could be dead already. I could be a distant family member come to pay my respects.

I can hear the rain hiss outside. I can hear pipes murmur as they flex somewhere in this big old house. I can hear these things, but I can't hear Anne breathing. I can't see the rise and fall of her chest beneath the quilt. She's just a shadow amid other shadows. Hardly real at all. A dream.

In Italy, just after it all happened, I hardly slept at all, but when I did, finally, nod out, then I dreamed of Sheldon and Anne a lot. The two of them hand in hand. Looking at me and smiling, showing all their teeth. Like they had joint enterprises I would never be part of. I could never recall any other details after, but I would jerk awake, heart racing, covered in sweat with the sense of having narrowly escaped something terrible. But of course I hadn't escaped.

Now my eyes begin to get used to the murky light, which in any case is growing stronger by the minute. I have no idea of how long I've been standing here. The body in the bed is tiny. She takes up almost no space beneath the heavy cream of the quilt. Her face becomes a pale shiver in the night. From here it seems unlined and the only giveaway to her age is the hair that falls across it. It is expensively, carefully, blonded. She used to be so dark. For a second I have the lunatic urge to stroke that new hair, touch that face. To see her scars.

Her eyes don't twitch or flicker behind her lids.

I have to make something happen. I can't just stand here like this. There are some essential tasks as detailed for me by Lulu. The first of them is to cross to the bedside table where, next to a glass of water, a mobile phone is charging. Another of those winking green lights by which we measure out our life these days. I disconnect that. Take out the battery. Put the useless phone back on the

table. Then the plan is to just be here when she wakes and somehow or other make her see the sense of withdrawing her statement.

While we'd sat for hour upon hour in Lulu's car eating crisps and listening to the full range of radio voices, she had asked exactly what I hoped to achieve from my meeting with Anne. What would success for this mission look like?

I'd explained that I was thinking I could persuade her, even now, to retract her statement to the police. She could say she was having a breakdown, hallucinations, false memories. Maybe she could tell them that her cancer medication was – is – playing havoc with her thinking, that her oncologist warned her this might happen. We know, don't we, about how prescription drugs can interfere with rational thinking.

I'd told Lulu how I was hopeful that if Anne knew about the life I've built – about Ella, Jack, Katy, the Bump – she'd see sense. If I had to I'd tell her about teaching – the parade of lost boys who have ended up saved. Some of them more than saved, some of them proper success stories. The hoodlums who have become historians, the thugs who have become theologians. The truants who have become good teachers in their turn.

If she withdraws her statement she'll be helping herself too. Bim told us that she's out on police bail right now, but if she sticks with her story then she's looking at her final years or months spent inside and – despite what you sometimes read – prisons are no picnic.

We had rehearsed the conversation, Lulu and I. She had taken the Anne Sheldon role, her job to be as intransigent as possible, and every time we ran it Lulu pronounced herself won over in the end.

'But I still think you should have a plan B,' Lulu said.

She had more tips about how to approach Anne too. She warned me that I couldn't just launch in. Said that if you wanted people to listen carefully to you, then you had to get them to open up first and you did that by listening to them. I told her, probably slightly tetchily, that I knew this rule already.

At work, at home, with children, with everyone everywhere, listen before you talk. *Listen more.* Or, at the very least, look as though you are listening. My tattoo itches.

'Knowing something and doing something can be very different,' she said.

It comes to me now that I haven't checked the other bedrooms. Only now do I consider the possibility that there might be other people in the house. God, we are so useless at this. So unfitted for this kind of action. I can't believe we've been so sloppy. But then I'm an amateur. Haven't watched enough television. I listen hard. There is creaking from downstairs, rustling. Lulu probably, or it could be the house stretching and sighing the way that old houses do. I need to be sure. It could get very messy if there was a guest or a relative staying here, someone who could be alerted by a shout or a scream.

I tiptoe out, complete a tour of the upstairs rooms. No posters anywhere now. I wonder what happened to the old adverts for the theatre shows and the exhibitions. When did they get binned?

A few stealthy minutes and I'm back at the door of Anne's room. Only this time the bed is empty. Shit.

Back down the stairs, not worrying so much about noise now, heart beginning to race, my breath becoming

shallower, sweat breaking out under my arms. My stomach cramping.

Adrenalin. Just adrenalin. All it is.

A hotly whispered conversation with Lulu who tells me that no one has got past her. She shows me that the doors at the front and back are both closed, and surely anyone escaping would have left them open behind them, would be up and down the street already, screaming for the neighbours. Yelling for the police who could be back at their station by now; there's been none of that, so Anne is still in the house somewhere. She was probably still in the bedroom when I came back to it. In a wardrobe maybe. Or under the bed. Wasn't it possible she'd been faking sleep while I did the business with the phone, while I did all that dumb standing and staring, while I was thinking about stroking her face?

Back up the stairs. All this to-ing and fro-ing, all this up and down-ing. Too much. Painful. Almost comical.

But if I'm methodical I will find her.

It seems that Anne has reached the same conclusion because by the time I'm halfway up the stairs, she is there on the landing. She is wearing white pyjamas with some kind of design printed on them in pink. They don't seem very Anne-like somehow. The 1990 Anne wouldn't have worn them. She's holding a pair of scissors in one hand and her useless mobile phone in the other. Her face, so peacefully closed as I was gazing down upon it minutes ago, is alive now. Alive and fierce. Cat-like.

I move towards her. I recognise the distinctive spice of her scent. Still the same after all these years. I shudder slightly. I can't help it, that fragrance will always take me back to places where I don't want to go. Places that I never left.

I keep my arms down by my side, make myself as unthreatening as possible, even while keeping my steps up the stairs purposeful and determined.

Anne seems to make a decision. As I reach the landing, she darts forward, slashing at me with the scissors. She's deft and she's quick, I can feel the point of them graze my shirt. I lean back, have to grab at the bannister to keep from falling. She stabs up towards my throat now, the point scraping my neck.

I grab her wrist as I step up onto the landing. It's so twig-like I could snap it with no effort at all. I squeeze and twist. Not too hard, just a Chinese burn really, no more than that, but she gives a little gasp, just a sharp breath, and the scissors drop to the polished wood of the floor with a clatter. Too loud. Too fucking loud.

Still holding her wrist, I grip the collar of her pyjamas and sweep her legs from beneath her fast with my left foot. It's a judo move, one I picked up from watching Jack and Ella's coach go through it on a hundred Saturday mornings. As she hits the floor, I see what the little motif is that covers her pyjamas. Love hearts. Little pink love hearts. I have time to wonder if that's who she is now. Is this what I'm dealing with now? A woman who covers herself in tiny love hearts? Do people change that much?

She gasps again, but makes no other sound. She makes much less noise in hitting the parquet than the scissors did. Neither of us has said a word. There's just been these quick hot breaths. It takes no time for me to have her on her knees, her arm bent up behind her back, my hand over her mouth and nose.

I stop myself. I need to be careful. She is what? Sixty? Sixty-one? Not properly old but on the way to it. And ill. Even without cancer, soon she'd be entering the zone of

routinely holding on to handrails, of not going out in the snow. I have to remember that she is fragile, breakable. I need her goodwill.

Of course I remember now that we loved each other once, that we spent days and nights wrapped up in each other. That my skin carries the memory of hers in every movement I make.

I am calm, soothing. I tell her she'll be okay. I just want to talk. That there are things I want to tell her, things she needs to know. And, staying calm, staying soothing but keeping my palm tight across her lips, my voice as steady as rain, I explain that I can't allow her to shout or scream and she should nod if she understands this. I feel a movement against my hand, probably an attempt at a nod, but I need to be sure.

I keep my voice even as I tell her how desperate I am, how I will break her neck if I have to, that I could do it. That a hurt and angry part of me wants to do it. Does she understand me? If she does I need a proper sign. A proper nod.

She makes sure there's no doubt about it now. A fervent bobbing of the head. Still, I wait a few seconds before unpeeling my hand from her lips and moving it to her hair. I help her stand.

Now she speaks. Her voice a tired whisper.

'Enjoy that, did you?' But she gives me no time to answer. 'This is a mistake, Mark. What you might call a strategic blunder.' She rallies, becomes brisk, seems to decide to take charge. The old authoritative voice is back. The languid smile hiding in it, just as it always did. With the old voice comes an old question. 'Coffee? Or shall we have wine?'

55

We have wine. Of course we do. There's a rack in the kitchen next to the kettle where most people keep their tea and coffee. Anne tells me that down in the cellar there are still a few bottles of the professor's really good stuff, the stuff they were drinking all those years ago.

'Saved a couple of bottles for a really special occasion,' she says. I don't know if I believe her.

She sits compliant in the living room while I light the stove. She doesn't seem intimidated by Lulu. She just ignores her. Pointedly addresses no remarks to her as she tells me where to find candles.

Once they're lit it's weirdly cosy. We even do small talk. Of a kind. I tell her she looks well. She tells me that I look fucking old. Knackered. That I've let myself go and no mistake. I don't rise to it, because sticks and stones and all that. Words will never hurt you. She sits opposite me on the sofa now, wrapped in a blanket, savouring her wine like a duchess. I notice that all the sculptures have

gone. No obsidian ladies or babies. No orbs and cubes. The house could be any suburban home now.

'Almost romantic,' she says. Her eyes shine with mischief and I feel some of the old tug at my heart.

From her chair in the corner Lulu snorts.

I don't say anything. But I feel sort of hopeful now. I'm wondering if this – getting me here – was maybe the whole point of the confession in the first place, like a child having a tantrum to get attention. I can imagine that. As the light dies you want to be noticed, you want your former lovers to gather around to reassure you that, hey, you were quite something once. You broke hearts, made strong men cry. Had boys queue to carry your books. You want to call out into the dying light and have people, men, come running like they used to. Just another way of crying for help.

She's cried out and here I am. Now we can sort it.

First, I apologise for breaking in. For hurting her. I tell her I'm just desperate. There's a silence. She coughs wetly into her hand. Sighs.

'You didn't hurt me,' she says.

'Good. Good,' I say.

'You can't hurt me now. No one can.' She coughs again, takes another sip at her wine, makes a face.

I don't answer. Instead I ask how she's been.

'Didn't we have a rule once? About not telling each other sad stories?' she says. I tell her it's a rule we've maybe outgrown. She sighs and says if I'm going to insist, then she's going to need a cigarette. Not a real one. An eFag.

'Absurd, isn't it?' she says. 'I'm trying to give up and these digital dummies, they're meant to help.'

'Do they?'

'Not really.'

Her story is a sad one, though she tells it matter-of-factly, without self-pity. Twenty-odd years of bad luck and bad choices. The men who are happy to go to bed with her but cagey about living with her. The men who are desperate to live with her, but whom she can't bring herself to go to bed with. Her French husband was in that category actually.

I hear about the jobs she gets easily, but can't be bothered to actually do. The jobs she loses. Then there are the illnesses. The disorders. The breakdowns. Not hers – her daughter's.

Dorcas begins with self-harm before her twelfth birthday and moves steadily through the phases like she's following some carefully worked out timetable. A demonic twelve-step programme of her very own. Anorexia, shoplifting, drinking, dope, expulsion from a string of posh schools, the running away, Ibiza, the wrong men, the hard drugs, the hard men, the wrong drugs, the stays in hospital, the therapy that encourages her to blame her issues on her mother.

Anne tells me all this with a resigned, ironic tone that implies her main problem with this series of fuck-ups is that they are so predictable. That she is disappointed that her daughter has bought into all the clichés of contemporary crashing and burning. That it is just embarrassing more than anything.

'After having been away fuck knows where, doing fuck knows what with fuck knows who without a word for nearly three years – she ends up back and she's so angry, Mark. Really angry. All the time. Unbearable.' She sighs. 'Except when it's your children you sort of have to bear

it. One night she tells me that she is sure I was responsible for Philip's death.'

I remember a child's face at an upstairs window. The solemn look, a little hand waving.

'Of course we were drinking. I tried not to when Dorcas was around but you know sometimes…' her voice trails off. She sits staring into the stove as if there are answers in the glowing coals. I prompt her a little, taking care to keep my voice paramedic-mild, bereavement counsellor-soft. The way I'd practised with Lulu. I don't want to spook her now I've got her this far.

'What happened then?'

Anne looks at me reluctantly, like it takes her a real effort.

'Well, it just spilled out, the whole sorry fucking mess. Next morning Dorcas said I had to go to the police but I didn't, not then. I told her not to be so bloody stupid. But after she'd disappeared again and the months passed without a word from her I thought… I thought…' she tails off, then makes an effort. 'I suppose when I got my diagnosis I thought maybe it had been what I did – what we did – that was making me ill. That keeping a secret like this had become corrosive, become a disease.'

So there it is. Voodoo. She thinks that it is her secret that is killing her.

It's all too much for Lulu. There is an explosive breath from the dark corner where she sits. We'd forgotten about her.

'How dumb. How utterly, utterly stupid.'

'What?' Anne's voice is sharp and I am reminded of all the times she mocked me for using this word. The way she once told me it was my catchphrase, the way it should be on my gravestone. What? What?

'Makes me furious when people say things like that. Makes me sick to my stomach,' Lulu says.

I try to throw her a warning look, try to will her into silence. But she won't be stopped. 'Cancer doesn't care about secrets like it doesn't care about stress or worry or your memories. Cancer is not psychosomatic. It's not a psychological illness and it's not punishment for sins. It's caused by genetics, or poor diet or bad luck. It has medical causes. Christ. I was told you were clever.'

I know Lulu is right. Secrets can be damaging, of course they can, but only if they are handled recklessly. They aren't corrosive in themselves. They react with air. They're like cyanide, sarin, smallpox – potentially lethal, yes – but safe enough if properly stored.

'Charming girl, Marko,' says Anne. 'Where did you find her?'

I know I need to go carefully now. Because if I do the thing about my wife, my life, my lovely accomplished children, it could do more harm than good. I'll be asking Anne not to rock the boat so my children can go to grammar schools, drama clubs, oboe lessons while she is busy dying and her own child is maybe trading blowjobs for ketamine in some rat pit somewhere – and well, that might not be good politics. I need to be subtle, nuanced. I need to undo the damage done by Lulu's intervention.

'Maybe you can boil a kettle, love,' I say.

'Don't you "love" me.' But Lulu heaves herself up from her chair and moves out of the living room with a petulant toss of her head. I'm irritated at her taking offence because I only called her love to avoid saying her name out loud.

Anne laughs, which annoys me. Maybe this little spat with Lulu has disrupted my concentration or maybe I've

been made stupid by stress, by driving, by adrenalin, by tiredness, by all the fucking listening I've done. Whatever, something makes me forget where I am, lose sight of what I'm trying to accomplish here.

'Only it wasn't actually the whole story that spilled out, was it Anne?' I say.

There is a long silence. A suck on her glowing tube. Little puffs of non-toxic water vapour. An anxious ducking towards her glass. Sip. Sip. Sip. In the old days she was never a sipper.

She tops up our drinks. Her hand shakes so that the bottle neck taps an erratic rhythm on the glasses. Her wrist is as delicate and as fragile as a sparrow's leg. There is a red mark on it where I held her. A spreading bruise. She is, I see now, still very beautiful. Her skin might be webbed with a mesh of delicate lines, but she's still beguiling. She still has that power. She looks up at me quickly. It's as if she has noticed a new charge in the room, a quickening in the atmosphere.

'Yes, you're right,' she says. 'I maybe did downplay my role in things for Dorcas's sake. And maybe I did build your part up. He was her father after all. You and I Marko, we were in it together, weren't we?'

Does she really think that? Can she really think that?

'Where's Dorcas now?' I say. I am bone tired, shivery, depressed by the thought that there is still quite a lot of negotiating to be done. But I need to keep the conversation going.

'God knows. On past form I should see her again sometime in late 2020. Or would if I was likely to still be around then. Earlier maybe if she gets herself busted, or pregnant or sick. I was hoping she'd maybe hear about our arrests and come back then.'

Sip. Suck. A long breath out.

'I don't want to die without seeing her again.'

'Kids. Always a worry.'

She laughs. 'Thanks for that insight Dr Spock. You got children?'

'Two. Nearly three.'

Now's the moment: I explain about the Bump. I'm about to tell her – carefully – about my life, about to seize the opening she's given me, about to appeal to her better nature, when her eyes flicker to a point behind my left shoulder.

I turn my head, just in time to see a small black shadow moving fast. I have time to see the wild-eyed bearded face behind it. A moment later the speeding shadow hits me full in the face. The world explodes into all the colours of flame.

I am on the floor. I am being struck over and over again with savage force, my body is revealed as nothing more than a leaky bag of liquids. From the remote place my consciousness has been flung to, the blunt force of the weapon hitting my flesh becomes a strangely distant, abstract thing. Between the frenzied blows I still somehow have time to try and work out what it is he is hitting me with. A golf club from the cellar maybe? Or one of those heavy pans from the pot rack? A cricket bat?

My ribs, my head, my back, my hips, I am hit everywhere. Impossible to imagine I will ever get up again.

I am certain I am going to die. I have my arms over my face. I'm all curled up but still I can feel my bones crack, my skull splinter, my skin rip. I bite my tongue, taste hot blood in my mouth. The blows keep coming and all I want to do is sleep. Weird.

'Jimmy. That's enough.'

Seems like the beating keeps on for a while though. I can't tell how long exactly this Jimmy keeps it up – could be a minute, could be ten. He hits me so fucking hard. I can feel the blood running into my mouth from my nose, see light bursting behind my eyelids like fragmenting wishes, like missiles falling among fishermen's shacks.

Suddenly there is the beautiful floating weightlessness of the cessation of pain. The sudden blue sky of it. The rainbow of it. Maybe I am actually dying now.

When Anne speaks again it's like a voice is coming from a far-off galaxy. No disguising the triumph in it, however.

'Marko. You remember Dr James Masterson. Still looking out for me.' The sound of a kiss. 'Never considered that I'd have a lover did you, Mark? I won't lie, I'm a bit insulted by that.' And, brusque now, 'Hold him there my sweetheart, while I call the police. Where's your phone?'

I'm lying there, running through my options, thinking that there'll be some faff, that the phone won't work. There'll be confusion. If I can just get a breath then I can get up, fight Masterson off, make a break for it. They won't catch me. You see, it's hard to kill off hope. Hope is really fucking resilient.

Where's Lulu? I hope she's already out of the house, back in the car, already leaving this place behind her, already taming the night into a harmless story, a quirky anecdote. I hung out with this guy who was on the run once. Only there's a whirr above me, the sudden whine of metal through air, and another effortful grunt, another explosion on the side of my face.

No point doing anything now. It's over.

I lie back on the dark teak of the floor, put my stinging

cheek against the beautiful cool of it, the welcoming dust of it. How old was the tree when it was felled? Five hundred? A thousand? Just to make this floor. The dust, all that's left of our ancestors. Our ancestors and their pets. How we all end up.

I remember something now, Anne crouching above me on this very floor, maybe on this very spot. Lowering herself carefully onto me while telling me quietly but firmly what do with my hands.

Another sharp crack and then my face is on fire again.

'James!'

'Okay, okay. I'll stop now. Just, ah, feels so good.'

I open my eyes, see the world as if through a thick reddish fog. I hear Anne breathing heavily close to me, it's definitely her, I know all the rhythms of her breathing, even after all this time. I can smell the spice of her. She cradles my head. Her touch is light.

'You stupid boy,' she whispers. 'Exquisite, but stupid. Philip always said you had a third-rate brain. Never quite thinking things through.'

Nothing to do but wait. To wait for the end of everything. Relief comes over me like a second duvet on a chilly night. Like your wife snuggling up against your back on a Sunday morning. I burrow into the comforting warmth of it. I am beyond fighting now. Sleep. Please let me sleep.

My face is wet. Blood and tears.

Anne says, 'Oh, and Jimmy, he has an accomplice in the kitchen, if she hasn't made a run for it. A slip of a girl.'

'Not in the kitchen. Right here. Come on big man, let's see what you got.'

Through sticky, half-closed eyelids I can see the outline of Lulu standing in the doorway, arms by her sides gunslinger loose.

Turns out Dr James Masterson doesn't have all that much. She might be a slip of a girl – and one with limited mobility at that – but Lulu is too quick and too fierce for him. I can't see clearly, the fog in front of my eyes refuses to lift, but I can hear well enough. A series of gasps and grunts sounding curiously sexual, like the noises we heard on the badly dubbed and grainy Scandinavian pornography we all watched back in high school. Like the noises I heard coming from Jake and Lulu's bedroom not three days ago. Seconds later, there's the sound of a grown man crying.

'She's broken my wrist, Anne. She's broken my bloody wrist.' No gloating in the voice now.

Uneven steps across parquet. Laboured breaths.

'Well, this is all a bit of a mess, isn't it?'

Lulu's voice is resigned. She could be complaining about a dropped teacup. I raise my head, try to speak. Fail. Try again. Fail again. Don't fail better. Fail worse.

'Come on, Marko, you're going to have to work with me here. Up you come.'

'No,' I say, as firmly as I can. 'No. Get the fuck out of here. Go on, go.'

The last I see of Lulu is her face frowning in disapproval of my unimaginative use of language, before she walks carefully, so carefully, back towards the kitchen.

'Arrivederci,' I say. I close my eyes, try to think of nothing. It hurts. Every single part of me hurts. A concerto of pain played by a bad amateur orchestra. When I open them Lulu has gone, instead there are two police officers – an Asian woman wearing smart casual

and a pale uniformed bloke with a straggly beard. Syima and Alex I presume. The police, anyway.

'Mr Chadwick,' says the woman. 'You've been leading us a merry dance I must say.'

56

A&E to get my injuries sorted. I have some broken ribs, a shattered nose and several cuts on my face including a particularly nasty one under my left eye, which needs fifteen stitches. These are put in by a jolly nurse who reminds me of Mrs Boyd, my old cleaner from university, much younger but same open-hearted manner. She's unphased by my being accompanied into the treatment room by the police.

'You'll have a scar I reckon. Pretty big one. It'll give your face a bit of character.' She frowns in concentration. I tell her what I know about scars, about them being stronger than skin.

She puts me straight. 'Actually, that's not true. Scar tissue has around 70% of the tensile strength of unwounded skin. Although there is more collagen in a scar, it isn't efficiently structured, and the skin's elastin fibres are not regenerated at all.'

That's me told. Wrong about this, like I've been wrong about pretty much everything my whole life.

The hospital wants to keep me in, but the police officers, well, they're not keen and to be honest I don't care much either way. A bored doctor says he'll discharge me if I'll sign a waiver saying any fits, seizures, strokes, aneurysms or embolisms will all be my own stupid fault – and I find I'm happy to do this.

When we get back to the London nick there's breakfast. Porridge with golden syrup. Then toast and marmalade. Lots of coffee, as many refills as I like, as if I were a customer in a decent unpretentious caff, as if I were somewhere like Ken's Kabin. There is banter, chat about football, some moaning about the weather, the government, how things today are all going to shit, about how everything is broken. Same old chat you hear everywhere. Then I'm left alone in a cell with the newspapers and the information that someone will be along to talk to me in a while.

It really is quite a while. It is the afternoon before we get started. The police read me my rights. All the stuff about not having to say anything but how it will harm my defence if I rely on something in court that I haven't mentioned to them first. They tell me that if I do decide to remain silent a jury will have the right to draw ominous conclusions. I don't really take in the actual words. In fact, I almost giggle. It sounds so fake. It sounds so TV. The carefully neutral, breathily monotone intonation of the reading of the rights sounds borrowed from one of those shows about jaded cops battling crime while dealing simultaneously with complex home lives. But I guess the police learn about how the police are from crime dramas just like everyone else does.

I am careful to make a long, determinedly cheerful-under-the-circumstances statement at the beginning of the interrogation about how I am happy to co-operate with the police investigation and will do everything in my power to help, and that if I say no comment to any question it is not because I am being difficult, but because I am taking the advice of my solicitor, or because I genuinely can't recall the answer and need proper time to think. That it is important to me not to give the police a bum steer, or unintentionally mislead them in any way. I know they are just doing their jobs.

When it comes to court, I want them to have to tell the judge and jury just how goddam co-operative I've been.

I steadfastly no comment my way through the next seventy-two hours.

It's hard. Harder than you'd think. Much harder. Human beings are programmed to speak, to tell stories, to communicate with each other. Seventy-two hours of silence when people want you to talk is a very tricky thing. I only manage it by imagining that I am doing something for school. That this is a sponsored no comment to raise money for a new minibus.

My solicitor is Katy's friend, Amanda Campbell. The last time I saw her we had been sipping peach Bellinis from plastic champagne flutes at the Latitude Festival while our kids roamed the site, happily free-range for an hour or two. That was only a couple of months ago. Imagine that.

Amanda has twins the same age as Jack. She has always seemed flaky to me but Katy always said that if she was ever in trouble, then out of all her solicitor friends Amanda would be her go-to girl.

Here she is, professional in her bible-black trouser suit, giving the steady hum of competence – her very presence irritates the detectives – she gave me a hug when she came to see me in the cell and I almost cried. She asked me how I was and I said fine, about as well as, etc.

I asked about Katy and the kids.

'They'll be fine, Mark. Let's worry about you for now, shall we?'

Amanda's view is that I should plead guilty but argue youth, infatuation, a man led astray, and also play up what a bully and a brute Philip Sheldon was. I ask her what she thinks I'll get and she is brisk in confirming what I have always known.

'Outlook is not good, Mark. I won't lie. Best scenario? Could be ten years. A little less maybe. If you're lucky. Depends on the judge. If they're feeling really vindictive they could even go after you for murder. Joint enterprise.'

She feels the need to explain the concept of joint enterprise. A concept fetishised by the modern courts and hard to beat, no matter how smart the lawyer. At one time – a less viciously unforgiving time, a more nuanced time – it was different. There was room to argue about these things. Nowadays everyone connected to a crime is as guilty as the worst offender. If a bunch of career robbers go into a bank and one, defying orders, packs heat and shoots some dumb have-a-go hero, then everyone from the brains to the getaway driver faces the consequences exactly as if their hands were on the trigger too. How can that be fair?

I know all of this of course, but I let her talk. It's just nice to listen to a more or less friendly voice. Someone on my side.

'I don't think they'll go for that in this case, but they might.'

I'm left thinking whoopee, out by the time Ella is twenty-one. When the Bump is fretting about going to high school.

That's if I'm lucky. If the judge is particularly soft-hearted.

I'm meant to be grateful for that.

Back in the interview room, back to the resolute no commenting, and I think how arrests may be more civilised than they once were, but the sentences – different story. Thirty years, even forty years. At some point in the future there's going to be a substantial cohort of very old men in our jails. Every prison will be a kind of overcrowded Spandau. Full of men who need treatment for Parkinson's and dementia. Men who need oxygen cylinders in their cells, who need wheeling from cell to shower block and back. Men who will need a special class of prison officer to wipe their arses for them.

Maybe that's the future for all those retiring without pensions. Jobs wiping the arses of child-molesters. Doesn't seem right somehow.

These are the kind of thoughts that drift through my mind as I say nothing for hour upon hour. Not productive. I should be thinking hard about finding another way out.

The trouble is – I can't think of it and after a while I stop bothering to try. Instead I dream of escape, of daring breakouts from court.

Even while the detectives are asking me about the events of September 1990 – even while I am steadfastly no commenting – I am running through the plots of every prison breakout film I've ever seen. I am fantasising about hiding in the laundry van as it leaves prison. Of

manufacturing files on the prison lathes. Of helicopters landing on the cell block roof. Of riots and shootouts and hostages. Of tunnels, of ladders and grappling hooks. Of waking up and suddenly finding I am able to fly. The guards' amazed faces as I soar into the clouds from the exercise yard. Suddenly from where I am, up in the sky, they look like frightened little boys.

I'm getting close to the seventy-two hour no comment target – the imaginary minibus almost paid for, hurrah! – when they tell me they've got another forty-eight hours to question me. What do I think of that? It almost breaks me.

They show me some of the press coverage of the story so far. I have been properly monstered.

I am, say the papers, a weirdo loner. I am someone the kids at school all knew was a wrong-un. Creepy. I have no real friends, apparently. Where are Anthony? Jim? Raj? Where are the colleagues I play five-a-side with? Nowhere, that's where. Instead there's the bank guy, Ian, saying how my presence gave him chills, how he knew there was something not right about me. Dead behind the eyes, that's Ian's phrase.

There's the girl from the flat above the Orwell gallery, Jezebel on her hip, apparently my face made her baby cry. And of course I hear Ella saying, 'Your face!' to everything we say. Your face needs to practice; your face needs a good tidy up. Your face is all over the papers.

They say I am aloof, stand-offish, arrogant, odd. There is a photo, taken God knows when, where I am staring straight at the camera unsmiling, eyes slightly bulging. I look like Ian Brady. The neighbours – and they have names I don't recognise – wax lyrical about Katy and the

children, how lovely they are, but they also damn me by saying how quiet I am, how I keep myself to myself and that looks bad, doesn't it? Keeping yourself to yourself in this day and age? Why would anyone do such a thing?

The papers point out that I don't even have a Facebook page. More damning evidence of pathology right there.

There are two detectives questioning me. Syima, the young woman who did the arrest in Selwyn Gardens, and an older guy who introduces himself as Jeff ('with a J'). Jeff points out that once I'm charged it'll all calm down.

'Has to, mate. By law. They're not allowed to prejudice a trial.'

Syima asks me how I feel about my kids reading this kind of stuff? Tells me that I should take the opportunity to tell my own story. It's as if she is a red-top journo herself.

I get so tired, I can feel myself fading, disappearing into a greyish smudge in the slow air and dead light of the interview room where it always feels like it's 3 a.m. There are no windows in this room but somehow there is a fly. A fly literally on the wall, high up. An elderly fly I guess, doesn't move much. Maybe it's not old, maybe it just finds the air as heavy and thick as I do.

Amanda Campbell sits next to me through most of the interviews, but her presence is not comforting. Somehow I begin to sense that she's just going through the motions, that she too can't wait for all this to be over, to get outside, breathe some fresh clean air and get back to defending ordinary decent rapists or whatever.

It's like she knows this is what I'm feeling because she puts her hand on my arm and I'm so grateful that I almost lose it. Almost burst into tears, but I don't. I keep it together. Just.

Suddenly I know I am about to crack. So does everyone else. They all sense it. Amanda Campbell rustles next to me. Jeff and Syima sit up that bit straighter. There's an expectant pause. Now. I'm going to do it now. I know it. They know it. I'm about to break. I can feel the anticipation of the detectives building. Their hearts must be thumping, pulses racing, but they maintain an admirable calm.

Once I've done it, admitted it, volunteered to make a statement, signed a full confession, all that, well, then they can gather their papers, step outside and hug and high five. Maybe they'll go for a pint or ten. Maybe – carried away by the moment – they'll sleep together, they seem like the kind of colleagues that might share those kind of benefits – but whatever they'll do later, for now they wait with exaggerated patience, keeping quiet so as not to spook me. Keeping their breaths small.

Yet, still, somehow, I hold out, delaying the inevitable. The fly takes to the air and I decide that when it lands again, that's when I'll start confessing. The long seconds tick past. Until the tension is broken by the door to this faceless interview room being opened. Both detectives exhale noisily and spin round with a scraping of chairs. I lose track of where that fly zigzags to.

It's Syima's sidekick from the arrest. Alex. Amanda sighs.

'What?' says Jeff, tetchy.

Syima remembers the protocol. She says 'For the benefit of the tape, PC Alex Matthews has entered the room.'

Matthews asks for a word and all three of my companions get up and leave the room. I feel strangely bereft.

Alone I wonder if they still use actual tape, or if it's just an expression. It must all be digital now surely? The

break allows me to harden my resolve again. I decide that, actually, I won't confess. Not just yet. I'll ask Jeff and Syima about the tape business. That might piss them off, pass a minute or two. Pissing off the police, passing the minutes, that is pretty much all I have left.

I have sat there on my own for over thirty minutes and when the door opens again it's just Amanda. No Jeff. No Syima. I stand up, which is when I notice the weird look on Amanda's face. Half puzzled frown, half smile.

'You're free to go, Mark,' she says. 'Congratulations. You can collect your belongings at the front desk.'

She tells me what she's been told and I feel my legs go from under me, I flop back on my plastic seat. The dead light hurting my eyes. The fly lands on the desk in front of me.

57

The officer at the desk is giving me back my possessions with an ill grace. The cheeriness extended towards prisoners has disappeared now that I am a free man. I get my wallet with a crumpled twenty and about 80p in change. I get the last of the Cash Converters phones.

'Stroke of luck for you, wasn't it? Very fucking convenient. Sign here.'

The pen is broken, I just scratch the paper with it, which won't do. She rolls her eyes as she gets another, which works for the time it takes to scrawl a signature, but then leaks a sticky black blob onto my fingers. Her mouth twists and she doesn't offer me a tissue, leaving me with dark, coagulating ink over the back of my ring finger. It looks like the blackest, thickest blood. She smirks sourly. She has something else to say. 'We were never really chasing you, you know. Your case was never really a priority.'

She's saying don't get above yourself, don't go thinking you're important.

Anne Sheldon is dead. A fall down the stairs in Selwyn Gardens while drunk. A broken neck. She was ill, she was shaky on her pins, she was an accident waiting to happen. Amanda Campbell reckons she might even have done it on purpose, who knows?

I try to decide what I feel. I won't weep for Anne, I know that, but I also know that she'll be with me always. Her crooked smile. Her lunatic driving. Her flashing me her breasts one summer's day a lifetime ago. An earring dangling against her perfect neck. Her kiss. The secret paths she showed me. The ones that took me from the world I'd been born into to a brighter place. Even if it was a place I was too afraid to stay in. Every time I pour myself a glass of wine I'll think of her. And I know a part of me – not the best part, but an important part – has died with her.

Amanda is still talking. In a few dry sentences she tells me that by the time poor James Masterson discovered her Anne was already stiff, already cold. She tells me that without her evidence the CPS have no realistic prospect of conviction. Or to put it another way, 'The old bill have fuck all on you and they know it.'

'What about Dorcas? What if they find her?'

'She was a child back then. Her evidence would have been useful back-up to her mother's testimony, but on its own? Thin, very thin. Decent QC would dismantle that no bother.'

'What about the other charges?' I mean the breaking and entering, the assault rap the police had been very keen to pursue along with the murder just a little while ago.

'Again, chief witness is no longer with us. The only one who got hurt was you. You might even have grounds for a civil case against the boyfriend. I think you could argue he used disproportionate force in restraining you.' She gives a tired smile. 'I don't recommend it, though. Judges and juries are pretty anti-those-who-break-in-to-property. They tend to think people who do that deserve all they get.'

I get the feeling that this is her own opinion too.

She tells me she has to go, that she has other cases, but before she click-clacks off in her lawyer's shoes she has time to tell me that I'm not to worry about Katy. 'She's nails, Mark. Really. A tough cookie.'

'I know,' I say.

'Ella and Jack will be fine too. Wherever they end up. They'll come through all this. Kids are resilient.'

Which is what people say, but I have never really believed it. Previous generations of kids might have been resilient, but not this one. What does she mean wherever they end up?

Amanda turns to go, then turns back. Hugs me again. Tells me that if was up to her she wouldn't bill me for her time, but you know how it is.

I do. I also know that I won't ever see her again. There will be no more festivals. No more peach Bellinis in plastic flutes.

58

I wake just as the boiler fires up. I wait under the yeasty duvet while the radiators clank and all the old wood in the house groans as it expands. These reclaimed floorboards, these salvaged doors. The whole place sighing as it stretches and wakes. Since I've been back I've been keeping the house tropically warm.

As the heat spreads through the empty rooms it brings with it the smells of my missing life. The biscuity smell of children. The sharp, gingery tang of the shampoos Katy likes to use. It's already fading, but for now, if I work at it, I can still catch a hint of them. Concentrating hard I can get a sense of something like the scent of freshly washed school uniforms drying.

While the heating is on, they're still here somewhere, though just out of reach. When the heating's on, the house has the illusion of life.

That's something I'm learning, that if you want to keep a dead house fresh, you keep it warm.

I put the moment off for a while – of course I do – but eventually I find I am slipping out of bed and walking down the landing.

Yes, time to get up now, it's been days and there's stuff I need. Basic stuff. Proper coffee, eggs, bacon, bread, for a start. Toilet roll. No more wallowing. Days of dozing in this nest of quilts, only getting up to piss, or to fix myself some cereal, or to make a cup of instant coffee. It's definitely enough.

I am just wearing boxers and a random t-shirt I've had since uni and I smell as rank as the den of an urban fox. So that is something else I will do today. I will have a bath. The house doesn't smell great either. I take a breath. I notice now how the place smells. How the sly stink of unemptied bins and stale milk has crept into all the corners.

I pause at the door of Jack's room. As the damp light seeps in through those thin blue curtains we never got around to replacing, I begin to make out all the figures on the floor. I'll pack them away today. Whatever story Jack was in the middle of, it ends here. I peep into Ella's room and I am hurt by the reproach of its tidiness, this ordered oasis amid the dust and the debris of the rest of the house.

There's a spider in the corner. A garden spider come in now the weather is turning colder. *I'll be a spider, a butterfly, a moth, a wasp. I'll be the annoying insect that won't leave you alone.*

How ridiculous.

In the living room I light the stove. The radiator alone never seems to warm this room. Maybe it's because its effectiveness is muffled by being behind the sofa, maybe it's simply dodgy plumbing, maybe it's a bit of both. But I like having the stove on anyway. I like the fizz and crackle of the logs, the orange glow behind the glass.

I cheat of course. I'm not using proper wood that I have collected and chopped. I'm not even using logs bought from the shops. I'm not messing around with kindling and rolled up balls of old newspaper. I don't even need firelighters. I'm using something called a home fire heat log. High-calorie, long-lasting, made out of real recycled wood pulp that's been treated in some special way. Mess free, fuss free. You simply put your safety match to both ends of its wrapping and voila. Fire. From rubbing two sticks together in an ice age, to a home fire heat log. From Prometheus to every 7-Eleven. As a species we've come a long way, baby.

I stand, rub my hands together though I am not cold. It's just what you do in front of a fire. A reflex. Outside there is a determined rain falling steadily. An aggressive wind is shaking the trees that line the street, but in here it's going to be pretty toasty soon. I watch the paper around the fake log twist and coil and shrivel in the stove. Small yellow flames begin to dance. I shut the little glass door.

I will have breakfast and then I will make lists. Making lists is the quickest way to put order back in your life. Or to pretend that you have, which is nearly as good.

I called the obvious people when I first got back here but no one was talking. Some were friendly, some were distant but they all claimed they didn't know anything. It was like they'd all signed the same oath. Tell Mark nothing. Give him no clues. Make him work for it. Make him sweat.

The first people I called were the in-laws. Katy's dad was coldly adamant. They didn't know where she was and if they did they wouldn't tell me.

'If she wants to get in touch she will, Mark. You'll

have to wait.' Then he hung up. So no help coming from there.

Maybe Claude is right. Maybe I don't want to be pushing my wife, wherever she is. Left to herself she might just start to miss me, miss the life we shared. The easy companionability of it. Yes, maybe I should just let them alone. Time might be my ally here. She'll have our new baby soon. She'll need me around then. Surely.

After a few days I went to the school too, endured the frankly curious stares of the kids, the sly glances of the parents. The quick perfunctory nods from people I used to have good old chinwags with. They haven't seen Jack or Ella either. The deputy-head tells me that the whole school community is missing them, thinking of them, hoping that they see them again soon. The place isn't the same without them.

'I know,' I say. 'I know.'

The house is too quiet. To pretend that a dead house is actually alive, you need noise as well as heat. But not music, not yet. So I put on the radio. Sport. Voices talking earnestly, passionately, about nothing at all. City came back strongly in the second-half, the home side looked distinctly uneasy as the game progressed. Then the whole atmosphere changed with one moment of brilliance. Who gives a shit? Empty arguments, lame jokes, fake excitement, heartiness. Men slapping each other on the back. Meaningless noise. Perfect.

The kitchen door bangs open. I start. She is suddenly just there, tiny, but somehow filling the room. Something to do with her stillness. Her serious quiet. Lulu. It's as if I somehow conjured her up just by thinking about her, like she's a fairy in a kid's story.

Now she says, 'Throwing Muses? Who are they when they're at home?'

She's talking about my t-shirt. I look down at it, tightish now where once upon a time it hung off me. Strange that this tee, never a favourite, should have survived all the moves, all the culls and clear outs. Escaped all the boot sales and charity shop drops.

'You nearly gave me a heart attack.'

'Soz. Maybe I should have knocked politely, only…'

'Not really your thing, I know.'

She laughs. 'How are you?'

'Oh I'm all right. It's the others.'

Where did that come from? This was always my dad's standard response to enquiries after his well-being. He must have said it dozens of times a night in the pub. I've never said it before.

Lulu settles carefully into a chair

She looks at me in silence now. I don't meet her gaze. In my head I go over my shopping list. Washing up liquid. Olive oil.

'I've been calling.'

Jam. Cheese. A TV.

'Mark?'

'I know. I just…', I shrug again. Words are increasingly pointless I find.

'Yeah. You're bound to feel weird.'

Vegetables, I think. Pulses. Lentils. Chick peas. I could make some nourishing winter soups. Spicy dahls. Stews. Begin to be a bit healthy. My eyes flicker to the recipe books piled high on their shelf next to the cooker.

Lulu looks around her. I wonder if the kitchen passes whatever audition is being set for it.

'You happy staying here, in this place, on your own?'

'Katy and the kids will be back soon.'

'She's not been in touch?'

I don't need to answer. Lulu nods. 'You going to offer me a drink or what?'

'Yeah, sorry. Coffee? Tea? Beer?' I am suddenly aware I have no idea of the time. I have a sense from the radio that the early kick-off is into the second-half, so that makes it, what? One o'clock? Respectable time to start drinking on a Saturday.

'Green tea if you've got it thanks.'

I look at her now. She looks sheepish. She's not blushing exactly, but there are twin pinkish dots high on her cheeks. Her brow furrows. 'Got to start looking after myself. I'm getting to that age. Can't live like a student all my life.'

Why not? I think. Why the hell not? Live how you like, we're only here for a minute.

'You want a slice of lemon in it?' I say.

'Yeah, go on then.' Only turns out there are no lemons. Lulu tells me not to worry, on its own is fine too.

I turn the radio down. I can still hear the comforting burble if not actual individual words.

We talk about this and that. We chit and we chat. We are careful to say nothing real, nothing important. She tells me where she's going.

'Suffolk obviously. Stebbing Bardfield maybe, do my bit for the half-millennium of creativity. Try to make sure people drive carefully through the village.'

I tell her wherever she ends up, she'll be fine. She tells me she knows this. There's silence again. I finish my mental shopping list. Some tins. Some stuff for the freezer. Some new sheets.

'I came to give you this,' she says.

She hands me an A4 envelope with my name hand-written in beautiful cursive. Inside a black and white headshot on glossy paper. My own face in close-up. The photo from Felixstowe. It's a good picture. Lulu has managed to give me a haunted film star quality. Eyes half-closed, sharp cheekbones, a two-day stubble. The camera lying like it does when handled by anyone good. It's certainly not how I see myself. I put it back in its envelope.

When I look at her again, she has tears in her eyes.

She stays maybe half an hour. When she goes to leave we shake hands like wary strangers.

'Stay safe,' I say. She nods, serious.

'You too,' she says.

There's a pause. She looks at the floor. Then she looks up again. Stares at me hard. Eyes like searchlights through fog, dazzling and smoky at the same time.

'Last chance to come with me. Doesn't have to be Stebbing Bardfield. I'm open to suggestions. We could go to Italy.'

'I don't think so.'

My phone chirrups perkily. I don't look at it. Not straight away. Lulu and I embrace and I breathe in the vaguely citrusy scent of her. She's getting sweat and self-pity in return. Doesn't seem a fair swap somehow. She seems okay though, she holds me tight. There's a moment when I think yes, Stebbing Bardfield. Felixstowe. Italy. Talent shows. Twitter even. We could do that. Live like students for the rest of our lives. 'You smell nice,' I say.

She smiles at the inanity of it. 'Cien mandarin. Lidl. 45p.'

'Bargain,' I say. We'll never see each other again, but we'll always be friends.

When she goes, I remember the text. It's from an unknown number and it makes my heart cramp. *Love you to the furthest thing in the universe and back x*

I want to text back, want to tell Jack and his sister and his mother that I'm coming to get them, that I'm going to bring them back where they belong. But I don't. Maybe they don't belong here. Maybe I don't deserve to be with them. Maybe I deserve to be alone, just one of the many kinds of ghost.

I take another look at the photo Lulu gave me, then I place it on the glowing heat log. It's a curious thing to watch your own face blister and burn.

I turn off the radio. The silence grows around me.

ACKNOWLEDGEMENTS

Many thanks to all the people and institutions that have helped make this book possible including Arts Council England, Arvon Foundation, Joe Compton, Robert Davidson, Keara Donnachie, Dr Jim English, Keira Farrell, Sue Foot, Moira Forsyth, Helen Garnons-Williams, Caron May, Herbie May, Carole Ockelford, Hannah Procter, Layla Sanai, Catherine Smith, David Smith and Chris Wellbelove.

The information about the real tensile strength of scars is adapted from *Robbins Pathologic Basis of Disease* - 6th edn., Kotran et al.

www.sandstonepress.com

 facebook.com/SandstonePress/

@SandstonePress

This book should be ret
Lancashire County Library